THE LETTER READER

THE LETTER READER

Jan Casey

HEAD
of ZEUS

An Aria Book

9 7 5 3 1 2 4 6 8

A catalogue record for this book is available from the British Library.

ISBN (PB): 9781803283845
ISBN (E): 9781803283821

Cover design: Jessie Price/HoZ; background: Rory Kee

Typeset by Siliconchips Services Ltd UK

Printed and bound in Great Britain by
CPI Group (UK) Ltd, Croydon CR0 4YY

Head of Zeus Ltd
First Floor East
5–8 Hardwick Street
London EC1R 4RG

WWW.HEADOFZEUS.COM

To my beautiful grandchildren. With all my love. XXX

Prologue

June 1941

Connie hitched her skirt above her knees and ran to catch the number fifty-three as it pulled away from the stop. Grabbing hold of the rail, she hauled herself up onto the platform, nodded to the conductor and found the last empty seat upstairs.

Whilst Connie watched, the man next to her rubbed a spyhole in the condensation on the window and tried to peer out at the rubble and debris before the glass fogged up again.

'It's a filthy day,' he said, the combined smells of soot, wet dog and fried sausages rising from his wool coat when he turned towards her. 'Got far to go?'

'The recruiting office,' Connie said. 'In the West End.'

'Oh, yes,' the man said with enthusiasm. He had a kind, fleshy face and a scar over one eye where it looked as though a deep layer of skin had once been peeled off. An injury from the Great War, Connie guessed. 'Good on you,' he said. 'I wish I could do my bit, but those days have long gone I'm sorry to say.'

Connie smiled at him. 'I'm sure you've done more than enough.'

'What's it to be?' he asked. 'WAAFS, ATS, WRNS or something closer to home? I was reading just the other day that women are going to be conscripted into all sorts of jobs – construction, air raid wardens, drivers, working in munitions factories, as well as the usual nursing and teaching.'

'My husband's in the Navy so I'm hoping to be a Wren,' Connie answered.

'Lovely uniform,' the man said. 'Much more sophisticated than the … Damn, another detour.'

The bus turned sharply left and Connie, along with everyone else, stretched her neck to see which route the bus was going to take, but there must have been an unaccounted-for obstruction in the road because, without warning, the front wheels tipped violently and the bus lurched forward before teetering this way and that.

Several cries could be heard from passengers all around the bus as they were hurtled out of their seats and their heads and arms and knees bashed against windows and metal poles and each other. A child started to sob and a young woman shouted, 'Mum, Mum, can you hear me?' Connie had only been able to steady herself by leaning against the man next to her, but his head had been flung forward against the handrail and when he stared at her – a dazed look in his eyes – a rivulet of blood streamed down over the already damaged part of his face.

'Here,' Connie said, taking a handkerchief from her pocket. 'Let me help you.' She dabbed at his wound as best she could then untied the belt from her mac and wrapped it around his head.

'Thank you, my dear,' the older man said as he laid his trembling hand on Connie's arm for a moment.

Those who were able began to stand and shuffle about and try to make their way up the central aisle that was now an alarmingly steep incline, but the bus shifted again with the change of weight. A pregnant woman moaned and a man, nursing his swollen, misshapen wrist, tried to calm the person next to him who might have been his mother or an aunt or a complete stranger.

'Stay perfectly still,' a voice called from downstairs. 'The emergency services are on their way. Is anyone seriously injured?'

The passengers appraised each other, all of them stoically reluctant to give themselves preferential treatment.

'Yes,' Connie shouted. 'There's a gentleman with a nasty cut to his head, a woman who doesn't look injured but is heavily pregnant and a man with a broken arm. I can't see any of the others very well.'

'Are you able to walk as lightly as possible around the seats and give me a roundup?'

'Yes, perfectly able,' she said, although her heart was thumping and her legs felt as if they were filled with loose wadding rather than anything solid.

On tiptoes, Connie made her way from seat to seat, trying to look reassuring and as if she knew what she was doing. She shouted down that there was an elderly man with a very sore shoulder, a young woman who had bashed her cheek against the window, a child who'd been forced under a seat and had heavy bruising to his knees, an older woman who'd fainted but had now come around and many who were in shock.

Every time she took a step, or someone moved, the bus pitched forward and the passengers couldn't help gasping or groaning. It felt as if they were dangling on the edge of a cliff and it would take nothing more than the slightest shift to send them into an abyss. Then there was the frightening smell of fuel.

Not wanting to alarm the others, Connie slowly and deliberately made her way to the top of the steps and signalled her fears to the man at the bottom. Glancing back over her shoulder, she saw the faces of the passengers staring at her. Some were ghostly and pale, others red and sweating, quite a few waxen and bewildered, all of them trusting and expectant. Her stomach lurched when the implications hit her. These people had somehow been led to think she was their spokesperson, their leader; the woman who would ensure they were led to safety.

I hope I can live up to the looks on their faces, she thought as she realised that whilst she'd been concentrating on the others she'd begun to feel much less jittery herself. The man with her belt wrapped around his head nodded and gave her the glimmer of a smile, and in that instant she knew that whatever happened she would do her best to remain in control and useful to these people who had put their faith in her.

'Right, the rescue services are here,' the man called up to her at last. 'Can you bring the passengers down one by one?'

A surge of fear travelled through Connie's arms and legs and a wave of cold sweat broke over her. But what else could she do? Run down the stairs and leave those who had fared less well than her to their own devices?

Taking a deep breath, she manoeuvred the others down the steps that stood at a giddy angle and handed them to the safety of the ambulance crews. When she got to the man who'd been sitting next to her, he said, 'I'm terribly sorry, my dear. That's probably my blood on your mac.'

She smiled at him. 'Don't give it another thought,' she said. 'Just worry about yourself.'

When the bus was empty, Connie was handed out onto the pavement where she stood for a moment taking in the scene. Ropes had been secured to the vehicle where it seesawed over a large pothole, fire and rescue crews shrouded in smoke and murk deliberated what course of action to take next, piles of refuse and wreckage were heaped on the pavements and Connie thought the whiff of stale food on a damp coat was much more preferable to the strong stench of leaking gas.

The ambulances had clanged their way towards the nearest hospital and for a moment, Connie felt overwhelmed with sadness that she'd never know the fate of the people she'd helped. Then she reminded herself that if everyone chased after someone they'd looked out for during these last months, no one would achieve anything else.

A small group of passengers who were well enough to continue their journeys under their own steam had congregated under the overhang of a shop and one of the women beckoned to Connie. 'Ta very much,' she said. 'I'm glad someone knew what they were doing.'

Connie laughed. 'I don't think any of us could have had previous experience of being in that precarious situation. Look at how it's leaning.'

They all stared at the faltering bus and a collective shiver ran through them.

'Are you a nurse?' a man asked. 'Or a teacher? You just got on with it.'

'No.' Connie smiled. 'Neither of those, but I was glad to help out.'

The small crowd began to go their separate ways and Connie wondered how many incidents would bring her close to others for a short period of time before the war was over.

Suddenly, a chill passed through her and she went to tighten her belt then remembered it was wrapped around her fellow passenger's head. So instead, she pushed her hands deep into her pockets and walked the rest of the way to the recruiting office, cautiously excited and hopeful that signing up to the WRNS would give her the same opportunity to feel – as she'd done today – that she could be of use in these uncertain times.

I

Wednesday. That could only mean one thing. Or two, to be fair. Liver and onions for lunch and a lavender-coloured tabard washed and drying on the line.

From the kitchen window, Connie watched the nylon overdress dance backwards and forwards in the wind, then leaning a bit closer, she inspected what she could see of the clematis she'd planted the previous weekend. It seemed to have taken hold and she crossed mental fingers that it would continue to thrive. The flowers on the little label she'd nestled in the soil were a delicate blush and she imagined them clinging and climbing and covering the back fence. If it did well, she might secure some kind of lattice to the top of the wooden panels and train the plant along that, which would go some way to blocking out the sight of the cooling towers that loomed, like monstrous concrete sentries, over everything for miles around.

She stared at them now, mesmerised by their foreboding size, the clear definition between their dark grey rims and pale lengths and the clean austerity of their shape that was like an egg timer with the top cut off. Burrowed amongst the six towers were two cloud-scraping chimneys that spewed out a ceaseless torrent of smoke or steam infused with clouds of whatever it was the funnels themselves belched into the atmosphere. Her poor clematis probably didn't stand a chance.

When Connie mentioned to Arthur the potential hazards of living so close to the power station, he would laugh and say there was nothing at all dangerous in any of the emissions, but she wasn't so sure.

The kitchen timer buzzed and, folding a tea towel into a pad, Connie took the casserole out of the oven. She turned over the two pieces of liver, still pale and soft in the middle, stirred the onions around in the gravy, put the dish back on the hot shelf and set the timer for a quarter of an hour. Potatoes simmered in one pan and runner beans in another. Somewhere in the labyrinthine workings of the power station, Arthur would be hanging up his overalls and hard hat, taking off his steel toe-capped boots and shrugging on his mackintosh. As Connie laid the table, she imagined him bending to fasten his bicycle clips around his trouser legs, then straightening to secure his cycle helmet under his chin. He would wheel his bike through the grounds of the industrial site to the gate, set it in motion, clamber onto the seat, salute the security guard and be home in fifteen minutes, ready for his dinner.

Most of the other men they knew on the estate stayed at the works for their midday meal and came home in the evening to whatever their wives decided to cook. Millicent next door often served fish fingers that she kept in the small freezer compartment of her refrigerator. Sometimes she heated up frozen chips, too, or gave the breadcrumbed sticks of cod to her family with mashed potatoes and baked beans. Shirley on the other side concocted dishes made with an Italian staple called pasta. Arthur laughed when Connie described the recipes to him and shook his head if she suggested they try – just try – one or other or anything different.

'No,' he would say. 'Millicent and Shirley and their ilk are too young to remember what we had to go through, so they're always looking here, there and everywhere for something different and exciting, but the war was enough excitement for us, thank you very much. You must have had your fill, too. Anyway, I, for one, am happy to stick to our routine.'

But Connie, for another, was not.

She sighed, sat on the edge of a dining room chair and threaded the tea towel first through one fist and then the other. She realigned a pleat in the heavy, flowery curtains and tucked the material behind the sash holding them open around the patio doors. Of course she knew Arthur didn't really mean the war had been exciting. That was merely his way of saying they should be grateful for the serene and ordered lives they lived now. But, she beat her hands on her thighs to make the point to herself, a little more excitement wouldn't go amiss or, if nothing else, perhaps a slight deviation from their same-old, same-old. Chicken in a basket at the pub once every few weeks, or a film at the cinema, or a picnic, or – *I don't know*, she thought – chops instead of pie on a Saturday.

But Arthur would have none of it, so it was a roast dinner on Sunday with leftovers on Monday. On Tuesday they had shepherd's pie, Wednesday liver and onions. Thursday was stew with dumplings, except at the height of summer when they ate salad with cold cuts; Friday was fish and on Saturday they had steak and kidney pie. And there was a different coloured tabard for each day of the week, too, which she wore around the house and garden to carry out the housework she performed on a strict rota.

If only Arthur could be persuaded to have his dinner at the power station once or twice a week, she could, for a start, see more of her neighbours. They were all kind and included her in invitations to coffee mornings and get-togethers, even though they were younger than her. But time was tight, as she was busy preparing Arthur's hot meal before lunch, and every afternoon was spent shopping for the next day's food. Sometimes she was able to nip in to see one of them in the afternoon for a cup of tea, although by that time of day they were walking to collect their little ones from school and nursery, and if they did have others in their homes, it was inevitably friends with children who could amuse each other.

Perhaps she could linger in Barnby Dun on market days, although there wasn't much there. Or catch the bus to Doncaster and explore the Minster and cobbled streets without Arthur checking his watch and fussing about the weekend being the only time he had to weed the garden or sweep the paths.

What she really longed for was a job that would get her out of the house for a few hours every day. She'd spoken to Arthur on countless occasions over the years about finding a position behind the counter in a bakery or manning a reception desk in an office, but he wouldn't give his permission. Just last week Millicent had told her about a job as a dinner lady at the local infant school. But when she brought up the subject with Arthur, he'd shaken his head and said, 'I didn't fight a war only to have to suffer the embarrassment of having others think I can't provide for my wife.'

She'd stood behind him in her blue tabard, duster in hand, silently mimicking his words as she guessed verbatim what he would say. And as always, she'd dropped the discussion because she knew she wouldn't get anywhere.

What was the point in torturing herself; Arthur was immovable on the subject of her working and really, she should be used to it by now. But if anything, her relentless, monotonous schedule was becoming more and more difficult to bear.

Craning her neck to peek over Millicent's fence, Connie could make out the top of her neighbour's head bobbing around in her garden. She was probably trailing after her toddler on his tricycle and as she did so, the breeze caught tufts of her short, auburn hair and sent them skywards. From this distance it looked as if the younger woman had had it cut again, something she did often, and Connie was intrigued to see the finished style. Her neighbour's head disappeared from view and shame engulfed Connie at the thought that Millicent might have glimpsed her peering in her direction. An almost irresistible urge came over her to open the door and shout to Millicent that she wasn't a prying, meddlesome busybody, really she wasn't – but luckily she stopped herself in time.

With a humourless chuckle, Connie thought about how she'd been ordered to be inquisitive and interfering during the war; although that wasn't how the work was viewed – then or now. The responsibility had been exciting and tense and in turns, deeply satisfying and unnerving. It had taken her out of London, too – a fact Arthur wouldn't let her forget whenever she mentioned how she would like to do something different for a change.

'Liverpool. Most of the ports in the country.'

'Yes, but that was—'

'And now Doncaster,' he would cut her off. 'You've seen more in your life than most, I reckon.' And that's where the conversation would come to an end because, no matter how many times she tried to explain, he wouldn't accept that her war work didn't make up for her being stuck in the house day after day with nothing to look forward to except a mind-numbing routine.

Needles of rain tapped on the window and Connie ran to rescue the almost-dry washing. After she'd scooped it together, she peeked at the clematis hugging the tepee of willow sticks Arthur had put into the ground for the plant to climb. *The rain will do you good*, she thought, *if it's not tainted by whatever erupts from that ominous power station*, and once again she willed the fragile plant to stay with her.

The kitchen timer buzzed again and she abandoned the damp clothes in the tiny utility room. She took the dish from the oven and as she was straining the potatoes, Arthur's key turned in the lock.

'Hello, you,' he called from the hallway.

'Yoo-hoo,' she replied.

'Mmm.' Arthur wandered into the kitchen, fussing with the strap on his cycle helmet. As he released his head from the sweaty, smelly leather, his hair stood out like a thin, greying halo around a flat circle on the crown. The dark, heavy brows that met at the top of his nose had recently begun to sprout white, unruly wires as thick and indomitable as an animal's whiskers. His nose twitched and he pretended to follow the aroma of their dinner around the kitchen. 'Liver and onions,' he said, naming the meal to match the day of the week, as if she needed to be told. 'It must be Wednesday.'

Despite the predictability of the remark, Connie managed a smile as she dished up. Constance's Constant was how Arthur referred to himself and what she ought to do was concentrate on how hardworking and faithful he was rather than dwelling on his annoying traits. But that was difficult to do as they sat and ate their meal in dispiriting silence.

When they'd finished, they laid their cutlery politely across their plates. 'Nice bit of liver that, thank you my Treasure,' Arthur said.

Connie nodded and exchanged their dirty plates for bowls of apple pie and custard, then Arthur wiped his mouth with a napkin, used the facilities – as he called them – resettled his helmet on his head and cycled off for the afternoon shift at the power station.

Busying herself with tidying and washing up, Connie kept her eye on the clock knowing that if she timed her chores correctly, she could leave for the shops just as Millicent and Shirley were closing their doors to collect their children from school and she could saunter along with them for a bit of company.

After the kitchen was restored to order and she'd dealt with the clean clothes, Connie changed her tabard for a mid-calf brown skirt and a taupe short-sleeved blouse. Smoothing down the disobedient wisps of hair around her double crown, she pulled the soft waves behind her ears, twisted the whole lot at the nape of her neck and secured the bun with a couple of pins. Then she gurned at herself in the mirror and applied a layer of red lipstick to the contours of her mouth.

At the bottom of the stairs she drew on her navy mac, laced her black shoes, grabbed her handbag and left the house in time to see Millicent and Shirley, each holding a toddler by the hand, strolling towards the end of the road.

They hadn't seen her, so she didn't think it unseemly to jog a bit to catch up, although she didn't want to give herself away and be out of breath when she reached them. As luck would have it they halted at the kerb, looked down at their tots and went into a lengthy explanation about how to safely cross the road, which gave her enough time to slow down and greet them with dignity.

'Hello, ladies.' Connie tried to make the meeting sound like a happy coincidence. With exaggerated surprise she widened her eyes, looked down at the little ones and said, 'Hello Tracey and hello Adrian. It is so lovely to see you. I love your teddy, Tracey. What's his name?'

Tracey held up well-loved brown and white soft toy and waved it around in front of Connie's face. 'Teddy,' she said.

'Well, hello to Teddy.' Connie smiled. 'No cuddly with you today, Adrian?'

Millicent's little boy shook his head, his soft bottom lip protruding from his mouth.

'Don't get him started, Connie,' Millicent said. 'He dithered so long about which toy to bring with him that we had to leave the house empty-handed.'

Shirley laughed and Adrian burrowed his chubby fingers into Connie's palm. 'Oh,' Millicent said. 'I think Connie is Adie's teddy today.'

As Connie gently grabbed onto the padded, sticky fingers, she felt snivels surfacing. They should have dried up long ago when month after month came and went with no announcement of a baby for her, but here they were again, threatening to spill over her eyelids and follow a well-established course down her cheeks.

She managed to quell her tears in favour of a beam that split her face and was pleased to see the smile returned by her neighbours. Although her age and unfashionable looks were nothing akin to theirs, they banded together comfortably as they walked along road after passage after cul-de-sac of look-alike houses in this corner of South Yorkshire, which none of them could call home.

Connie had been right: Millicent's hair had been restyled again. This time the dense fringe, cut with exacting precision, tapered to a point next to her ears, then was snipped sharply upwards. It looked as though the nape had been shaved. Very bold and brave, Connie thought, wondering how something similar would look on her. Not at all the same, was her conclusion. Her hair no longer had the shine and movement of Millicent's and her skin was nothing like the younger woman's fresh, taut complexion. Shirley was not as daring or confident as Millicent, but she looked lovely with a daisy print band around her shoulder-length, light brown flip and a block-print minidress in primary colours over her baby bump.

'Your new hairdo is fabulous, Millicent,' Connie said. 'It suits you.'

Millicent's hand went to her head where she picked up a few strands of hair and moved them around. 'Thank you, Connie. Richard suggested this. I had a few misgivings but let myself be persuaded in the end.'

'Richard?' Connie was confused. Millicent's husband was Brian.

'Richard at *New You for a Snip*,' Shirley put the record straight. 'You know. The salon on the high street in Barnby Dun. Everyone goes there.'

Everyone except me, Connie thought. 'And your boots,' she enthused. 'I love them.'

Shirley and Millicent looked down at their identical white boots and giggled. 'We ordered the same pair from Littlewoods,' Shirley said. 'Pure coincidence.'

'Good taste, that's what I say.'

'Would you like to have a look at the catalogue, Connie?' Shirley asked.

Connie didn't know what she would buy from a shopping catalogue – certainly not a pair of white boots – but she was intrigued. 'I'll have a look,' she said. 'If you don't mind me being non-committal.'

'Of course not,' Shirley said. 'It can be helpful as there's so little around here in the way of shops.'

'Or anything,' Millicent chimed in.

There were schools, a chemist, a doctor's surgery and a hugely overpriced Spar dotted around the estate. All the brickwork was red, each roof tile dark slate. Some windows were leaded, others were clear; the semi and detached types had garages, the terraces a block for car parking. It was all lovely and new and fresh and should have been their dreams come true; instead, the lack of variety or quirkiness or personality made it soul-destroying. And then there were the towers, casting their cold, forbidding shadows over everyone.

'I worked at Littlewoods during the war,' Connie said. Then she could have bitten off her tongue as she was sure Shirley and Millicent's eyes glazed over.

'Really?' Millicent said. 'Was there mail order then?'

Connie laughed. 'Not really. It was mainly the football pools, but their head office in Liverpool was requisitioned for war work and I was stationed there.'

'Oh,' Shirley said. 'How strange. Tracey, don't dare put that leaf in your mouth.' She made a dash for her little girl but was hampered by her bump, so Millicent beat her to it and took the offending bit of greenery out of the child's hand. Then she and Shirley laughed again at their toddlers' antics, and Connie's stint at Littlewoods was forgotten. Probably just as well as she didn't think these young women were particularly interested in what she, or anyone else, had done during the war years. And why should they be. None of it had any relevance to the carefree lives they led now – and that, she thought, was what they'd fought for more than twenty years ago, although she hadn't known it at the time.

'Thought any more about the dinner lady job?' Millicent asked.

'I wish you would take it,' Shirley said. 'You have such a lovely way with little ones.'

That made a glow, like the flare of an incendiary, burn in Connie's chest. She wondered if her neighbours really did think she was good with children or if they merely felt sorry for her. Everyone knew there wasn't anything much more painful to contend with than wanting children and not being able to have them. A lump as hard as a stone formed in the base of Connie's throat and threatened to swell in size until it crushed her heart.

'No,' she said, swallowing forcefully. 'I don't think I could fit it in.'

From the corner of her eye, Connie caught Millicent and Shirley exchanging a look. *They must think I'm mad*, she thought. In comparison to them, she had all the leisure time in the world. Or perhaps they suspected that Arthur didn't approve of her working, or doing anything at all, for herself.

To stem the flow of embarrassment she felt, she looked down at Adrian, his plump hand still snuggled in hers and pointed out a purple clematis snaking up the side wall of a house. 'I planted one like that but in pink. I'm keeping my fingers crossed it grows to be just as beautiful.'

Adrian stared, put two fingers in his mouth and slurped loudly. 'Oh, I do wish you wouldn't do that, Adie,' his mother said.

'I hope you don't think I'm a nosy cow,' Shirley said. 'But I saw you planting it at the weekend when I was in the bedroom sorting out nappies for the new baby.' She touched the top of her round stomach with gentle fingers.

'Of course not,' Connie said, relieved at not being the only one to take an interest in her neighbours' trivial day-to-day activities. 'I'm not one of those who wants to keep herself to herself.'

'Good.' Shirley laughed. 'Because neither are we, are we, Millie?'

Millicent shook her head. 'I can't think of anything worse in this place,' she said. 'Can you imagine not trying to make friends here?' She looked around as if she had that minute landed in a foreign country and a shudder ran through her. 'I mean, what else is there to do?'

Shirley put her arm around Millicent and hugged her close until her friend smiled.

'Oh now, what do we think?' Millicent asked, pointing with her chin to a pair of flashy zigzag-patterned curtains that had appeared in the downstairs windows of a terraced house.

'Lovely,' Shirley said. 'Do you think she'll put a matching set upstairs?'

They all looked at the upper-floor windows, shrouded temporarily in old sheets.

'She should,' Connie said. 'They're delightful.'

'Come on, Tracey.' Shirley pulled her little girl away from the fascinating sight of a ladybird crawling along a low wall. 'I'm surprised, Connie,' she said. 'I thought your tastes were more …' She shrugged. 'Traditional.'

'Oh, really?' Connie was a bit taken aback, although the tone of the observation was not in the least critical. She thought about the décor she and Arthur had chosen and she knew it was dull, heavy, uninspired and rather dated. In the soft furnishings department she had caressed lightweight, paisley curtain material in shades of yellow and orange and imagined it billowing softly in a summer breeze, but Arthur had taken her by the elbow and steered her towards the grey serge shot through with brocaded flowers in dark greens, reds and golds. 'We have got money to spend,' he said. 'But the pot's not bottomless, and if we go for something modern and frivolous, you'll only want to change it again in a year or two.'

But I'll want to change this from the outset, Connie had thought. She hadn't argued, though, as she knew Arthur wouldn't change his mind. They played out the same scene when they'd shopped for flooring. She'd wanted a light, fluffy carpet she could wriggle her toes into; Arthur had manoeuvred them to coarse, woollen burgundy-and-blue swirls – and when it was all in place with dark wooden furniture, Connie tried to appreciate the elegance as that was what she would be stuck with for years to come.

Connie kneaded the top of Adrian's little hand. 'What are you having for tea tonight, Adie?'

The little fellow took his fingers out of his mouth and saliva ran down his chin. 'Oh, Adie,' Millicent said, mopping up the mess with a tissue she took from her sleeve. 'Sausages with frozen chips and peas. One of Adie's favourites. Janet likes it, too.'

Adrian nodded.

'And you?'

'Egg and cress sandwiches,' Connie said. 'With a custard tart for afters.'

'Sounds good,' Shirley said. 'We're having lasagne I made earlier.'

Connie didn't have a clue what that was, but murmured some kind of approval.

They walked single file through a chicane built to slow down pushbikes and when they came out at a crossroads, Millicent took Adrian's hand and held onto it. 'That was nice, Adie, wasn't it? Holding Connie's hand all this way?'

Connie smiled and thought it was probably much more of a treat for her than it was for the toddler.

'Now we have to go and get Janet and Simon and let Connie get to the shops. Say bye.'

'Bye,' the little boy waved with his free hand.

'You hold my hand, too, Tracey,' Shirley said. 'See you, Connie.'

'Bye for now,' Connie called out. 'Lovely talking to you.' They didn't turn around again and just like that, her diversion for the day disappeared towards the opposite end of the red brick estate.

2

July 1941

Connie thanked the Wren who handed her the blue bundle, but when she tried to claim it, the woman held on to the folds of clothing with a firm grip. '*Mam*,' the officer in charge of supplies said in a flat voice.

Mam. Connie wondered if that was how she was going to be addressed from now on, although she'd never heard that title bandied about when the WRNS had been mentioned in conversation or on the news or in the paper. The two women stood staring at each other, both holding onto corners of the uniform. Confusion about what to do or say next caused irritating prickles of sweat to crawl under Connie's armpits. All she could think to utter was thank you again, in a slightly louder voice this time in case the officer hadn't heard her.

'Thank you, Mam,' the other woman said, letting go of the uniform and nudging it towards Connie. 'All superiors in the WRNS are addressed as Mam.'

'I'm so sorry,' Connie said.

As a gentle reprimand, the officer raised her eyebrows and Connie hastily added the missing word, 'Mam.'

The officer allowed herself a smidgen of a smile, leaned a

tiny bit closer and said, 'Don't worry. You're here to learn. You'll get the hang of it.'

Connie drew herself up and to prove she was capable of taking instructions said, 'Mam,' once again and turned to walk past the queue of recruits who would, no doubt, have to go through exactly the same ritual when it was their turn.

She made a point of looking at the two girls next in line and grimaced at them in mock terror. The third girl along had tears welling in her eyes and, astonished, Connie stopped and quietly asked if she was unwell.

'No, it's not that.' The recruit snivelled and shook her head. 'I was told the uniform was the smartest of all the services but this is horrible.' She pinched Connie's bluette overall between her thumb and index finger, then drew her hand back brusquely, as if the garment were harbouring something contagious.

'I'm sure it's not forever,' Connie offered, although she had no idea if that really was the case. 'It's to get us started and it looks practical and easy to move around in.'

That turned out to be just as well, as the initial two-week introduction consisted of square bashing, route marches and learning naval terminology, which meant that 'scrubbing the decks' translated to washing what seemed like miles of freezing cold corridors in their training centre at HMS Pembroke not once for practice, but over and over again. Working in the galley meant taking turns to prepare and serve food to their colleagues, sleeping in cabins amounted to tossing and turning in a three-bunk bed, and as if they weren't already aware, they were taught about the tasks that were considered suitable work for women – cleaning windows; washing cutlery; polishing shoes; heaving buckets of coal up and down stairs; peeling potatoes; scouring pots and pans; making beds in a strict, ascribed manner with the anchors on the blue and white bedsheets the right way up to avoid causing the ship to sink.

Apart from that first day, when the girl in the queue behind her had shed a few tears, none of the recruits let the daily timetable of menial tasks get them down. After all, if they hadn't been polishing and washing and cooking in the WRNS, they would have been working their way through the same list of chores in another aspect of war work or at home. At least they could put their hands on their hearts and say they were doing their bit, and Connie was proud of herself for that.

Interspersed with the physical activities were talks, which Connie looked forward to, mainly because they were an opportunity to rest on a chair for an hour or two, although she did try to look interested in the *King's Regulations and Admiralty Instructions* fed to them under the strict supervision of a Second Officer. Then there were lectures about Jackspeak, badges and ranks and upholding the reputation of the WRNS with proper behaviour, something the new recruits accepted with varying degrees of compliance. Two of the girls who shared Connie's cabin were put on detention on day three of their training for singing a rather bawdy song whilst they swabbed the decks. Neither of them seemed to mind and they whispered the fruity lyrics again that night after lights out, which sent the rest of the Jennies to sleep with a giggle. That ditty went round and round in Connie's head for the next couple of days until the two girls came up with something even more salacious.

Then they were interviewed and tested individually and in groups about what they might want to do in the Royal Navy. The options seemed endless, although they were all jobs that men, presumably, had deemed suitable for women. Connie was able to weigh up the pros and cons of working as a wireless telegraphist or a bomb range marker, parachute packer, radio or vehicle mechanic or cook. If she applied and was accepted, she would be allowed to drive cars and lorries short distances, operate radar communications equipment or be responsible for putting up and taking down barrage balloons. Then there was helping to plan operations or forecasting the weather, which she felt quite drawn to. She imagined herself confidently writing up the daily, weekly and monthly weather forecasts that would help the bigwigs shape their bombing campaigns and organise troop manoeuvres accordingly. Then, when the whole thing was over, it would be such fun to use her forecasting skills to tell the children she and Arthur were going to have when they needed raincoats or when they could go out in sandals – they would think she was a genius or a magician.

It was explained that none of them would ever experience active duty on sea-faring ships. Their role was to enable men to take up those positions. If they hadn't understood that before they were recruited, it was reiterated relentlessly – this was as close as they would get to a life on the ocean waves. A few Wrens would be used to operate small harbour launches and tugs close to the shore, but what they had to go through to prove their sea legs didn't make the process worth the effort. Connie didn't mind. She had no great hankering to work on the water. When she peered down at the Thames as she was crossing the river at London Bridge or Blackfriars, she sometimes swayed with the ripples beneath her and had to look up quickly to stop herself from coming over giddy.

The girls sitting on either side of her during the final lecture decided to opt for clerical work because they'd all been told that was the area where the women could be most useful. That made sense to Connie and she knew taking that course of action would enable her to work for any number of different sections. But it seemed too safe, if such a thing were possible with a war going on all around them, and didn't fill her with the sense of eager anticipation she'd hoped joining the WRNS would provide.

Of course, she'd written to Arthur about her conundrum and he'd replied that she should definitely request a clerical role, expounding the same reason that her two colleagues had given her. *Don't forget, Treasure,* he'd written.

That it's my duty to keep you safe and the best way you can help is by taking up a little job that allows me to do just that. I know you're strong and clever and capable and brave, but only insofar as undertaking roles that are suitable for women, and clerking is definitely one of those. Let's not forget our plans for when the war is over and we're together for the rest of our lives – a house, days out, high teas, a nice garden and our own brood running around in it.

The letter dropped from her hand. She knew Arthur was only thinking of her well-being and safety, and what he wanted for their future was what she dreamed about, too. Nothing would please her more than having two or three little ones, Arthur's key turning in the lock as he arrived home at six o'clock from a safe and secure job. But that's not where she was or where Arthur was or where the world stood – and couldn't this wretched war be a chance to do something more than pander to others' basic needs?

Not for the first time she wondered whether supporting the troops was the one and only reason women were being called up to participate in war work. With a bitter taste in her mouth she supposed it was, and most women seemed happy to play that ancillary role – or any role, as long as it was suitable – if it meant they were helping to defeat the enemy. And she was, too. But whilst she was in a WRNS uniform, why not have a go at something that would never have otherwise been within her grasp. A job or a trade or a skill that men could choose any time they liked without having to wait for the dictates of war. Holding onto that thought, she filled in her form with clerical as her first option and weather forecasting as a wildcard and kept her fingers crossed she'd get lucky.

When the list of who was going where to train for what role was pinned on the wall, Connie joined the crowd of girls craning their necks to find out where they would be headed next. As they found their names, they pointed and patted each other's arms and nodded, stood tall and lifted their chins. A fizz of exhilaration coursed through Connie when she found her name towards the top of the first column. Her breathing was shallow and she could feel herself becoming a bit light-headed as she followed the row across to discover her fate.

It wasn't weather forecasting. With a sudden drop, she felt let-down and deflated in the chilly, dark, corridor. She was to report to Westfield College in Hampstead the following Monday at eight hundred hours. She drew her finger along the row to assure herself she was reading the correct posting, then tapped the writing a couple of times, because it wasn't clerking, either.

For some unfathomable reason she'd been given postal censorship. All those letters that laid bare the private and personal thoughts of mothers, fathers, sons, daughters, grandparents, lovers, friends. She remembered a few occasions when she'd been waiting for her turn to post an envelope and had wondered what was written in the letter being dropped into the cavernous belly of the red pillar box by the person ahead of her. A confession? A declaration of love or lust? A telling off with what amounted to a handwritten slap. Maybe a plea for money or blackmail for some misdemeanour. Perhaps she'd been given quite exciting war work after all.

3

April 1967

When Connie and Arthur had moved to Barnby Dun from London, Connie thought the damp air indigenous to South Yorkshire, then she'd hit on the idea that it was something generated by the power station, and she couldn't get that out of her mind.

'Of course it's not to do with the stacks or the funnels.' Arthur had laughed at her. 'It's humidity, that's all. Silly billy.'

As usual, Connie had dropped the conversation and conceded the point to Arthur, which was exactly what happened when they, or he, had decided to move to Doncaster.

It was not long after Mum died – three weeks or a month at the most. Connie had been in her mother's bedroom sorting through a pile of dresses and cardigans and paste brooches ready for her sister-in-law to look at later and decide what she wanted to keep. Pulling out an oyster-coloured blouse with mother of pearl buttons that had been one of Mum's favourites, Connie held it to her face and breathed in the warm, talcum powder scent that had followed her mother around for most of her life. She'd laid the garment out on the bedspread, as if it was ready for her mum to pick up and slip over her fluffy, white hair and thin, creased face. With tears clouding her vision, she'd tucked a shiny, iridescent necklace under the collar and stood back, almost able to convince herself that her mother would be wearing it any minute now, as she'd done so many times in the past.

A shadow made her start and she'd looked up, expecting to see Mum smiling at her from the doorway, but it was Arthur, slumped against the wooden frame and watching her with his mouth turned down, his excessive eyebrows heavy with sympathy.

Connie had cleared her throat, disassembled the outfit and moved the pieces back to their respective piles.

'I miss her, too,' Arthur had said, sitting on the edge of the bed.

She nodded. 'I know you do.' They'd lived with Mum for almost twenty years, so of course he felt her loss. But not as much as she did. With no children to care for and no work to keep her occupied, she'd spent so much time with Mum that her grief was as much for the loss of her closest friend and her main purpose in life as it was for her mother. She felt as if one of her limbs had been wrenched from its socket and thrown on top of a pile of rubble.

Tears had pooled in her eyes. 'I'll have to do something with my time, Arthur,' she'd said, plonking herself down next to him. 'Once I've got everything straight in the house.'

Arthur hadn't offered any comment on that but said, 'I think, my Treasure, that it's time to sell this house and move on.'

Connie hadn't been able to believe what she was hearing. 'Sell Mum's house?' she'd said. 'But where would we …?'

'I've been talking to Ken,' Arthur said.

'I've been talking to Ken, too. Just this morning. But he didn't mention anything about selling the house.'

Arthur had taken her hand in his and laid it on his knee. 'Your brother,' he said, 'is entitled to half. You know that. And he and Dora would like to move from their flat to something bigger for the boys.'

'Of course,' Connie had muttered glumly. 'I'd forgotten about that.'

'So,' Arthur carried on. 'Ken would like his share and with your half, we could put a hefty deposit down on a new build somewhere like ... Doncaster, perhaps.'

'Doncaster? Where on earth is that?'

Arthur had laughed. 'For someone who's travelled extensively around the country you—'

'That was war work,' Connie said. 'Hardly extensive travelling. Or travelling of any sort.' All she'd seen were the scissors or indelible pencil she'd held in her hands and all she'd heard was *snip snip* and *scritch scratch*. 'So,' she said again, unable to keep the frustration out of her voice. 'Where is Doncaster?'

'South Yorkshire,' Arthur said.

Images of windswept moors and sheep wandering over lofty, bracken-covered hillsides passed through Connie's mind. 'Whatever for?' she'd asked.

Arthur told her about the job he was going to apply for at a new power station close to the quaint and unlikely sounding town of Barnby Dun, one that would give him a good promotion and a sizeable increase in pay. There they could buy a brand-new house subsidised by the company and furnish it with what was left of the proceeds of Mum's house.

'Think about it, my Treasure,' Arthur had said. 'No bomb damage to work around. Windows that fit properly. A toilet that flushes without making the entire house shake.' He'd walked to the window and Connie wondered if he was concentrating on the cranes and patches of defaced land in various states of renovation or if he was staring at the empty spaces where they'd hoped to watch the children they'd never had skipping and running and playing.

Then a sudden thought had made her heart thud – perhaps the move would be a new start. Maybe Arthur would realise that they didn't have to follow a prescriptive way of life. They could be spontaneous and even happy-go-lucky once in a while. Maybe she could get a job and they could have a bit of a social life with people other than Ken and Dora.

So Connie agreed to take the train to Doncaster and have a look around. It was whilst they were there, being led from one type of house to another by a representative of the power station, that she realised Arthur's mind was made up and it didn't matter what she said: they were moving to Barnby Dun.

How strange, Connie had thought at the time. That a man like Arthur – who would not deviate an inch from his routine of meals on certain days; Friday night baths; the same walk through Springfield Gardens every Sunday morning; winding the mantel clock at exactly 10 p.m. and bed by 10.30; the exact make and colour of shoes for years – seemed to relish the idea of moving hundreds of miles from home.

But after they'd settled into their new surroundings, Arthur sank deeper into his strict routine. Connie sighed and wondered again now if the unvaried and orderly estate was what had attracted him to the whole set-up in the first place.

Walking past a row of detached properties identical to the one they lived in, she heard the high-pitched yap of a small dog from behind one of the doors and gazed at a dark green pram parked in front of another.

One of those outside the front door or under the shade of a tree in the garden would have made all the difference in the world, Connie thought. She had to walk on apace so she wouldn't dwell on the sight of the corduroy cover, pulled back enough for her to catch an anguished glimpse of a dishevelled powder blue blanket and the baby nestled inside.

Month after month Arthur had come home to her defeated tears, and although he'd tried to be stoic, she sometimes heard him sniffling and snuffling behind the bathroom door. Eventually, he must have become accustomed or immune to the disappointment because on the final two occasions he hadn't noticed, or had turned a blind eye to the silver, shining residue around her eyes and nose. Then the inevitable happened; the sliver of hope she'd clung to ceased to exist and neither of them mentioned the subject again.

Stepping off the zebra crossing, Connie hoisted her bag up on her shoulder and made to turn right to the butcher's but there it was, right in front of her: *New You for a Snip.* And in the window, wearing denim hip huggers, an orange roll neck and winklepicker boots – with such keenly pointed toes they could have had an eye out – was a young man who she thought must be Richard. In one of his pale, elegant hands he brandished a comb and in the other a pair of shiny, silver scissors that danced around the backcombed blonde hair on a client's head. Every chair in the steamy salon was filled and every hairdressing station was a hive of activity. Taped to the door were photos of Twiggy and Cilla Black and Jean Shrimpton who, Connie supposed, you only had to point at and you would be magically transformed into. Connie felt for her thin, wavy bun and spiralling double crown and knew that would not be how it worked out for her.

'Can I help you, Madam?' The door opened a crack and a grinning Richard leaned out, the sickly sweet smell of shampoo and hairspray whirling around him. Close up he was boyish, but older than he appeared to be through the glass and Connie could see that he definitely dyed his own hair.

'Oh,' she said, embarrassed at being caught loitering. 'I'm afraid I've been admiring the photos for too long. I do beg your pardon.'

'I won't charge you for looking,' Richard said, flashing a charming smile. 'Come in and make an appointment.'

Alarm coursed through her. She didn't think she could possibly do that. 'Oh no,' she said. 'You couldn't do anything with me.'

'Let me prove you wrong,' he said, stepping back from the door and beckoning her to follow him. 'Come and have a look around.'

'Well, maybe just for a minute,' Connie said.

A babble and a fug greeted Connie when the door was closed behind her and she stared openly at the women sitting under dryers reading magazines, or wearing huge sheets tied around them to catch the inches of hair being hacked from their heads almost without thought. In the background, 'Release Me' blared out from a wireless.

'I'm Richard,' the hairdresser said.

'My friend mentioned you,' Connie said. 'Her name is Millicent. She lives next door.'

'Ooh,' Richard swooned. 'Millicent has gorgeous hair. And she's very adventurous with it.'

'Yes,' Connie said, feeling flustered and out of place. 'But I'm not, so I think I should ...' She moved towards the door.

'Hang on one mo,' Richard said, pointing towards a row of empty chairs. 'Have a seat and I'll be right with you.'

Connie perched on the edge of a chair that felt as if it was about to swallow her whole. She crossed and uncrossed her legs, ran her hands around the straps of her bag, wiped her nose. She could not remember the last time she'd been in a hairdresser's, but it was probably on her wedding day in 1934, or perhaps once since then. Yes – the other occasion was after she'd been stood down and she was waiting for Arthur to be demobbed. She and Mum had done each other's hair after that, and when Mum was no longer capable, she'd turned to Dora. Now she managed it by herself.

Swinging her head around to follow Richard's fair-haired client as she approached the desk to pay, Connie caught a flash of herself in a mirror and thought she looked more like a woman who *mis*managed her hair.

'Two and six, Mrs Dempsey,' the girl behind the reception desk handed the blonde woman a chit.

Connie's eyes widened. That seemed like a huge amount for the privilege of being able to walk out of the salon looking like Veruschka, but the woman didn't turn a hair.

Looking at the clock, Connie decided she'd wasted enough time. The shops would soon be closing and if she didn't get the prerequisite groceries she would have no other choice but to serve Arthur something completely inappropriate for his dinner tomorrow. Faced with that stark reality, she broke out in a cold sweat and stood to leave.

'Madam,' Richard called to her as he swept needles of hair from a swivel chair with one hand and invited her to sit in it with the other.

Feeling as though she was getting into deeper and deeper water, but somehow unable to turn and make for the shore, Connie sat and faced the mirror. 'Now,' Richard said, deftly freeing her hair from the pins and fluffing out limp, greying strands between his graceful fingers. 'What did you have in mind?'

She shook her head and shrugged. 'Something a bit … different, I suppose.'

'Well,' he said, making eye contact with her reflection. 'How do you feel about sleeping in hair curlers at night? That would get rid of the wave.'

'I don't think so,' she said in a high, squeaky voice that she hardly recognised. She couldn't begin to think what Arthur would have to say about that.

'Hmm,' Richard mused. 'Then there's no point in a fringe. And how much length are you willing to lose? Anything you cut off will instantly give what's left more volume and movement.'

Connie liked the sound of that, but she knew Arthur wouldn't.

Richard swung her chair around and pointed out a woman with a razor-sharp chin-level bob. 'Shall we chop off that much?' He pivoted the chair back with force.

'I don't think I'd want to go above my shoulders,' Connie said.

Richard nodded sagely. 'This is what I'd do, my lovely. First, I'd put a rinse on to bring you back to your rich, dark colour. Then I'd cut you to here.' He chopped his hands against her shoulders. 'Next, I'd backcomb the top, which would hide that cheeky double crown, and lacquer you all over so that nothing, not even the steam from those wicked towers, would stir the style. What do you think?'

She thought it sounded nothing short of a miracle. But it didn't matter what she thought. It was what Arthur thought that counted.

'I can fit you in tomorrow at 12 p.m.' Richard leaned on one of his narrow hips and waited for her reply.

'No, I'm sorry,' she said. 'I have a prior appointment.' She was relieved that she didn't have to add that her engagement was with Arthur's stew.

'Then nothing until Saturday,' Richard said. He picked up a book from the desk and opened it. 'I have ten in the morning or two in the afternoon.'

Studying her hands, Connie's eyes widened. By two o'clock dinner would be out of the way and she wouldn't have to think about tea until later in the afternoon. 'Two,' she said quickly, before she could persuade herself that the idea was completely impractical.

'Fabulous,' Richard said. 'Your name, my lovely?'

'Constance Allinson. But everyone calls me Connie.'

'All booked for you, Connie,' Richard said. 'Look forward to seeing you on Saturday.'

Richard showed her to the door, then turned to usher another woman into his mystical revamping chair and Connie was left to hope there was a bit of decent stewing beef still to be had at the butcher's.

As Connie suspected, the last of the meat she needed for Arthur's stew was an unsavoury dark grey and sat in a puddle of congealed red sludge. The butcher looked at her forlorn face and pointed to a display of plump, pink meat they would have fought over during the war. 'How about a nice chop?'

'No,' Connie said. 'It has to be stewing beef, I'm afraid.'

'Well, you won't get anything decent from this,' he said, shovelling up a scoop of the stomach-churning offcuts. 'I'm about to consign it to the bucket of dog slops. But,' he said, 'there's a lovely bit of shank. It makes a great stew if you cook it slowly.'

Connie stared down at the round cuts of beef and thought she saw the outline of Arthur's disapproving face etched in the marbled fat running through the meat. He would most certainly taste and smell the difference and he wouldn't be happy. Then he'd ask why she hadn't bought the usual stewing beef and one thing would lead to another and she'd have to come clean about *New You for a Snip*, but she'd have to tell him about the hair appointment at some stage as she'd have to hold out her hand and ask him for extra housekeeping to pay for it.

'The shank breaks down whilst simmering,' the butcher was going on. 'And the gravy it produces is rich and full of flavour.'

The urge to force Arthur's hand by serving him something different overwhelmed her, and if the revolutionary change to Thursday's menu was the catalyst for a discussion about getting her hair done, all well and good.

'I'm most grateful for your suggestion.' Connie smiled warmly as the butcher piled four rounds onto the scale, wiped his sticky hands on his apron and wrapped the meat in paper.

Whilst she was tackling the shank with a sharp knife the following morning, Arthur came up behind her and laid his hands on her shoulders. She stiffened with such a start that he took a step back, then peered around to try and look at her face. 'Alright, Treasure?' he asked. 'Oh, I can see why you're upset. That stewing beef looks a bit strange. Might be time to try a different butcher.'

Connie's knife slipped and caught the end of her finger. 'Ouch,' she said, putting the cut to her lips.

'Here.' Arthur jumped to attention. 'Let me see to that for you.'

'It's alright, Arthur,' she snapped. 'I can manage.'

With her back to him, Connie turned on the tap and waited whilst the water pouring over her hand changed from pink to crystal clear. Then she took a deep breath and said, 'I'll need extra housekeeping on Friday, Arthur, if you please.'

Not a murmur or a rustle or a sharp intake of breath came from Arthur's side of the kitchen. When Connie turned around to grab the tea towel and press it against the wound, Arthur was standing stock still, staring at her as if she'd put a gun to his head and asked him to hand over the entire proceeds of his bank account.

She waited for him to get over the shock and speak. He waited, she guessed, for a further explanation. Eventually, he asked if the extra money was for her to buy a better cut of stewing beef.

Despite her throbbing finger, the thumping in her chest and her dry mouth, Connie wanted to laugh out loud. Arthur did not have the capacity or the imagination or the interest to think beyond his own needs and wants. Quite suddenly she felt anger rising up inside her. She was nothing more than a bit player in the drama of his undramatic life and she was tired and fed-up with it.

Throwing the tea towel onto the worktop, she tore at the buttons on her tabard and shrugged it to the floor where it lay in its own pale pink polyester pool.

'Connie.' Arthur took a step back. 'Whatever is the …'

'If you must know,' Connie heard herself shouting. 'I want to get my hair done at a proper hairdressing salon.'

Arthur held up his hands as if he were under arrest. 'Alright, Treasure,' he said. 'We can talk about it.'

'We shouldn't need to talk about it.' Her voice went up a few decibels and Arthur skirted around her to close the kitchen window. 'I shouldn't have to ask if I want to spend some money on myself.' Then with a shudder and a few ragged breaths, the outburst abated, and Connie felt spent, her limbs heavy with fatigue.

Arthur cupped his hand underneath her elbow and led her to the sofa. He sat beside her but she inched away and rested her forehead in her hand. After a minute or so, he quietly moved towards her again and started to rub her back and she let him, too drained and frustrated to do otherwise. 'We agreed on how much housekeeping you would need each week,' Arthur said. 'And I believe it's an adequate amount.'

Had we? Connie wondered. No, they hadn't. Arthur had stated how much he thought fair and she'd acquiesced, knowing that the small amount offered no leeway for her to have any change for herself. She hadn't put her case forward, though, because she knew Arthur's mind had been made up. 'We didn't,' she said.

'Didn't what?'

'Agree. You told me and I didn't argue.'

'No, you didn't. We never argue.' Arthur let his hand drop and exhaled a heavy, frustrated sigh. 'That's why this is so unlike you, Treasure. Quite frankly, I'm a bit worried.'

Connie looked at her husband and wondered how a man with an engineering degree, who had served as an officer in the Royal Navy and now managed a team of employees at the power station could be so ludicrously stupid.

Bitterness surged through her again and she could not hold her tongue. 'No, I never answer back,' she spat. 'But perhaps I should, about the ridiculous pittance you give me for housekeeping and moving here and spending all of my money on this …' She looked around, her top lip curling in distaste. 'This poor excuse for a proper house.'

Arthur drew back, his eyes registering shock and disbelief. 'You wanted to move here, too,' he said, genuinely taken aback.

'No, you did,' she said. 'I didn't have a choice.'

'But, Treasure.' His voice was pleading.

'You acted as if my half of the money from Mum's house belonged to you and you decided what to do with it.'

Arthur's nostrils flared and Connie could tell she'd insulted him deeply. But she would not or could not backtrack and swallow her words.

'That's because I'm in a better position to deal with—'

'With what?' She fired her question before he had a chance to finish his sentence.

'Finances. Provision for the future. You've never had to deal with the ways of this world. I've protected you from all that.' He pointed to his puffed-up chest. 'You haven't had to work since 1945.'

'And whose fault is that?' Connie wailed. 'I've begged you to let me take a job. I would love to go out to work. But oh no,' she aped his voice as best she could between her sobs, '"I didn't fight in a war just to have my wife going out to work."'

That stopped any further outpouring from either of them. Silence hung in the air, chilly and foreboding, like the aftermath of a bombing raid. 'Well,' Arthur said in a hangdog tone of voice. 'Seems I can't do right for doing wrong.'

Connie made no comment.

Arthur looked at his watch and said, 'We'll talk more about this at dinner time.'

He went into the hallway and she heard him clumping about as he gathered his bike helmet and trouser clips and put on his jacket. 'See you later, Treasure,' he called from the doorway. When she didn't reply, he slipped back and peered at her from the kitchen. 'I like your hair as it is,' he said in a meek voice. 'You always look lovely and well-turned out.'

Still she couldn't look at him, but knew she should say something as he was waiting for a kind word from her. 'Thank you, Arthur,' was all she could manage through the bile rising from her stomach.

'Okay then,' he said. 'Bye from Constance's Constant. Put a plaster on that finger.' He stood for another minute, waiting for her to turn and smile at him and when she didn't, he shuffled to the front door and closed it behind him.

Surely, she thought, he must be able to see that it made her feel worthless to have to ask permission for anything that deviated from the routine he dictated. Why did he think he had the right to allow or forbid her to do whatever she wanted with her time? And why did she let that happen? There were things she had no control over – the lack of children, Mum dying, the position of the towers, but thought she was entitled to have some say in how she wore her hair or if she worked at some unqualified job in a school or haberdasher's.

Serious tears started to flow and Connie put her face in her hands, folded in on herself and rocked back and forth. She felt ashamed for treating Arthur so shabbily and reminded herself that he was faithful and caring and steady and, pushing aside how livid she felt, she knew he truly believed he always had her best interests in mind – and that he knew better than she what they were. But she'd lived and worked through the war, too, and hated to think she'd gone through all that tortuous upheaval and heartache just to find herself tied to the house, delivering a specific meal to the table at a specific time on each specified day of the week. That thought was crushing.

4

July 1941

Until a week ago, Connie hadn't been aware that the Navy was involved in cutting out bits from letters sent backwards and forwards between service personnel and civilians. Now she had so many questions – how would she know what to cut and what to leave standing; would she have the final say about what to strike out from every letter she read, or would some phrases and paragraphs have to be checked by a superior; where would she be based; how would she be able to tell if a letter held a secret code. In a heartbeat, her spirits lifted and she felt an electric shock of intrigue.

Alone in the corridor and staring at the list, Connie quickly scanned the column of roles to find out if anyone else had been posted to the same situation. There was one other girl, Angelique Allard, whom Connie hadn't met but she determined to seek out.

The Mess Hall was noisier than usual, the Wrens bubbling and buzzing with the news they'd been given. Connie tagged onto the end of the queue waiting to be served lunch from a hatch and whilst she waited, she looked around for a woman who lived up to the very French-sounding name of her fellow censor.

'Thank you,' Connie said when she was handed a chipped tray holding a steaming main meal, a piece of bread and butter and a bowl of pudding. If she'd been asked exactly what she was saying thank you for, she wouldn't have been able to answer with accuracy. But it looked stodgy and filling and smelled of fatty meat and pastry and she was hungry, so knew she'd mop up the gravy with the bread and not leave a scrap of her afters, either.

'Connie.' Bea, one of the girls who shared her cabin, half-stood and beckoned to an empty chair at her table. 'What did you get?'

'Postal censorship,' Connie answered, sitting down. 'And you?'

'Oh!' Bea seemed surprised. 'That's different. It's clerking for me.' She sounded buoyant enough, then her mouth curled into a look of distaste when she added that she'd been assigned to the supplies department. 'I was hoping for something a bit more exotic,' she said. 'But it needs to be done, I suppose.'

Connie nodded between mouthfuls. 'It might not be exotic, but writing out chits for men's undershorts might turn out to be quite erotic,' she said.

Bea laughed. 'I hadn't thought about it that way, but I will from now on.' She lowered her voice. 'Don't let Chief Wren hear you talking in that unsuitable manner or she'll have you in detention even though it is our last couple of days.'

The dessert turned out to be peel and raisin steamed pudding with watery custard. Connie found two raisins and not many more pieces of peel in her portion and Bea said the cook must like her as that was more dried fruit than she'd had in her slice.

'Anyone else posted with you?' Bea asked. 'There are ten others with me.'

'Only one,' Connie said. 'Angelique Allard. I don't know her, do you?'

Bea shook her head, then turned to the girl on her other side, who after scouring the room through squinting eyes, nodded towards a group of Wrens in the far corner. 'Over there,' Bea reported back to Connie. 'The thin girl with her back to the wall.'

Crisscrossing between tables and chairs, Connie saluted and said, 'Wren Ordinary Wren Allard? Wren Ordinary Wren Allinson. I understand we're to be posted together.'

'Oh,' Angelique said in perfect, clipped English. 'I'm very pleased to meet you.' Her hair was collar length as was every other Wren's, but it looked as though putting a pin in it to hold it off her forehead had been too much of a chore. Her lips were flaking and her blouse caved in around the buttons rather than straining outwards. So much for French glamour, Connie thought.

Angelique pulled out a chair for Connie and the two women sat facing each other. 'I'm not sure why I was given censorship,' Connie said. 'I wonder if I'm going to be posted as a clerk in the department. You know, filing and so forth, because clerking is what I listed as my first, safe choice and weather forecasting was my second.'

'Perhaps.' Angelique didn't sound convinced. 'But I think the list would have made that clear by stating clerk and then censorship. Not postal censorship as is next to both our names. Do you have languages?'

'No,' Connie said. 'Only English. Do you?'

'My father's from France as my name suggests,' Angelique

said. 'So I speak French along with German and a bit of Italian.'

'Do you think there might have been a mistake given our surnames both start with the same three letters?' Connie felt alarm at the prospect of being out of her depth amongst Wrens who were probably much brighter and more well-educated than her.

'Of course not.' Angelique was genuinely earnest. 'The Royal Navy knows exactly what it's doing and if they think you're suited, then you are.' She beamed and Connie was struck by how the girl's face transformed when she smiled, revealing two rows of lovely, even white teeth.

They made arrangements to meet at their quarters in Hampstead on Sunday evening so they could nab a cabin together if possible and then prepare for Monday morning. 'It seems so silly,' Connie said. 'I could stay with my mum in Acton. It's only twenty minutes away on the Tube.'

'That would have been lovely for you,' Angelique said. 'But I suppose it wouldn't fit in with Navy life or the secrecy surrounding our jobs.'

Intrigue was the first word Connie had used when she'd become aware of her posting. But that was excitement about learning the intricacies of the job and being privy to the ins and outs of other people's lives. Secrecy, though, was a different matter, and Angelique made it sound as if there might be aspects of their jobs in censorship that would have to be kept under wraps from everyone else – including Arthur and Ken, her mum and Dora. When Connie thought that she could have been posted to weather forecasting, the idea came and went with a fleeting sense of indifference.

'I must admit to not giving the secrecy aspect much

thought,' she said. 'But to be completely honest with you, I really have no idea what the job entails.' She leaned closer to Angelique. 'Can you tell me a bit more about it?'

Angelique laughed. 'I don't want to spoil it for you,' she said. 'I'll let the training do that.'

'What other roles did you list?' Connie asked.

Colour rose from Angelique's neck and washed over her pale features. 'None.' She shook her head. 'I was ordered to go for censorship, so I stuck with that.'

That was the first Connie had heard of anyone being commanded to take a posting, although that was what had indirectly happened to her. She studied her younger colleague and thought that behind the wan appearance that made her look as if a breeze would knock her off her feet, there was something much deeper, more substantial and robust.

The atmosphere felt a little awkward between them, which Connie didn't like, so she said it was probably something to do with Angelique's flair for languages.

That seemed to do the trick and the tension eased. 'Yes,' Angelique agreed readily. 'Cup of tea?'

'Yes, please,' Connie said. 'With a pinch of sugar if there's enough to go round.' She watched Angelique make her way to the hatch and stand in line to have tea poured for her from a huge, industrial-sized pot. The thought flashed through her mind that she might have been better off doling out socks and drawers and vests with Bea as, whilst there was certainly something enigmatic about both the job and her fellow censor, there was nothing mysterious about Connie herself.

She took her tea from Angelique and whilst they drank

it, the two women exchanged small talk about their families, their lives before the war started and how many times they'd each had to mop the decks during the last couple of weeks. 'I must have lost a good half a stone,' Connie said.

'Me too,' Angelique laughed. 'And I was nothing but skin and bone to begin with.'

'Reading through letters will be a doddle after this,' Connie said.

But Angelique only smiled. She didn't pass comment or offer any more information about the role of postal censor. *Never mind*, Connie thought. She would find out soon enough. And whether the posting was an error or not, she was determined to carry it out to the very best of her abilities.

At last they were given their tailored uniforms of three white shirts, a black tie, black stockings, very dark blue jacket, unpleated skirt, greatcoat, navy mac, two pairs of shoes, white gloves, a round hat with turned-up sides, which was adorned with a Navy ribbon, their pay books, ships' card and railway warrants. Connie was pleased that there wasn't a brass button in sight. The promise of black buttons for the lower ranks, which didn't need to be polished every day, was a bonus for some girls and the deciding factor in choosing the WRNS instead of the WAAFs or one of the other services. Then, after a brief passing-out parade, they were sent off for a weekend's leave before their next posting.

'Can you believe we've only been here for two weeks?'

Bea asked Connie as they walked through the lustrously polished corridors for the last time.

'I know,' Connie said. 'It seems like months ago we were standing in that line waiting to get our bluettes.' She nodded towards the queue of new recruits waiting to claim their bunks, their chores, the tables in the Mess and their chairs in the lecture hall.

'I have no idea what they're going to do with themselves,' Bea said. 'These floors are so shiny I can see my shoes in them. Look.' When she lifted her foot Connie could indeed see the reflection of Bea's sole in the well-scrubbed tiles.

Connie laughed, and when they reached the gate to go their separate ways, they aimed an awkward hug in each other's direction but then settled on a more seemly farewell salute. It had crossed her mind that they should exchange addresses, like so many of the girls had done, but neither of them mentioned it, so perhaps it had been nothing more than shared circumstances and close proximity that had made them feel close. At the corner, Connie turned and watched Bea's back as she hurried down the road, stepping out much more smartly than when they'd first met. With a sudden wrench of wistfulness, she realised there would probably be many more people she would be thrown together with over the course of this war who, when the situation changed, she would lose contact with, and the knot in her throat made her feel as if she were mourning those friendships already.

5

Connie's nose was running dangerously close to her top lip. She went to dig out the tissue she kept in her tabard pocket then remembered the pink puddle of material in the middle of the kitchen floor. That made her sob again and she wiped her tears and snot on the sleeve of her cardigan instead. What had brought all this on now, she wondered. Was having to go to Arthur, cap in hand, for the money to get her hair done the final straw? Or had it enabled the worm to turn. Any of those cliches would do, she thought.

Wandering into the kitchen, Connie retrieved the tabard from the floor and decided there was nothing else for it but to start simmering the shank of beef for Arthur's dinner. He'd be home at quarter past one, bringing with him the promise of talking in greater detail about her hair and the money she needed for it, and this time she determined not to let it go without having her say. When she was younger, tall and proud in her WRNS uniform, excited about the prospect of tackling her war work as a letter censor, she would have laughed if anyone had told her she couldn't get her hair trimmed or serve a meal of her own choosing. Tears threatened again, then a small smile of impending victory crept across her face at the thought of Arthur having to like or lump the cut of meat that wasn't his usual Thursday stewing beef.

She circled a plaster around her finger then set about the shank again, cleaving it into chunks and throwing them into a large non-stick saucepan. Next she peeled and chopped onions, carrots, potatoes and tossed them in with the meat. She'd prepared this meal so many times before, that she coated the whole lot in flour and stirred in water without registering what she was doing. Instead, she played out her squabble with Arthur in her mind and prepared her defence for the second round.

Opening a tin of peas over the sink, she caught sight of the clematis. It was a breezy day and the spindly plant swayed precariously in the wind. Later, she would go out and check that the pebbles covering its roots had remained in place; she would pull any offending weeds, too, which was one of her chores for Thursdays at this time of year.

Steam as thick and damp as the billows from the towers filled the kitchen, the aroma from the stew rich and hearty. Connie reached up to open the window and sighed, furious again that Arthur had closed it as their barney began. *He doesn't want me to do anything other than work in this house*, she thought. *Then he can't leave me alone to get on with it – he has to interfere.*

As soon as the latch gave way, Shirley and Millicent's voices drifted in and Connie froze, suddenly aware that Arthur had closed it so the neighbours couldn't be privy to their overheated discussion. Her cheeks burned at the thought that one or other of them might have heard her tears, her rant and rave and unkind words.

As she stirred the contents of the pan, there was a tap at

the front door. Connie paused, saucepan lid in hand, and thought about who it could be. Taking a couple of steps backwards, she looked down the hall and saw Shirley's fuzzy, obscured figure through the stippled glass.

Any other day she would have tripped over her own feet as she ran down the hallway to wrench the door off its hinges and say hello to Shirley. But this morning she could have done without the intrusion. Patting under her nose and around her eyes to wipe away any evidence of her upset, she managed to greet her neighbour with the semblance of a smile.

'Connie,' Shirley said, as if she was surprised that Connie had opened her own door. 'Everything alright?'

That could have been an innocent question, but Connie was quite sure her neighbour had heard at least some of what was said between her and Arthur.

'Morning, Shirley,' Connie said. 'I'm fine, thank you.'

Shirley rested one open palm on the little hill that filled her maternity smock and in her other hand she carried a large, colourful book. Connie couldn't be sure, but for a beat she thought the younger woman looked a bit disappointed with her reply.

'And how are you today?'

'Oh, I'm okay,' Shirley said.

Then there was an awkward pause during which the saucepan lid emitted a thin, watery whistle and the warm smell of simmering meat and vegetables drifted towards them.

'Oh,' Shirley said again. 'You said you might be interested in looking through my Littlewoods catalogue.' She held the book out towards Connie who thought that conversation must have taken place weeks ago, not yesterday.

'Of course. I remember,' Connie said, taking the catalogue from Shirley and flicking through it so mixing bowls and models, bikes and bathroom cabinets blurred into one.

'Also,' Shirley said. 'A few of the others are having a cup of coffee at my house in half an hour, if you've got the time?'

Connie turned to look towards the jiggling saucepan in the kitchen and the unweeded garden beyond that. *Why not?* she thought. Arthur could dish up for himself if she wasn't home in time, that would definitely give them something to discuss later. 'How nice of you, Shirley,' she said. 'I'd love to. See you soon.'

She turned the heat under the saucepan right down, fixed her face and drew pins through the bun that she hoped would soon be non-existent, and when she marched to Shirley's front door she no longer felt pent-up rage, but a potent sense of defiance.

Toddlers squirmed all over Shirley's living room like tadpoles in a pond. They were pushing toy cars on road mats, looking through Thomas the Tank Engine books, scoffing biscuits and trundling along behind replicas of their own baby buggies, dolls without eyes or hair or clothes hanging alarmingly from gummy, unbuckled straps.

'Hello, Connie.' Millicent looked up from her cross-legged position on the carpet. She seemed to hold Connie's gaze for a moment too long, as if they shared a secret, before she turned her attention to the children and said, 'Welcome to the madhouse. Take that out of your mouth right now, young man.'

A piece of red Lego swam on a stream of drool from Adrian's mouth to the carpet, where he immediately proceeded to dig it into the tightly packed fibres. 'Mucky pup,' Millicent said, wiping her little boy's mouth.

'Coffee, Connie? Or tea?' Shirley asked, Tracey hanging onto the hem of her dress.

'Tea, please,' Connie said. 'One sugar, if I may.'

'Anyone for a refill?' Shirley looked around the room and each of the young women held out an array of mismatching mugs.

Susan from across the road balanced on a squat, red pouffe, concentrating on a catalogue in her lap whilst her little boy repeatedly banged a truck of wooden bricks into a deflated football. Without looking up, Susan grabbed the handle of the cart and said, 'Enough, Edward. Go and find something else annoying to do.' When Connie settled next to her on a dining room chair, Susan smiled and rolled her eyes in her toddler's direction.

'You know Connie, don't you, Mandy?' Millicent asked a fair-haired woman wearing thick, wire-rimmed glasses. 'She's the lovely neighbour between me and Shirley. I tried to get her to apply for the job at the infants' school. You know, for a dinner lady. But she's decided against it.'

All eyes turned to Connie and she felt hot blotches of red creeping up from under her collar. It seemed as if they were all waiting for her to affirm Millicent's statement, so Connie shook her head and said, 'No, it's not for me.'

Excitement over, the other mums resumed their chattering,

but Millicent studied her for a few extra moments. 'Shame,' she said. 'It would be good for …'

Connie waited for her neighbour to finish.

'… the children,' she said at last.

'Well,' Connie said, smiling towards Adrian. 'They're all so lovely, I'm sure they'll like whoever gets the job.'

Adrian picked up a book of fairy tales and clambered up Connie's legs, pointing to a picture of Little Red Riding Hood and a grey, slobbering wolf. 'Read,' he demanded. Connie's heart turned to liquid.

'Say please, Adie,' Millicent chastised, then she laughed. 'You certainly are his favourite, Connie.'

Before she could stop herself, Connie kissed the little boy on his head and immediately wondered if Millicent thought she was taking liberties, but her neighbour was oblivious, helping Shirley with the tray of hot drinks and a plate of biscuits, which she passed around after popping one into her own mouth first.

The talk turned to what everyone was buying from Littlewoods and how much they could afford to put into the club each week. That's what they called it, although it was the same as buying things on tick or the never-never, as Mum used to say. Connie wasn't able to offer much to the chat as she was sure she wouldn't be purchasing anything – Arthur would be struck deaf, dumb and blind if she dared to ask for extra money to pay for goods in such a foolish, frivolous way.

'Connie might be joining,' Shirley said, giving her a sweet smile. Connie wondered how much commission Shirley made for all the trouble of ordering, delivering packages, sending unwanted purchases back and collecting payments each week. And the poor girl probably ploughed it all back into Littlewoods for nappies and nursery equipment and little treats for her children.

Millicent explained Connie's situation. 'She doesn't have any children and her house is absolutely per-fect.'

'All kitted out,' Shirley chimed in. 'And no muddy feet or greasy handprints to ruin things.'

'Then maybe a piece of jewellery?' Susan said. 'Or a nice coat or electric hoover?'

A murmur shot through with longing bubbled around her.

'So it's luxury goods for you,' Mandy said.

'Well, not exactly,' said Connie, wondering what they would think if she told them she had to plead with Arthur for a few bob to have her hair cut. Tightening her hold on Adrian, who was reciting the story to himself as he turned the pages of his book, Connie thought that one like him was worth more than all the paraphernalia up for grabs in the catalogue and she would trade everything – carpets, clothes, necklaces, hairdos, saucepans, stockings, radiators, her clematis – for a child she could call her own.

That subject ran its course and the next twist in the chat led to husbands and she listened in astonishment as they pulled the poor men apart, with affection and humour, but scathingly, nevertheless.

'Every morning when Graham leaves the house,' Mandy said. 'I have to go behind him and pick up his pyjamas, put the top on his tin of shaving foam, mop the milk he spilled making a cup of tea. He's worse than the children.'

'Tony says he'll mow the lawn, but then he never gets

around to it. So muggins here,' Susan pointed to herself, 'has to do that as well as everything else.'

Connie couldn't believe what she was hearing. She'd never disrespected Arthur to anyone no matter what she thought about him in her innermost, private musings and wouldn't dare go crying to Dora or Ken or a neighbour about his shortcomings. But here were these young women sharing all their complaints as if it were an everyday occurrence that made no difference at all to their marriages.

Millicent laughed, her hair shimmering around her head. 'Brian often doesn't get dressed until lunchtime at the weekend,' she said. 'He lazes in his undershorts scratching his arse until I shoo him up the stairs to make himself decent.'

Connie laughed with the rest of them but couldn't imagine Arthur doing anything like that; on Saturdays and Sundays he was up, dressed and ready to tackle his weekend list by eight o'clock at the latest – and he expected her to have his breakfast on the go by that time, too.

'Connie,' said Shirley, 'and her husband, Arthur, seem happy to do everything together. Don't you, Connie?'

Connie was sure her two neighbours were doing their best to make her feel welcome, but every time they tried to drag her in she felt guarded and uncomfortable. If they'd overheard the argument coming from her house that morning, they might be trying to glean more information from her about that. Each face in the room was focused on her and suddenly she felt sorry for all of them, including herself, because what else was there to do on this new housing estate besides gossip and watch each other's children and compare their houses and themselves to each other. 'We're in a different position to all of you.' She shrugged. 'You know, we're older and ...' She couldn't say the words – childless; grandchildless; friendless – not without them sticking in her throat, so she let them hang in the air.

'Arthur even comes home at 1.15 on the dot every day for his dinner,' Shirley persisted. 'Doesn't he, Connie? I couldn't bear to see Trev in the middle of the day. Not that I don't think the world of him, because I do. But what would we talk about? Oh no, would you look at that?' She pointed to bloated billows of smoke or steam pumping out of the towers. 'Do you think I should get the Babygros in?' Her hand massaged the top of her distended stomach.

'Why bother?' Mandy pushed up her spectacles. 'If you save them this time, they'll only get smothered in the stuff tomorrow or the next day.'

Connie gazed at the towers with all the others, hypnotised by the shape of them from this slightly different angle. One of the concrete giants looked closer than the others and seemed to be leaning towards them like an obnoxious Tower of Pisa. 'That one looks ready to topple,' said Mandy.

'Oh, they do worry me,' Shirley said. She got up, took a snivelling Tracey's hand and walked towards the patio doors overlooking the garden.

The other women muttered their agreement. Whilst Connie, too, was fearful of the emissions, she wanted to say something to put Shirley's mind at rest. 'Arthur assures me that whatever it is that gets puffed out, it's completely harmless.'

'He's Tony's manager,' Susan said. 'So I'm sure he knows what he's talking about.'

Connie wasn't convinced that was the case, but Shirley gave her a relieved smile and she felt as if she'd been helpful.

Someone started talking about cooking and when that topic was exhausted they turned back to orders from the catalogue. Adrian slithered off Connie's lap and squatted in front of a Noddy puzzle. No one addressed her again and she felt her neck and shoulders soften.

She watched the children play and squabble and hold out little orange beakers for their mums to fill with diluted squash. In the background, the women jabbered and giggled, grabbed minuscule choking hazards from their toddler's hands and wiped at tiny button noses and cherry red lips. Outside, the wind changed direction and the smoke from the towers dissipated into thin wisps that stretched across the pale blue sky. It seemed as if all of them were filling in their time, waiting for something to happen. But this was it. This was how they passed their mornings and with a jolt of surprise, she realised she'd had enough for one day and wanted to leave the endless round of hot drinks and lukewarm chatter.

'More tea, Connie?' Shirley asked. 'I'm making a pot.'

'No, thank you,' Connie said, getting to her feet. 'I've had a lovely time but I must be getting back.' Again, she noticed a look pass amongst them – a flicker of incredulity mixed with annoyance, perhaps because she hadn't shared more of the early morning argument that had transpired between her and Arthur.

All she said, though, was goodbye and thank you as she caressed Tracey's satin hair on the way out.

'Maybe we'll see you when we fetch the children from school,' Millicent said.

'Perhaps,' Connie said. 'I enjoy our walks.' Which was true; she loved holding Adrian's hand, and Tracey's wonder at the world of insects and fallen leaves and chips in brick walls was contagious. But now she couldn't believe that coffee morning was the mysterious social life she'd craved. Her heart plummeted and seemed to hit the short path back to her house when she realised that the much-anticipated diversion had lost its awe.

By the time Arthur appeared at quarter past one, the stew was thick and bubbling, fluffy dumplings languishing neatly on top of the gravy. 'Hello, you,' he called from the hall.

'Yoo-hoo,' Connie answered flatly, feeling obliged to complete their customary dinner time greeting.

Little muscles tightened around her mouth as she willed him not to say what he always said: 'Mmm. Stew with dumplings. Must be Thursday.'

Thankfully he gave that sentiment a miss when he shook his head almost imperceptibly at the unweeded garden. Connie chose to ignore the reproachful gesture and not make any attempt to justify herself, although she knew she'd have to fit that chore in amongst her others during the afternoon.

Arthur took off his outdoor things and Connie dished their meal into bowls and set them on the table. They sat down and she waited with a somersaulting stomach for Arthur to take his first mouthful then begin the deferred discussion. The shank was so tender that he cut a forkful as easily as if he was drawing a hot knife through butter. His eyes narrowed and he held up the meat, inspected it from different angles, put it in his mouth, chewed and swallowed. 'This is not the usual stewing beef, Treasure,' he pronounced. 'But I must say it's excellent.'

Connie almost choked on her own tasty mouthful and decided to spin out her reply and watch Arthur flinch under the discomfort of her having the upper hand for once. 'Thank you, Arthur,' she said. 'But it's not stewing beef.'

Arthur waited, his jaw slack, for further explanation but Connie gazed over his shoulder and ate another morsel of meat with a wedge of dumpling.

'But,' he spluttered, 'we always have stewing beef on Thursdays.'

'We always *had* stewing beef on Thursdays,' she said, hardly able to keep a spark of triumph out of her voice. 'But not this Thursday.'

Arthur pushed the meat and vegetables around in the thick, silky gravy. 'What is it then?' he asked.

'Another cut of meat I thought we'd try,' Connie said. 'It's called shank. Aren't you going to eat yours? You said it was excellent.'

There was nowhere he could go after that other than back to his bowl.

'Didn't you?' she insisted.

Arthur closed his eyes for longer than a blink and nodded. 'Yes, Treasure,' he said. 'It is. But if it's more expensive, which it must be, please go back to stewing beef.'

'Same price, Arthur,' she said with a small lift of her chin. 'Different meat.'

All that could then be heard for the next few minutes was the scrape of cutlery on china, cups of tea being picked up and put down, the faint sounds of gnawing, nibbling and munching and Arthur clearing his throat. With warmth beginning to irritate around her waistband and along the nape of her neck, Connie wondered when Arthur would address the issue of the extra housekeeping, but he seemed intent on getting the ball back into his court after her coup with the meat.

Connie watched her husband as he mopped up the last of his gravy with a forkful of dumpling, laid his cutlery straight and said, 'Thank you, Connie.'

She sighed, started to stack the dishes and thought she might have to resign herself to washing any hope of a new hairdo down the plughole with the residue of dinner.

Then Arthur said, 'One minute, Treasure.'

Connie stood, hands full with the crockery, waiting for him to carry on.

'Back to this morning's discussion.'

She sat back down with a bump.

'Here,' he said, leaning back and reaching into his trouser pocket. 'Is this enough?' He pushed three shillings across the table towards her, but kept a finger firmly on the tower of coins. Connie looked down at his hands, the wiry black hairs on his knuckles standing out against pale skin.

'Yes, thank you,' she said, meeting his gaze.

'Well I believe hairdressers expect a tip.' He pushed the money the last inch or so, then let it go. After a pause he said, 'I've been thinking about some of the things you said this morning.'

'So have I,' she said.

'I must say, I was rather stunned. Don't you think you were more than a bit hasty and unfair?'

Connie thought for a minute. 'Perhaps about one or two

things,' she said. 'But I would so like to do something else besides ...' She swept her arm around the dining room. 'A job. Or a little job, as you call whatever women do for pay.' She could feel herself becoming infuriated again when she remembered Arthur using that very expression about the important work entrusted to her during the war.

'Not that again,' he said. 'Why am I and our home and our life together not enough for you? I don't understand.' He shook his head slowly from side to side as if trying to extricate a piece of enlightening knowledge that was lodged deep in his brain. 'During the war that's what everyone wanted to get back to, didn't they? This was what we fought for.'

'Not quite, Arthur,' Connie said softly. 'We hoped for more of a family than the two of us.'

Suddenly on the defensive, Arthur's nostrils flared and he crossed his arms over his chest. 'But we didn't get that, so I've devoted my life to keeping you happy and safe and providing for us. All I've ever wanted is for you to be by my side.'

'Arthur,' she said. 'I appreciate how hard you work and how you try to look after me, but me having a job won't change that. It would be a diversion from these four walls, that's all.'

Arthur studied her and Connie felt hopeful that he might be weighing up what she'd said in her favour. 'I do think you need to do something different from time to time,' he stated. 'A distraction to look forward to.'

Connie caught her breath. What could he mean? She waited with wide eyes and fidgeting hands for him to carry on.

'I would be willing to give my permission for you to

visit Ken and Dora let's say … Once every two months? You could spend two nights and the best part of three days with them and the boys and come back refreshed after a little break.' He sat back, folded his arms and looked rather smug. 'What do you think?' he asked, his face eager and boyish.

Connie didn't know what to think. Never in a million years had she expected that to be the answer Arthur would come up with to resolve her brooding unrest. She was utterly speechless, so he carried on.

'I am understanding, Treasure,' he said softly. 'And I do know how women feel at your time of life.'

'You know nothing,' she blurted out between clenched teeth.

Arthur's face hardened. 'That's quite enough, Constance,' he said. 'I am trying my best to make things easier for you, though God knows I give you a good enough life. The least you could do is be grateful.' He stood and walked towards the hall to retrieve his cycling gear. 'You haven't even bothered to ask how I'll manage on those few days without you every other month.'

No, she hadn't thought about that, but now that Arthur mentioned it, she imagined it would involve huge amounts of planning and preparation on her part. She took a deep breath and told herself to stay calm and think before she spoke.

'Arthur.' She followed him into the hallway where he was adjusting his cycle clips. 'I appreciate the offer and lovely as it would be to spend more time with Ken and Dora, *I*,' she emphasised the word, 'don't think that's what I need.'

Arthur stood, his face beetroot from either bending over or from the fact she was standing up for herself.

'I think that a part-time job that won't interfere with anything I have to do in the house would solve my ...'

'Your what?' Arthur said with a touch of anxiety.

'My disquiet?' she offered, holding his gaze. 'My desire to be purposeful? The need to fill my time? Any and all of those things.'

For a moment, Connie thought Arthur was seriously considering what amounted to an entreaty from her to be understood.

But he twitched his head, his helmet moving clumsily from side to side. 'No, Treasure. I've said it before and I'll say it again – I didn't fight in a war just to have my wife ...' He stopped himself short mid-sentence, then carried on. 'Well, you know what I think and why.'

'What about what I think and why?'

For a moment, his raised eyebrows disappeared under his bike helmet. 'Treasure. A new hairdo and a trip to your brother's every once in a while is my offer. You shouldn't look a gift horse in the mouth.' With one foot in the hallway and the other on the front path, he turned back to her for a moment. 'Oh, and that meat,' he said. 'Whatever it was, please feel free to buy it again.'

That afternoon she tidied the kitchen, weeded the garden, mopped the linoleum floors, dusted the ornaments and waited until Millicent and Shirley were well out of sight before she set off for Barnby Dun. When she passed the park, she thought she distinguished a flash of the two young mums heading towards the swings with their little ones in tow. But she marched on and didn't harbour the slightest desire to take up where they'd left off earlier that day.

Feeling in her pocket for the three shillings Arthur had handed over, she held on tightly to the hope that the shine of a new hairdo on Saturday wouldn't tarnish as quickly as the coffee mornings she'd endlessly hankered after.

6

August 1941

On the first day of training at Westfield College, Angelique was proved right when Connie and all her fellow Wrens had to sign a secrecy document that stated they wouldn't gossip about censorship practices or disclose any information they read in the letters they opened. In no uncertain terms, they were told that in times of war, censorship was necessary, but in a democratic society the population should be entitled to send and receive private correspondence, and they were to honour that ethos whenever possible by cutting only what was necessary. The motto they were told to live by was: What does not concern the war does not concern censorship. They were also instructed that as much private mail as possible should be quickly released and letters should only be stopped when they contained what amounted to organised propaganda against the Allied interests. Which in practice meant anything that gave away the position of troops or where they were being moved to and from; manoeuvres; deployment; military strategy; descriptions of equipment; the effect of enemy action.

At that point in the training Connie put up her hand. 'So political opinion isn't to be censored?'

'Correct up to a point, Wren Ordinary Wren Allinson,' the training officer replied. 'Everyone is entitled to their opinions. You must use your discretion, but you must only censor if statements against our cause appear to form part of a propaganda campaign. Free speech is one of the principles we are fighting for and we must uphold that right.'

Connie swallowed and a few of the girls sitting near her whispered to each other in disgruntled tones. That edict was most admirable, but certainly went against the grain. How Connie would have loved permission to tear up every letter that had just one word or sentence against Churchill or the government or the Allies. How dare anyone, she thought, speak out against what was right and just.

The training officer, surveying the Wrens over her spectacles, let them have a few moments to talk amongst themselves then called them to order. 'Remember,' she said. 'That you are here to do a specific job and you must not, under any circumstances, take it upon yourselves to set your own guidelines based upon the morals we in the Royal Navy uphold. You must stick to the rules. When you get to your cutting stations and the letters pile up on your desks, you won't have time to worry about Mrs Jones and her silly opinion that the Allies should surrender so she can have real milk in her tea again, or old Mr Smith's prediction that Germany will be victorious because his waterworks forecast they would.'

Connie laughed out loud with the other girls.

'You will soon be able to spot the difference between those kinds of daft statements and the ones engineered by an organised body of people working against the Allies, or statements that are likely to circulate and influence such a body.'

Put that way, it all made perfect sense and Connie felt reassured.

A couple of rows in front of her, Angelique put up her freckled hand. 'What about things written that might lower the morale of the troops?' she asked.

'Or civilians, for that matter,' another young woman added.

'That's a tricky one,' the training officer said. 'The public should not be exposed to disturbing content. If letters home from service personnel discuss the horrors of war in too much detail, they should be kept from families for fear that public opinion would be routed away from support for the war effort. As you are well aware, civilians are encouraged to write about day-to-day life at home. Trips to the shops, chats with friends, children's birthdays. Anything written that could cause despondency and despair should be blacked out. There's much more about that in *The Manual for Censorship of Naval Mail* and it will become much clearer when we go through some drills later.'

They spent a good deal of time learning about the espionage, secrecy, codes and spying that Angelique had alluded to. Although there were special divisions that dealt with that kind of thing, they had to look out for secret messages that might be written into the text of letters. These could consist of numbers spaced out evenly in the paragraphs. 'For example,' their instructor said. 'The letter could mention that a friend had moved to number 11; it was little Freddy's second day at school; they celebrated

Great-Aunt Bertha's ninety-seventh birthday and the fifth stair in the house had developed a creak. An agent would know what each of those numbers stood for and be able to pass on vital information to the enemy.'

Connie gasped involuntarily and put her hand on her heart, but quickly pulled herself together when she realised that was just the beginning. They were given examples of plain language codes, Playfair method codes, secondary meanings codes, en clair codes, number codes, alphabet codes, name substitution codes, musical note codes, sophisticated codes, unrefined codes and schoolboy codes. In pairs, they were asked to read through concocted letters and determine whether or not the writing contained code and if it did, to attempt to break it. Some Connie found easy and others were harder to detect.

'Clues,' the training officer said. 'Will be in awkward wording or reasoning or when the writer jumps from one totally unrelated subject to another.'

They were told that they must hold each and every envelope up to a strong light and look for secret writing or an inner sleeve that could conceal code or something written under the postage stamp. 'And if any currency or jewels are included in the letters, they must be handed over with the complete contents to the officer in charge of your table.'

'Even the diamonds?' a very slender, smart young woman asked.

The officer laughed at that. 'I'm afraid so,' she said.

Then they were instructed to deal with one letter at a time and never pick up the next envelope until the first one's fate had been decided. How to precisely open envelopes along the short side, if possible, with their regulation letter opener, and how to reseal them with their examiner's label. To always pass letters upwards if in any doubt; never take correspondence out of their section in their hands or bags; never write down information in a notebook or on a piece of paper for their personal use at a later date.

Then there were the ever-changing blacklists, watchlists, inspect lists and statutory lists they must refer to constantly.

Again, they had to learn the lingo and abbreviations and acronyms that went with the role and where to find the Postal Liaison Group circulars that came into all censorship offices at a great pace. They were given a week to read through the official tome entitled *Instructions for the Use of Postal Censors*, then they had to attend a question-and-answer session about the contents.

At the end of the course, before they were given their next postings, they had to sit and pass a number of examinations to make sure they'd taken it all in.

'I'm sure I don't belong here,' Connie said to Angelique when they were drinking cocoa during their evening recreational break. 'I can't imagine I'll pass the exams.'

'Don't be so silly,' Angelique said. 'We're all struggling with the new information that's being thrown at us. It's overwhelming. I know my head's swimming with it.' But Connie felt sure the girl immediately understood every piece of information she was given and was merely being kind.

In a letter to Arthur, Connie reiterated that she felt a bit out of place and hoped he would allay her fears. He replied saying he was in no doubt she would do a grand job but – there was always a reservation with Arthur – she must not do anything that would put her in harm's way. She must keep herself safe until he could come home and do that job for her.

Connie lay on her bunk and read his words again.

> I'm aware we're in the middle of a war, but if you think your own safety is compromised, please tell the Chief Wren you're out of your depth and unhappy and want a transfer to a clerical position. After all, Treasure, I'm fighting this war so we can build a family together – I wouldn't want that with anyone other than you.

She wasn't unhappy, although she thought she was rather out of her depth, but that served to spark a determination in her and spur her on to pass her exams, get on with the job efficiently and effectively and prove to everyone, herself included, that her allocation to censorship had been the right decision.

When the results of the final examinations were posted, she'd passed with excellent marks and been promoted to Leading Wren. 'Do you see?' Angelique said, her mouth pulling back from her white teeth. 'No mix-up.'

'No,' Connie agreed. 'Apparently not. And if we didn't already know it, your perfect score confirms there was certainly no mistake about you, Petty Officer Wren Allard.'

'Guesswork,' Angelique said in her usual deferential manner.

When they'd finished their training and had to go their separate ways, Angelique, along with another woman who had languages, was sent to somewhere in Buckinghamshire called Bletchley. This time, Connie asked if she could take

Angelique's address, but her new friend said she wasn't allowed to give it to anyone.

Connie was taken aback. 'That's very odd,' she said. 'What if your mum needs to get in touch with you?'

'There is a way for a limited number of people to do that,' Angelique said, looking sheepish.

Connie studied her, but once again the girl didn't offer any other information. Then an idea almost floored her. 'Are you going to be a spy?' she whispered. 'Or something along those lines?'

Angelique met Connie's stare and put her finger against her lips, white and taut with knitted tension. 'You give me your address and I'll send you a note when I get settled.'

Looking back at various conversations with Angelique, Connie became convinced her fellow Wren knew all along she was destined for a job in espionage and that she herself had not been earmarked for anything as exciting.

Two of the others in the contingent were sent to Bristol and the rest to Liverpool. Connie alone was posted to HMS Holborn and had to move her quarters no further than the Chelsea Embankment.

Gleaming brass buttons winked from the Chief Wren Censor's jacket as she and Connie saluted each other. They were the only spots of colour in the otherwise stark room and with one sweep of her eyes, Connie took in whitewashed walls; highly polished wooden floors of an indeterminant colour; windows boarded against bomb damage; circulars and official leaflets standing to attention in a wire rack along one wall; pigeonholes stuffed with various divisions of mail and Wrens stationed six to a countless number of round tables, an officer presiding over each of them. Working on one letter at a time, the women's heads hung over piles of envelopes. When one or another looked up or wandered to confer with a colleague, Connie saw that they all wore the merest scrape of makeup, no jewellery whatsoever except plain wedding bands and their hair off their collars – as per strict orders. Her hand went to the nape of her own neck where she felt for the ends of her lobbed off strands, which still felt odd to the touch and looked strange in the reflection that stared back at her from the mirror. *But if that's all I lose during this war*, she thought, *I'll be doing alright.*

'Welcome to HMS Holborn, Leading Wren Censor Allinson,' the Chief Wren said, her hand glued to her temple in a salute.

Connie stood straight and tall until the officer's hand floated down and a shadow of a smile crossed her face. 'Please,' she said, pointing to a chair across from her desk.

'Mam,' Connie replied. She removed her hat and placed it on her knees, hoping it hadn't squashed her double crown to a flat mess, and folded her hands in her lap.

The Chief Wren flicked through a file of papers on her desk, then looked up at Connie. Out of habit, or so it seemed, her finger and thumb went to touch tiny holes that had been drilled into her earlobes and Connie guessed she had hung jewels from them before the war had seen fun and frivolity take a back seat. 'I read through your ships' card earlier,' she said. 'And I must say I'm very impressed. You enjoyed your training?' she asked. 'Although I see we weren't your first choice.'

Connie could feel the officer waiting for her reply. The only noise was the shuffling of papers, the ticking of a large clock on the wall, the *snip snip* of scissors and the *scritch scratch* of pencils. It crossed Connie's mind that perhaps this job was not going to live up to its enchanting appeal and she might have been better off insisting on forecasting the weather. But it was too late for that now. 'Mam,' Connie said. 'The training was very interesting and I'm committed to doing the job effectively and efficiently.'

The Chief Wren sat with such a ramrod back, Connie thought her spine must have been hewn from metal and she hoped her own posture was equally as impressive. 'Excellent,' the older woman said. 'If you'll be so good as to follow me, I'll introduce you to your table and your presiding officer.'

'Mam,' Connie said, gathering together her hat, coat and bag and following closely behind the Chief Wren as she chicaned through the labyrinth of tables.

Each chair was occupied until they came to the far side of the room where there was one empty space, a pair of scissors, an indelible pencil, a pile of examiners' stickers, a letter opener and a lamp waiting on the desk. All five Wrens and the presiding officer stood and saluted. 'As you were, please,' the Chief Wren dismissed them back to their duties with a salute of her own. For a split second, a cloud of discomfort at their deference came over the superior officer and once again she stopped her fingers short of fidgeting with her earlobe. Connie was struck at how difficult it must be, for so many people, to take on roles and titles and uniforms they never would have chosen for themselves.

'Petty Officer Wren Censor Saunders,' the Chief Wren

addressed the only Wren left standing. Then she indicated Connie with the flat of her palm and said, 'This is Leading Wren Censor Allinson. I'll leave her in your very capable hands.'

Connie addressed her presiding officer as Mam and the two women saluted each other.

'This way, Leading Wren Censor Allinson,' the Petty Officer said. She turned on her heels and led Connie through a door and into a cloakroom where tatty, worn benches were interspersed amongst tiers of dark green lockers. 'This one's yours,' she said, stopping at a tin cupboard that stood open, a lock and key dangling from the door. 'Number 43.'

Connie peered inside the gloomy depths and saw dust and grime swirling in the corners. It looked as if the last girl who'd used it had brought in half the debris from the Blitz with her.

'Vera only left yesterday for Liverpool,' the Petty Officer said, shrugging her shoulders. 'No time to clean, I suppose.'

'Thank you, Mam. I can bring in a duster and sort it out,' Connie said, rather taken aback at what she saw when she turned to look at her superior properly for the first time. They all called each other girls, but the Petty Officer was no more than that; she looked as though she was barely out of a gymslip. With thick, fair hair cut to the required length, the thinnest veil of makeup on her flawless face and dark brown eyes that hadn't lost their huge, round innocent appeal, she was the mirror of a porcelain doll Connie had carried about as a child. And, she couldn't believe it, the officer was slouched against the locker next to hers picking at her cuticles.

'Mam?' Connie offered.

The Petty Officer looked up from her fingernails and smiled, her round cheeks pulling towards her ears. 'Dotty,' she said.

'I beg your pardon?' Connie was confused.

'Out of earshot, my name's Dotty,' the officer explained. 'And you are?'

'Constance. Everyone calls me Connie. But, Mam,' Connie was concerned, she didn't want to be reprimanded.

Dotty shrugged again. 'It's fine,' she said. 'In here or out on the street or in the pub. You do like the pub, don't you?'

Connie nodded, although she wondered if Dotty was old enough to drink.

'And if someone above us,' she pointed upwards, 'does happen to hear, what are they going to do, make us walk the plank?'

Despite her jaw resting unhinged on her chest, Connie couldn't stop herself from laughing out loud. Dotty laughed, too, in a high-pitched giggle that added to her schoolgirl mien.

'Shove your things in there,' Dotty said, pointing to the open locker. 'And I'll get you started on your first stack of letters.'

Not exactly Naval rhetoric or even Jackspeak, but Connie followed orders and hung up her bag, hat and coat, turned the tiny key in the huge lock and stood facing Dotty.

'Right, back out to the main room,' Dotty said, her hips sashaying from side to side as she led the way.

Much to Connie's amazement, the girl's demeanour changed the minute the door opened into the workspace and she was once more Petty Officer Wren Censor Saunders. She stood taller and the way she walked changed from sassy to smart; her voice became colder and more clipped; she looked straight ahead to her desk with a no-nonsense gaze. 'This is your equipment.' She pointed to the items on the table in front of Connie's chair. 'Please put them in your desk drawer at the close of business. They are your responsibility. I distribute copies of the blacklist and watchlist every morning and collect them at the end of the day.'

'Mam,' Connie said. She thought Dotty's eyes might be impish when they met hers, but they were steely and hard without the slightest hint of the playful anarchy they'd displayed a couple of minutes earlier.

'The best way to start is to begin,' Dotty said. 'Open your first envelope, read it and make a decision. For the first few days at least, I will be asking you to show me every letter that passes through your hands so I can verify your judgement. Understood?'

'Yes, Mam,' Connie said.

'And until you are completely happy with the system, I will supervise you when you go to the pigeonholes to refresh your pile of letters.'

'Mam.'

'There you are then.' Dotty offered her a much more controlled, grown-up smile than the one that had been plastered over her face in the cloakroom. 'You may begin your war work.'

Connie made herself as comfortable as possible in the hard chair. She surveyed her equipment and clicked on the bright, high-powered lamp. Turning over her wad of labels, she saw that they read *Examiner 7364* and her heart thumped once in her chest before it settled back to a steady rhythm. As she aimed the letter opener under the side flap of the first envelope she picked up, she forgot about Dotty and the Chief Wren's earrings and Angelique in Bletchley, the last letter she'd received from Arthur, her mum on her own at home in Acton, the detritus in the bottom of her locker and the hole in her stockings she would have to mend later. All she thought about was the letter in front of her.

7

Determined to use the opportunity of having her hair done to show Arthur that she could manage the house and have time to herself, Connie served an exceptional dinner of steak and kidney pie, mashed potatoes, carrots and broad beans, cleared up in the kitchen, hung out washing to dry, baked a Victoria sponge and hoovered the stairs before it was time to leave for her appointment.

'I'll be off now, Arthur.' She peered around the door of the bathroom where Arthur was regrouting a row of tiles he'd taken off the wall because he thought they were misaligned.

'Yes, yes. See you later.' Arthur dismissed her with a wave of his hand. 'I hope it's worth it,' he called down the stairs after her in a rather sulky voice.

Connie smiled to herself as she left the house and the sun hit her face. Perhaps now he'd grasp how she felt stuck in on her own day after day, working her way through a list of mundane chores.

The afternoon was fresh and bright, cotton balls of smoke from the towers puffing across the sky in slow motion. She'd been so organised that she didn't have to rush and she enjoyed the soft air and the flowers that crowded pots and clung to the sides of houses.

At first, she'd given no time to Arthur's suggestion of sending her to London six times a year. How dare he forbid her from doing what she wanted to do in the first place, then presume to tell her what would be good for her. She'd agonised over how he made her feel no more capable than their neighbours' children, but she wriggled away from that thought as every time it surfaced she wanted to hide away, hurt and humiliated.

Then she began to think about it in a more logical way. It might be rather fun. She imagined looking around the shops with Dora or asking her brother for gardening tips or playing board games with the boys – all without Arthur steering the conversation or monitoring the time he'd assigned to the visit. They could go to the pub and the pictures, and Dora might like to visit some of Mum's old neighbours with her. The idea grew in her mind and she saw herself on the train with endless time to read a book or, if Arthur gave her enough money, sitting in the restaurant car with a cup of tea and a bun, the scenery rolling away beside her.

Eventually, she'd convinced herself that the trips would be of great benefit. She would hold Arthur to his suggestion and insist it come to fruition. The best outcome would be if it taught him that her having a part-time job would be much easier than her being away for days at a time, although she doubted that would happen, because of course it was the principle that mattered most to Arthur. But if nothing else, it would be a break from her routine and give her something to look forward to other than fish on Fridays.

The park was packed with families and dog walkers making the most of the best weekend of spring so far.

Spikes of white flowers, like candles waiting to be lit, stood upright on horse chestnuts and silver birches swayed in the breeze that played around the new greenery. Cutting across the grass on a diagonal path, she stopped when she heard someone shouting her name from near the play area. Squinting, she caught sight of Millicent waving, her arms above her head as if she were bringing in a plane to land.

Connie waved back and Millicent pointed her out to Shirley and both their families. Then she beckoned for Connie to join them. When Connie put up her hand and shook her head, Millicent released Adrian from her grasp and sent him running towards her.

The sight of the little boy, his shorts slipping from his waist, made her laugh out loud. She walked to meet him and when he was almost upon her, he opened his arms wide and called out, 'Connie, Connie, oh, Connie.' Connie's hand flew to her chest and she had to fight to take a proper breath. Putting out her arms, she caught him in a hug. Then she was duty bound to carry him back to where the others were waiting.

'Hello, Connie,' Brian said. 'Millie keeps telling me how much Adie thinks of you. Now I have evidence for myself. Do you want him?' he asked, a beam on his face.

Millicent hit her husband playfully on the arm. 'How could you say that? If we gave him away you'd have nothing to moan about, would you?'

'Oh, I'd think of something,' Brian said, kicking a ball with his hands in his pockets.

'That's for sure,' Millicent said.

Brian, short and square with the bald patch in his fair

hair catching the sunlight, and Trev, taller and sporting a dark, trim beard, turned to each other and started to talk about football. With one eye on Simon and Janet as they scaled the climbing frame, Shirley asked Connie what she was up to.

Connie could barely keep her excitement in check as she told them she was heading to see Richard at *New You for a Snip*.

The two younger women stared at her, Shirley's mouth wide enough to catch any passing fly. Then she clapped her hands together and Millicent said, 'Good on you, Connie. What are you having done?'

Connie explained as best she could and was grateful when her neighbours gave their approval. 'Sounds lovely,' Shirley said.

'Yes,' Millicent agreed. 'It will really suit you.'

'Oh, I hope so,' Connie said, touching her wrapped-around bun and twining double crown. 'I've had it this way for so long that I can't imagine how it will look.'

'Fantastic, that's how. Next you'll be wearing a pair of these.' Millicent pointed to her and Shirley's white boots.

'Well, I'd better make a move,' Connie said. 'I really don't want to be late.'

'No,' Shirley said. 'It wouldn't do to keep Richard waiting.'

Millicent grimaced and wiped her brow with mock trepidation. 'It certainly wouldn't,' she said. 'If you do, his scissors will be working overtime, like this.'

Connie watched as her young neighbour chopped away at the air as if snipping and trimming and layering. For a fleeting instant she was taken back to the war when she'd held a pair of scissors in her hands for hours every day. *Snip snip*, she thought.

'Can't wait to see the result. Adie, say goodbye to Connie.'

Adrian looked up at Connie forlornly, his fingers disappearing into his mouth.

Connie traced the side of her finger over the silky skin on the toddler's cheek. 'Bye, Adie. See you soon.' There was no question about it – she would love to have him.

He nodded and waved, then his smile turned to tears until Millicent distracted him with the promise of a Zoom ice lolly.

Richard greeted her as if she were royalty. He helped her off with her coat and made sure she was comfortable in the chair that went up and down on a whoosh. Like a matador, he snapped a bright blue nylon cape out to the side then settled it over her lap and tied it around her neck. She felt apprehensive but expectant at the same time, her lips quivering slightly when she smiled at him in the mirror.

'So, Connie,' Richard said. 'Still up for what we talked about?'

'Yes,' Connie said, sure Richard could hear her swallowing nervously. 'Please.'

'Good,' he said. 'First I'll colour, then wash, then cut, then dry and style. In that order.'

She nodded. 'And could you please tell me what I'll need to do every day to look decent?'

Richard took a theatrical step back, his eyes wide with

feigned hurt. 'Decent?' he spluttered. 'You're going to look more magnificent than decent.'

That made Connie laugh.

'But of course, my lovely,' he said in a kindly voice. 'I'll even let you have a tin of our best lacquer.'

Connie hoped he wouldn't charge her for it as she didn't know if her three shillings would stretch.

Condensation ran in runnels down the window Connie sat next to, which was just as well as she didn't relish the idea of every passer-by getting a glimpse of Richard dragging strands of her thin, greying hair through the tiny holes in a funny, rubbery cap he'd pulled over her head. Heat prickled around her neck and radiated in waves from the elastic waistband of her petticoat and she hoped the whole procedure wouldn't take too long.

Once more, every chair in the salon was occupied and the burble of women's voices filled the space. Connie surreptitiously glanced at other customers as they chatted away to the stylist who was working on their hair as if they were talking to their closest friend. Perhaps they were. Millicent seemed to be on very good terms with Richard. It seemed to be the done thing, so Connie racked her brain for some topic of conversation but everything she almost said sounded silly and banal when she played it out in her head.

Then Richard came to the rescue. 'Is this just because?' he asked. 'Or is it for a special occasion. You know, anniversary, big birthday, holiday?'

Connie hesitated. She could tell him that she and Arthur had recently celebrated thirty-three years of marriage with fish for their dinner as it fell on a Friday and a ham sandwich with pickles for tea. Or she could say that she would be fifty-five this year, but not until October, and that Arthur had turned fifty-eight in February. Neither cause for a knees-up in their house. But how could she tell Richard that the new hairdo was more than just because and it qualified as the only thing she'd done out of her weekly routine since Ken and Dora had visited for two days last Christmas. She sensed he already felt some kind of pity for her and didn't want to say anything to compound that notion so blurted out, 'I'm going to London. To visit my brother and his family.'

'Fantastic,' he said. 'I love London. Will you see a show whilst you're there?'

'I don't know, but that's a good idea. Any suggestions?'

Richard took up a small, flat brush and painted a dark colour on the strands of her hair that stood out from the cap. 'I don't really keep up with it, I'm afraid. But I have read that *Funny Girl* is fantastic.'

They chatted about what they liked to do in London, Richard much more interested in art galleries and museums than she was, but she listened and nodded and murmured in all the correct places. 'Right.' He used the last scrape of tint from the plastic bowl to coat the one remaining filament of hair and said, 'This won't be as dark as it looks now. When it's washed out you'll be a lovely shade of chestnut brown.'

'A bit like a conker, then,' Connie said.

'A gorgeous, shiny conker. Now, under the dryer for you.' He led her to an empty chair and pulled a contraption that looked like a space helmet over her head. 'Coffee, my lovely?'

Connie usually drank tea, but didn't want to sound unsophisticated so said, 'Yes, please. With milk and one sugar, if possible.'

'Anything is possible here,' Richard assured her. He picked up a few magazines and handed them to her, then set what she presumed was a timer on the hood and suddenly she was cocooned in her own snug world. All she could hear was the low buzz of the dryer, which made the radio and the chatter of the salon a hum of background noise. She thought she could get used to drinking coffee, and the magazines were a wonder of information all laid out in colour. *Tatler* and *Vogue* were good to flick through, but her favourite was *Good Housekeeping*. If she could eke out her money, she might buy a copy to keep her company on the train to London.

When Richard lifted the hood to check her hair, the noise and commotion of the salon hit her like the blare of an air raid siren. He proclaimed her ready then ushered her to the backwash where a junior spent an inordinate amount of time rinsing, washing and conditioning.

Then back to Richard's chair where she could see her new colour for the first time. 'What do you think?' Richard said, picking up lengths of her dark hair and running them through his fingers. 'It will lighten up a bit when it's dry. You'll see what I mean.'

'I think,' Connie said, turning this way then the other. 'That it's very different and I like that.'

He smiled. 'Now, the scissors.' He held the blades between his fingers as if they were a weapon.

Connie couldn't watch as the sharp, pointed ends fluttered in and around her long, stringy locks. She didn't want to appear silly and close her eyes either, so she concentrated on her hands in her lap. Richard must have been lost in concentration, too, as this time there was no small talk. She was aware of chunks of brown falling onto her cape and carpeting the floor around her and she could hear the decisive snips and clips as Richard made judgements about where to direct his scissors, how much to trim and what would be best left behind.

For the second time that day, her mind went back to rooms full of young women with scissors in their hands. They opened letter after letter and cut or pencilled out what shouldn't have been written in the first place and what shouldn't be read by the people whose names and addresses were on the envelopes. Those names swam in front of her eyes – Drew Morrison, James Stanton, Albert Higgins, Maude Grimshaw.

An electric shock passed through her – although they'd occupied so much of her time years ago, she hadn't thought about those names and specific letters for years.

Then Richard was leaning towards her, trying to get her attention. 'Do you think that's enough, Connie, or shall I take off a bit more?'

'Oh,' she said, able to scrutinise Richard's handiwork at last. 'I wouldn't know. Can I be guided by you?'

'Well, once it's cut it can't be glued back. Let's play it safe. If we want to, we can always snip off a bit more when it's dry.'

She nodded. 'That sounds like a good idea.'

Rollers were placed symmetrically in her hair, the pins keeping them in place pulling enough here and there to give her scalp the shivers. Once again Richard settled her under the hairdryer, but this time *Good Housekeeping* lay unopened in her lap as she sat perfectly still, stared straight ahead and recalled more of the names in those letters. There was Agnes and her sister, Alice; Chas and Rosamund Sinclair, Harold Hargreaves and his wife, Lily; a poet from Hackney; Clemmie and her friend Elsie; Peter Carstairs; the godmother who drew pictures of flowers; Mairead and her Auntie Kathleen; Ted Adams and Beryl Smythe. She'd agonised about all of them during the war; worried about each of their dilemmas; been privy to their deepest, darkest thoughts and most hopeful moments. She thought she'd let them go, so why was she seeing them so distinctly again now? She shook her head, top-heavy with curlers. Must have been the incessant, abrasive *snip snip* of scissors so close to her ears.

'Back you come, my lovely,' Richard said. 'For the grand unveiling.'

In front of the mirror again, he carefully unwound each roller then stepped back, his hands wide. 'Voila!' he said.

Connie gasped, then giggled and gasped again. All thoughts of the letters she'd read more than twenty years ago swept from her mind as if they were no more valuable than the strands of clipped hair lying discarded on the floor. She could not believe the reflection staring back at her was the same woman she'd seen in the mirror an hour and a half ago. Her hand automatically searched for the bun and the double crown. 'I know where the topknot's gone.' She pointed to the floor. 'But what have you done with my squiggly bit?'

'Artfully disguised under layers of glamour,' Richard said. 'Now watch and I'll show you what to do each morning.' He picked up a long, tapered comb with fine teeth and backcombed her hair all over from roots to ends. 'Don't be afraid to give it some welly,' he said. 'Then smooth down the top, like this, make sure it's even by digging in the with the end of the comb and patting it down. And finally.' He shook a huge tin of lacquer. 'Spray this all over. Oh, mind your eyes.'

Connie covered her face with her hands and tried hard not to breathe in, but taking in some of the spray was inevitable. She had to laugh to herself, as Millicent and Shirley complained about what the towers might be spitting out yet never said a word about gulping down this stuff. Now she would be doing the same.

'Richard,' she said, unable to take her eyes off herself. 'I cannot thank you enough. I feel …'

'Lighter?' the hairdresser offered. 'Younger? You certainly look both.'

'Yes, that's it exactly,' Connie said.

'And we can get a proper look at those green eyes now. Beautiful.'

At the desk, Connie paid and had just enough left over for a tip, which she took back to Richard who was talking to his next client. 'These are for you as it's your first visit,' he said, handing her a new can of hairspray and a special comb. 'But don't tell Millicent, she'll never forgive me for not treating her to the same.'

'Thank you very much, Richard. For everything.'

'My pleasure,' he said. 'See you in six weeks.'

Connie felt her eyebrows lift in confusion.

'You'll soon look like the old you, my lovely,' Richard said. 'If you don't keep it up.'

That put a damper on her walk home. She felt rather

silly; how could she have thought the new hairdo would be a one-off, which is what it would turn out to be if Arthur couldn't be persuaded to give her extra on a regular basis. So she decided to make the most of the new style whilst she had it and deal with the next step when necessary.

Millicent and Shirley were nowhere to be seen and Connie wished she'd bumped into them after, not before, her transformation. They rarely saw their neighbours on Sundays either, as families tended to keep that day to themselves. Never mind, she told herself, it would soon be Monday and she would definitely see them then.

As soon as she set foot in the door, Arthur called to her from the living room. 'Hello, Treasure. I've put the kettle on.'

That was the most he'd ever do towards making a cup of tea and he sounded as if he wanted a medal for it. She busied herself with the cups and the tray and sliced the cake she'd baked earlier. Carrying it all in to where Arthur sat – his eyes glued to the newspaper in front of his face – she waited for him to acknowledge her with some kind of reaction. Begrudgingly, he folded the paper and when he caught sight of her he gawked, a look on his face she hadn't seen since around 1952. 'Constance Allinson. Is that really you?'

She nodded. 'What do you think?'

'I ... I don't know,' he stammered.

Her heart sank and she thought she could say goodbye to future visits to the salon.

'You look ...'

'Younger and lighter?'

He nodded. 'And to see you smiling,' he said. 'Is worth the extortionate amount the salon charges.' He nibbled a forkful of cake, declared it very good and opened his paper again.

That was the sum of Arthur's verdict so asking him for the money again in six weeks would be hit and miss.

But that night it was Connie's turn to be surprised when he reached for her across the cold, cotton sheets. It wasn't their usual night to be intimate, so she could only presume her new hairdo had charged up his libido. Turning to him, Connie hoped this was a good sign about how the night's events would unfold but that was too much to ask. His left hand went to her thigh, his right to the back of her neck. One quick kiss, a set number of caresses and thrusts and it was over – exactly as it had been for years.

8

August 1941

My dearest Chas

I wish I could find words to tell you how much I miss you. You are everything to me – my moon, my stars, my sun; wherever you may go, don't forget that I love you more than anything else in the universe.

The girls miss you, too. They've been billeted in a different house, but they're still in Lowestoft. Their new host family sounds much nicer and cleaner than the first lot and at least they can still go to the same school with their friends. Did you get their little notes I sent last time I wrote? I hope so and I hope you're alright as it's been a while since I've heard. I try to keep busy, as you said I should, and not dwell on where you are and what you're having to do, but that's easier said than done.

Anyway, I dug over the flower beds and planted beetroot, potatoes, onions and leeks, so I shall be able to have a hearty stew some day! I sweep and clean and wash and polish, queue for rations and visit Auntie Clara and Iris. I asked last time I wrote if you had any preference for the war work I should take up, but as I haven't heard from you I made up my own mind. I've decided to be a mechanic – yes, you did read that correctly! I went along to a recruiting office and, amongst many other jobs, women are needed as mechanics on the buses, so I just thought, why not? Now, of course, I can think of a number of reasons why not, but I'm committed and start on Monday next. If you get this letter by then, think of me holding a monkey wrench, up to my elbows in grease.

Other news is that poor Mrs Bartlett from down the road lost her old cat in an air raid and the bottom of Whitehill Road no longer exists after it took an almighty hit.

Please, please write to me soon as your loving letters keep me going here in Epping. Keep your chin up and I know we'll be together again soon.

Your adoring wife

Rosamund XXX

Well, Connie thought. *What a lovely letter to receive.* She and Arthur always wrote that they missed each other and wanted the war to be over so they could start their proper life together. Last time she'd received a letter from Arthur, he'd said that the words she wrote to him kept his eye on the ball more than anything said by Winnie or the King or the Admiral of the Fleet put together. Scanning Rosamund's letter again, she made a mental note of the wording in the first paragraph, which was so simple and heartfelt, and thought she'd try to replicate some of it when next she wrote to Arthur. She hoped he'd like that.

Connie felt certain there was nothing untoward in the

writing in her hand, but she wanted to read through the letter again to be sure. She drew her chair a bit closer to the table and started over at the beginning. When she'd finished, she thought she would never forget this, the first letter she'd read as a censor. For a moment, she placed the pages on her desk, a knot tightening in her stomach as she stared into the distance. Where was Chas and why was it taking so long for his letters to get to his wife?

She turned over the envelope and reread the address. It was written strictly according to regulations with the only information Rosamund would have been given about her husband's location – his full name and rank followed by the regulation wording 'On Active Duty', his number and HMNB Portsmouth, which must be his operating base. He could be anywhere in the world. Or – Connie could feel tears stinging the backs of her eyes and she had to blink quickly to disperse them – he could have been killed in action. But Arthur's letters were often delayed. Sometimes Connie spent weeks imagining them sitting in a sack on some dock or another waiting to be picked up in the jaws of a crane and thrown into the hold of a ship heading back to the UK. It was a miracle any letters to or from naval crews made it into the right hands at all. Looking at the writing again, Connie decided she wasn't about to give up hope on Rosamund's behalf and she wished her and Chas the very best of luck.

Connie felt Dotty's eyes on her from where she sat at the next station along and she held up the letter for her presiding officer's approval, but Dotty's only reaction was to widen her bushbaby eyes.

For a beat, Connie thought Dotty might have resorted to her silly side and waited for what would happen next. Then Dotty pointed to Connie's lamp and mimed holding something up to the light. 'Oh,' Connie mouthed in a whisper and she heard a giggle escape from a Wren sitting directly opposite.

Holding the envelope under her lamp, she looked around the postage stamp to see if it had been tampered with, then she held it up to the light to check for a second skin nestled inside that might hide another, more sinister communication and lastly, she tried to discern any hidden writing. All clear.

Dotty stood behind her and read the letter over her shoulder. Connie watched the young girl's eyes as they followed the writing from left to right, top to bottom and wondered if she would ever get to the stage where she could scan letters as quickly and confidently. 'Now seal it with your label,' Dotty said, sounding as sedate and solemn as a wireless newsreader informing the nation of the latest news from the Front.

Connie stuck out her tongue and went to lick the label, which caused the same giggler to laugh again. Dotty shot a look across the table and the girl hung her head over her work, quiet once more. 'Where's your sponge?' Dotty asked.

Throughout all the hours of training, Connie had never heard a sponge mentioned. She was about to say she'd left it next to the sink in her quarters, but was saved from embarrassing herself again by Dotty opening the desk drawer and producing a discoloured, springy lump sitting in a small bowl of brown water. Both women stared at the unsavoury dish, then at each other. Vera, it seemed, had not been as bothered about cleanliness as they were. 'I'll requisition a new sponge for you,' Dotty said. 'But for now ...' She pressed the label into what reminded Connie of jelly made from very old vegetable water, wet it thoroughly and wrapped it around the envelope.

'Next one if you please, Leading Wren Allinson.'

'Mam,' Connie said, reaching for the next letter on her pile. Peeking around, she noticed that the other girls at the table were getting through their envelopes at an alarming rate. It seemed as if they were reading twenty to her one, but she told herself that at this stage it would be better for her to be accurate rather than fast, so she held her nerve and plodded along.

Letter after letter passed her scrutiny that first morning. Some of them functional, others loving and intimate; none of them suspicious. Apart from the clock, which seemed to have the loudest *tick tock* Connie had ever heard, the rustle of envelopes, the *scritch scratch* of pencils and the constant background noise of scissors meeting with a *snip snip*, there was hardly a sound in the vast room. When the Wrens walked from one table to another they did so with quick, light steps, and when they had to talk to each other, the tone they adopted was hushed. The covered windows and the bright lights made it seem as if there was no passage of time; it could permanently have been nine in the morning or two in the afternoon or eight at night.

'Leading Wren Allinson.' The Chief Wren was at Connie's elbow, the trace of a smile on her face again. 'How are you settling in?'

'Mam.' Connie rose to her feet and brought her hand to her forehead in a salute.

'As you were,' the Chief Wren said. 'Any problems?'

'Not as far as I'm concerned, Mam,' Connie said, looking towards Dotty for confirmation.

'Leading Wren Allinson is working very efficiently and at an excellent pace, Mam,' Dotty said.

Connie felt her face colour with a mixture of pride and chagrin.

'Good,' the Chief Wren said. Connie followed the older woman's gaze as she looked up at the clock. Eleven on the dot. They'd been hard at it for three hours although she would have sworn on oath it had only been twenty minutes. 'Your table's break is coming up quite soon. Petty Officer Wren Saunders will show you where you can freshen up and get a cup of tea.'

'Thank you, Mam,' Connie said.

As the Chief Wren progressed around the room, Dotty said, 'One more letter each, Jennies, then we'll take our break.'

An almost imperceptible sigh of relief rose from the girls around the table. A couple of them shifted in their chairs and the Wren across from Connie looked at her with a smile of expectation so wide she thought the girl had been told to ready herself to meet the Queen. None of that boded well for the day-to-day excitement Connie had hoped the role would provide. But whether it was because this was her first day or because she'd been lucky and found her niche, Connie loved the anticipation of picking up each new letter, slicing the envelope neatly with her opener, taking out the pages and reading what amounted to a glimpse of other people's lives – in fact, it felt as if she'd been given permission to be nosy without having to worry about the embarrassment that would bring under normal circumstances. What a privilege. She thought she'd never tire of it and felt disappointed when Dotty told her to down tools and follow her to the canteen.

All seven Wrens from the table stuck together like a pod of navy-blue dolphins as they headed for the door that led to the locker room. Once inside, they drifted in ones and twos to retrieve their bags, then banded together again to walk up the two flights to the canteen. 'The lavatories are over there.' Dotty pointed behind her. 'And there's more on each floor. I should have said earlier that if you need to be excused from the table, just ask.'

'Thank you, Dotty, you've made me most welcome.'

Dotty grinned. 'Fancy more of a welcome at the pub tonight?' she asked. 'One of the perks of this job is that we finish every evening at five. No night shifts at all. That means there's plenty of time to go back to quarters and get ready for a night out.'

'Well, I don't usually,' Connie demurred.

Turning a corner in the staircase, Connie noticed that Dotty had left her officer guise in the censoring room and was once again flouncing her hips from side to side. She thought it must be exhausting to flit between identities like that, and what would happen if the girl got mixed up and strutted when she should have been saluting or vice versa? Connie was intrigued – which was the real Dotty? A bit of both, she guessed.

'What do you usually do after work then?' Dotty asked.

'Read,' Connie said, 'or write to Arthur, my husband. Visit my mum in Acton when I can. Wash, iron, clean my cabin …' She trailed off when she heard how staid and mundane she sounded, especially compared to such a radiant young woman as Dotty.

The corners of Dotty's mouth and eyes turned down with a semblance of scorn. 'Well if you can tear yourself away, you're invited to join us tonight at the Commercial Tavern in the King's Road. We'll be there from about seven. Won't we, Josie? Race you!' And she took the stairs two at a time, jostling the giggling girl who sat opposite Connie for position.

Connie laughed, it was hard not to. Another Wren, about Connie's age, joined her and together they climbed the stairs at a more decorous pace. 'I thought I was a young thirty-two,' the other woman said, 'but they make me feel ancient. I'm Norma, by the way.'

'Connie. Pleased to meet you. I'm a decrepit thirty.' She grabbed the handrail and pretended to limp up a couple of steps.

'I don't know how Dotty does it,' Norma said. 'She switches from work to play seamlessly without missing a step and she's so full of energy. Mind you, I couldn't ask for a better presiding officer. She is wonderful at her job. Fair and helpful, too. But outside of work …' Norma shook her head. 'She certainly knows how to have a good time.'

'Do you go to the pub with her?'

'Sometimes,' Norma said. 'But I rarely go on to a club afterwards. I'll go for a drink tonight if you do.'

'I think I should,' Connie said. 'As Dotty said it's to be

my welcoming party. Although ...' Arthur had said many times he thought she should be very wary of going into pubs without him.

'Oh, pay no attention to that. Dotty can think of something to celebrate every night of the week. It would be a nice introduction to everyone. Mind you,' she lowered her voice, 'it would just be the four of us. Those three,' she lifted her chin towards the women from around the table who Connie had yet to meet, 'don't approve of Dotty so keep themselves to themselves. Dotty calls them the Absolute Miseries.'

Connie wasn't sure she approved of Dotty either, but hearing a squeal of laughter from the young officer as she raced ahead, she realised that part of her was envious of her superior's audacious joie de vivre.

The canteen was as spacious as the work room downstairs and just as devoid of ornamentation, with boarded windows and another large, loud clock ticking on the wall. The aroma, though, was mouth-watering. Bacon or spam frying in oil joined the heady waft of yeast and wheat that whirled to meet them. 'The scrambled egg on fried bread is very good, if they have any today,' Norma said. 'Or the spam sandwich.'

Neither were available by the time Connie got to the front of the queue, so she opted for a carrot and leek fritter with a slice of toast and sat next to Dotty at a large table. Looking around at the expanse of navy-blue, Connie was about to ask which other WRNS departments had their offices in the requisitioned insurance building, when Josie shouted what amounted to a private joke across the table and Dotty laughed.

'Same to you,' Dotty said, sticking out the tip of her tongue. Again, Connie was shocked but found it hard to stifle a giggle of her own.

'Time, Jennies,' Dotty trilled just as Connie finished her last bite.

'That was quick,' Connie said. 'Is this our only break?'

Dotty shook her head, her full hair bouncing with her. 'We get half an hour for dinner and another fifteen minutes in the afternoon.' She beamed. 'It's not too bad.'

Connie thought the girl was so exuberant that nothing on earth would get her down.

The afternoon flew by. Connie was so engrossed in her letters that she could have happily foregone all her breaks. There was one from a woman telling her son she was moving yet again as the flat she'd been in for a mere two weeks had caught alight and been declared unsafe to live in by the inspector. The couple of unopened boxes of possessions she'd brought with her had gone up in flames. The poor mother was probably close to breaking point, but with stout defiance, she stuck to the advice about not allowing servicemen and women to hear the full extent of the suffering at home and kept the tone of her letter fed-up and resigned rather than distraught.

Then there was another from a man who had penned a poem about Hackney, of all places, for his nephew; one from a woman saying sorry for something she didn't specify and begging her fiancé not to leave her; another from a Wren's aunt that contained the recipe for flapjack and one that Connie thought was written in musical notation code. Her heart flipped and her eyes bulged when she saw it. Imagine, she thought. On my very first day.

Signalling to Dotty, her hand shook with the slightest of tremors as she held out the pages. 'Excellently observed, Leading Wren Allinson,' Dotty said as she scanned the writing. She read through the letter again, then once more. 'I think this really is a score of music someone has written for their friend. But let me check with the Chief Wren.'

Unable to start on another letter whilst that one was being discussed, Connie waited at her desk and turned over in her mind some of the things she'd read that day. How she would love to know more about Rosamund and Chas, but the likelihood of their letters to each other ever reaching her desk again were so slim she'd never find out if and when a letter from Chas arrived or how Rosamund got on with her mechanic's job. She'd never discover if the poet went on to write poems about Tottenham or Earl's Court or Fulham Broadway, or if the woman's fiancé gave her the push for whatever it was she'd done wrong. For the few minutes she held each letter in her hands, she felt as if she were a part of the writer's and recipient's lives and the lives of everyone they mentioned. A chilly veil of bereavement passed over her when she realised she'd have no contact with any of them ever again. Looking up, she caught Josie studying her, bemusement furrowing her forehead. She smiled and the girl quickly shifted her gaze back down to her desk, but she knew she could never tell anyone how close she felt to the cast of characters in each letter she read. They would think she was mad.

'All okay to pass.' Dotty was back at her side. 'But the Chief Wren and I both think it was very well spotted.' She leaned a bit closer to Connie's ear and whispered, 'Deserving of a drink or two tonight, I think.'

Connie attached her label to the envelope, reached for another letter and decided to put Arthur's rumbling disquiet to the back of her mind. A celebratory drink would be very nice to look forward to.

9

May 1967

Tuesday. Shepherd's pie. A coral tabard. In the past four weeks Connie had been to five coffee mornings, as she didn't know what she could say to get out of them, and the same round of hot drinks, bland biscuits and chat about catalogues, recipes and husbands who didn't live up to expectations prevailed. She always came away thinking the women wouldn't moan if they had to live with Arthur. It would be her turn soon to host but she hadn't quite figured out how she would do that, get cleared up and have Arthur's dinner on the table by quarter past one.

She'd been managing her new hairstyle well, but now it was growing and grey strands were beginning to poke through the brown at her roots. Arthur hadn't mentioned it, so she supposed she would have to get out her begging bowl again and ask him to cough up.

Tender green stalks were shooting up from the woody root of the clematis as it climbed upwards and she'd spent a good deal of time dwelling on James Stanton, Maude Grimshaw, Mairead, Chas and Rosamund, Harold Hargreaves and Beryl Smythe.

The timer trilled and the front door opened. 'Hello, you,' Arthur called from the hallway.

'Yoo-hoo,' Connie murmured, her voice a monotone.

'Oh, there you are, Treasure.' Arthur was in the doorway, fiddling with his cycle helmet. 'I didn't hear you. Mmm. Shepherd's pie. Must be Tuesday.'

This time she could not find it within herself to raise a smile.

They sat at the table, picked up their cutlery and began to eat. 'Have you changed greengrocer?' Arthur asked. 'The potatoes these past few weeks have been of a very high quality.'

'No, Arthur,' Connie said, unable to force her voice from its flat drone. 'But I might do so.'

'No point,' he stated. 'When the current one is top notch.'

'There is a point,' she said. 'It would give me something to do.' Forcing the allegedly excellent potatoes down her throat, she waited for another argument to begin.

'You have plenty to do here. That would just be a waste of your time.'

Connie had to fight not to throw her plate of food into his face. She imagined cubes of carrot and dark gravy lying on his bald patch and streaming from his heavy eyebrows.

After a few minutes of intense chewing, Arthur looked at her with a secretive smile and asked if she liked surprises.

He has to ask me that, she thought. *There have been so few as the years have gone by.*

The only thing Connie could envisage was a scone at a café in Doncaster on Saturday, but she knew she had to humour him if she had any hope of getting the money to get her roots done. 'Yes, Arthur, I love surprises,' she said. 'Why?'

'Well, Treasure.' He dug around a tooth with the edge of his fingernail. 'I have three for you.'

'Really?' Connie was intrigued, despite herself. Perhaps something exciting and different was about to happen.

'Yes, three,' he said. 'Let's count them.

'I.' He patted his chest. 'Arthur Ernest Allinson. Have been given a promotion that I didn't have to apply for.'

Connie's eyes grew wide; she knew that would please him. 'Well done, Arthur,' she said. 'I didn't know that was in the pipeline.'

'Nor did I,' he said. 'Until last week. I thought I'd keep it a secret until I received the official say-so.'

She smiled, but her first thought was that getting extra housekeeping out of him might be easier on the back of his announcement.

'The money will really help with our savings,' Arthur gloated.

'What are we saving for, Arthur?' She held his gaze without smiling.

'Retirement, Treasure. It's a mere seven years away.'

Connie hadn't given that impending date much thought, or perhaps she hadn't allowed herself to think about the future. Now though, she broke out in a cold sweat at the thought of Arthur here in the house monitoring her every move hour after hour of every single day. The image of him calling out that he'd put the kettle on and therefore expected a cup of tea filled her with horror. He would huff and puff about the place, wiping over windows that she'd buffed to a shine the day before and reminding her that she'd better get a move on if they were to stand any chance of a decent bit of liver the following day.

She'd survived when the front wheels of the number fifty-three had tipped into a pothole during the war; she'd been the first at Mum's bedside, holding her hand and smoothing her brow, when she'd been taken to St Pancras after that sideboard had fallen on her leg during the blackout; she'd witnessed scorched limbs and babies barely alive in their mothers' arms; her ears had been battered by barrage after barrage from the Luftwaffe; she'd lived through incendiaries plummeting from the skies like hundreds of vicious, overfed fireflies, but she didn't think she could survive a retirement with Arthur.

If she felt stifled and smothered now, she would probably look back upon these days as breezy and full of excitement in comparison. Her heart raced and she felt as if she would explode. 'And what are we going to do with the money when you retire,' she said in a voice laden with sarcasm. 'Take a trip around the world? Buy a motorcycle and speed along hairpin turns in the Lake District? Sign up for dance classes and spend weekends at the Blackpool Tower Ballroom? Watch the television you won't consider buying for us?'

But Arthur didn't bite. 'Oh, my Treasure,' he laughed. 'You are a funny one sometimes. You know the war was enough excitement for us.'

'For you.' Connie couldn't help herself. 'Not for me.'

His face changed in an instant; his dark eyes narrowed and a ticking twitch appeared next to his mouth.

'I'm sorry, Treasure,' he said at last. 'That I don't do enough to make you happy. Though God knows I try.'

She looked down at the remains of her shepherd's pie, shamed into submission again.

'To answer your question, we are going to use the money

to have a comfortable, safe, worry-free life in this lovely house I worked to buy for us – our family of two. The sort of life I fought for during the war.'

'That's not quite true, Arthur.' Connie looked up at him again. 'We used my share of the money from Mum's—'

'That's neither here nor there,' he interrupted.

They were quiet for a few moments, then Connie could feel him studying her. 'Constance,' he said. 'I'm willing to let your unkind words go as I know these upsets are due to your age.'

Her nostrils flared and she was surprised she didn't snort enough steam to compete with the towers.

'But perhaps you can tell me what it is you do want?'

She could have thrashed about and wailed. She'd made that clear on so many occasions. 'I want a job. So I can get out of this house and away from my strict routine which, I'll tell you in no uncertain terms, I cannot stand.'

Arthur's unbroken caterpillar of an eyebrow lifted towards the ceiling.

'Routine is good for you.'

'Just me?'

'Don't be silly. Everyone.'

'Oh, Arthur,' Connie begged. 'It would be so good for me and I wouldn't have to ask you every time I wanted to get my hair done or buy a magazine. I could manage those things with my own contribution.'

Arthur looked at his watch. 'Connie,' he said. 'Despite what you think, I'm not an unfeeling man.'

'I didn't mean that. Of course you're not. I know that better than anyone.'

He made his way to the hallway, Connie at his heels. 'I

had noticed your hair is not quite the same as it was when you first visited the salon, and I was going to suggest I give you a bit extra every eight weeks so you can get it redone before your visits to Ken and Dora – that was surprise number two.' When he turned to look at her, his eyes were those of an innocent Labrador puppy. 'I'm Constance's Constant. Not a monster,' he said.

She cringed inwardly. No, he wasn't. But his behaviour was inconsistent and confusing and this was a perfect example. He'd missed the point entirely and made her feel bad about having her say. It was almost as if he couldn't help himself sometimes, which was baffling.

Arthur stood with his back to her, his hand resting on the door handle. 'Sadly, the third surprise will have to wait until later.' He shook his head and left her standing alone in the doorway, the empty, echoing house behind her.

Without thinking, Connie cleared the kitchen, dusted the ornaments, straightened Arthur's newspapers, sat down and waited for Millicent and Shirley to pass by, then waited a bit longer to create some distance between them. She should have ruminated on the words she'd had with Arthur and how she could temper what she said to make the outcome more favourable for her next time. Instead, she thought again about Maude Grimshaw and how the contents of her letter had made her gut twist, as if a knife had been plunged deep inside her. She brooded on Jim Stanton, too, as she'd first done years ago. She'd decided then that he must have been very young, which would make him in his early forties now, still a relatively young man if he'd survived those terrible years and any number of mishaps that might have seen him off since.

Shaking her head to clear it, she began to gather together her outdoor shoes and clothes. She stuffed her purse and a see-through, concertinaed rainhat into her pocket, and started for the shops. She would love to know what had happened to Maude Grimshaw and Jim Stanton. Realistically, she knew that was the last thing on earth she would ever be able to discover, so she might as well dismiss it from her mind. Easier said than done now she'd started to ruminate on them. A few fat drops of rain landed on her lacquered hair and she tied the plastic bonnet under her chin. Head down, she did her best to concentrate on the puddles at her feet and what she needed to buy from the shops.

That evening, Connie gave Arthur his Tuesday tea of pork pie and Branston pickle but substituted the usual sliced tomato for something different. He picked up the small, crimson replacement and examined it as if it were potentially life-threatening. 'Whatever is this?' he asked.

'It's called a cherry tomato,' Connie answered, popping one between her teeth. 'Aren't they lovely?'

Arthur ignored that but said, 'What's the point of them?'

She tried to remain enthusiastic. 'They're pretty for one thing. And for another they're much sweeter than larger tomatoes. They make a change. Try it.'

Taking the tiniest amount from his fork, Arthur took ages to chew and swallow. 'I suppose it is rather sweet,' he said. 'But there's nothing wrong with the tomatoes that have stood us in good stead right through the war until now. And I'll bet these are more expensive, aren't they?' He eyed her suspiciously as if she were trying to get away with buying a ruby ring.

'A little,' she admitted. 'But not much.'

Arthur finished his tea and in protest pushed the tomatoes to the side of his plate and left them there uneaten. Whilst she cleared up, Connie took great delight in squirting a thin drizzle of juice from one of them into Arthur's cup of tea before scooping it into her mouth and savouring the succulent remains.

'I think I might like to plant a vegetable patch,' Arthur said, looking out on the garden from the patio doors.

'As you wish, Arthur,' Connie said from her station at the sink. She didn't mind what he did in the garden as long as it didn't affect her clematis. She picked out the plant, trembling in the shadows cast by the towers. It had gained momentum during the last few weeks and she'd lovingly manipulated the twirling filaments in the way she wanted them to spread. When she had a peek close-up, tiny pink buds had begun to appear, and she checked on their progress each day.

'It would go nicely just there.' He pointed to the fence on the left, between them and Shirley. 'And I'm going to start with tomatoes,' he mumbled under his breath.

'Yes, Arthur,' Connie said, laughing to herself about how petty he could be. Then the inward chuckling stopped abruptly when she realised that it wasn't really funny at all. If this was how Arthur's retirement was going to play out, she would have to change things now or …

Or what? she asked herself. Leave him? How could she do that. She had no money of her own and no means of earning much. No grown-up children or mother to turn to.

There was only Ken and Dora and she hated the thought of being a burden on them.

Arthur sat in his chair, produced his pencil and found the crossword in his daily newspaper.

'Was that the third surprise?' she called to him.

'What, Treasure?' He would never get up and come to her, she always had to stop what she was doing and seek him out.

'The veg patch. Was that the other surprise?' She wouldn't put it past him to think that was a cause for major celebration.

'I'll tell you all about it when you're sitting down,' Arthur said.

Intrigued, Connie sat in an armchair, picked up the threads of the lemon matinee jacket she was knitting for Shirley's baby and waited.

'So, Treasure,' he said, a rather pompous look smeared across his face. 'I have joined the Thorpe Marsh Power Station cricket team. Well, the managers' team to be precise.'

The needles slipped and Connie dropped two stitches. 'But you don't like cricket,' she said. 'You've always preferred football.'

'I do like cricket.' Arthur was quick to come to his own defence. 'I've just never had an opportunity to play. But now,' he smiled broadly, 'I have been asked so I've accepted.'

Connie didn't know what to think or how to react. It was certainly not something she ever thought he'd agree to as it would mean a huge change to his weekly routine, but that couldn't be anything other than a good thing, she reasoned. On the other hand, she thought she had every right to feel bitter as he'd ignored her pleas for years and now one word from the power plant and the next thing you know he's having a go at something he's never shown an interest in before.

Arthur sat beaming, waiting for a comment from her. Playing for time, she diligently picked up the wayward stitches with a spare needle and set them back in their correct place. This could mean at least one evening when she would be able to do as she pleased whilst he trained, and then there would be long hours whilst he played in matches on Barnby Dun Green or away. But, she wondered with suspicion, why did he think this surprise involved her? 'Well, Arthur,' she said, picking up her needle again. 'I'm pleased for you.'

'For us,' Arthur corrected her.

Connie laughed out loud. 'I won't be playing cricket,' she said. 'I'm the last person they'd want on the team.'

'Don't be silly, Treasure,' he said. 'Of course not, but you'll get to meet all the other managers' wives who you will have much more in common with than those little girls on either side of us.'

'Millicent and Shirley?' Connie felt she had to stand up for her neighbours despite the fact their coffee mornings had turned out to be such a let-down.

Arthur nodded. 'And that one across the road.'

'Susan,' she said. 'You know her name. And they're all very lovely young women.'

'But think about how good it will be for you to mix with a different … type of person,' he said.

In theory, she thought she would like to meet the managers' wives. It would widen her circle of friends so she wasn't going to argue with Arthur on that point. 'How will you joining the cricket team enable me to meet them?' Her forehead creased in confusion.

'You've walked past cricket matches before. I know you have.' Arthur looked bemused. 'You must have noticed women sitting in deckchairs and on blankets, enjoying the sunshine and watching their husbands score wickets.'

'Yes, but ...'

'Well there you are,' he said. 'That will be you soon. Hobnobbing with the best of them. There are teas and sandwiches and cakes to make and serve. Kits to wash. We'll get your first trip to London done and dusted and then you can join in. I've put your name on the rota for when you get back.'

Connie opened her mouth and made an effort to form words but as hard as she tried, nothing came out and Arthur, true to form, took that as her being too thrilled and grateful to speak. 'Of course,' he carried on. 'It will take a lot of organisation on your part to fit it in with the house and garden and meals here. But if anyone can manage, you can. That's what I told Clive, my counterpart on the electrical side.' He turned to her. 'I'll take bets you're in charge soon.' He picked up his paper and turned to the crossword again.

At last she found her voice and had to make a monumental effort to keep it subdued and passive. 'I don't want to,' she said.

'Sorry, Treasure?'

'I don't want to do any of that.'

'Any of what?'

'I'm very happy for you to pursue playing cricket,' she said with control. 'And I would love to meet the other wives.

But it will be your hobby, not mine. So on that basis, I'm not prepared to be a skivvy.'

Connie felt her lips tighten and knew she was making the little lines around her mouth deeper and more harsh. She kept her head down and concentrated on purling her way from one edge of the tiny garment to the other.

Without looking up, she heard Arthur take a deep breath, then exhale with a grumbling sigh. 'I do understand, Treasure,' he said. 'That you want the nice things. The good, fun things, but I'm afraid that in order to partake of those you have to make a bit of tea and sandwiches and wash a few whites. The two things go hand in hand.'

'And what are the fun things, Arthur?'

'Supporting your husband whilst he plays cricket. Meeting his colleagues' wives. Compromise, Constance, is what marriage is all about.'

Connie felt ablaze. Her hands were shaking and her face was throbbing. With great care, she put her knitting down in case she pulled it apart in frustration. 'There is no compromise in this marriage,' she spat out. 'You do what you want to do, when you want to do it and I am your ... lackey.'

'That's not true!' Arthur was crestfallen. 'What about—'

But Connie couldn't stop herself from interrupting him this time. 'It's the truth,' she said. 'All I do is shop, cook, clean and wash for you and now you've signed me up for more of the same. And I'm supposed to be over the moon about it.'

Neither of them said anything else. All Connie could hear was Arthur's short, sharp, heavy breaths and the ticking of the clock hanging over the mantelpiece. Her heart was pelting and she clenched her teeth so tightly it felt as if they would crack.

'I thought you'd be happy for me.'

'I am.'

'Proud, even.'

'I am.'

'You're always on about doing things differently and I thought this would make a change.'

'It will, for you. And some of it will for me. But only some of it.'

'I thought you wouldn't mind as I've come up with so many different things for you to do. Your hair. London.'

Connie closed her eyes and rested her head against the back of the chair. 'Arthur,' she said. 'I can come up with things I want to do all by myself, believe it or not. I am quite capable.'

'From that I take it you mean a job,' he said. 'I'm sorry, Connie, but that just isn't practical. The household would be chaotic if you went out to work and as head of said household, I cannot let that happen.'

'But, Arthur,' she said in an innocent, syrupy voice that was laced with fury. 'I thought you said marriage was all about compromise.'

A violent blush reddened Arthur's ruddy complexion. He picked up his paper and hid behind it. Connie marched into the kitchen and set about preparing supper. After a few minutes, Arthur traipsed behind her. He looked so forlorn that for a moment, she wondered if he was going to apologise, although it would be the first time he'd condescended to do that. 'Treasure,' he said, in an appeasing voice. 'Let me suggest something that might be agreeable.'

Connie didn't think she could bear the sight of him at that particular moment, but to keep her back to him would be disrespectful because it did seem as if he was trying.

When she turned, he took her hands in his. 'I will look extremely foolish if I go back to Clive now and ask him to cross your name off the rota.'

She waited, hope against hope that if she agreed to brew tea and slice the crusts off cucumber sandwiches, he would relent and say she could find a job.

'And that wouldn't be a great way for me to start my new position,' he carried on. 'I think you'd agree, wouldn't you?'

She refused to say anything now that she would regret later.

'So,' Arthur said. 'If you could stick with it this season, then I will surreptitiously make sure you're not included next year.'

Connie's heart sank. Nothing she said or did would make any difference to him.

He bent and looked into her eyes. 'You wouldn't want your Constance's Constant to look ludicrous, would you?'

She pictured him arriving at work each day with his brown, leather cycling helmet balanced on his head, his bicycle clips snapped into place around his beige trousers, his abhorrence of the canteen and thought he did a good job of looking absurd without any help from her. But of course she didn't want his colleagues to laugh at him or talk about him unkindly behind his back, so she said, 'No, Arthur, I wouldn't.'

He smiled and said thank you in a passive tone of voice. 'And I do believe,' he added. 'That by next year you will love it so much that you won't want to be removed from the list.'

Arthur Ernest Allinson – purported head of the household. He would always make sure he had the final say. With a grin on his face, Arthur returned to his crossword and Connie to the task of preparing fish paste sandwiches for supper.

IO

August 1941

Alcohol was the only difference between the pub and the canteen as the Commercial Tavern was crawling with Wrens and naval personnel.

On first perusal, Dotty and Josie wore their uniforms for the night out identically to Connie and Norma, but when they took off their jackets, their sleeves revealed just a bit more arm than the older women's, their collars were inched up to frame their faces and they hiked their skirts to show an extra slice of leg when they sat down. The result was that every sailor in the place stared at them, Dotty in particular, an experience the girls clearly enjoyed.

Connie wondered if she would have behaved in the same way if she were single and had been blessed with Dotty's angelic yet worldly wise looks, but she doubted she'd ever have been able to give herself that amount of free rein. Anyway, it was too late now as she was committed to Arthur and her marriage and the family they longed for.

'Good to have you on the team,' Dotty said to Connie

'It's good to be occupied in a proper job,' Connie said. 'And thank you for being so helpful.'

'Cheers!' They clinked their drinks together in a rousing hurrah of solidarity.

'Sorry about the Three Miseries,' Josie said.

Dotty threw back her head and trilled with delight. 'Well, I'm not bothered. They'd only put a damper on the evening. Oh ...' Her face fell and she looked downcast. 'I forgot to introduce you, didn't I?'

Connie nodded. 'Don't worry, Norma performed the honours.'

Dotty's hand flew to cover her mouth. 'Oops,' she said. 'I am very sorry. How rude of me.'

Connie thought the girl really did try to do the right thing, but sometimes her natural exuberance overtook her good intentions.

'Anyway,' Dotty said. 'I can see you're more like us than one of them, so no harm done.'

That, Connie thought, remains to be seen. But they seemed to enjoy Norma's company so they might tolerate her, too.

They couldn't talk about their work as they'd been sworn to secrecy, and the war in general seemed too dull a topic for a lively night out. So, they discussed what they had planned for the next weekend; how they would wear their hair, if they had a choice of styles; their various quarters; the food in the canteen and the films they'd seen recently.

The hubbub in the pub grew until Connie found it difficult to hear without cupping her ears. So many tipsy men crowded around the bar, that it would have been a dawdle to pressgang them into the Navy if they hadn't already joined up. Every time the door opened, another crew crammed themselves in on a shared guffaw or a shout to others they recognised. Dotty espied each newcomer from the corner of her eye or with a quick glance over her shoulder, and Connie realised she must be waiting for someone in particular to make an appearance.

Eventually it was easier to concentrate on Norma, whilst Josie and Dotty carried on a conversation with each other. 'How long have you been posted at HMS Holborn?' Connie said.

'About six months,' Norma answered. 'I'm quartered near London Bridge.'

Dotty nudged her and mouthed the name of a club as if Connie were familiar with such places. 'No, thank you,' Connie shouted. 'I'm about to head back to my bunk. This has been enough excitement for me.'

Her mouth open and her eyes glistening, Dotty was about to protest when the double doors flew open and two young men strode in with an air of casual confidence that commanded centre stage. Connie was pleased to see the flush of colour that veiled Dotty's face because it made her appear less seasoned and knowing and more in keeping with her guileless, girlish appearance. So, these were the fellows Dotty and Josie had been waiting for. The lads stood loose-limbed, the pretence of boredom dulling their features as they surveyed the crowd. Then their browsing eyes stopped short on Dotty and Josie and their faces lit up.

The taller of the two made for Dotty, whilst the shorter, fairer man staked his claim on Josie with a strong, capable hand on her shoulder. They reminded Connie of muscular, mythical warriors who, in one seamless movement, would have thrown their women over the backs of their horses and galloped away towards the horizon, never to be seen again.

Quickly, as if to get the mandatory courtesy out of the

way, Dotty carried out the introductions and Connie was able to give her superior's beau a detailed once-over. She wondered how he would be able to see when he put on his cap because it would inevitably slip over his eyes before it came to rest on half-mast ears. But she was being picky. Apart from that one flaw, he could have been a film star and if Dotty's melting doe-eyes and the brazen thrust of her hips were anything to go by, she couldn't give a hoot about that slight imperfection.

'Drinks, ladies?' Dotty's fellow asked in a strong Midlands accent.

'Not for me, thank you,' Connie said firmly. 'I'm just about to take my leave.'

'Same here.' Norma followed suit.

'I hope we haven't scared you off,' Josie's protector said.

'Of course not,' Connie laughed. 'But be quick. The minute we stand up you must grab our seats or else someone else will nab them from under us.'

Dotty and Josie laughed as they made a lunge for the chairs Connie and Norma vacated so the two men could sit close. 'I knew right away that you'd be great fun, Connie,' Dotty said. 'See you tomorrow.'

'Enjoy the rest of the evening,' Norma said with a quick wink.

The night air was cool after the heat of the pub and Connie breathed out a relieved sigh. 'Was I ever that young?' she asked. 'If I was, I don't remember it.' She thought about how she and Arthur had never been ones for dancing in clubs or staying out late, although she certainly thrived more on being with other people and having a social life than Arthur did – she seemed to be enough for him. In one of his letters he'd written that as his only family, her safety was his main concern and he wanted to be her haven, her refuge and her sanctuary. That filled her with guilt when she imagined the betrayed expression on his face if he found out she'd been to a jam-packed pub on a Monday night.

'Josie's only twenty, but Dotty isn't as young as she looks,' Norma said. 'She's all of twenty-four although you'd think she was about twelve. When she's forty-five she'll look thirty, lucky girl. But do you know …' Norma looked over her shoulder and Connie knew something scandalous was to follow, which made her feel a bit uncomfortable; she wasn't sure she wanted her view of Dotty to be tainted by gossip, true or not. 'Dotty was off sick a few months ago and when she came back, she was terribly thin and pale. Whenever I asked how she was, all I could get out of her was a shrug and a cursory, "Alright." The Absolute Miseries told me she'd been pregnant and got rid of the baby by some underhand means.' Norma lowered her voice. 'And she doesn't have a mum or a nan. In fact, Josie told me she doesn't have anyone at all.'

Connie was surprised, but not shocked. Dotty's attitude and behaviour made that piece of news perfectly plausible. She didn't pass judgement either, but her heart went out to the girl she'd come to feel fond of after only one day and who had to go through that terrible experience in complete isolation.

When she turned to peer at Norma, her features obscured by shadows in the blackout, she expected to discern a haughty, pious expression but all she made out was softness and solicitude. 'Poor kid,' Norma said, squeezing Connie's arm. It was then Connie thought she and Norma might become great friends. They seemed to have a lot in common.

The following weeks turned into months as Connie's days formed as firm a structure as possible during such an unpredictable war. Under the shadow cast when she turned the strong, artificial light of the desk lamp out of her eyes, she began to work faster and with more competence through her never-decreasing pile of letters and her fascination for reading about the lives and thoughts of other people didn't wane for one moment.

Once a fortnight she and Norma joined Dotty and Josie for a few drinks, which seemed to satisfy the younger women that they hadn't become Absolute Miseries themselves, but Connie formed a solid friendship with Norma and they spent a great deal of their free time together. They occupied themselves with the cinema; reading in silence or comparing bits of their husbands' letters; dodging potholes and bomb craters; sharing meals; visiting Mum in Acton; knitting for Connie and cross stitch for Norma.

At least once a day, each of the girls at the table thought they'd found a code, but the majority of them turned out to be false alarms or misinterpretations or unsophisticated attempts by writers to use encryption to enliven their letters. 'Time wasters,' Dotty tutted. 'Do you know that some boys' comics are running pages on how to send letters in simple code?'

'That's right,' Norma said. 'And my sister said her sons' Scout group was doing that as an activity. I told her to get the Scoutmaster to put a stop to it right away.'

Most of those letters were passed and sent with the addition of a leaflet informing the recipient to remind the writer of censorship regulations and that if they continued to write in code their name would be placed on a watch list. Until one Wednesday afternoon when Connie came across something most peculiar.

The letter was from a godmother in Surrey to her godson serving on a ship somewhere in the world. There was a paragraph about food, or the lack of it, as there was in most letters. Next, she wrote about an evacuee she was billeting whom she called her 'little poppet'. Then she talked about the communal bomb shelters she refused to use before mentioning everyone in her family by their Christian names and her neighbours by the numbers of their houses. And lastly, she wrote about her artwork and an exhibition of paintings that were to be hung in the local church. Signing off with a row of three kisses, that seemed to be that except for a tiny ink and pen drawing of flowers at the bottom of the page.

Scanning the writing again, Connie frowned and wondered if she should question the discussion about the shelters, but the woman hadn't mentioned their exact location or how many people they held, so that would pass. Perhaps the numbers of the neighbours' houses? She would check with Dotty on that one. But it was the drawing that was strange. Or was it? The writer was an artist, after all. Connie held up the page for closer inspection, then put it down again on the table, retrieved her magnifying glass from the drawer, scrutinised every flower and there it was – each petal was filled in with a different amount of shading. One had been inked in the shape of a half-moon, the next sported a dot in the middle, the top third of another was coloured in and so forth. It was clearly some kind of ingenious code and Connie held the pages out to Dotty.

'My word,' she said. 'The lengths some people will go to. I'm not sure whether it's sophisticated or childish but either way, it's definitely inventive. I'll get this over to the Chief Wren right away.'

Connie felt herself puff up with pride, although she tried hard not to appear self-satisfied. When Dotty returned, she told Connie that the letter was being sent upwards and it wouldn't pass through her hands again so she should get on with her next envelope. 'I insist you come out for a special drink to celebrate your excellent find. Norma, too. I'll let the Miseries know, just in case.' She sent a withering glance towards the three girls who refused to join in. 'But I'm sure they won't take up the invitation.' She shrugged. 'Their loss.'

The following morning, her head a bit thick from three Gimlets, Connie alerted Dotty to a number code and a more complicated symbols code, both of which had been written by serving sailors in an attempt to let their wives or mothers or girlfriends know where they were and that they were okay. None of them were involved in organised propaganda against the Allies, but had to be condemned nevertheless, a stern message of reprimand sent to each of the writers.

Much more interesting to Connie was the letter from Leading Signalman Drew Morrison telling his wife about the mist that had surrounded their ship for three days and which, in the middle of a vast sea, had made him feel claustrophobic. Would that information give away his position? Foolishly, he'd mentioned the name of his vessel and that it was escorting a convoy of troops, so she scoured through that with a *scritch scratch* of her indelible pencil.

He went on to say his quarters in the bowels of the ship were cramped and sometimes he'd wake thinking he couldn't catch a breath. Jokingly, he said it reminded him of the time he'd had to rush out of the pictures before the end of the film because he felt too confined, and Connie felt dreadfully sorry for him, climbing the walls in his small cabin with all those other men when he couldn't stand being boxed in.

He said the bunk room smelled, too, of odours he couldn't mention to a lady such as his wife, but he would leave it up to her imagination and when he was home for good, he would buy her some lovely perfume to make the stink dissipate from his nostrils forever. Poor Drew, Connie thought as she smoothed her label over the envelope. Hopefully his wife would find words to appease him.

Five minutes until morning break and Connie thought she would have a raisin scone with lemon curd or a powdered egg and a rasher of streaky bacon, depending on the available rations. Norma pointed to the clock and Connie nodded. Time for one more letter.

The envelope of this one looked a bit bashed about, as if it had been kicking around in the sender's bag for ages before they'd slipped it into the post box. Taking out two pages of equally forlorn paper, Connie started to read the most gut-wrenching letter she'd come across to date. Sitting up straight, she felt her fingers leave damp patches on the corners of the paper and as she continued, she slumped and slipped down, hunched over in her chair.

It was from a woman named Maude Grimshaw to her Dearest Mikey. She told him she was writing soon after she'd last written because she wanted to let him know how much she missed him. Then the letter took a more serious turn.

Also, there's something between us that I haven't been able to tell you about all these years. Not because I haven't wanted to or because I didn't think it was the right thing to do, but because I was warned, in no uncertain terms, that I mustn't. But now, what with this bloody war and how none of us know the ending in store for us, I feel I must tell you in case I never get another chance. Mikey, I hope you're sitting down or lying on your bunk or leaning against a wall because I'm not your sister, I'm your mother and I love you dearly, as only a mother can. I've always loved you in that way. But Mum and Dad – or Nanny and Grandad as they should be known to you – said I must agree to them bringing you up as their own and that I would have to love and care for you from afar as your sister. It was either that or lose you altogether.

They have no idea I'm sending this letter to you. When they find out all hell will break loose and they might never forgive me. But Maurice, who is really your stepfather and not your brother-in-law, knows everything and he agrees that this should come out in the open, as you deserve to be told the truth. I know this is a lot for you to grasp, but can you forgive me? Please write back as soon as possible and say you will at least try.

Your ever-loving Mum. XXX

The bruised and battered envelope made sense now. It had probably been hiding in Maude's pocket for days whilst she worked up the courage to post it.

'Jennies, down tools,' Dotty announced.

When Connie didn't move, the letter still in her hand, Dotty asked her if there were any problems.

'No, Mam,' Connie answered softly. She checked the name on the envelope, Able Seaman Michael Johnson, and the sender's address, resealed it with her label and feeling heavy with sadness, placed it in the bag to be sent onwards.

Trailing to the canteen after the others, Connie went over and over the words in the letter, committing them to her memory. The thought that she'd never know whether Mikey forgave his mother and grandparents was almost unbearable. She felt crushed under the weight of anxiety for all of them.

'Everything alright?' Norma asked.

'Yes, fine, thank you,' Connie answered, feeling as if she were being pulled back from another world.

'What delicacy are you going to have today?'

Maude and Mikey appeared with stark clarity in her mind again and she felt so drawn to them and their dilemma, that she knew her churning stomach wouldn't manage anything other than a strong cup of tea.

11

Connie had been peeved when Arthur told her he'd made arrangements with Ken for her trip to London. 'I could have organised it myself,' she said. 'If I'd known when I was going to go.'

'No need, Treasure.' Arthur had seemed offended that she wasn't effusively grateful. 'You'll be going at seven thirty-five on the Monday morning. That way I will have time to put you on the train and get back for work.'

'Arthur, really. It's good of you but I can get to the station and find the right train by myself.'

'It's not a problem, Treasure,' he'd said, oblivious to her exasperated tone. 'Anything for you. Dora will meet you at King's Cross and then she'll see you back on the train on Wednesday. She's taken the day off work especially to be with you.'

Deep shame had flooded through Connie when she thought of how silly and immature Arthur made her seem to other people. 'There was no need for Dora to do that. I can find my own way around London.'

'When I wrote to Ken, he said Dora was more than happy with the arrangements.'

Connie didn't know how she'd stopped herself from clobbering him.

'Anyway,' he'd carried on. I'm telling you now so that next week you can sort out meals that I can easily heat up whilst you're away.'

She'd hinted that he might use the opportunity to try out the works canteen, but he'd shaken his head and said something along the lines of not having fought in the war only to have to line up for a tray of mediocre, lukewarm dinner. So on the day she was travelling to London, Connie was downstairs first to prepare Arthur's breakfast and put the final touches on the meals she'd cooked and covered and stacked for him in the refrigerator.

When Arthur came down, carrying her small suitcase, he asked if she was joining him for porridge but she was too churned up with nerves or excitement to eat.

Arthur shook his head. 'You'll regret it later,' he said. 'When your tummy starts to rumble somewhere around Newark.'

Refusing to be convinced, Connie preferred to imagine herself settled in her seat with a cup of coffee and an iced bun on the small table in front of her.

She thought she'd despise the walk into Barnby Dun and the bus ride to Doncaster station with Arthur fussing about her case and reminding her to check for her ticket and not to leave her bag unguarded when she had to use the facilities on the train. Despite the dominating towers that seemed to sidle and shift as they monitored their progress to the bus stop, the crisp morning air, twined with the heady scents of summer, captivated them and held them enthralled. It almost seemed as if they could have been a different couple to the Connie and Arthur who had emerged from their younger selves. A more adventurous couple who enjoyed each other's company and had more to talk about than what cut of meat went into the stew and if the garden had been weeded. If that was the case, it would be lovely to be going off somewhere together – Scotland, perhaps, to explore lochs and forests, or Cornwall to sit by the sea and eat pasties and cream teas, or somewhere more mysterious and sensuous like France or Italy.

'Listen.' Arthur stopped and held Connie still with a hand on her arm. 'I think it's a wren, looking for a mate.' Despite the rattling, grating churr, they smiled at each other as they stood and listened. 'Lucky for me I've found mine.' He gave her shoulder a squeeze. 'When it's very quiet you can sometimes hear blackbirds, robins, thrushes and chaffinches, too,' he said as they continued towards the bus stop. 'Their songs are loud and strong at this time of year, but once they've found their companion they become less vociferous. Too busy building a nest, I suppose.'

That keeps all creatures busy, Connie thought. But if the nest is never filled – then what? The chatter and enthusiasm and expectation peters out and the only thing the lonely pair have to do is snipe at each other in less than harmonious tones. That's what it seemed she and Arthur had descended to when their hopes for a feathered nest had failed to materialise.

As Arthur was in charge of the expedition they arrived at the station in plenty of time, but Connie didn't go into the newsagent's to buy a copy of *Good Housekeeping* as she didn't want him to think the few shillings pocket money he'd given her was enough to burn.

Connie protested, but Arthur went ahead and bought a platform ticket and insisted on carrying her case right into the carriage. He cross-checked her ticket with the seat number and when he was satisfied she was in the right place, heaved the case onto the rack above her head, helped her off with her coat and reminded her again to wait at King's Cross for Dora if her sister-in-law happened to be late.

Beginning to feel embarrassed that any potential fellow passenger would witness Arthur's fussing, Connie tried to shush him along by saying she would be fine, she knew what to do when she got to London, he would be late for work. She walked back to the carriage door with him but before he stepped out onto the platform, he tilted her chin and kissed her vigorously and for rather a long time in a way that reminded her of another kiss in a different cold, busy station when they were both in uniform. 'Arthur,' she laughed when they drew apart. 'I'm only going for two nights. I'll soon be back.'

With a look that flashed across his face so swiftly Connie thought she might have imagined it, he appeared lost. 'You will, won't you?' he whispered. 'Come back.'

Might this be an opportunity to say she didn't think she could carry on unless something changed dramatically? But she couldn't do that to Arthur. Not here on the draughty station in Doncaster and not now. She smiled, rubbed the sinuous muscles under his jacket and said, 'Now who's being a silly billy? But …'

'But what?' he asked. Then he changed the subject and the moment passed before she could say she wanted him to take her seriously about finding a job, the rut she was in with her strict routine, having a social life. Pointing to her hands, Arthur said, 'Your bag. You mustn't leave it unattended on your seat, Treasure, or you'll have no money for London and no ticket to get home.'

'Yes, Arthur,' she said. 'And don't forget to water the clematis, please. Not today. Just tomorrow.'

He nodded then wagged his finger in the direction of her seat.

The last few minutes before the train pulled away were painful. Arthur stood right outside the window where she was sitting, putting his hand up every few seconds or checking his watch and mouthing three minutes or two minutes twelve seconds or one minute thirty-seven. She walked two fingers along the table and pointed for him to leave, but he stayed rooted to the spot.

The doors slammed shut one by one; the whistle blew; Arthur waved and for one terrible moment, Connie thought he was going to run next to the train until he could no longer keep up, as servicemen had done during the war. But he didn't and her last sight of him, for a few days, was the desolate shape of his slumped shoulders, beige-clad legs and dark brow staring after her from the grey, concrete platform.

Connie closed her eyes and put her head back against the flocked seat. She took a long breath in, eased her feet out of her shoes and wriggled her toes about in their stockings. The conductor opened the sliding door from the corridor, punched her ticket and said he hoped she liked her own company because there was no one else booked in the compartment until Peterborough. 'The dining car's open in fifteen minutes and you can order a light meal to be brought to you here,' he said.

Connie thought she would like that when her stomach

began to grumble near Newark, as Arthur warned her it would. For now, she was content to sit and watch the world go by. There were a few bomb sites still waiting to be renovated and repaired, largely unchanged since the attacks that had razed them to the ground years ago. Hastily built accommodation, with yards that ran down to fences bordering the train tracks, looked flimsy and barely serviceable. Lines of washing fanned lazily backwards and forwards, and she caught glimpses of rusting prams and bikes and motor scooters propped against lean-tos and sheds. Perhaps she should be grateful that Arthur was so careful with money and they had their comfortable, warm house with its tidy rooms and neat garden. But, she reminded herself, most of the money had rightfully been hers and she hadn't had a say in what to do with it, which she thought was most unfair.

That was the dilemma she always found herself in when it came to Arthur. Just when she thought she'd had all she could take of him and the strict, structured life he insisted they live, one of his good traits came to mind and she acquiesced again. Backwards and forwards she shifted between the two incongruous ways of thinking about her husband.

That kiss was the perfect example. Up until that moment he'd been finicky and controlling and treating her like a child and then from nowhere, he'd been both passionate and vulnerable. No wonder she wavered between not being able to stand the sight of him to feeling sorry for him to thinking that he really was a good man after all.

Doncaster was behind them now and the train slowed down for a scheduled stop at the much smaller town of Retford. Hanging baskets swayed on the edges of the wooden overhang above the one southbound platform and a few women, shopping bags in hand, boarded the train. When they started again, Connie took in lush green pastures, ripe with growing crops. Ribbons of smoke rose from a few cottages in the distance and she was sure everyone was aware of what they were inhaling from that, unlike the vapours that streamed over them in Barnby Dun. Three horses stood close together near a fence, probably waiting for their owner to arrive with their feed. Cows grazed, oblivious to the train chugging by and sheep meandered single file across a field.

Newark came and went and Connie was hungry, which made her smile inwardly because if Arthur were with her he would smugly say he'd told her so. She remembered her bag and headed to the dining car where she asked for a pot of coffee, two rounds of toast and jam and a cinnamon bun. She showed the woman behind the counter her seat number and was told her order would be with her in a few minutes.

Not long after, another woman in a navy-blue tabard steered a trolley into the compartment, placed the coffee and breakfast on the table and said, 'There you are, my dear.' Then she went off, swaying with the movement of the train to take similar orders to other passengers. Connie could easily imagine doing that woman's job. She could meet and chat with all manner of people and look out at the passing scenery in between. She was eminently qualified for the position as she already had the uniform and she'd been waiting on Arthur for years, without receiving a pay packet for the privilege.

The toast was warm and the coffee not too strong. When she finished, she dabbed her mouth with the serviette and went to put it on top of the crockery but stopped, her hand dangling above the plates. As if in a trance, she put the soft material to her face again and the ghost of Arthur's firm lips on hers a few hours earlier flooded her with a deep feeling of loss and regret.

When had the affection between them trailed off? Perhaps the war had eroded what they'd had together and stopped their optimism in its tracks, or maybe it was the lack of children, or when Arthur had begun to insist they keep to a regimented lifestyle.

A week or so ago, during a tedious coffee morning, her neighbours had started to talk about how they'd met their husbands. Susan and Tony first set eyes on each other in a discotheque in Bedford; Mandy and Graham had worked together in a printing firm in Brighton; Shirley and Trev met at a vocational college in Surrey and Millicent, preoccupied with counting triangles, squares and circles into a brightly coloured shape sorter, said she and Brian had first noticed each other at infant school. 'He was horrible,' she'd laughed. 'He had a permanently runny nose and scabs on his knees. Wait – I'll say it first – no change there, then.'

Susan had turned to Connie and asked, 'How did you and Arthur meet?'

'I'll bet it was during the war, wasn't it?' Shirley joined in.

'No, the war is not to blame this time,' Connie said. 'We were children when we met. His auntie lived on the same road as me and when he came to visit, which was often as his mother was poorly, we played together in the street with lots of other children.'

'Oh, how lovely,' Shirley enthused.

'And I suppose he was your one and only?' Susan asked.

'Not quite, but almost.'

Connie thought they were going to question her further, perhaps about how long she and Arthur had known each other before they married, but little Adrian knocked over a vase and put paid to any more chat on that subject. She remembered how he'd cried, tears streaking down his face and how he'd turned to her for comfort, clambering onto her lap and snuggling into her cardigan.

If they'd returned to the conversation after the mess had been mopped up, Connie would have told them that when she was nineteen, she'd been dating a lad who was an apprentice bookbinder. Looking back, she remembered everything about him as average. He was of medium height with a build that was still building; he had rather nondescript brown, wavy hair that he combed back from his forehead and a few whiskers were beginning to push through his baby-soft skin. But when he threw back his head and laughed, his Adam's apple bobbing up and down in his throat, the joyful sound was powerful enough to fill an auditorium. That, and his great sense of humour, was what Connie liked about him. When he called to take her for a walk or when he treated her to the pictures or when they had tea with his mum or hers, they would spend the entire time choking on their jokes and clever observations. As soon as one calmed down the other would start and off they'd go again.

Then Arthur reappeared. She'd thought nothing of the fact she hadn't seen him for some years and vaguely remembered hearing some adults mention that his mother had passed away and he'd gone off to train as an engineer in the Navy. Stepping out of his aunt's house one morning, he'd caught her eye as she left for work and he was everything her young, dappy boyfriend was not. Tall, with thick, dark hair, those striking animated eyebrows that from a distance almost blended into one and good prospects ahead of him. She was drawn to him as if he were a forceful magnet. The only disadvantage was that his laugh, when it surfaced, sounded as if it was dragged out of him against his better judgement, but she put that down to Arthur being older and therefore more mature and worldly wise than the boy she'd been seeing.

She recoiled now when she thought about the hurt look on that poor lad's face when he saw her and Arthur walking arm-in-arm along their road. Eventually, he'd married a pale girl from Tottenham and they had three thin, fair-haired children before he tragically took a packet in Tripoli.

Arthur had proposed very quickly and when he was commissioned two years later and came home with sub-lieutenant stripes on his left sleeve – a smart maroon flash between them to denote he was an engineer – they set a date, the banns were read and Connie walked down the aisle towards the rest of her life.

When she thought back to her wedding day, she had an image of herself as impossibly young and slim in a white dress, her dark hair curving over her shoulders. When she'd first glimpsed Arthur beaming at her from the altar, her heart had seemed to skip a beat – he'd looked so handsome and tall and capable in his uniform. In her hands she held a bouquet of red roses and in Arthur's, he held her.

Once when she was feeling particularly frustrated about the relentless round of housework she had to perform week in, week out, she'd put down her cloth and tried to calculate how many times she'd dusted their wedding photo that stood on the sideboard. She arrived at a sum of 1,822, but thought the figure must be higher as sometimes Arthur asked, as a special favour, if she would run the rag over things again because he thought they needed an extra polish. At the time she wondered why she'd bothered working that out because it only made her more resentful and nothing would change just because she had hard evidence of how her life was spent.

Peterborough was a busy, bustling station and three people made their way into her compartment, bags and cases, coats and hats filling the space. Connie made sure her shoes were back on her feet and looked out of the window so she wouldn't be dragged into superficial conversation – she was too intent on thinking about how her life with Arthur had developed. Regardless, everyone exchanged pleasantries about the weather, timekeeping on lines from the north, if Harold Wilson was living up to his landslide victory.

When Connie turned to the window again, flat earth as far as the horizon was all she could see, which made the sky seem infinite and immense and as if it were balancing on top of them, but nothing about it was inauspicious as the towers were in Barnby Dun. A shiver ran through her when she thought about how those imposing pillars seemed to lord it over all of them.

The countryside on the Dorset coast, where she and Arthur had spent a four-day honeymoon, was undulating and fertile and smelled of salt from the sea. Their special time together had been loving and passionate, although Arthur's predilection for being intimate in a certain, set pattern should have been a warning to her about how their future life together would unfold. But how could she have had an inkling when that short break was the only time they would live on their own until after Mum died. As soon as those few days and nights were over, Arthur rejoined his ship and Connie went home. War was declared, they worked at their separate jobs and spent any coordinated leave in the same house Connie had lived in all her life.

When those six terrible years came to an end and no children materialised, they'd drifted into life with Mum. She'd found distractions: Dora popping in and out with the boys and a few friends she'd meet for tea, and there had been myriad routes to take to and from the shops that consisted of more to look at than other houses and steam from a power station. No wonder all this business with Arthur was coming to a head now, they'd never had the chance to iron it out before.

'Almost there,' a portly man stated with confidence.

'Yes, I believe so,' said one of the other women.

Taking in the packed terraces, the yellow sodium lights, the zebra crossings, the new high-rise flats, Connie could smell, taste and feel London. She turned to her fellow passengers to share her excitement with them, but they looked as if they were preparing to go into battle. Not to be discouraged, she stood and swung her case down from the parcel shelf. She couldn't believe it had been so long since she'd been home and she was determined to make the most of the visit.

★

Peering over numerous heads, Connie saw her sister-in-law waving with twiddling fingers. Even when she was standing still, Dora bustled and bristled with energy and Connie found it both infectious and exhausting.

'Snap,' Dora said, hugging Connie to her. She pointed to her hair, cut short and dyed a dark blonde. 'New hairdos.'

Connie laughed and touched her lacquered, back-combed strands. 'About time for me,' she said.

Dora went to take her case, but Connie beat her to it. She noticed that Dora was wearing a pair of the ubiquitous white boots and over her shoulder she carried a bag that sported alternating pink and green chevrons. 'Very trendy,' Connie said. 'I think that's the expression, isn't it?'

'Absolutely,' Dora said, leading the way to the Underground. 'We're with it. That's another.'

Connie thought Dora was very with it, whilst she was more without whatever it was.

As they stepped off the moving staircase, Dora put her arm through Connie's and said, 'I can't believe you're here. I never thought you'd convince Arthur to let you ...'

Connie waited for Dora to continue, but Dora looked away as if she'd said too much. It was enough, though, for Connie to know that her brother and sister-in-law were under no illusions about her life with Arthur.

When they were sitting on the Tube to Islington, Dora squeezed her close again and said, 'I've got so many things planned. We're going to have a fantastic time.'

'Thank you, Dora,' Connie said. 'I'm looking forward to

anything we do, but I'd be just as happy to sit in with you, Ken and the boys. That would make a big change for me.'

'Well, we'll do more than that,' Dora said, her hands fluttering whilst she talked. 'There's the pub, the cinema, a trip down memory lane and Somerset House.'

'Somerset House?' Connie echoed.

'I've just started to trace my family tree.' Dora became more animated as she explained. 'It's very interesting. I'm going to look for documents relating to my great-grandparents on my mum's side.'

'Goodness,' Connie said. 'I wouldn't know where to start.'

Dora crossed her legs and turned so she was facing Connie. 'It's quite time-consuming. I've told myself not to expect too much too quickly, but just to take one piece at a time. It's a bit like being a detective.' She laughed. 'Ken's going to have a go with your family when he has the time. Maybe you could help him.'

'That might be difficult,' Connie said. 'I don't seem to have much time, believe it or not.'

'Oh, I believe it,' Dora said sharply.

'Also, I wouldn't have access to records in Doncaster. Besides, if Ken wants to do it, there's not much point in me doing the same.'

Connie looked through the glass and stared until she made out the eerie black and grey shapes of the tangle of tunnels they were travelling through. 'That's what it must be like to search for someone,' she said. 'You go down one route and that leads you off at a tangent and then another and another after that. I imagine it's very easy to get mixed up.'

'Yes, but it's fascinating, too. If you did have a go, who would you choose to investigate? Your grandfather, an aunt, a cousin?'

'Maude Grimshaw or James Stanton,' Connie said without a moment's hesitation. And the look on Dora's face, thrown back at her from the window, was more bewildered than when she'd been talking about the conundrum that was Arthur.

12

Dotty had ordered them to follow her – quickly. In single file Josie, Norma, the three Absolute Miseries and Connie, bringing up the rear, turned on their heels and followed their superior down into the depths of the nearest Underground station. Others piled down the stairs with them, then dispersed to the far reaches of the platform in a more sedate, dignified manner.

'Well,' Dotty said in a bit of a huff. 'So much for our big night out. I hate Hitler.'

Connie laughed. 'You never fail to amuse me, Dotty,' she said. 'Don't you think we all hate Hitler?'

'Yes, I suppose so.' Dotty would not allow herself to be cajoled into a better humour. 'But not as much as I do.'

That remark made Norma catch Connie's eye and smile. 'It's probably nothing more than a tip and raid,' she said. 'We'll be sitting in the pub in no time.'

Connie agreed for the sake of Dotty's mood, but felt guilty in doing so. Referring to any bomb onslaught in such a glib manner demeaned the suffering of all those poor people taking this packet or any of the bombs and incendiaries the Jerries dropped on them.

The little ways in which everyone adapted and became accustomed to the most dire of circumstances never failed to amaze her. Last week after she and Dotty had been for a cup of tea and a slice of eggless ginger cake, the siren had wailed its sad lament and they'd hurried under the overhang of a shop. Connie had thrown herself to the pavement as they'd been instructed to do, but Dotty had stayed on her feet, folding herself into a space near the door. 'Dotty,' Connie admonished, pulling on the young woman's hem. 'What are you doing? Get down.'

But Dotty had shaken her head. 'No fear,' she said. 'These stockings are almost new. I refuse to allow them to kiss the dust and dirt. If one of the bombs has my name on it, at least I'll look presentable when I get blown up or down or sideways or wherever.'

It was then Connie had become aware of a number of feet and legs surrounding her. She was the only one who had taken to the ground for safety, everyone else taking their chances in a more refined manner. Sheepishly, she scrambled to her knees and took the hand Dotty held out to help her up. Brushing mud and bits of concrete off her coat, she'd wriggled in next to Dotty who made an attempt to smooth the hair around her double crown. 'Next time don't be so silly,' Dotty had said.

'Mam,' Connie replied.

The Three Miseries distanced themselves from the rest of them and Connie thought they would have probably been quite pleased to spend the entire evening in the musty tunnels of Victoria station rather than amongst the fusty crowds in the Commercial Tavern. And although it couldn't be helped, she agreed with Dotty's disappointment and felt cheated that they might not be able to say their goodbyes to Norma in the proper naval tradition.

'Let's make camp over here,' Josie said, taking off her dark navy greatcoat so she could sit on it under the much too cheerful red, white and blue Underground sign. The others followed suit. 'Try not to look so glum, Dotty,' Josie carried on. 'Or that will be Norma's lasting impression of you if she ever thinks of us again.'

Norma laughed out loud. 'Josie,' she said. 'I can assure you that Dotty sulking won't be how I'll remember her. There are her huge brown eyes, the way she flits so easily between being Dotty and Petty Officer Wren Censor Saunders, how she …'

'Hang on one minute,' Dotty said in such a loud voice the families on either side gawped at her. 'It's not flitting. It's …' She looked to the tiles on the ceiling for inspiration. 'It's consciously remodelling myself to fit the situation.'

'Take advantage of the situation, more like,' one of the Miseries whispered to her friend.

'I heard that,' Dotty said. 'And if you don't like it, you can go elsewhere.'

Connie's attention was taken by a loose thread in the lining of her greatcoat and Norma decided that was the perfect moment to brush dust off the tips of her shoes. Connie peered at Norma from the corner of her eye and her friend grimaced in solidarity – Dotty pushed her behaviour to the edge sometimes and she should be careful when she was wearing her uniform in a public place.

'Anyway,' Dotty said. 'I feel bad for Norma.'

'You mustn't,' Norma insisted. 'I wanted to spend the

evening with all of you and here we are. It really doesn't matter that we're in the Underground and not the pub, does it?'

'That's the spirit,' Josie said.

Dotty mimicked Josie in a sing-song voice, her waved hair moving on her collar as she waggled her head from side to side. Then to Connie's astonishment, the three miserable Wrens stood up and said sorry to Norma, but they were actually going to do what Dotty suggested and move somewhere else. Connie watched as they wished Norma the best of luck, saluted and walked right to the other end of the platform where they plonked themselves down next to a large group of women playing cards.

Gathering her mouth back up from where it had hit the concrete, Connie said, 'Well, I would never have believed that happened if I hadn't seen it myself.' She looked around at Dotty, Josie and Norma who were staring after their colleagues, eyes wide with disbelief, and when they turned their attention back to each other, they burst into laughter.

'Good riddance,' said Dotty. 'But how rude. Especially as it's your leaving party, Norma.'

Norma, as easy going and amenable as ever, shrugged and said, 'It doesn't matter. I didn't think they'd make it this far with the rest of us.'

'Yes,' Dotty said, lying across her coat with her hands beneath her head. 'Let's forget about them and hope the siren stops soon so we can make the most of what's left of the evening.'

That filled Connie with sadness and a feeling of trepidation. Other colleagues had come and gone and that, she knew, was the transient nature of friendships during a war. But she had grown close to Norma and would miss her very much. There would be a hole in her life that Norma, with her practical nature and sensitivity, her dry humour and love of tea, cake and cross stitch, had filled very snugly. They were both married with husbands away in the forces and that meant they could excuse themselves from late nights in smoky clubs and dance halls without fear of being told they were spiralling downwards into absolute miseries themselves.

Another lovely, companionable Wren might fill the chair vacated by Norma, but looking over at her friend listening intently to Josie and nodding to encourage the younger girl along, Connie knew she would be difficult to replace.

Producing a small notebook from her bag, Dotty handed it to Norma with a pencil and asked for her forwarding address. 'It's for all of us,' Dotty said, indicating Josie and Connie with a nod of her head. Her voice sounded uncertain and timid and as wispy as if she were nothing more than the last child left in the school playground, looking up and down the street for her mum and praying she hadn't been abandoned.

'Thank you,' Connie said, although she and Norma had exchanged addresses as soon as Norma had received her posting to Manchester, and unlike the way in which she had lost contact with Bea and Angelique, Connie felt sure they would stay in touch.

Dotty kept her head down as she took back the notebook and busied herself with putting it in her bag, but Connie noticed that the girl's eyes had clouded over. Knowing that to draw attention to her show of emotion was the last thing their fun-loving, mischievous presiding officer would want, Connie looked away and gave Dotty the chance to pull herself together – they all did. Connie's heart went out to her when she remembered that Dotty didn't have anyone and she wondered if each time someone she felt close to left her life, she had to cover up her feelings of abandonment with bigger and bolder displays of bravado.

True to form, it didn't take Dotty long to recover. 'Look at them.' She shot her best scathing look towards the Three Miseries. 'They're talking to those women as if they've known them all their lives, but they won't give us the time of day.'

'Leave them,' Josie said. 'They're not worth bothering with. So, what do you know about Manchester, Norma?'

'It's north,' Dotty said. 'I know that much.'

'Not much more than Dotty,' Norma said. She and Connie had talked about that very subject a few nights previously and now Norma repeated what they'd discussed. 'The train leaves from Euston and takes about five and a half hours. It's an industrial city and they were blitzed just after London. The locals called it the Christmas Blitz because it happened during December. Oh, and there's a football stadium called Old Trafford which took a packet, too.' Norma's husband was an avid football fan.

Dotty sighed and smoothed down her already perfectly shaped eyebrows. 'Well, I suppose it won't make much difference where you are,' she said. 'You won't see anything during the day as you'll be cooped up in another airless room looking through endless letters.'

'*Snip snip. Scritch scratch*,' Josie added. 'That's all you'll hear.'

'Don't forget the *tick tock* of the clock,' Connie joined in.

'You're right,' Norma said. 'It doesn't matter where any

of us are posted, the work will be the same. And although I know I couldn't possibly be stationed with a lovelier bunch, I hope the Jennies in Manchester turn out to be reasonably good company.'

Hearing that statement made Dotty scowl again in the direction of the Three Miseries, but Connie thought the idea of being posted to Manchester rather glamorous and exciting and she envied Norma to a certain extent. As for the work of ploughing through other people's letters, Connie could not get enough of legitimately prying into other people's business.

At last the all-clear sounded and they breathed a sigh of relief. They wouldn't have to spend the entire night in the confines of a stuffy yet draughty tunnel with people they would never choose to sleep next to under normal circumstances. Wearily, they followed the crowds up the steps and into the smoky night air. They ducked around a pile of rubble and Josie and Dotty each took one end of a shattered door and moved it from where it could so easily have been tripped over.

'Good job, girls,' Norma said.

Brushing muck off her hands, Dotty said, 'Still time for one or two?' She looked at each of them hopefully.

None of them were enthusiastic and if the dark rings under their eyes, their jaded skin and lank hair was anything to go by, they weren't up to a night out. Yawning, Norma shook her head. 'I'm afraid I'm done in,' she said. 'My train leaves early tomorrow and I haven't quite finished packing.'

For once, Dotty didn't argue the point. Instead, she put her arms around Norma's neck and hugged her, holding on for a moment too long. When she pulled away, the tears had misted her eyes again and she reached for Josie's arm, both of them looking over their shoulders once for a final wave goodbye.

'Oh, dear,' Norma said. 'I'll never stop worrying about that girl. You will keep an eye on her, won't you?'

'As best I can,' Connie said. But she thought that watching Dotty's antics from a distance might be as far as it went. The girl was too troubled and free-spirited to take advice from the likes of her. There wasn't much she, or anyone else could say that would rein her in.

When she and Norma parted company, Connie felt the pressure of a tear or two in her own eyes. 'I am so sorry you didn't get a proper send off,' she said.

Norma laughed. 'You know me,' she said. 'I'd much rather have an hour's chat with tea and biscuits.'

'We've had plenty of those,' Connie said.

'And I've enjoyed every single one. Thank you for being a great friend, Leading Wren Censor Constance Allinson.'

'Here's to you, Petty Officer Wren Censor Norma Trenton.' And she mimed lifting her hand in a very special farewell toast.

13

Connie had been foolish to think there might be games with the boys as Victor was nineteen, out to work and courting, and Gregory was almost seventeen. When they'd all visited her and Arthur last Christmas they'd played Monopoly, draughts and Cluedo they'd brought with them – although Twister stayed in the box as Arthur wouldn't entertain the idea. When they left, Connie tried to persuade Arthur to let her buy a boxed game they could play in the evenings, but he'd scoffed. 'Cards, then,' Connie had said. 'We used to enjoy a hand of Whist or Crazy Eights with Mum.'

'No need now we live here,' Arthur had said. 'There's more than enough to keep us busy during the day and by the evening we're tired out.'

She fumed when he spoke for her and dared to presume she agreed with his endless mandates.

Now she had to be content to watch from the sidelines as her nephews flew in and out, enjoying the years as they transitioned from adolescence to adulthood. Ken was at work, too, and left early in the morning for his job as a maintenance supervisor in a big hotel in the West End, so Connie and Dora were on their own.

They hauled themselves onto high stools at a long worktop Dora called the breakfast bar. 'It serves for anyone who only has time to eat quickly before they get on with what they want to be doing. That's the boys most of the time.'

'You do seem to lead a whirlwind life,' Connie said.

Dora shrugged. 'We all have a lot of interests. Do you want to try some of this?' she said, holding out a brown jar.

'Nutella,' Connie read the label. 'I've seen that in the shops but I've never tried it.'

'Have a go now,' Dora said. 'Let me get you a clean knife.' Connie smeared some of the sticky, sweet-smelling substance on her bread and took a bite. It melted on her tongue, stuck to the top of her mouth and tasted wonderful.

Laughing, Dora pushed her finger into the goo, scooped out a blob and savoured it. 'Go on,' she encouraged. 'Have some more.' Connie did the same and decided that she might take a jar back to Doncaster and hide it away where Arthur couldn't find it.

'Connie,' Dora said suddenly, as if she couldn't stop herself. 'What's going on?'

'What do you mean?' Connie said, licking the last of the Nutella from her finger.

'Come on,' Dora said. 'You're talking to me now and I know this is unprecedented. The visit, the time away from Arthur, the new hairstyle, Maude Grimshaw and James Stanton. I know Arthur's difficult ...'

Dora was forthright and practical and they'd known each other for years, so of course she wouldn't let an event like this pass her by unchallenged. Although she and Ken tried to bite their tongues when it came to Arthur, they didn't hide their opinion of him very well and this wasn't one of the Barnby Dun coffee mornings, so why shouldn't she confide in her sister-in-law?

Connie looked down at the jar of nutty, chocolaty sweetness that had held such promise of fun a mere minute or two ago. Now it was no more than another piece of excitement that hadn't lived up to the high hopes she'd had for it. She supposed her trips to London would lose their shine in the same way.

She tried to gather her thoughts, deciding what to say and what to leave out, but before she could find the right words, Dora picked up a satsuma from the fruit bowl and held it out to Connie. 'Want one?'

'No, thank you, Dora.' She shook her head.

'Oh, Connie.' Dora let her hand rest on her sister-in-law's arm for a moment. 'Ken and I are worried about you and we only want to help.'

'I know,' Connie said, swallowing to stop tears flooding her eyes. 'But I'm alright. We're alright. Really. I just need a break from the same old routine and Arthur came up with this idea.'

'So, it wasn't your solution?' Dora put her head to one side in sympathy. 'What would you like to do to break the monotony? Oh, don't answer. I can easily guess. You'd like a job.'

'Yes, I would.' Connie met Dora's gaze. 'But you know Arthur.'

Dora nodded. 'I'm afraid I do,' she said.

That seemed to be enough of an explanation for the exceptional turn of events they both found themselves embroiled in, so they sat in silence for a couple of minutes.

'I had a thought a couple of weeks ago,' Connie said.

'Oh, Ken would say "that's very dangerous".'

Connie laughed. 'A lot of men would say that. Especially about thoughts that women have. I suppose that's why so many women just share things with each other.'

'Ken doesn't mean it like that.' Dora was quick to come to her husband's defence. 'He's only messing about, you know that.'

'Of course I do.'

Dora nodded. 'So, what was the thought you had?'

Connie hesitated and part of her wished she hadn't broached the subject, but she carried on. 'I wondered if perhaps Arthur can't help the way he is sometimes.'

'Hmm,' Dora murmured in a sarcastic tone. 'We all have control over our attitudes and behaviour, don't we?'

'I've always thought so,' Connie said. 'But there are times when he seems to be so vulnerable that I almost feel sorry for him.'

Dora huffed. 'Like when?' she asked.

'Like when he said goodbye to me at the station. He was so forlorn I thought he was going to cry.'

'Those would have been the tears of a man who had to get his own meals and cups of tea for a few days.'

'Yes,' Connie laughed. 'That's probably the sum of it.'

'Have you tried talking to him about it?' Dora asked.

There was no need to reply. All Connie had to do was raise her eyebrows to make her point.

'Even if you did bring it up with him, he would deny there was anything untoward going on so you wouldn't get far.'

Connie knew that to be the truth of the matter. Arthur would never admit to there being anything wrong with his attitude towards her and he would scoff at any suggestion that he'd shown her signs of being susceptible to his emotions. He would probably say something about not fighting in a war just to have his wife tell him he was weak and sappy. Weariness washed over her and the mere thought of trying to talk to Arthur in the way Dora suggested exhausted her. 'Anyway,' she said. 'What about your work whilst I'm here?' She didn't like to add that neither she nor Arthur had given that much consideration.

'I don't work Mondays and Tuesdays,' Dora said. 'As you know. And I've taken a day's annual leave on Wednesday.'

'I know Arthur asked you to take the day off to be with me.' Connie turned away to hide her embarrassment.

'I don't mind at all,' Dora said. 'Seeing you like this is a rare treat.'

'Yes, it really is lovely. But if I visit every two months, you'll soon use up your holidays looking after me.'

'Yes,' Dora said, pouring boiling water into the teapot. 'That wouldn't be practical.' She bit her lip and studied Connie. 'But I needn't take a day's leave every time you visit, need I? We could give you a key and on Wednesdays you could come and go as you pleased then see yourself onto the train.'

A thrill so violent shot through Connie that she was surprised she didn't find herself on the floor. A day to herself in London – utter freedom was so close she could almost reach out and touch it.

'Of course, you'd have to muck in as we'd all be going about our day-to-day business.'

'I've never minded a bit of muck,' Connie said, barely able to keep the glee out of her voice.

'I know,' Dora said. 'Although there's not a trace of anything close to that in your life in Doncaster. So what do you think? Would that suit?'

'Very much,' Connie said. 'It's most generous of you.'

'Now, what about August?' Dora said.

'What about August?' Connie parroted.

'That should be the month of your next visit, but we've got a holiday cottage booked in Wales for a fortnight. You could come before we go away or postpone your trip until September or …' She pointed her finger towards the ceiling as a thought struck her. 'How about you have the run of the place whilst we're away?'

Connie let out a near hysterical squeal that instantly plummeted to a deep moan. 'Arthur,' she said. She knew he would either forbid that to happen, explaining that the whole point of the trips to London was to spend time with Ken and Dora or, worse still, he might insist on tagging along to take care of her and have a little holiday himself.

'Arthur.' Dora puckered her mouth as if she'd accidentally licked a lemon. Then she smiled and said, 'Well, I won't tell if you don't. Nor will Ken and the boys.'

The very idea filled Connie with a buzz of excited trepidation. But could she see it through? What if Arthur found out? She imagined first his enraged face then his hangdog look of betrayal that she'd wanted to be completely alone in Ken and Dora's empty house rather than with him. Apart from following her, which she didn't think even Arthur would stoop to, she could not think of how she'd be caught, so before she could change her mind, she blurted out, 'That would be fantastic, Dora. I would love that.'

'Good,' Dora said. 'That's settled then.'

'Now. Who are James Stanton and Maude Grimshaw?' Dora asked. 'Neighbours in Doncaster?'

Connie leaned across to the fruit bowl and picked up a satsuma. 'May I now?' she asked.

'Of course,' Dora said. 'But come on. Who are those people?'

As Connie peeled the satsuma, a fine, fragrant spray misted the air and she wished the steam from the cooling towers smelled as fresh and wholesome. 'Jim Stanton,' she said. 'Was someone whose letter I read during the war. When I was based in Liverpool. And I read Maude Grimshaw's whilst I was serving in Holborn.'

Dora's eyes were so wide, Connie thought they might never fit back into their sockets. 'Goodness,' Dora stammered. 'They must have been very important letters if you can still single them out from the thousands you had to plough through.'

For some reason Connie couldn't fathom, tears crept into her eyes again. 'No, they weren't,' she said. 'In fact, they were insignificant. It's just that I …' She shrugged. 'I'd love to know what happened to them and the other people they mentioned in their letters. I'd like to know that they're alright.'

'Well,' Dora said, emptying tea leaves into the sink. 'I never imagined you'd be able to recall any of those letters, let alone dwell on them to that extent. Any others?'

'What do you mean?'

'Just Maude and Jim or can you remember the names and circumstances of others that passed through your hands?'

'I can recall quite a few,' Connie said. 'Of course, some had more of an impact than others.'

'Those wartime jobs,' Dora said, shaking her head in disbelief. 'So many of them were an oddity buried in that period of time and now it hardly seems possible that they existed, let alone were carried out by us women.'

'That's it exactly,' Connie said, energy rushing through her when she heard the expression of her own thoughts. She threw her arms around her sister-in-law. 'How did we let it happen?' she asked. 'How could we have given up our skills and independence?'

'We didn't have a choice,' Dora said. 'Remember? When the war ended we had to give our jobs back to the men. The status quo, that's what we fought for. Besides, once it was over there was no need for half those jobs. Yours and mine included.'

'Did you ever miss yours?' Connie asked.

'What, miss driving tanks off assembly lines and onto lorries for distribution? Do you know, I did. It's a terrible thing to say about anything that happened during the war, but we had a lot of fun.'

'Yes, we did in our quiet, solemn censoring offices, too. Probably because we were thrown together in such extraordinary circumstances and we had to make the most of it.'

'Some of the other girls were such a good laugh. Do you remember that girl named Eunice who used to come home on leave with me sometimes?'

A short young woman with solid, square shoulders and permed hair that frizzed in the rain played around on the edges of Connie's memory.

'And then there was that lovely woman, Norma. You were great friends with her. Do you still keep in touch?'

'I did for quite a while, then she moved to Australia with her family and the letters petered out.'

'None of the others?'

Connie shook her head. There had been Bea and Angelique, Dotty, Josie, Marjorie and Ivy, but after the war Mum and Arthur and trying to have a baby had become her priorities and their friendships had gone by the wayside.

'Such a shame,' Dora said. 'Funny though, that you're more interested in the likes of Jim Stanton and Maude Grimshaw than you are any of those old friends you'd been close to. Anyway, who am I to talk.' Dora shrugged. 'I've lost contact with all my old ATS pals except Bertha. But do you know, next year I'll have the chance to drive again. We're going to get a brand-new Ford Cortina so we can have weekends away without having to worry about trains and buses.' Dora beamed, grabbed Connie's hands, pulled her off her chair and jumped up and down with her on the spot.

Connie bounced in time with her sister-in-law and said she was thrilled for her. She was, but her delight was tinged with envy – a car, weekends away to look forward to, a job, two lovely boys. Perhaps these few days would provide her with more unrest than she'd arrived with.

When the bobbing stopped the conversation came to an end, too. 'Right,' Dora said. 'Let's get our coats, we're off to Oxford Street where I'm to buy you an early birthday present.'

Connie started to protest, but Dora cut her short. 'Orders from your brother,' she said. 'And he made it quite clear I'm not to stand for arguments.'

Murmuring her thanks, Connie was acutely aware that

Ken's edict was playful and impish, the complete opposite from the way in which Arthur doled out his decrees. The contrast made her feel cheated.

Oxford Street was brisk and busy and brimming with people. Dora fitted right in as she bustled them from one shop to another, all of which she seemed to know so well. She told Connie she often spent the day having a look around or meeting a friend from work for lunch on one of their days off. It was a way of life that Connie found hard to imagine. The hoops she would have to jump through to get Arthur to agree to her spending the better part of a whole day wandering around Doncaster gazing at shoes and bags and household gadgets would not make the outing worth it.

They went into Miss Selfridge and had to shout to hear each other over the endless Beatles and Monkees records that were definitely not background music. Miniskirts hung from overhead pipes and brightly coloured boas lay tangled together in huge woven baskets. 'These,' Dora pointed out a rack of thigh-high dresses, 'are made from paper.'

'Paper?' Connie echoed.

Dora laughed. 'Feel one.'

Connie caressed a hot pink and orange sleeveless shift between her fingers and was astounded when it felt like a page from Arthur's newspaper. 'I can't believe it,' she said. 'Wait until I tell Millicent and Shirley. But what's the point?'

'Wear once then throw it away,' Dora said.

'Well, we've come on since the war, haven't we?' Connie said. 'When we never got rid of anything.'

'I like this one.' Dora held a purple and yellow patterned

dress with a nipped in waist against herself and looked at her reflection in a mirror hanging from a crazy angle on the wall. 'But I wouldn't trust it not to rip apart when I sat down.'

'Yes.' Connie laughed. 'That would be sure to happen to me and I'd show the world my very old-fashioned knickers.'

They spent a lot of time in Debenhams and Bourne and Hollingsworth and John Lewis, then had a sandwich lunch on the fourth floor of Peter Robinson. Light flooded through the domed ceiling and fell on the tables and chairs and plants and sliced through the painted murals that ran the length of the walls underneath the high windows. Connie offered to pay for her meal, but Dora insisted on taking the tab for both of them. 'I don't think Arthur and I worked this out very well,' Connie admitted. 'Although in my defence, Arthur took all the planning out of my hands.'

'Oh, you do surprise me,' Dora said in a sarcastic voice.

'I've got my ticket back to Doncaster and a bit of money, but not enough to …'

'It's alright,' Dora said. 'Ken and I are pleased to have you. This is as much of a treat for us as it is for you.'

Connie chewed slowly and deliberately on her ham and salad roll. Arthur had been so pompous when he'd given her a few bob spending money, but all along he must have known that her brother and sister-in-law would have to fork out for her. The fact that he expected them to do the same every two months filled her with shame. She knew that Ken and Dora would do anything for her, but a terrible embarrassment crept from her toes to her scalp and she felt every inch the barren, middle-aged burden she knew herself to be.

Dora pointed at Connie's cup. 'Another coffee?'

'Thank you, Dora.' Connie said.

Whilst Dora was at the counter, Connie twisted and turned to take in as many of the murals as her neck would allow. They each seemed to depict a dramatic scene set in a long-forgotten period of time and in a place far away – Italy, perhaps. A wedding was obviously taking place in one frame and all the characters portrayed were dancing, playing musical instruments and smiling. In another, a man was on one knee in front of a young woman who was leaning towards him.

Turning to look at the murals on the opposite side of the restaurant, Connie was faced with one that forced the breath from her lungs. A man in a white, flowing toga was pointing a finger at a woman who had fallen on her knees in front of him, begging for all she was worth for his mercy. Connie stared and thought that despite paper miniskirts, coffee on tap, white boots, lacquered hair, cars, money to spend and plenty of food, some things remained unchanged. She wondered what the woman in the painting was prostrating herself for – something as mundane as a handful of Roman coins to get her hair styled or perhaps, Connie thought, she was on the verge of being banished because she wanted to work outside the villa. The painted scene made her think of her own life and she wanted to stand up and scream in defiance. She had no idea what the painting was called, but she named it *Connie and Arthur* and thought she would always remember it as that when she brought it to mind.

'Beautiful, aren't they?' Dora said, placing a tray with two cups of coffee and two cream buns on the table.

'Yes,' Connie said. 'They're fascinating.'

'They all illustrate operas.'

'I thought they were Italian,' Connie said. 'Thank you for the bun. I'll make this up to you when I next visit.'

Dora smiled but didn't offer a comment. 'Right,' she said. 'How about this birthday present. Seen anything you'd like? How about a pair of white boots?'

That made Connie laugh. 'I do love them,' she said. 'But how would they look with the rest of me?' She spread her hands to encompass her dependable grey checked skirt, white blouse and the faithful navy mac that was hanging over the back of her chair. 'I'd need a complete overhaul to go with them and I don't think I'm up to that.'

'Perfume?' Dora offered.

'It's so kind of you,' Connie said. 'But I don't really go anywhere to …'

'I know.' Dora laid her hand on Connie's. 'But there must be something.'

Connie took a sip of her coffee. 'I'd much rather you and Ken kept the money and put it towards all you're having to spend on me these few days.'

Dora squeezed Connie's hand in hers before she let go and took a bite of her bun. 'Let's go to Littlewoods next,' she said. 'I love having a mosey around in there.'

Out amongst the throng again, Connie draped her arm through Dora's and told her about Shirley and her catalogue club. 'Do you remember me working in the Littlewoods building during the war?' she said.

'Where was that?' Dora asked. 'Liverpool?'

'That's right,' Connie answered. Then she related the story of how she'd been interrupted whilst telling Millicent and Shirley about her wartime job. 'To be honest, I don't think they were very interested.'

'No,' Dora said. 'Young people aren't bothered with all that. Oh, quick.' She herded Connie into a shop doorway. 'It's raining.' A number of other women ran for shelter with them, each of them pulling lovely silk scarves out of their handbags or pockets – Dora included.

Connie fished around and found her clear plastic cap and tied it under her chin. 'Sorry, Dora,' she said, feeling as if she had to apologise for herself. 'This is what I use in Doncaster. But look at you so smart. Everyone else is, too.'

'That's very practical,' Dora said, eyeing Connie's pleated rain bonnet. 'But you've given me an idea.' Clutching each other, they joined crowds of women who squealed with laughter as they ran out into the rain, detouring around puddles and aiming for the nearest department store or boutique.

In Littlewoods, Dora headed straight for a display of scarves in every size, colour and pattern imaginable. 'This is where I get mine from,' she said. 'And I'm afraid they're polyester, not silk, but you wouldn't know, would you?'

They were very reasonably priced, so Connie let Dora purchase one for her in a dark blue material shot through with purple and grey and green. It would go with her mac and she thought it would make her feel sophisticated and stylish when she wore it into Barnby Dun on rainy days. 'Thank you, Dora,' she said when her sister-in-law handed her the gift wrapped in a plastic bag. 'And I'll thank Ken tonight. It's gorgeous and I love it.'

Dora hugged Connie there in the middle of the aisle and when they pulled away from each other, Connie was puzzled to see the first signs of tears in Dora's eyes. 'Oh no,' she said. 'Have I said something to upset you? Or perhaps you had your eye on this one for yourself? Here, you must …'

'No, nothing like that,' Dora said. 'It's perfect for you and I'm glad we found it. Now I think it's time to head home.'

Although Ken said he was pleased that Connie liked the scarf, he rubbed the back of his neck and disappointment creased his face when he saw that was all she'd chosen. From the corner of her eye, she saw her brother shoot Dora a questioning look and his wife shrug in return.

She helped Dora prepare a pork and orange casserole that looked and smelled wonderful and when it was in the oven, each of them sitting in the living room with a gin and tonic, Ken said Dora had told him that Connie would be staying in the house for a few days whilst they were in Wales. 'I think it's a great idea.' He tipped his glass towards his wife.

Spurred on by the shock that had coursed through her when she'd studied the mural on the wall of the Peter Robinson restaurant, Connie knew she had to do something to emancipate herself from her own subservient position. It was a huge leap from swapping Arthur's stewing beef for shank; or putting cherry tomatoes on his plate; or insisting she get her hair done at a proper hairdresser's to seeing her and Dora's plan to fruition, but the thought of it made her feel as if she was making a concrete stand.

'I really appreciate it and I know you're both worried about me, Dora's told me as much,' Connie said.

Another very quick look passed between Ken and Dora

and Connie noticed her brother's knuckles whiten as he gripped his glass.

'You've done so much for me already, but can I ask that you please don't communicate with Arthur any more about my visits? I'm all grown up now so I can talk to him and I can talk to you. There's no need for the pair of you to organise things without any involvement from me.'

Ken blushed a deep crimson.

'I told you, Kenneth Watkins,' Dora pounced. She pointed an accusatory finger at Ken, then stood and gathered their glasses together for another round. 'You and Arthur carried out all the arrangements about your mum's house, too. You didn't let Connie have a look in.'

'That was because Arthur just … took charge,' Ken said, glumly. 'I hoped he was discussing all the details with Connie.'

Dora grunted. 'Then it was the same again with these few days. Let Connie organise things for herself, I said to you. She's perfectly capable.'

Ken sighed and looked as desolate as a cornered animal. 'Dora's right, Connie,' he said. 'Arthur wrote to me, so I wrote back to him and it went on from there. But that's the way it's always been between the two of you. Arthur in charge and you …'

Connie waited for him to sum her up and when he didn't, she imagined what he would have said. She let Arthur boss her about; she was subservient to him; he dictated her life.

'That doesn't excuse me going along with it, though,' Ken carried on. 'I'm really sorry, Sister of Mine.'

That made Connie smile, Ken hadn't called her that since before they were both married.

'You've nothing to be sorry for, Cheeky Cherub.' Connie took great pleasure in using her childhood nickname for her younger brother.

'Shh.' Ken pointed to the stairs. 'Don't let the boys hear you or they'll never call me dad again. Anyway, of course I know you're more than competent,' he carried on. 'From now on, we'll make all arrangements directly with you.'

'Thank you, Ken, that will be very helpful.' Connie held out her little finger and Ken hooked his around it, as they'd done to cement their solidarity when they were little.

'Wait for me,' Dora demanded and joined them in a three-way symbol of unity, then she doled out the replenished glasses, rattled a packet of peanuts in front of them and tutted once more for effect in Ken's direction.

'But what if Arthur writes to me again?' Ken said.

Making the most of the confidence she'd gained at taking some control for herself, Connie turned to her brother and smiled. 'Just reply and say all arrangements will remain the same for every visit.'

When they'd downed their drinks, Dora shouted upstairs for the boys to come down for dinner and they bounded into the dining room, playfully pinching their dad's jowls and calling him a Cheeky Cherub.

After the meal, Connie made to clear the table and start the dishes, but Dora was adamant that the lads took care of that. 'The three of them clear up every evening,' she said. 'Come on, let's put our feet up. Then we can have some pineapple upside-down cake in front of the TV.'

Guilt made Connie hover in the kitchen, stacking plates and rinsing cutlery. She wondered what Arthur would think if he could see these three strapping men doing what he always referred to as women's work. She knew he would be appalled and would whisper to her later, when they were alone, that to wash dishes wasn't what he'd fought for in the war.

'Go on, Auntie Connie.' Victor pushed his spectacles up on his nose and looked at her. 'Sit down like Mum told you.'

'Yeah,' Gregory joined in, flicking a damp tea towel across his brother's rump. 'Might as well whilst you have the chance.'

They poked and prodded each other with serving spoons and knife handles and Ken plodded backwards and forwards, managing to stay out of their way whilst he put things in their proper places. Connie watched them for another few moments and thought that Arthur wouldn't know where anything went in the kitchen, at least not until something was out of place and he could rub her nose in it.

With bowls of pudding in their laps, they watched an instalment of *Z-Cars* together, the boys stretched out on the soft, pale carpet with their backs against the sofa. Summer sun flooded the living room and the aromas of gin, pork, pineapple and something zesty that Victor wore on his freshly shaved face floated around them. *What a lovely, easy, happy life they have*, Connie thought. *If only Arthur and I had children, our lives would be more like this, too.*

The episode finished, the theme tune blared out, the credits rolled, then from nowhere a shrill ringing noise pervaded the living room.

Victor jumped up and grabbed the phone from a small table huddled in the corner – an address book, notepad and pen spread out on it with care. He pulled the cord, tight and taut, into the kitchen where he spoke for a few minutes in a muffled voice. Then his face appeared in the doorway and he said he was going out to meet his girlfriend.

'Wait for me,' Greg shouted. 'I'll walk with you as far as the courts.' He dragged on his tennis shoes, retrieved his racquet from the cupboard under the stairs and joined his brother on the doorstep.

The house was heavy with quiet when they left. Dora smiled at Connie and at the same time, they each asked the other if everything was alright.

Dora shook her head. 'They're growing up so fast,' she said. 'It's wonderful in one way but on the other…'

'It's heart breaking,' Connie finished for her.

'Nothing like you've had to endure, though,' Dora added.

What a weighted choice of word, Connie thought. It conjured images of emaciated children and penniless beggars, disease, hardship and anguish. Connie hated to think that was the view others had of her life and that they felt sorry for her to such a tragic extent.

'Anyway,' she said. 'Nothing one of these won't cure.' She raised her glass towards Dora.

'Then another is in order,' Ken said. 'Let's make them doubles this time.'

Half-cut, Connie held out her glass to be filled again.

'I'll have to go to the off-licence if we carry on at this rate,' Ken said.

But clever Dora had thought ahead and squirreled away another bottle in the cupboard, as if she knew the evening would come to this. Jumping up, she pulled 'Twist and Shout' from its cover and put it on the record player, then turned to drag Connie from her chair.

'I can't do this sort of dance,' Connie protested, her drink sloshing over the side of her glass and running down her arm.

'Of course you can,' Dora slurred. 'Even Ken can put one leg in front of the other, swivel his hips and pretend he's stubbing out a ciggie with his foot. Can't you Ken?'

As if to prove a point, Ken cavorted around the living room, first holding his wife's hands, then his sister's. Connie couldn't remember when she'd had so much fun; she threw back her head and whooped with laughter. Dora changed the record and they had a go at something called the Watusi, then Dora shouted, 'The Pony!' and led them galloping from one room to the other. They were making so much noise, they didn't hear Victor and Lyndsey until they were standing in front of them, watching their procession around the house.

Lyndsey, a petite, dark-haired girl in a blue and green dress that might have been fashioned from paper, tore off her jacket and said, 'Here's another one, it's called the Mashed Potato. Follow me.'

And they finished the night in spectacular fashion with one more drink and a lesson in a dance that Connie would never again think of as a mere kitchen chore.

14

February 1942

The shadow of a headache throbbed in Connie's temple and she moved a little to the left so the lamp didn't shine directly into her eyes, managing a half-hearted smile for the Jennie who now occupied Norma's chair. She thought her new colleague very nice – but she wasn't Norma.

She'd written and told Arthur about Norma being posted to Manchester and how much she would miss her friend, but she had no intention of telling him that she regretted they hadn't had a last evening at the pub – Arthur would probably ask for compassionate leave right away to rush home and make sure she was alright. At the very least, his return letter would be filled with deep worry and concern. *Treasure*, he would reply.

I am sorry you didn't get to say a proper goodbye to your friend before she was sent elsewhere, but I'm relieved that you didn't have the opportunity to sit in a pub for hours on end. As amiable and cosy as they seem – and believe me I miss the welcoming atmosphere and a pint or two – they're not the best place for women on their own, as we've talked about before. Perhaps a nice café would be a better option until I'm home?

She sighed and reached for another letter. This one was from a Mrs Alice Mayberry who lived in Kent and was addressed to a Wren based in Belfast. As Connie slit the envelope, she wondered what personal news it would contain and what tone of voice it would be written in. Gently chiding, like some of Arthur's letters? But nothing could have been further from the truth.

Dear Agnes

How are you, my lovely sister? Keeping your end up I hope, so to speak. I wish I was – keeping my end up, I mean, but that would be difficult to achieve with this baby on the way. Anyway, enough of that nonsense as that's how I got into this state in the first place. But you mustn't mind me, I'm only trying to make you laugh – did I? I'm happy to be pregnant and it's a bright spot in the otherwise dull days that seem to go on indefinitely without Stewart by my side. Oh, my dearest, I know reading that will probably push you right back down again as you're missing your Philip so much, but as we said before, not talking about my husband won't bring back yours.

Have you settled into your job again? I'm so glad the powers that be didn't get someone to replace you when you were on leave as I know you enjoy your war work. And it does sound fascinating, keeping the WRNS quarters clean and tidy and supervising their food and laundry. They sound like a good bunch, too, although one or two seem a bit slovenly which goes against all the WRNS rules and regulations, doesn't it? I think you should report them to the Chief Wren.

Connie smiled and thought about the state of the locker left by Vera and that filthy sponge swimming in germs. Orders and directives were one thing, but getting thousands of people to strictly abide by every single petty regulation would be impossible, and if a monumental effort was made to do so, what would happen to the likes of Dotty and those two girls who sang the lewd songs at HMS Pembroke? There were many more important things to think about than a Jennie not picking up her stockings from the floor or allowing a swirl of dust to settle in the corner of a locker.

Arthur thrived on rules and structure. He'd always been a bit of a fusspot, officious and a little too fond of having the final say. That wasn't much of a problem as what did it matter if they always saw his choice of film at the pictures or if he insisted they walk clockwise around Springfield Park every Sunday morning. He was away with the Navy most of the time, so it was easy to let him have his own way when he was at home. That made for a much happier leave. And she should bear in mind how lucky she was. There were so many girls, like Dotty, who chased after men in the hopes of finding one who would be as caring and steady and faithful as Arthur.

Connie quickly found her place in the writing in front of her again. It was amazing how these letters had the capacity to make her think about so many aspects of her own life and take her away from them at the same time.

Now, what about the one named Nellie you were telling me about?

Nellie Wright, I think it was. Carrying on with that married officer. Really, she should be ashamed of herself. What would happen if the Navy found out? Would the pair of them be court-martialled or posted somewhere else miles away from each other?

Connie picked up her scissors and shook her head. No, she didn't think they would be sent for trial if they were found out; court-martials and summary hearings were saved for things like absence without leave or malingering, fighting, theft or careless cycling. But they might very well be summoned in front of their superior officers and given a stern warning about respectability and keeping their minds on their work – as the distraction of thinking about each other could prove to be dangerous.

Connie jabbed the pointed tip of the blade into the flimsy paper, snipped out the paragraph that named Nellie Wright and let the chopped section float down to her desk. For a beat, she felt as if she were being judgemental and had cut through the essence of the woman herself. Perhaps she'd been too hasty – she could have pencilled out the name and left the surrounding paragraph standing as there was nothing else in it that gave away sensitive information. She stared down at the writing and felt sorry that Agnes would miss part of her letter, but there was nothing to be done about it now.

News from this end is not very exciting. I've joined the local WVS and my duties include helping to organise Warship Week next summer.

Connie reached for her pencil – *scritch scratch* – that would have to go.

I work at the Centre two afternoons a week and it's good to be doing something in the company of other women. Although I don't know if I shall continue when the baby comes along as it might be better to be evacuated away from this Hellfire Corner.

Connie's pencil *scritch scratched* out the locals' nickname for Kent.

But if I do stay to be near Mum and Auntie May, I might be able to take the little one into the centre with me if my duties allow. Some mums do and it seems to work out well. The only other thing worth reporting is that the milkman's old horse has been put out to pasture and the new, much livelier one leaves piles of manure in the street. Mum shovelling the stuff into a bucket to spread on the vegetable patch is a very funny sight indeed.

I do miss you being here. Although I know the reason for your leave was horrid.

Mind yourself.

All my love,

Alice and the Baby xxx

Connie watched Dotty lean in and follow a line of writing on the letter being read by one of the Miseries. Without a word she picked it up in her most efficient manner, held it to the light and placed it back on the desk. For a minute she stood bowed over, considering a word or a line or a paragraph. Not for the first time, Connie wondered about what effect playing with other people's lives had on the writers and recipients of the letters. Not much, in reality, if their letters were innocuous. She'd come to learn that in the majority of cases when people gave away too much it was not through malice, they simply got carried away and spilled out their news without thinking. Despite the warnings and posters and examples of what to leave out of letters, people wrote from their hearts in a familiar manner. All they were trying to do was to keep their spirits up and feel close to their loved ones during a time when the next letter they wrote might be delivered to an empty bunk or sit on a dock waiting for a ship that would never arrive or be sent back from an address in London or Bristol or Essex that no longer existed.

But reading all of that intimate information, no matter how trivial or banal, was bound to have an effect on her and Josie and Dotty, the Three Miseries and the countless censors in HMS Holborn. None of them talked about the intricacies of the letters outside the censorship room – they wouldn't dare, neither did they talk about the job in general terms. It was nothing more than another aspect of war work that had to be done. But the letters Connie read spun around and around in her mind and she wondered if it was the same for the other girls. Unless, like Dotty, they could switch from one way of thinking and behaving to another in the time it took to wrap an examiner's label around an envelope.

Dotty must have let the letter she was analysing pass because she came and stood behind Connie and watched her whilst she plucked another missive from her pile. 'That took you a while,' she said in a low tone. 'Did you have a query about it?'

Connie shook her head as heat spread across her face. How could she tell her presiding officer the letter had made her think about the details of her own life? 'No,' she said. 'It was just a bit ... complicated. I wanted to be sure of a couple of things before I made a decision.'

'You're extremely conscientious,' Dotty whispered. Then leaning in closer she added, 'And great fun, too. Don't ever forget that.'

'Mam,' Connie said, watching Dotty walk back to her chair. She gave Connie a shred of a smile and when she looked away, the bright light from her lamp played like a fierce spotlight on a silvered tear in her eye.

Connie stood and made to go to her side, but Dotty spoke in a loud, authoritative voice. 'Next letter, Leading Wren Censor Allinson. If you please.'

'Mam,' Connie said and dutifully picked up another envelope.

That evening, Connie ate a meal in the galley and before tidying her cabin, she mended the hem of her skirt and turned the heel of a sock she had nearly finished knitting. But her mind was firmly on Dotty. She thought about relating Dotty's baffling behaviour in a letter to Norma, but decided against it as Norma, in turn, would ask Dotty if she was alright and that would leave Connie open to never hearing the end of it. No, she would wait and see what Dotty was like tomorrow and the next day before she bothered Norma.

★

The following morning, the Chief Wren clipped across the room and came to a stop behind Connie. 'Mam,' Connie said, rising to her feet.

'Leading Wren Censor Allinson, follow me if you please.'

'Mam.' Connie, sure she must be guilty of some unthinkable misdemeanour she couldn't bring to mind, hung her head as far as regulations allowed.

In an office Connie hadn't known existed, the Chief Wren pulled out a chair and sat behind a large wooden desk. Paperweights held down piles of neatly stacked memos and lists and clippings from Postal Liaison Group circulars. An unmarked sheet of paper waited in the roller of a dark, heavy typewriter and a black ink pen, stapler and box of indelible pencils were laid out at the ready. Pins held additional information to a corkboard and the windows were boarded like all the others in the building. The small space was as hushed as the censoring room and all Connie could hear, except the sound of her pulse pounding in her ears, was the *tick tock* of the regulation clock on the wall.

When the Chief Wren beckoned for Connie to sit opposite her, all she could do was perch on the edge of her chair, her back as inflexible as her superior's. Flicking through one stack of papers then another, the Chief Wren found what she'd been looking for, read through it quickly then held it out to Connie. 'It might surprise you,' she said. 'Although it doesn't me in the least, that you've been promoted to Petty Officer. You're to preside over your own section of seven. Congratulations and well done.'

Connie glanced down at her jacket – she'd have to get used to polishing brass buttons, like it or not. Skimming through the piece of paper she held in her hand, she could see that what the Chief Wren said was fact.

'If you read further,' the Chief Wren carried on. 'You'll see that you leave for HMS Eaglet Monday next after a weekend's leave. All your instructions are there.'

'But where ...' Connie faltered, trying to listen to the Chief Wren and read the promotion letter at the same time.

The Chief Wren tapped the paper. 'Liverpool,' she said. 'It's the centre for British censorship.'

Disbelieving, a chill – or was it a thrill – passed through Connie. All she could do was find the spot on the memo, read it for herself and say, 'Mam.'

The Chief Wren sat back in her chair, put her head on one side and stopped her fingers short of her earlobe. 'We will miss you, Petty Officer Wren Censor Allinson. You are particularly diligent and fastidious. Good luck in your new posting.'

The Chief Wren stood, saluted and Connie left the office clutching her letter of promotion.

She headed back to her desk, plucked the top letter from her pile, reminded herself that she must bring in a cloth to clean out her locker and smiled when she thought about Liverpool.

15

June 1967

In what was usually Victor's single bed, Connie watched as the ceiling above spun and rolled and tipped. She and Arthur rarely had a drink, an exception being made for Christmas and perhaps when Ken and Dora stayed with them for a few days once or twice a year. Dance moves swam before her eyes and she thought she should feel guilty about overindulging in such an uncharacteristic way, but try as she might, all she could think about was how much fun they'd had.

Turning on her side, she hugged the pillow and tasted the residue of gin as it made its way up from her churning stomach. She knew she'd feel terrible in the morning, but as she drifted off she wondered, for a fleeting moment, if there would be alcohol at cricket matches or if they would stick to tea.

Well before dawn she woke with a jolt. It took her a few seconds to get her bearings and recall why her head thumped and her stomach pitched. She was sweating, too, her nightie and the bedclothes sticking to her arms and legs.

She tiptoed to the facilities and refreshing summer air cooled the perspiration on her skin. Ken and Dora's bedroom door was ajar and as she hurried past she caught sight of Dora's arm flung over her husband's shoulders as they rose and fell with his rhythmic snores. They seemed to be cosy and comfortable and in tune with each other. Nothing like her and Arthur who slept back-to-back with a wide berth between them except on the specific nights when they were intimate in the customary manner.

Tucked up again, the alcohol guaranteed that sleep evaded Connie and she knew she'd be lucky to get another hour before it was time to get up. She'd have to give her teeth a good scrub in the morning on the off chance that Arthur got passionate at the station again and detected the presence of drink on her breath.

'Wah-Watusi', 'Twist and Shout' and 'Mashed Potato Time' played over and over in her mind and she smiled when she thought about how silly they must have looked last night. She thought, too, about the lovely scarf tucked away in her suitcase and the television set, the unusual combination of pork and orange, Peter Robinson's restaurant, the boys tackling the washing up. The idea of going home later that day, back to her old routine, filled her with an empty, hollow feeling in the pit of her stomach.

Lulu's face on a poster advertising *To Sir, With Love* stared down at her as one searing tear slipped across her face and landed on the pillow. She brushed at it roughly with the back of her hand. Then she remembered she had August – and three whole days here on her own – to look forward to. That felt like a huge victory.

She fell in and out of a fitful sleep, dreaming in fragments about Jim Stanton, Millicent, Shirley, Ken, Maude Grimshaw and Mum. Despite her semi-conscious state, she realised that Arthur was nowhere to be seen in her visions and that didn't worry her in the slightest. Snippets of conversations she'd had with Dora floated in and out of her awareness and that word – *endure* – continued to nag at her. Then there was 'stylish' and 'let Connie organise things' and 'can you remember the names and circumstances of others that passed through your hands'.

Rubbing her eyes, Connie saw the first signs of dawn creeping under Victor's blind; the birds, too, told her it was almost morning. She yawned extravagantly, stretching her arms and legs to get some energy into them. There had been others – thousands of them. She'd dwelt on them and fretted about them endlessly during the war years and now they were back to bite her on the bum, as Ken would say.

The letter from Maude haunted her and was as intriguing now as it had been in 1941. The words on the lined, stained paper torn from a notebook swirled and roiled their way into her consciousness, demanding her time and attention.

She shifted and tugged her nightie from where it had bunched up around her waist. *Now, what were the exact words in the letter?* She squeezed her eyes together and conjured up the opening paragraph verbatim. Then an alarm went off in Ken and Dora's room and she bolted upright. Plumping the pillows, she listened to the sounds of Ken getting ready for work. Dora groaned and Ken's voice was gravelly when he laughed at his wife's salute to the day. Light from the bathroom edged in under the bedroom door; the rhythmic whirr of the extractor fan pulsed through the rooms and the smell of minty toothpaste and Imperial

Leather floated on the air. The toilet was flushed, and then Ken's footsteps trailed down the stairs.

Connie waited a few minutes for her brother to get the kettle on, then she wrapped Victor's dressing gown around her nightie and followed him into the kitchen.

For a beat, Connie and Ken stared at each other then, as if on a silent signal, they both started to laugh. 'Good on ya, Sister of Mine,' Ken said. 'What a night. My head's telling me I've caused myself serious damage.'

'Mine too,' Connie moaned, pressing her fingers against her temples. 'It was great fun, but I wouldn't want to repeat it too often.'

'That's me off the gin and beer and anything else until Christmas.'

She watched as Ken filled a flask with coffee, milk and three teaspoons of sugar. 'I'm going to need this today,' he said. He poured them each a cup of tea, but as he cut a couple of rounds of sandwiches and wrapped them in greaseproof paper she had to look away – the comparison with what Arthur expected for his midday meal was too raw.

Ken took a cup of tea up to Dora and when he came down Connie said, 'I want to thank you for giving me such a lovely few days.'

'I'd do anything for you, Connie. I hope you know that.'

'Yes, I do,' she said, another round of tears forming in her eyes. 'And I'll love wearing the scarf.'

He shrugged as if the gift was nothing. 'Oh, I almost forgot.' He took an envelope with her name on it from behind a packet of biscuits. 'I asked Dora to give this to you as I didn't think I'd see you myself.'

'Whatever is it?' she asked.

'Just a letter,' he said. 'As we're going to bypass the big man and write to each other, I thought I'd start now.'

'Thank you for that pact. I don't expect you to get it as you probably think it's trivial, but it's given me a real boost.'

'You'd be surprised at how much a mere bloke like me understands,' Ken said.

The envelope felt thick and padded and Connie wondered when he'd found the time between their drunken capers last night and this morning's hangover to write so much. She went to open the flap, but Ken folded his hand over hers. 'Save it for the train,' he said.

He held out his arms to her and she rested in his anchoring embrace for longer than usual. 'We'll be in touch soon,' he said when he pulled away. 'Bye, Dora love,' he called up the stairs.

The only response was another guttural grunt.

'She'll be down soon,' Ken chuckled. They blew a kiss to each other and then he was gone.

A slice of dry toast and a glass of Andrews Liver Salts each and Connie and Dora felt ready to make their way to Somerset House. 'If we manage your case between us, we can go straight from there to the station,' Dora said.

'Are you forgetting?' Connie pointed in Dora's direction. 'I am able to get myself on the right train at the right time.'

Dora laughed. 'Okay,' she said. 'I agree that you are indeed adept.' Then she lowered her voice to a whisper. 'Just don't tell Arthur I left you to your own devices.' She sliced a finger across her throat. 'Or I'll be for it.'

'No, we've finished with all that nonsense of passing

messages back and forth about me.' She raised her arms and clenched her fists until her biceps formed mounds under her sleeves. 'I am mighty and I can speak for myself. But not too loudly,' she said, hands over her ears. 'At least not today.'

On the Tube, Dora told Connie that she'd requested, in advance, the birth, death and marriage certificates pertaining to her great-grandparents and any of their brothers, sisters, aunts, uncles and cousins that could be found.

'Do you have to order the documents in advance?' Connie asked.

'It definitely helps. You can walk in off the street although you might have quite a wait whilst the assistants search. One of them told me there are almost nine miles of vaults on the premises.'

After coming up into the light at Temple, they walked down the Embankment past crowds of young people sitting in groups around Cleopatra's Needle. Again, the girls wore short, colourful dresses, dark eye makeup and hair that either shone as it moved in the breeze or was immovable with lacquer. The boys strutted around like peacocks in flared trousers, with turned-back cuffs on their patterned shirts and curly tendrils that touched their collars. None of them gave her so much as a glance and who could blame them – she was invisible next to them in her dull, buttoned-up, watered-down clothing. It was obvious they wanted nothing more than to distance themselves from their elders in terms of how they presented themselves to the world and probably in their thinking, too. No matter how she and Dora restyled their hair or played around with pointed boots or dared to wear a skirt above their knees, it was clear they were has-beens. A rush of sadness passed through her at the thought that her young days had been spent in uniform, fighting a war, with no chance of expressing herself by rebelling against the establishment or wearing any kind of flowery, floaty alternative clothing. For once, Arthur's proclamation about what they had fought for in the war rang true. Was everything they'd been through just so this younger crowd could wear what they liked, throw it away when they got tired of it, dictate what was and wasn't fashionable and ignore the likes of her and Dora? *Yes*, she thought, *that is most certainly the sum of what our victory was all about*. Freedom for the next generation to turn their backs on them in disdain.

Changing her suitcase from one hand to the other, Connie glanced back over her shoulder at five or six of the laughing, jostling youngsters, cigarettes dangling from their fingers, their movements as graceful, slick and effortless as if they were performing ballet. She singled out a girl with shoulder-length dark hair, wearing lipstick so pale it was almost white, and smiled at her. The young woman beamed back with such easy candour that Connie could not begrudge her the pink minidress she wore, the magenta band in her hair, her paisley tights or a second of the carefree time she was sharing with her friends in a peaceful, calm, happy-go-lucky London.

'Before I go in, I always have a look across the river from the bridge.' Dora pointed to the Waterloo crossing. 'I read somewhere that it's the best view you'll get of London.'

They made their way to the halfway point and stood, gazing first at St Paul's and then in the other direction towards the Houses of Parliament. After a couple of moments, Dora said, 'How about you ask to look at any documents pertaining to Maude … sorry, what was her name?'

Surprised, Connie turned to face her sister-in-law. 'Grimshaw,' she said.

'You did say if you were going to research anyone it would be her or that other person whose letter you remembered.'

'Jim Stanton.'

'Well, now's your chance to find out how it's done. Wait and see, you'll soon get the bug.'

There wouldn't be any harm in it, Connie thought, and it might give her some peace of mind. 'Good idea, Dora. I'll give it a go.'

Dora breathed in deeply and said she would never grow tired of the sights of London. 'Especially now when there are no bombs or incendiaries dropping all around us to obscure the view. This time of year, too, is always the loveliest. No fog or smog.'

'And everything's better when the sun shines,' Connie added. She put her elbows on the bridge and followed the progress of a pleasure boat as it made its way upriver. But even as she said it, she knew that wasn't the truth. What waited for her in Doncaster would be the same no matter what time of the year it happened to be.

Connie had never been in the grounds of Somerset House and when she and Dora walked across the quadrangle, she was amazed. 'I had no idea this was behind the façade,' she said.

'Beautiful, isn't it?'

'It's a massive place,' Connie said. 'What else is here, besides where we're headed?'

'Offices and more offices.' Dora shrugged. 'Some to do with taxes, stamps, inland revenue.'

Connie took in the balustrades, the grand steps and the dome of St Paul's, which seemed to be perched right on top of the roof like a huge, green jelly mould. With a soft hiss, elegant fountains of water danced upwards then cascaded back down.

'Here we are,' Dora said, holding open a heavy door. A notice next to it read *Registry of Births, Marriages and Deaths* and a number of assistants were stationed behind a long, ornate counter in the hushed foyer, each of them occupied with a customer. Connie and Dora joined the queue waiting behind a thick, red rope and Connie took in the high ceiling and lofty windows, the marble tiles on the floor and the discreetly patterned, flocked wallpaper – very grand for a place that housed certificates pertaining to people's everyday lives.

'They do probate, too,' Dora whispered. 'I imagine that's what a lot of these people are here to investigate.'

Connie nodded. 'Is this where Arthur and Ken came to get the paperwork sorted out after Mum died?' Those first few weeks had passed in a blur of utter and desolate grief and now, when she looked back, she couldn't remember how anything had been finalised.

'No,' Dora hissed. 'That was all straightforward. These people probably want to query probate.'

When it was their turn at the counter, a man wearing a charcoal suit smiled at them from under a broomhandle moustache, the moistened ends stained yellow and brown.

'Hello,' Dora said. 'I've ordered some certificates.' She produced a sheet of paper. 'Here's my documentation.'

The assistant's eyes flickered backwards and forwards through Dora's paperwork. He asked her to wait in the Reading Room whilst he retrieved the files she'd ordered, and Connie watched as he shuffled through a door flush with the wall behind them that looked as though it could be the entrance to secret tunnels or passageways lit by sconces.

Then it was her turn. She gave the assistant the names of Maude Grimshaw and Michael Johnson and waited whilst she wrote them on a form.

'Any other information that might help with the search?' The woman looked at Connie over the rim of her slightly wonky spectacles. 'Dates of birth, middle names, marriages, deaths?' she asked hopefully.

Connie thought for a moment. 'Maude Grimshaw was married to a man named Maurice and they lived in Finchley during the war,' she said. 'At 187 Southgate Road, to be exact. Oh, and Michael Johnson was an Able Seaman in the Royal Navy. Portsmouth was his base.' She grimaced to show the woman she was sorry for being a nuisance by offering such paltry information.

The assistant made a note and Connie tiptoed into the depths of the Reading Room. The atmosphere was hushed and studious and all that could be heard was the *scritch scratch* of pencils and the clock on the wall that had a tick to rival the one in the censor room at HMS Holborn during the war.

She arranged her notepad and pencil on a desk close

to where Dora was seated, her head bent over a pile of documents, and just when she thought she might have been forgotten, the assistant appeared in the doorway carrying a skimpy folder and scanned the room. Tentatively, Connie raised her hand and the woman nodded to her. 'These,' she said, leaning over Connie's table, 'are the only documents I could find without doing an enhanced search.'

'Is that different?' Connie asked.

'You have to pay for it,' the woman explained. 'And we need at least a fortnight's notice but we can usually uncover much more or, at the very least, point you to where you can find the information. But here are some certificates relating to hatch, match and dispatch that might be of interest to you.'

Connie frowned and waited for an explanation.

'Sorry,' the woman said. 'Births, marriages and deaths.'

'I like that.' Connie smiled when she understood.

The woman lowered her voice. 'Newspapers use that disrespectful terminology, too. I'll just write down your table number then leave you to it. Please bring everything back to the main desk when you've finished. Good luck.'

'Thank you,' Connie said, but didn't think she'd be long rummaging through the scant number of papers in front of her.

Opening the folder, Connie gently and reverently picked up the first document and found herself gazing at Mikey's birth certificate. She found it hard to believe she had this piece of evidence in her hands. Then guilt engulfed her. When she was a censor, nosing about in other people's business was legitimate but that wasn't the case now. On the other hand, she wasn't up to anything illegal. All she wanted to establish was how Maude and Mikey's lives had unfolded after the family secret had been brought out into the open.

With a shaking hand, Connie transferred the details from the birth certificate to her notebook. Mikey was born Michael Alfred Johnson on 13 September 1922. She jotted down a quick calculation in the margin and came up with Mikey's age at the time Maude's letter was written – eighteen. He'd been so young that it hardly seemed possible boys like him had fought as soldiers and sailors and airmen. Connie closed her eyes and tried to imagine what he might have looked like. Fresh-faced, she imagined. With fair, wavy hair and blue eyes that bulged, stunned and shocked by everything he was forced to experience.

According to the certificate, he'd been born at home, which would have made it easier to hide his mother's true identity, and his parents were listed as Alfred and Anne Johnson. Connie let the certificate fall from her hand as she harrumphed out loud – she knew for a fact that information wasn't true. Glancing at the document again, she took in the insignificant details of Alfred's occupation – a stevedore – and Anne's maiden name, Peters.

She turned her attention to the rest of the papers in the folder. There was Maude's birth certificate and Connie felt deeply upset that the girl had been just sixteen when Mikey had been born and she wondered if her sweetheart had left her in the lurch. Or perhaps her mother had failed to tell her how women got pregnant and she'd had no idea until she was showing. At least she'd had a mother with her, grim as the woman sounded, unlike poor Dotty who'd had to endure that whole wretched experience on her own.

Oh, it's all so unfair, Connie wanted to scream into the corners of the still room. *I couldn't have longed more for a baby and so did Arthur, yet there are girls who get pregnant at the drop of a hat without giving any thought to what it means to be a mother.*

Although if Maude's letter was anything to go by, she'd wanted to be Mikey's mum despite the most undesirable of circumstances and that option had been coerced or encouraged or forced from her. No doubt the poor girl had been one more victim of not being allowed or not having permission. To be fair, perhaps her parents had been doing the best they could for their daughter and grandson given the constraints of the time and place they lived in. How could a sixteen-year-old have cared for a newborn and how could her parents have stood back and let her try knowing she would be stigmatised by family, neighbours and friends. Connie thought about how hard it would have been for Shirley – or any new mum in her twenties – without a whole network of people to help her, and that was before the financial implications came into play.

Another quick add-up and Connie came to the conclusion that Maude would be sixty-one now, if she were still alive. Frantically flicking through the documents, she found death certificates for Alfred and Anne and Maurice, Maude's husband, but not for Maude. Relief flooded her. Then she smiled when she turned over a marriage certificate for Mikey and two birth certificates for his sons – a lovely dollop of icing on the cake.

Connie sat back and closed her eyes. She'd established the bare bones of Maude and Mikey's lives, that was all. It was accurate and impersonal but what she longed for was the story beneath those facts. She itched to know what had been said at the time and if the words had been spoken calmly or harshly; if Mikey accepted the situation but continued to refer to Maude as his sister and his grandparents as his mum and dad, as he'd always done; if he'd been repulsed and shamed by the fact that he was illegitimate or had been a very mature young man and understood the reasons everyone involved had said what they did and behaved as they had. But how she could go about ascertaining any of that seemed impossible.

Dora beckoned to her and Connie pulled up a chair next to her sister-in-law. 'How did you get on?' she whispered.

'Okay, I think,' Connie answered. 'I found out a few bits of information about Maude but wouldn't know how to follow them up.'

'That's a big problem,' Dora said. 'What to do with the information once you have it. I'm drawing up a family tree, but Maude isn't your family or even a friend so you can't do that. I suppose all you could do was go knocking at her door and ask her to tell you her life story, which might be taking your research a bit too far.'

That, Connie thought with sudden clarity, *is the only possible solution to finding out the rest of Maude's story.* She looked at the clock and decided that if she hurried, she could just make it to Finchley and back in time to catch her train. Her heart thumped at the thought of meeting the woman whose letter had troubled her so many years ago, but if she held her nerve she thought she might be able to go through with it.

'Want to help me?' Dora pushed a pile of documents towards Connie. 'You can look through these and put to one side any that have the surname Clarke and are from the District of Middlesex.'

'Actually, Dora,' Connie said tentatively, not wanting to appear rude. 'I was thinking I might push off now, if you don't mind. I'd like to grab a bite to eat before I get my train.'

'I'll come with you,' Dora said, shuffling her papers together. 'I could do with some lunch myself.'

'There's no need,' Connie insisted. 'You finish up here. I'll be quite alright and it will be good practice for my trip in August.'

The shadow of a frown crossed Dora's face. 'Are you sure you'll be okay?'

Connie gave her sister-in-law a long slow-burn of a look.

'Okay, I get it.' Dora held up her hands. She stood and the two women hugged for a long time. 'I have so enjoyed your company,' she said. 'As always. We'll write.'

'We certainly will,' Connie said. 'Thank you for everything.'

'Even the gin?'

'Especially the gin.'

Picking up her case, Connie made her way across to the reception desk to return her documents without turning back. She didn't want to spoil the moment by letting Dora see just how much she would miss her.

*

A sense of propriety slowed Connie's stride as she headed to the Underground. Stopping under a shop awning, she waited a moment and thought about whether it was fair to call without announcement on a sixty-one-year-old woman who had no idea that a stranger had been privy to furtive events in her life. Maude might not be a strong person and Connie's sudden appearance could churn up all sorts of long-forgotten emotions that might lead to her having a heart attack or worse. But the age difference between her and Maude was no more than six years and Connie thought about how she would react to such a visit coming out of nowhere. It would be shocking, she decided, but not life-threatening.

Then again, Maude might be busy helping with her grandchildren or chatting with her son and his wife or sitting with a neighbour or reading a magazine; shopping, gardening or doing the laundry. Connie had no knowledge of Maude's comings and goings; in fact, she knew nothing about Maude at all other than the scant information she'd gleaned from the letter that had passed through her hands and the documents she'd seen in Somerset House. She could spend time and money going to Finchley on the Tube only to find that Maude hadn't lived in Southgate Road for years. She closed her eyes and leaned against the wall of the shop, feeling hot and bothered with frustration at how she would feel if that were the case.

So if she didn't knock on Maude's door now, when would she? The idea crossed her mind that 'never' might be the best answer to that question, but that would be like getting to the end of a jigsaw puzzle and finding one piece missing. Or meandering down a lane that stopped in the middle of nowhere, or having a dream that fizzled out without coming to a satisfactory conclusion.

Connie took a deep breath, made up her mind and before anything could change it, she plunged into the depths of the Underground and found the correct line for Finchley.

16

For a beat, bitterness rose from Connie's stomach when she remembered Norma saying it didn't matter where they were posted, the work would be exactly the same. Take an envelope from the pile; slit the flap with the regulation opener; *snip snip* or *scritch scratch* where applicable; pass upwards if necessary or reseal with the label marked Examiner 7364 and onto the next one. Then shame washed over her. Arthur would have rightly reminded her that fighting in this war wasn't meant to be an adventure. It was about giving them stability and security and standing up for what was right.

Despite the similarities of the job, there were differences between working in Liverpool and London, not least the scale of the censorship operation housed in the Littlewoods Building. From the outside, the immense edifice stood starkly white and proud with a central clock tower that seemed to melt down into columns of streamlined concrete alternating with barred windows. It reminded her of the Hoover Building in Ealing that Arthur said was designed in the Art Deco style. The clean, simple lines juxtaposed with the sheer expanse took her breath away. How the Jerries had missed it when they'd blitzed Liverpool she could not fathom – but she was so glad they had.

The censorship floor was vast, but crammed with table upon table of seven look-alike Jennies, the strong, bright spotlights of the regulation lamps trained on their desks and their scissors and pencils at the ready. It was impossible to see from one end of the room to the other and it seemed absurd that in such an enormous, light, ethereal building the huge room was still and stuffy and oppressive with the odours of stale perfume, face powder and well-handled paper. On her first day, Connie had felt small and insignificant as she'd been shown to her table and introduced to her team, and that feeling of being nothing more than a minuscule component revisited her every morning when she set foot in the building and made her way through arched corridors to her table in the censorship room.

By dint of sheer numbers her new surroundings were noisier than HMS Holborn and in the background, there was the incessant shuffling sound of documents spinning off printing rollers. 'You'll get used to that,' the Chief Wren said as she showed her the stacks of ingoing and outgoing postbags; circulars; the store cupboards; the copious pigeonholes that made one wall of the room look like an overwhelmingly busy beehive. The superior was short and squat and talked very quickly. 'The government has requisitioned the presses to print National Registration forms.'

'Mam,' Connie said as she followed the Chief Wren through what felt like mile upon mile of winding rabbit warrens towards what would be her table. Chancing a glance behind her, she thought it would take up most of her working hours to walk back and forth to get queries checked with the Chief Wren, but as if she'd read Connie's mind, the superior turned and said, 'Here the extra layer of a Third Officer has been added and she has responsibility for about twenty-five tables. You will take your queries to her and she will pass them upwards if necessary.'

The Chief Wren introduced her to the Third Officer, pointed out the stairs that led to the galley and the facilities, then she was standing in front of her own team of Wrens who stood and saluted her smartly. 'Mam,' resonated a number of times around the table and Connie wondered if she would ever get over the thrill that came every time she was addressed with that respectful title.

Now there weren't just the contents of the letters she alone opened to transport her into a whole new family or group of people, but all those that the six other Wrens at her table asked her to verify.

'Mam,' a girl with strawberry-blonde hair and sandy eyebrows held a page out to her. 'The second and third paragraphs,' she said.

Connie took the thin, translucent pages and read from left to right, top to bottom as she'd seen Dotty do so many times and hoped she seemed as effective and efficient to this younger woman.

Dear Auntie Kathleen

I have ricked my ankle in the blackout and feel most miserable about it. Every time I walk up and down the stairs to the attic it throbs and swells so much that I can hardly get my shoe on or off. But the minute I get up here I have to go down again to use the lav or fill the kettle so it never has a chance to heal.

Sometimes I have a game of Crazy Eights or Spades with Mrs Brown or Henrietta, and yesterday I won because I held an ace, the king and queen of hearts and laid down a run of four, five and six of clubs.

How I wish I'd listened to you and Dad and insisted on staying in Cork after I married Georgie. With himself gone to goodness knows where, although I'd take bets he's in Tunisia along with all the others, I'm awful lonely. His mother never stops by, although his sister sometimes pops her head around the door.

Please write soon as your letters keep me going.

Love from Mairead X

For a second, Connie's mind strayed from the paper in front of her. If she had a penny for every letter that declared the same sentiment about how the contact from others bolstered morale, she would be a very rich woman. She knew that looking for codes and ensuring no one recklessly gave away vital information was what the job was all about, but she thought it equally as important to keep letters moving as quickly as possible between loved ones. Always at the back of her mind was the motto drummed into her whilst she was training: If it doesn't concern the war, it doesn't concern censorship.

'Well spotted, Leading Wren Hadley,' Connie said.

The girl turned pink under her alabaster colouring.

'Have you looked under the stamp?' She held it to the white light and searched for any minute area that might harbour a swathe of secret writing.

'Yes, Mam,' the girl replied. 'And I've checked the watchlist and blacklist.'

'Excellent,' Connie said, although she knew the lists changed daily and if you were working with the enemy to send coded messages to other like-minded people, wouldn't you change your name in every letter you wrote? 'This will need more than a snip or a scratch. I'll take it to the Third Officer now.'

'Mam,' the young Jennie said. She folded her hands on her desk and waited for Connie to return with the verdict.

As expected, the Third Officer kept the letter back and Connie would never find out if Mairead was who she purported to be or someone who did not have the best interests of the Allies at heart. A flash of anger flared at how hateful it was for anyone to be involved in espionage, amateur or otherwise, that might hinder the Allied victory.

'Next letter, if you please, Leading Wren Censor Hadley,' Connie said and smiled at the girl across from her, who sat up tall and reached for another envelope from her ever-replenished pile. That would have been the perfect time to lean over, as Dotty had done, and say, 'We should all go out for a celebration drink tonight. As I'm new to Liverpool, you can decide where we meet up.'

But when she'd tried that during a break on her first day, the others had declined. The hurt that caused Connie intensified as the weeks went on and the others bandied it about that they went for a drink together once or twice a week. But she'd teamed up with Marjorie, a telegraphist from Leeds who shared her cabin, and together they often strolled around Sefton Park, which spread out opposite their quarters in Ackerleigh House.

'I wouldn't take it to heart,' Marjorie said. 'All your Jennies are younger than you. Perhaps they started at the same time so they've just ... I don't know.' She shrugged. 'Stuck together. And here it seems that rank socialises with rank. It's almost a tradition.'

'My presiding officer in London was very young,' Connie said, trying hard not to sound bruised. 'And we had a great time when we went out.'

'Well,' Marjorie said. 'I'll bet this lot isn't much fun anyway.'

Connie laughed and agreed. She could pursue the other girls' friendships only to find she then spent time and heartache trying to get out of meeting up with them.

'Let's take that path,' Marjorie said, tightening her navy-blue scarf around her neck.

They admired the lakes, summerhouses, bandstand, follies and boathouses and the hoar frost sparkling on barren trees. 'Can you sometimes kid yourself into believing there isn't a war happening at this very minute?' Marjorie asked.

Through the branches of oaks and planes, Connie looked up at slices of sky as bright and white as the lamps on the censors' desks. 'Yes,' she answered. 'For a second or two at the most. But it never lasts.'

Marjorie laughed. 'About the length of time it takes you to seal one envelope and pick up another.'

'Funnily enough,' Connie said. 'I get lost in those letters and although I know the war is the only reason I'm allowed to read them – and each and every one makes reference to that fact – I get so involved in the minutiae of the sender and recipients' lives that the war goes out the window.'

Marjorie wrinkled her brow and seemed to be giving that

idea a great deal of thought. 'I don't have that problem in telegraphy,' she said. 'But I think those letters would get to me, too. You must read some heart-breaking things.'

Connie thought about Maude Grimshaw and Drew Morrison and nodded softly. 'And some very funny things. You wouldn't believe the antics people get up to. And others …' She leaned in close to Marjorie. 'Are quite close to the knuckle.'

It was rather exciting to read a prurient paragraph or two, and secretly Connie hoped to receive an indecorous sentiment from Arthur at some stage. Although if the usually prim and proper Marjorie's burning face was anything to go by, her fiancé had already done so.

Connie looked down at her shoes to give the other woman a chance to calm herself and when she'd recovered, they both laughed out loud.

They passed gallops and statues and the Palm House, its camouflaged glass roof shattered by a hit. By the time they came to a statuesque obelisk, their hands and feet and faces were numb with cold. The monument towered above them. It was dedicated to Samuel Smith and on each side of the plinth were bronze plaques about his life.

'Hmm,' Marjorie said. 'Other than memorials to Queen Victoria, have you ever seen a statue dedicated to a woman?'

'Now you mention it, no, I haven't.' Connie stretched her neck to see the tapering pyramid at the top. 'Do you know, I always feel as if there's something looming over me. The Littlewoods tower, this obelisk, Big Ben, the clock in the censoring room, my pile of letters, the war, Ar—' She stopped there.

'I know what you mean,' Marjorie said. 'But there's

nothing to be done about it except move ourselves out from the shadows and into the full light.' She pulled on Connie's sleeve until they were standing on the other side of the pillar where the anaemic winter sun found them and warmed them for a few moments. 'See, isn't that better?' Marjorie asked.

'Much,' Connie said, watching dark clouds scuttle across the sky. 'Whilst it lasted.'

The evidence of Liverpool's Blitz lay all around her when she walked into the city on her days off. Tall shops and offices had crumpled like biscuits into dust and rocks and rubble. Burst gas pipes were in the process of being mended. The beautiful cathedral had taken a hit to its dome and Connie thought of Churchill's command that St Paul's must stand. How demoralised the Liverpudlians must have felt when they witnessed that missing chunk from the roof of their own beloved symbol of safety and strength. Empty spaces where families had lived and laughed and loved pockmarked every corner. Streets of devastated houses and row after row of shops and businesses as smashed and shattered and broken as they had been in London.

Then there were the people. Scousers, they liked to be called. They were funny and cheerful and endearing and spoke in the most charming dialect. A bus took the Wrens back and forth between the Littlewoods Building and Ackerleigh House and no matter which driver was on duty, he addressed each of them with a chirpy, 'Hop on, me queen,' that seemed to come from the back of his throat and out through clenched teeth.

'Me queen?' Connie couldn't help smiling when she repeated the sentiment to Marjorie as they walked alongside the river, their coat collars turned up against the biting wind. 'I'm sure that's against regulations.'

'Probably.' Marjorie shrugged. 'But they're not guided by WRNS rules so they couldn't care less. Besides, here in Liverpool, Mam means Mum so it would be much worse if they called us that. They're all the same no matter where you go – the shops, the pubs, the cafés. To tell you the truth, it gets a bit much sometimes.'

But Connie wondered how on earth she could ever tire of that level of buoyancy.

'Although I've been told,' Marjorie continued. 'That they are somewhat aggrieved that their Blitz was played down in the newspapers. I suppose it was vague in order to hide descriptions of damage from the Germans, but they feel that what they suffered has been overlooked.'

Busy with letters during the day; knitting, washing and cleaning in the evenings; firewatching and deck swabbing duties after work and walks in Sefton Park with Marjorie, Connie's weeks began to take on a structure. But whilst most of the girls moaned quietly on Monday mornings, Connie felt a shiver of anticipation at what she would find when she picked up the envelopes piled in front of her.

She'd had a busy morning snipping and scratching and checking her team's queries. Her own pile of letters hadn't diminished much and she decided to stay behind whilst her Jennies went for dinner and try to make a dent in it. The room was warm and fuggy, the swirls of cold air that laced around their legs in the corridors never reaching them in the vast expanse of the censorship room. The light from the lamp bored into her eyes again and she angled it slightly so it was out of her direct line of sight. Perhaps she should have gone for a break, after all – the change of scene would have done her good. *One more*, she thought. Then she would nip along to the galley for a cup of tea and whatever happened to be on the menu that day. Parsnip rissoles or spam stew or a slice of not-much-sausage roll, as Marjorie called the savoury pastries.

No untoward writing under the stamp. No inner lining. No jewels or money hidden amongst the folds of paper. Nothing written in code at first glance. She focused on the horizon at the top of the room and thought about those mysterious doors that were hidden behind the sweeping curves in the corridors. Marjorie had told her they were full of men deciphering codes. 'That's where the real work is done.'

Connie didn't know whether to believe that or not, but one morning when she was marching down the infinite corridor to her office, pockets of chilly air coiling around her legs, a man in a suit rushed from a doorway and nearly bowled her over. Full of awkward apologies, he carried on to another door where he knocked once with force and pushed inwards to a room manned by men in civvies, looks of intense concentration on their faces.

Perhaps the letter she held in her hand would end up in front of that harried young man and what if it contained a code that could be cracked and would lead to the beginning of the end of the war? Full of anticipation, she opened the letter, then her heart sank. If that did happen to be the case, she would never know as no one would trace her as the person to have discovered it. She was merely someone whose head moved in and out of the shadows as she got on with her job and she would never be privy to the next chapter in the lives of the correspondents.

Dear Hugh, she read.

How I wish there was a way for me to find out each and every day that you are fighting fit and in good spirits. But we must wait interminable lengths of time for our letters to go backwards and forwards to have the peace of mind that each other is soldiering on.

As you can see from the enclosed photo, taken with a borrowed Brownie camera, we celebrated the twins' first birthday party with my mum, your mum and dad, Marion and her little one and Amelia in attendance. Mainly ladies, for obvious reasons, but I do worry about children growing up thinking the world consists of women, older men and young boys, although there are always servicemen around on leave.

Mum and I saved our rations so I was able to put on a nice spread. We had jam sandwiches, fish paste on toast, jelly and condensed milk, carrot fudge and Amelia brought a small trifle with her. I tried my best to make a currant cake without the proper ingredients and it looked quite nice. But when we tasted it, well, Hugh, you would have laughed. It was horrible! All the grown-ups turned up their noses but we ate it anyway because we were hungry and we mustn't waste anything. The children gobbled theirs down and asked for more. Poor little things, I don't suppose they know any better.

Everyone went home about five, except for Mum who

ended up staying the night and I'm so glad she did. I put Martha and Martin to bed whilst she cleared up in the living room and kitchen, then we put up our feet and laughed again about the cake.

I can picture you now staring at the photo of the twins sitting up so straight in their little romper suits. I still don't feel confident about taking the pillows away from them when they're on the floor in case they topple over and bump their heads, but Martin is crawling properly now and Martha won't be far behind, so I'd better get used to them bumping and clumping and grazing themselves on all sorts of things.

I can't wait to receive a letter from you telling me how amazed you are at how the two M's have grown and you'll see a huge difference in them when you're next home – which can't be soon enough for me.

All our love to you always

Helen, Martin and Martha XXX

A perfect letter in terms of sticking rigidly to the directives distributed by the government about what to include in letters to men and women away with the Army or Navy or RAF. Keep it simple and relate the positives of what is going on at home – children's antics, walking the dog, flowers in the garden – not the rigours of rationing and bomb shelters and the remains of neighbours that had to be swept into the guttering along with gushing water from a shattered mains pipe.

She peered into the envelope and saw a small square pushed right up into the corner. When she turned it over, two perfect, smiling cherubic babies looked back at her and caused her heart to skip a beat. They both had masses of hair that their mother or grandmother or auntie had styled into swirling kiss curls. Their elbows and knees were dimpled and their matching outfits were different shades of grey, although Connie imagined one was blue and the other was pink.

She thought about Hugh putting the snap to his lips and pinning it over his bunk. No – he would put it under his vest so it was next to his heart – that's what Arthur would do. He longed for children as much, if not more than she did. Reluctantly, she tucked the photo back into the envelope but not before running a finger lightly over the soft contours of the twins' chubby cheeks.

That letter had exhausted her. What she would have liked more than anything was a brisk walk along the grimy, misty Mersey and to stand for a little while and watch the funnels on ships coughing out their sludge, a stiff slap of wind from the Irish Sea reviving her when it hit her face. But there was never time for that during the day and now her team was returning and she'd missed her break completely.

The Jennies greeted her with a series of Mams to which she replied, then they each picked up another letter and Connie was embroiled in the life of a man named Albert Higgins. He'd written to his niece, a Wren serving in Scotland, about a strange occurrence on his dairy farm in Lincolnshire when all his cows had stood as one, turned themselves around and sat back down facing the opposite direction. He seemed to think it was an ominous warning that something unsavoury and formidable was coming from the south. As Connie sealed the envelope, she smiled to herself and thought that she agreed with Albert – something could well be on its way from any or all directions of the compass – it was called Hitler and he had his sights trained not only on the farm in Lincoln, but on every single one of them.

17

June 1967

When she was seated on the Tube, Connie thought hard about what she could say that might suffice as an opening line if and when she came face to face with Maude. She could fabricate a story about undertaking research for the council on family relationships, but decided she wouldn't be able to carry out that charade for long. Perhaps she could say she was trying to create her family tree and Maude's name had come up on a document. But Maude would question her about that and how they might be related. After some consideration, she decided that telling the truth, with a few embellishments or omissions where appropriate, would be the best way forward. That might mean Maude would slam the door in her face – *And that*, she thought, heat creeping up from her neck to her scalp, *is probably no more than I deserve*.

After asking for directions from a helpful couple, Connie soon found herself standing opposite number 187 Southgate Road. She stared at a tiny front garden packed with zinnias blooming in every shade of orange, yellow and lavender; velvety red and white begonias; swaying foxgloves and purple sweet peas whose lovely scent she could detect even from that distance. Paint was flaking off the fence and it looked a bit rickety, but the brown front door was solid, and framing it was a pale pink clematis so abundant it took her breath away. For a beat she stood, hand on her throat, taking in the scene.

A young woman walking smartly down the road forced her back to reality. Connie watched as she turned up the path towards the house with confidence and opened the door with a latchkey. That most certainly wasn't Maude Grimshaw. If it was, Connie wanted to know the secret of her youth so she could use it herself. Perhaps she was a lodger. London was crawling with them, so she'd heard. She paced a few steps one way, turned and walked back to the same spot again, wondering if she could use the clematis as a starting point if she dared to knock on the door. Then she jumped when a woman's voice behind her said, 'Excuse me, can I help you?'

A short, round woman, her hefty arms crossed over a stained blouse, was staring at her.

'Oh,' Connie said. For an awful moment she was flummoxed, but the woman didn't wait for a reply before ploughing on.

'Are you poorly?' The woman's voice softened a bit.

'No,' Connie answered. 'Just a bit breathless. You know, the day's so hot. May I sit on your wall for a minute?'

The woman nodded and asked Connie if she'd like a cup of tea.

'No, thank you,' Connie said. 'I'm okay. Really.'

'Water?'

Connie shook her head.

'You've been outside my front room for a quarter of an hour,' the woman sounded distrustful again. 'Were you trying to get your breath that whole time?'

Connie avoided that question and decided, in a split second, that this meddlesome neighbour might be able to provide her with the information she needed. 'I'm actually looking for a Maude Grimshaw,' she said.

'Maudie,' the woman's voice rose an octave. 'What do you want with her?'

'I knew her during the war,' Connie said. Not the complete truth, but not entirely a lie either and that attempt at justification alleviated her guilt to a certain extent. 'I was in the area, so thought I would say hello.' Connie smiled, hoping she appeared breezy and nonchalant. 'You know her, do you?'

'Oh,' the woman said. 'I've been friends with Maudie most of my life. But she moved a couple of years ago. To the new flats around the corner.' She pointed to the right with a wave of her hand. 'You know, in Rosewood Avenue. Her son was anxious to get her in there. It's a bit closer to him and not so difficult to maintain.'

A thrill passed through Connie when she heard that. There hadn't been any other birth certificates with Maude listed as the mother, so the son had to be Mikey.

'They're nice places, but you wouldn't get me in one. No garden to speak of and if your neighbours are noisy, you can't get away from them.'

'Yes,' Connie said. 'I can imagine. What number is Maude in?'

'Now, let me think.' The woman's face hardened with concentration. 'I know how to get there and what the door looks like, but I can't remember the number. I think it's 17. Or might be 71.' Her face brightened. 'I could take you there. Just give me a minute to change into my outdoor things. And I could help if you come over peculiar again.'

Connie couldn't think of anything less helpful. 'I'm absolutely fine now,' she said, standing and brushing down the back of her skirt to prove the point. 'And it's getting late so I might not call today. Yes, I'll leave it for now. Thank you for your help,' she said, striding out in the opposite direction to the one the woman had pointed her towards.

'Well,' the woman called after her. 'Mind how you go. I'll tell Maudie you called when I see her. What did you say your name was?'

In response, Connie raised her hand but didn't say another word. Despite the heat, a chill from the woman's stare seemed to penetrate her light, summer clothing and find its way right to her bones. She shivered and pulled her jacket tighter.

Now another dilemma faced her. If she put off visiting Maude, the nosy neighbour would no doubt forewarn her old friend and Maude would be both worried and suspicious. Or it might be best to get back on the Tube and leave well enough alone – she knew Maude was in contact with Mikey and that was a better result than she thought she'd get. There was, though, a third alternative and that was to double back and knock on Maude's door now before the neighbour beat her to it, if she hadn't done so already.

Her mind and legs seemed to have a will of their own and without giving enough consideration to the pros and cons, Connie found herself heading towards Rosewood Avenue.

This time she didn't linger across the road, watching and waiting and deliberating. She knocked without hesitation on the front door of number 17 and whilst she waited, she listened to her pulse beating in her ears. At her feet, three empty milk bottles stood in a red plastic caddy and next to them, a yellow patio rose was growing in a clay pot. Scalloped net curtains swayed in the kitchen window that was open just enough to let in a breeze and hanging lopsided from the handle was a wooden sign that read *World's Best Nana*.

All the evidence pointed to this being Maude's flat, although it was likely that most of the occupants in the block were grandmothers. Connie lifted her hand to knock again, but let it remain suspended when she heard shuffling from inside. 'That you, Mikey?' a high-pitched voice called out. 'What did you forget this time?'

Connie felt sure her heart missed a beat. Here was Maude at last and she had no idea what to say to her. It now seemed preposterous that she hadn't been able to think of anything other than making contact with this woman. She knew she should turn on her heels and leave, but she was rooted to the spot.

The door opened and Connie was staring at someone who didn't look anything like the Maude Grimshaw of her imagination. And in turn, Maude Grimshaw gawped because the person she faced didn't resemble her son, either.

Connie had harboured a picture of Maude as tall, slender, fair and rather elegant with a ready and waiting smile. But the woman in the doorway was shorter than Connie, round and cumbersome in a pale green nylon housedress that left folds of skin exposed at her knees and elbows. Her eyes were a dark, watery brown instead of the imagined blue and her chin was the shape of a soft heart. 'Can I help you?' she asked. She sounded a bit cross and looked bemused.

'I'm … I'm …' Now was the time to say she'd knocked on the wrong door and head back to the station, but she'd come this far so faltered on. 'I'm enquiring about a Maude Grimshaw.'

'Who's doing the enquiring?'

On an impulse, Connie thrust out her hand as if it were a weapon and said, 'Censor 7364.'

Maude Grimshaw slowly averted her stare down to Connie's hand then back up to her face. 'Censor 7364,' she mumbled in a whisper. 'Are you from the council? Or the police? I hope I'm not in trouble for something I wrote years ago.'

'No, no,' Connie was quick to reassure. 'Nothing like that. I've just …'

Maude waited whilst Connie tried to think of the words to explain exactly why she was there.

'I've been worried about you,' she said softly.

Maude Grimshaw put her hand on her chest, peered behind her as if there was someone else lurking who this matter might pertain to, then appeared to be more confused than ever. Shaking her head, she said, 'My son says I shouldn't open the door to anyone I don't know, but I think you'd better come in.'

'Thank you,' Connie said. Stepping into the tiny hallway with her suitcase in tow, Connie could feel her legs shaking. She followed Maude into an equally small sitting room and sat in the easy chair that was pointed out to her. For a moment, Maude took her in from head to toe as if she were trying to commit her face, hair, clothes and demeanour to memory in order to pass the information on to Mikey or her neighbour from Southgate Road. Then she seemed to take pity on her and asked if she'd like a cup of tea. 'You seem a bit shaken up, my dear.'

'Yes,' Connie said. 'I think I am.'

'Won't be long,' Maude said, shambling back to the kitchen at the front of the flat.

Connie sat on the edge of the chair, her hands and the back of her knees slick with sweat. *Maude must think I'm mad. Connie* thought she was mad. But once she knew the circumstances of Maude and Mikey's lives after the letter was sent, she felt sure she would be able to put them to the back of her mind and concentrate on other things. Things that were important to her life and not to the lives of others. But what were those things, she asked herself as she looked around at little shells and painted stones, school photos of Maude's grandsons and a drawing of a burly woman holding onto the hand of a child, broad grins etched across their faces. Were they catering at cricket matches; coffee mornings that consisted of banal chitchat; a roast dinner on Sunday, leftovers on Monday; tiptoeing around Arthur; a hair appointment once every six weeks; the dread of Arthur's retirement? She'd rather be finding out about Maude and Mickey or Jim Stanton and George or Beryl Smythe and her fiancé, Ted.

'Now,' Maude said, placing a tray with two mugs on a small coffee table. 'What's this all about?'

Connie picked up the tea nearest to her and took a sip. 'Thank you,' she said. 'This is just what I need.'

Maude watched and waited.

'Mrs Grimshaw,' Connie started, trying to conjure up the words that might make her enquiry sound plausible. Maude no longer appeared baffled or annoyed. She looked expectant and interested, so Connie said, 'I was a censor during the war and a letter of yours passed through my hands.'

'That was par for the course,' Maude said.

'And Mikey, your son, would have received it with my number wrapped around the envelope.'

'He never said. But then I don't suppose he would. That was hardly cause for conversation in those days.'

'I didn't censor anything from your letter,' Connie went on, eager to get the whole story out in the open. 'There was no need. But it contained very ... personal, sensitive material. And I've been thinking about it – about you – ever since.'

'Ah.' Maude closed her eyes and rested her head against the back of the chair. 'Was that the letter telling Mikey that I was his mum, not his sister?'

Before Connie could answer, Maude sat up straight again. 'That wasn't a crime, was it? Nothing to get the government after me now, surely.'

Exhausted, Connie explained again that she hadn't been sent by the authorities. 'I'm here because your plight moved me all those years ago, and recently I've found it hard to settle without knowing you were alright.' Then from nowhere, she began to cry. 'I haven't a family of my own, you see. Not for want of trying, if truth be told. And I don't do much except ...' She held out a pleading hand towards Maude. 'I would so like to hear that everything has been good between you and your son.'

'Well, I never,' Maude said. She pulled her chair closer to

Connie and put an arm lightly around her shoulders. 'Bless your heart. You have restored my faith in human nature.'

The tears, which Connie had hoped to control, spilled hot and fast. Maude grabbed a fistful of tissues from a trolley laden with books and magazines. 'All these years,' she said. 'There must have been other letters that got to you as much as mine.'

'A few,' Connie said. She wiped her nose and face and took another gulp of tea. 'I desperately wanted Mikey to forgive you and for both of you to go ahead with a proper mother and son relationship. Which,' she managed a small laugh as she waved her hand towards the trinkets and tokens dotting every surface in the minuscule flat, 'I see you've achieved. But your parents. Were they upset at your revelation?'

'My goodness,' Maude said. 'I can't believe we've meant so much to you. Let me tell you the whole story.'

Bittersweet relief coursed through Connie at the sound of the words she'd been longing to hear. This was coming to a much better fruition than she'd dreamed possible. She turned, one leg tucked around the other in the comfy chair, to face Maude as she told her story. Mikey had been shocked and, he'd related much later when he had the vocabulary, appalled that the woman he'd thought was his older sister was, in fact, his mum.

Maude didn't hear from him for quite a few weeks as he didn't know what to say by way of reply to her startling news. But when he'd come home on his next leave, he'd gone straight to Maude and Maurice's house where they'd thrashed out the implications and decided they must try, now that the beans had been spilled, to live as mother and son. 'In fact,' Maude said. 'It proved not to be very difficult at all. What with the war and Mikey being away, the time and distance gave us a chance to adjust. Then when he was demobbed he got a job on the building sites, found a girl and now I'm a nana to his boys.'

Connie listened and nodded in all the right places. She didn't want to give any indication that she already knew some of those details.

'It seemed natural between us, so we didn't keep going back over old ground. We talked about it from time to time, but only to comment on what a cruel world it was that forced such a situation on people. And he's a devoted son. Sometimes it seems that he, of all people, tries to make up for those first eighteen years by falling over himself to be caring and helpful.'

'I don't have any other children,' Maude said. 'That never happened for me and Maurice. Much like it never did for you, by the sounds of it.' She smiled at Connie with a poignant sadness. 'So goodness knows where I would be without my Mikey.'

'You're very lucky to have each other,' Connie said from her heart. 'Can I please ask about your parents and how they took your having told Mikey the family secret?'

'Ohhh.' Maude looked as if the memory was too much to bear. She tried to squeeze her unwieldy frame into the folds of her chair and she covered her face as if waiting for a blow to hit. 'That was a different story.'

Connie was alarmed at Maude's reaction and the thought of that stroke or heart attack crossed her mind again. 'Please don't feel you have to tell me,' she said quickly, keeping her mental fingers crossed that Maude would ignore that statement. 'It's just that you said your parents had no idea you were sending the letter and that all hell would break loose when they found out.' Connie cringed a bit, too.

'It turned out okay in the end,' Maude said. 'But they were most unhappy to begin with. They'd brought up Mikey as their own and, to their way of thinking, had saved me from becoming a social outcast. Which was probably the case. So they thought I'd been disrespectful and ungrateful by telling Mikey the truth. My dad didn't stop, telling Maurice he would never have married me if he'd known the truth. Of course, Maurice did know the truth, and told him so.

'"Then you're a bigger fool than I thought," Dad had yelled. "To marry a woman who had a baby out of wedlock." On and on. They were different times, thank goodness. But do you know, I came to realise that the worst thing they had to endure was not having Mikey with them as their son. They'd been so used to having the lovely boy in their house, with me popping in and out as his sister, that they were terribly lonely without him.'

'But they gradually came around?' Connie ventured to ask.

'Oh, yes,' Maude said. 'It took a while, but once they understood that Mikey would love them in the same dedicated way, they got used to being his grandparents and we all settled into our new roles.'

They sat in silence for a few minutes, with Connie turning over the information she'd been given and Maude, Connie presumed, thinking about the twists and turns of her life.

'They've gone now,' Maude said rather wistfully. 'Mum and Dad and Maurice.'

'I'm sorry,' Connie said. 'My mum's gone, too.'

A look of understanding passed between the two women.

'I can't give you any more information on that story,' Maude said. 'As that's all there is to tell. But I can offer you another cup of tea.'

'No, thank you,' Connie said, unfurling her legs. 'I must leave you in peace. I've taken advantage of your kindness already.'

For a beat, Maude's face crumpled with concern. 'Has hearing all of that helped, my dear?' she asked. 'I do hope you can settle now.'

Connie allowed her shoulders to slump. She laid her hands loosely in her lap and said, 'You have no idea just how much meeting you and hearing your story has meant to me.'

When she stood, Connie felt weak and drained and she needed the loo, but wasn't prepared to take any further liberties and ask to use the facilities.

At the door to the hallway, she was about to thank Maude for her time and trouble when there was a rattle at the front door and a man's voice called out, 'Only me, Mum. You'll never guess what I forgot this time.'

Maude smiled at Connie and mouthed, 'Mikey.'

She swung open the hall door and a short, robust man in his forties was wiping his shoes on the mat. He looked up and froze when he saw Connie, so she was able to discern how much he looked like his mother, especially around the brown, liquid eyes and distinctive chin. 'Oh,' he sounded taken aback and looked to his mother for an explanation. 'I didn't know you were expecting company. Who have we here?'

Connie held her breath. She hoped Maude wouldn't tell Mikey what her business had been with his mother as she suspected this overprotective son wouldn't be as welcoming or forthcoming as his mum had been. But Maude seemed to pick up on her apprehension and without taking her eyes off Connie said, 'Just someone from the council with a survey.'

Connie nodded her thanks towards Maude imperceptibly, scooted around Mikey, grabbed her case and let herself out into the sweltering early evening. Turning, she caught Maude's eye and said, 'Thank you so much for your time, Mrs Grimshaw.'

'Take care of yourself, my dear,' Maude said.

As the door was closed behind her, the last thing Connie heard was Mikey berating his mother about having told her a million times not to let strangers into the flat. 'I hope you asked to see her ID,' he said in a gentle but frustrated tone of voice. 'Mum, did you? And what was she doing with a suitcase?'

London was busy and Connie didn't have many minutes to spare before her train left King's Cross. When she flopped into her seat she felt as if she'd been through a wringer, but relief flooded her, too, that she'd been able to put a line under Maude and Mikey's story. She couldn't believe how lucky she'd been that Maude, whose life she'd wondered about for so long, had been receptive to her intrusion. A smile crossed Connie's face when she recalled how worried she'd been about trying to glean the information and then how easy it had all turned out to be.

A woman with two amusing, well-spoken children occupied the opposite end of the compartment and Connie was engrossed in watching them surreptitiously until they alighted at Stevenage. That left her and a younger couple who were busy with each other. Leaving her case in the overhead rack, she took her bag and made her way to the refreshments carriage where she ordered a pot of coffee and a rock bun.

Hunched against a window with her snack in front of her, Connie tried to concentrate on the scenery; but the thought of returning to the thick of her weekly routine with the added duty of cricket teas to contend with made her feel morose and fed-up already, especially as her days with Ken and Dora had been filled with excitement and laughter and a feeling of freedom and independence. To think, after she'd been shown the rudiments of research in Somerset House, she'd found Maude and had a conversation with her entirely off her own bat. That made her feel proud and capable and it would be something to hang onto in the couple of months between now and her next trip.

Back in her compartment, she checked on her suitcase in the little mirror over the seat opposite and suddenly remembered Ken's letter. Her hand flew to her throat and she turned on her toes, struggling to release the case from its netting bed. Tearing under the flap with her fingernail, five ten-pound notes and a key fell into her lap. Goodness knew what the young man opposite thought when he saw those items. He raised his eyebrows and she quickly picked up everything and tucked it all back into the envelope. Fifty pounds! She couldn't believe she had so much money in her possession, plus the key to three glorious days on her own in London.

One thin sheet of paper in Ken's handwriting had been

folded around the notes and she held it up to her face, her lips moving as she read it.

I can't believe all you wanted for a birthday present was a scarf from Littlewoods. Treat yourself, Sister of Mine. And here's the key for August. Love you, Ken X

Retford came and went. Disbelieving of her brother's generosity, she lovingly wrapped the money, the key and the letter in her scarf and hid them in a pair of her underpants.

The train was slowing down for Doncaster and Connie shrugged her shoulders into her navy mac. It was lovely to have money behind her and she could use some of it to see a show in London, browse the shops and perhaps buy a little something, have lunch in Peter Robinson's, teas, coffees, cake and a small sherry. The possibility of doing that, without anyone to answer to, filled her with febrile anticipation.

And, she thought, huffing into her cupped hand to check for the last traces of alcohol, *I will definitely be spending a few solitary, uninterrupted hours in Somerset House sniffing out the records of other people's lives.* She smiled as she realised that what had seemed beyond the realms of her imagination on the way to London, was now within reach.

The train slowed down at the platform and there was Arthur, cycle helmet in hand and wearing what looked like the same beige trousers he'd been clad in on Monday morning. He was peering into each compartment with his dark eyebrows pointing towards each other and when he spotted her, he nodded once and held up his hand by way of a greeting.

There was no kiss on the mouth awaiting her, so she needn't have worried about Arthur detecting gin fumes on her breath. He brushed his dry lips across her cheek and asked if she'd had a good time.

She gave him her broadest smile. 'Lovely,' she said.

'Oh.' Arthur raised his eyebrows in surprise. 'It did you good?'

'It was a real tonic, Arthur,' she said.

He nodded and she let him take her elbow and guide her towards the ticket barrier. 'So my plans for you worked out,' he stated rather than enquired.

'Absolutely,' she said. 'I can't wait until the next time.'

A pompous, smug grin took over Arthur's face and Connie had to turn away so he couldn't see how the spread of her own wide, self-satisfied smile matched his.

18

April 1944

Connie was engrossed in a letter when she became aware of the Third Officer standing by her side. 'Petty Officer Wren Censor Allinson,' the Third Officer said. 'I require a word with you in my office, if you please. When you've finished with the letter in your hand, of course.'

'Mam,' Connie said, watching her superior walk away briskly.

The unfathomable shame Connie had felt when she was called into the Chief Wren's office at HMS Holborn surfaced again. She racked her brain to think of something she might have done that was against regulations. Perhaps she'd let too many letters go uncensored or maybe she'd sent too many upwards when she should have made those decisions herself – or there was always the possibility that her section was lagging behind in their letter count and she was going to be asked to crack the whip a bit harder.

Her concentration had slipped, so ever-diligent, she picked up the letter from James Stanton to his nana and started at the beginning again.

Dear Nana
    I'm getting by alright so please don't worry about

me. I have enough to eat and plenty of clothes to peel off when it gets warm and pile back on when the temperature drops.

Massaging her temples with her thumbs, Connie thought that probably wasn't the case and she reminded herself that services personnel had been told not to write about the horrors of war to their loved ones as it would drag down morale.

The lads are all envious of the scarf you sent and a couple of them ribbed me endlessly about getting you to knit one for them. So if you want to make an extra bob or two, just let me know.

But I'm worried about my mate, George. You remember him, don't you, Nana? He lived around the corner at number 24 and he used to call for me to play football. Well, he's lost his sense of humour and his appetite and he isn't sleeping. Can you go round and ask his mum to give him a boost when she next writes? I'm sure that will make a big difference to him. And to me.

All my love to you and Grandad

Jim X

Something twisted deep in Connie's stomach. They were just a couple of boys whose carefree football days had been cut short by a monstrous war in which they had to play their part as men fighting against other boys. But there was something more to it than that. There were plenty of childhood friends who joined up at the same time and whose loyalties to each other were fierce, but there was something momentous and powerful about this particular ardent petition. With a kick so ferocious it felt as if it stopped her heart, she realised that Jim's request for his nana to talk to George's mum was an entreaty; a begging prayer to get help for the boy he was deeply fond of. George, she thought, was Jim's beloved. That was illegal and wouldn't be tolerated in the Royal Navy.

She stared towards the far end of the room where she could make out a blur of navy-blue and white moving between one desk and another. Each heavy, rhythmic clunk of the printing press was interspersed with a tick of the clock; scissors snipped; pencils scratched; a cough from one corner of the room bounced off a wall and was echoed by another and another; the rustle of papers caused the sluggish air to move around languidly before it settled again.

She imagined Jim, tall and smart in his uniform with a Player's between his fingers, watching his precious George shuffle and slink around their quarters. She could hear him saying, 'Buck up' or 'Eat what's on your plate' or 'How about a hand of gin rummy?' And she could feel the knot in Jim's stomach tighten when none of those simple suggestions did the trick.

Staring down at the letter, Connie felt as if she were caught in the sticky web of a dilemma. She wondered if she should report her misgivings about the young men's relationship, but reading through the words again she was relieved to find that there was nothing incriminating in black and white or between the lines. It was possible that it was all in Jim's head, or heart, and George had no idea that his schoolfriend harboured any feelings for him other than those that came with sharing childhood experiences. Or perhaps it was all in her mind, but she shook her head to get rid of that thought. She'd immersed herself in the lives of enough people by now to know there was more to Jim and George than the words on the page would have her believe.

The letter didn't have anything to do with the strategy of the war or go into gory details, so it shouldn't have anything to do with censorship, but what about morale? George's mum would turn herself inside out with worry about her son and Connie was well aware that should be avoided, but wouldn't it be worse if George's state of mind plummeted further and had a detrimental effect on Jim and the rest of their battalion? She had to at least give George's mother a chance to get her son back on the straight and narrow, and releasing the letter uncensored seemed to be in keeping with her duty.

Looking at the front of the envelope again, Connie memorised the address in Nuneaton and then, as if on a factory conveyer belt, she plunged her label into the gelatinous sponge on her desk and sealed the envelope addressed to Jim Stanton's grandmother. The Third Officer was waiting, so she cut short her musings and pushed the letter, with forceful determination, into a burlap bag of outgoing post, her damp fingers sticking to the envelope momentarily and leaving their imprint on the flimsy paper.

'Take a seat, Petty Officer Censor Wren Allinson,' the Third Officer said when the salutes were out of the way. She was neat with petite hands, feet and features, and the desk she sat behind was well-organised. 'How would you like to go to Bermuda?'

Wrens were supposed to be well-composed, gracious and unflappable but Connie couldn't hide the astonishment she felt. She was sure the Third Officer could see the blood racing through her veins and colouring her face and neck. 'Bermuda?' she echoed. 'Isn't that in the Caribbean?' She'd heard a number of officers talking about censorship posts all over the world – Trinidad, the Bahamas, Bermuda, Ceylon, Egypt, Newfoundland, Malta and Mauritius – but she didn't think she'd ever get the opportunity to go somewhere that sounded so vibrant and alluring.

'That's right,' the Third Officer said. 'A few of the girls have come home to take up other positions so there are some vacancies. We're asking Jennies of your rank and above who are particularly conscientious.'

Again, Connie felt heat rush to her face. Bermuda. Rather than walks through a windswept, bombed-out grey city, days off would mean beaches, sunsets with a gin in hand, soft sand underfoot. If there was a form to sign, she would have put her mark on it there and then.

'Are you interested?'

'Definitely,' Connie said. 'When do you require my final decision?'

'We understand you'll want to consult with family, but as soon as possible, if you please.'

'Mam,' Connie said, barely able to disguise her beaming smile under a façade of refinement.

She wrote to Arthur and after an agonising wait, a return letter arrived. He said he'd seen some terrible things. He couldn't describe them to her in a letter, but he didn't want her to be faced with the same.

> I know you've been exposed to awful sights and sounds at home, too, but at least there you're near friends and family and amongst familiar places and I know where you are. The voyage would be hazardous and once there you would be in peril from everything from poisonous insects to drowning to sunstroke. I've even heard it bandied about that Wren Censors are thought so little of in the colonies they're referred to as Censorettes and one such Wren was murdered on one of the outposts.
>
> Treasure, I will be very disappointed if you knowingly compromise your safety and risk our future together, the thoughts of which keep me going and are the reason I am fighting in this war.

Tears refused to surface when Connie put the letter aside, but the frustration she felt welled in her chest. She balled the pages and threw them in the bin along with the prospect of slow sunsets and warm walks. She thought the Third Officer would be scathing or sarcastic when she told her she wouldn't be able to take up the offer, but she was neither. 'It's mostly single women who sign up for postings abroad. Husbands and fiancés aren't so keen.' She rolled her eyes and Connie smiled in solidarity. 'But there are positions in our mobile units. You'd be travelling around the country as part of a team and checking letters in post boxes throughout principle Naval port towns to detect evasion from censorship. It's gruelling work, but I think you're well-suited.'

'Thank you, Mam,' Connie said. 'I didn't know that such units existed. It sounds intriguing.'

'Well, Portsmouth isn't Bermuda. Nor is Inverness.'

Surely Arthur wouldn't have any quibbles about that? It was very important war work, she would be stationed in Britain and he would know where she was – more or less. 'Yes,' Connie said after a moment. 'I would like to volunteer for the mobile unit.'

The Third Officer raised her eyebrows. 'You don't want time to contact your husband?'

'No, Mam,' Connie said, in a voice less than convincing to her ears. 'There's nothing about the job for him to disapprove.'

By the time she wrote to Arthur the papers had been signed, she had instructions in her possession about what kit she needed to take with her, train tickets to join her mobile unit in Dover and a weekend's leave had been organised. Connie was sharing a fish and chip supper with Mum in Acton when the door flew open and Arthur stood in the doorway, his brows knitted together and shadows hollowing his cheeks.

'Arthur!' Connie's mum cried out. 'We weren't expecting you. At least I wasn't. Were you Connie?'

Connie shook her head and rushed towards Arthur where he took her up in his arms and held her for some time. 'Let me get you a cup of tea,' Connie said. 'And you can have the rest of my fish. I'm not very hungry as it happens. Is this planned or special leave?'

Arthur took off his cap and battledress jacket and sat at the table. 'I thought I should see you before you start on your posting,' he said.

'Oh yes,' Connie's mum chipped in. 'Isn't it wonderful that our Connie's going to be travelling around the country looking through letters for anything that might be amiss? How I envy her. What I wouldn't give for a week by the sea. Or in the country.'

Arthur stared at Connie, his eyes heavy with a sense of betrayal and a hint of icy anger. He drank his cup of tea, moved the chips and cold lump of cod around on his plate and was pleasant to Mum. But that night in bed he told Connie how annoyed and disappointed he was with her. 'I can't believe you went behind my back and accepted this mobile censor role,' he whispered.

'Arthur,' she said. 'I did no such thing. I never thought for a moment you'd be unhappy with the posting.'

'I am unhappy and worried about you,' he said. 'I'm trying my best to keep you safe in dire circumstances.'

'I worry about you, too.' Connie stroked his arm. 'But it doesn't really matter where we are, does it? London, Liverpool, on a ship somewhere in the middle of an ocean teeming with mines. We're at war and there's nothing we can do about that, I'm afraid.'

Nothing else was said and eventually she heard Arthur's breathing become less stertorous and more rhythmical and she knew he'd fallen asleep, so she turned on her side and followed his lead.

It wasn't until the morning they were both due to report for duty that Arthur reached out for her in bed. She responded with warmth and wrapped herself around him. They snuggled and caressed and shared the occasional giggle and Connie was pleased that he had seemed to put their quarrel aside. With Mum out at the shops and the house empty, it was as if he were driven by the thought that they were all that existed in the entire world and that this half an hour they had to themselves could very well be the last thing either, or both of them, would ever experience.

Arthur insisted on taking her to the train station, which was awash with people greeting each other or saying their goodbyes. Deep kisses and lingering embraces were exchanged, but Arthur handed Connie into the train with a quick peck on her cheek then stood outside the window looking at her with a face as grim and gloomy as ash settling after a conflagration. Disappointment washed over her and she was left wondering where his earlier passion and affection had disappeared to.

With a sigh, she put her small case in the luggage net and when she turned, there was Arthur blocking her passage out to the corridor where she'd planned to wave goodbye. Before she had a chance to question him, he threw his arms around her, lifted her from her feet and kissed her as he hadn't since their wedding day in 1934. When he released her, she touched her bottom lip with the pad of her finger, then reached up and traced the contours of his mouth, which was trembling as if he were lost at sea.

He leaned in close and said, 'Promise me you'll come back.'

'Of course I will, Arthur,' she said.

Then the whistle blew and Arthur jumped from the train and marched off smartly, his uniform blending in with the hundreds of others striding away from their loved ones.

19

July 1967

For the first few weeks after Connie returned home, she felt as if she were floating on air. She'd gone over and over her plan to stay by herself in Ken and Dora's house in London, honing the finer details until she was sure it was viable. She'd received the usual letters from her brother and sister-in-law, and Arthur, puffed up with pomposity that his idea for her had worked so flawlessly, hadn't heard from them at all.

'I suppose,' he'd said. 'That your visit in August will go ahead exactly like the first, given it went so well.'

'There's no need to change any arrangements, Arthur.'

'And I must say, Treasure. You seem much the better for it.'

The smile she'd aimed at him felt oily, but it failed to penetrate his self-satisfied shell.

As time went by and Arthur didn't mention the cricket club rota, she hoped he'd forgotten all about signing her up for making tea and sandwiches, or perhaps he was so pleased he'd given her a new lease of life that he was letting her off the hook. Then he announced he would be playing mid-wicket for the managers' team on the following Saturday and she would be serving the refreshments with

Clive Mullin's wife, Elspeth, and a couple of others he didn't name. Already the dull routine under the circumspect, watchful gaze of the towers had abraded the sheen off her trip to London. Now, as she gazed out at the rain dripping in a steady, humid stream, she couldn't think of one thing she'd like less than doling out cups of tea from a rickety hut on the village green. At least she could wear her beautiful scarf – that might cheer her up a bit.

'What time will I have to be there?' Connie asked in a flat voice.

'The match starts at one, Treasure,' Arthur said, tutting as he rubbed at a spot of congealed gravy on the worktop.

'Leave it, Arthur,' she couldn't stop herself from snapping. 'I'll wipe it over when you've gone back to work.'

He held up his hands in surrender. 'Just trying to help,' he said.

Connie wanted to reel off a hundred other things he could do to be useful, starting with scoring her name off that ridiculous roster, but knew she had to hold her tongue if she wanted to have her break in London. 'Surely,' she said in a measured tone. 'I won't have to be there until later. Teas aren't served until teatime, are they? Four o'clock?'

In her mind Connie kept her fingers crossed, hoping she would get a couple of precious hours to herself without any chores. But that was never going to be the case.

'Treasure.' Arthur's face crumpled. 'You wouldn't want to miss your Constance's Constant scoring some spectacular runs, would you?'

She thought she could live without that.

'Besides,' he said rather flippantly. 'I've put your name

down for the whole afternoon. It will give you a chance to get to know Elspeth.'

This time, Connie couldn't help herself. 'You seem very keen on me becoming acquainted with Mr Mullin's wife,' she said. 'But I can make friends for myself. Given the opportunity.'

Arthur ignored the jab. 'Clive sings her praises,' he said. 'Like I do yours.'

Connie thought the sum of what he said about her probably added up to nothing more than how good she was at cooking, cleaning and being the quintessential wife for whom he'd gone into battle.

There was a sheen about Elspeth Mullin that radiated an easy life. A good ten years younger than Connie, the skin on her face and hands was plump and as well-tended as the flesh on a Christmas goose; Connie thought she must use expensive lotions and potions or never have to burden herself with household chores. Practical yet elegant, she swept off her coat in one movement, swept her collar-length bob into place, swept around the pavilion showing Connie where the cups, saucers, tea, coffee and biscuits were kept, swept the floors with a broom, opened the fridge and swept milk and butter onto one of the shelves and managed to chatter non-stop at the same time.

'The others are bringing the cakes, so we can slice them later and put them on these platters,' she said, pulling a couple of huge, white plates from a cupboard. 'The sandwiches go on these,' she said, hauling out four more identical pieces of heavy-duty crockery.

'When do we make them up?' Connie asked.

'Denise and Catherine are bringing the bread and fillings,' Elspeth said. 'So we'll probably start to prepare about three.' Connie nodded as she followed her mentor around the kitchen area with its rickety wooden walls and creaking floor. 'When we've turned on the urn and laid everything out, we can sit outside and watch the match.'

Connie felt clumsy and awkward in Elspeth's wake, but busied herself organising rows of cups behind what would become a serving hatch when two small doors were opened later. The other women arrived and introductions were made and when they'd got on with as much as they could, they each picked up a deckchair and trooped around the perimeter of the cricket pitch to take up position under a small copse of oak trees.

The rain that had soaked them for the best part of the week had cleared up and bright blue patches nudged their way through the clouds. From the other side of the green near the pond, a lawnmower could be heard and the heady scent of freshly cut grass wafted towards them. Denise stretched out her legs and laid her hands, heavy with bracelets and rings, in her lap. 'This is the life,' she said.

The others muttered their agreement. Denise asked Connie where she'd lived before Barnby Dun, which was the standard conversation opener whenever women on the estate were introduced, but it was obvious that none of the others sitting under the swaying branches of the trees were interested in her reply.

'And you?' Connie asked. 'Where do you hail from?'

'I'm from London, too,' Catherine said. 'Putney, to be exact.'

'Glasgow,' Denise said, laying on a thick Scottish accent for effect. 'But Jem and I have lived all over the world.'

'And we're from Sheffield.' Elspeth was the last to contribute.

That information out of the way, the three women who knew each other began to talk about their lives in a way that made them seem more like rivals than friends.

'Clive's about to get that next promotion I was telling you about.' Elspeth swept away an insect with a well-fed hand in front of her face. Connie could tell she was trying hard to sound nonchalant, but why would she bother? Either she was proud of her husband or she wasn't.

'Fantastic,' Denise said, a hard edge to her voice. 'Now you can get that new telly you want.'

New telly? Connie thought. That meant they already had a television set and it couldn't be very old. So why would they want a new one?

'Hope so,' Elspeth grinned and held up crossed fingers. Then she turned to Connie. 'What model of telly do you have?' she asked, a shard of ice in her voice.

The others turned their gazes on Connie, but she held her nerve and answered that they hadn't made the decision to buy a television yet.

'Oh,' Catherine said. 'Whatever do you do in the evenings? Not sit and talk to each other, surely.'

Denise laughed. 'Or listen to your husband droning on about work, like my Chris does.'

Connie smiled politely, laced her fingers together, sat up as straight as she could in the sling of the striped deckchair and listened to the endless talk about private schools for their children; the horrible way they'd spoken to their cleaners; the next luxury item on their shopping lists; where they were going for their summer holidays; the next round of promotions they wanted their husbands to apply for. The chat was very different from that bandied about during the coffee mornings, but it was as endlessly unfulfilling.

She felt sure she was an enigma to them, with her new hairdo and incongruous clothes, lack of car, television, telephone or children, but she reminded herself that they knew nothing about her life during the war or the enlightening conversation she'd had with Maude Grimshaw or the three carefree days in London that would soon come to fruition.

The crack of a ball on willow seized their attention and they turned in time to see Arthur catch out an opponent. Even from that distance Connie could see her husband's broad grin as he held the ball above his head in triumph. They all clapped languorously, layers of jewellery jangling against each other. 'That's you in for a good time tonight.' Elspeth winked and nodded towards Connie. Denise and Catherine cackled and it was at that point Connie realised she really did not like any of them at all.

'It's that time,' Elspeth said, looking at her watch. Denise and Catherine grumbled and they all traipsed back to the pavilion, Connie carrying her deckchair under her arm.

'You could have left that there,' Denise said. 'When we've cleared up, we can go back and enjoy the last of the evening.'

'Never mind,' Connie said. 'I've brought it this far.' She had no intention of sitting with them again and listening to their moans and boasts and watching their eyes reduce to slits when someone else had something they coveted for themselves. She would present herself as a jolly good fellow by volunteering to stack the plates or polish the glasses or impeccably clean the floor.

'You can make a start on the sandwiches, Connie,' Elspeth gave out the orders.

Connie buttered slice after slice of the pillowy, pre-cut white bread that Arthur would not tolerate. He insisted on solid loaves fresh from the bakery and she looked forward to what he would say to get out of eating a couple of triangles when the game stopped for tea.

They opened the hatch and Connie found herself working with Catherine to offer sandwiches to each team member in turn. When Arthur appeared, he nodded surreptitiously and asked her with his eyes if she was having the time of her life with Elspeth and her gang. Connie didn't bite.

'Which type of sandwich can I give you, Arthur,' Catherine said. 'Egg and cress, cucumber? Connie made them.'

'Well.' He looked down at them and hesitated. 'I think I'll just have a cup of tea and a slice of fruit loaf.'

'You love a nice sandwich,' Connie said. 'Here, have two of each.' As she piled his plate, she made a point of pushing her finger into the doughy bread and watching his appalled face as the hollow imprints refused to spring back.

Arthur walked away to sit with his teammates, plate in one hand, cup in the other. Gingerly, he took a small bite from a sandwich and nibbled at it. Next time she looked over, his plate was empty and he was picking up the crumbs with a damp finger.

That evening after supper, Connie and Arthur sat in their usual places, Connie furiously trying to finish the matinee jacket for Shirley's baby and Arthur filling in the crossword. Arthur, however, could not concentrate for long and badgered her with questions about his exploits on the cricket pitch.

'You did see the catch, didn't you, Treasure?' he asked for the third time.

'Yes, Arthur,' she answered. 'I turned when you waved the ball in the air.'

'Clive said that catch ensured the game went our way.'

'Very generous of him,' she said, thinking back to how his wife and the other women watched each other with a tinge of jealousy. Each afraid the others were one step ahead.

'What do you mean?' Arthur drew his brows together. 'I don't think Clive would say it if he didn't mean it. He's not like that.'

'I didn't mean to suggest he was,' Connie said. 'It's just that he must have played well, too. It's a team effort after all, isn't it?'

'Of course, Treasure,' Arthur was a bit too quick to agree. 'How did you get on with Elspeth and her chums?'

Playing for time, she went to the window to count stitches in the brighter light. 'They seem to know each other very well,' she mumbled, a spare knitting pin dangling from her pursed lips.

Arthur grunted, picked up his paper then put it down again and looked into the distance. 'Do you think they'll keep me in the same position for the next match,' he said. 'Or put me somewhere else?'

Connie couldn't care less except that something inside her rolled over and played dead when she thought about going through the whole rigmarole the following weekend.

'Oh, and by the way,' Arthur said. 'Can you please find out what type of bread was used today? It was excellent.'

'I know what it was. I made the sandwiches. It's the pre-sliced brand I bought once and you said you'd never have in the house again.'

Arthur shook his head and cleared his throat. 'Can't be exactly the same,' he mumbled.

'Yes, it is, Arthur,' she couldn't keep the edge of victory out of her voice. 'Absolutely the same down to the last detail.'

And she intended to prove it to him by buying a loaf and making him eat each and every slice, even if it choked him.

20

May 1944

Connie stepped off the train onto the busy, sooty platform at Dover Priory, a small case in her hand that carried a change of clothes, toiletries and her equipment. She'd thought Dover would be less frantic than London and Liverpool, but the station was packed with servicemen and women rushing past.

Making sure her tricorne hat was lodged properly on her head, Connie waited for a gap in the pedestrian traffic and when one didn't appear, she flung herself into the throng and walked smartly towards the door where her papers told her to wait for her superior. Announcements over the loudspeaker were drowned out by blasts from whistles; mothers clung to the sleeves of their toddlers; newspapers were snatched mid-air from vendors. *What must it have been like during Dunkirk?* Connie thought. She and Mum had seen the Pathé newsreels of the evacuation and their jaws had dropped at the hundreds and thousands of men passing through Dover, filling the town and station, with stunned looks on their unshaven faces. It hardly seemed possible that such a feat had been executed and the mass of men in uniform made it difficult to think about them as individuals. Then the camera had picked out one soldier from the crowd and played on his features until Connie felt she knew him – he could have been a boy from school, or someone she'd worked with, her cousin or nephew or friend's fiancé. By the time the young lad had retrieved half a cigarette from his jacket, lit it with a cupped match, given the camera Churchill's V-sign and a cheeky grin, Connie thought that everyone in the pictures must love him in one way or another. It was then she felt the enormity of the situation for all the men who'd lived through that terrible ordeal.

A feeling of trepidation washed over her as she waited at the allotted meeting place, but her training stopped her from jiggling from foot to foot or pacing up and down. Another Wren of the same rank took up a position nearby, followed by another and two more after that. They all wore tricorne hats, the regulation amount of makeup and they all carried the same cases. Connie's instinct was to smile or nod and ask if they were going to be part of a mobile censorship team, but thought it best to wait and see if they were destined to work together when their superior arrived. The others must have made the same decision, because they all faced the doors, scanning the sea of uniforms for a Third Officer or Chief Wren.

Then from behind them came a woman's voice. 'Petty Officer Wren Censors?'

They jumped imperceptibly then turned as one. 'Mam,' they chanted.

'Move to the side, if you please.'

They stood next to a dark wooden counter in a quieter corner and the Chief Wren produced a clipboard and pen from her case. In a subdued tone, she read out each of their names and ticked them off a list. Connie was first, so she had time to study her superior, who looked at each of the Petty Officers in turn as if she wanted to etch their faces in the depths of her memory. She was tall and willowy and had elegant, expressive hands that Connie thought she could use to her advantage when telling a story.

'All accounted for,' the Chief Wren said. 'Follow me.'

They filed out of the station and into a gale that contested the winds Connie had battled against as they'd whipped across the Mersey. 'Hold onto your hats whilst we walk to the Cliffs. And please,' she lowered her voice, 'for security reasons, no talking until we arrive in our quarters.'

Cliffs, Connie thought. Could she possibly mean the White Cliffs that Vera Lynn sang about? How on earth were they going to censor letters there and where would they sleep – in tents? Security had always formed a large part of their job, but not to the extent that they weren't allowed to speak to each other in public. Perhaps there was more to being a mobile censor than she'd been told. They clipped along with their mouths firmly closed, avoiding what looked like the same mounds of bricks and debris, fallen walls and exposed pipes that lay all over London and Liverpool and the entire country, so Connie supposed. There was a long queue of jaded women outside a bakery and another winding away from a dairy. A child hobbled past in odd shoes, the black one more worn down at the heel than the brown, and Connie had to look the other way, both ashamed of her warm, tailored uniform and proud to be wearing it at the same time.

The sky was darkening as the houses and shops thinned out and Connie heard waves crashing against the cliffs. She thought they must be nearly there – wherever that was – when they turned sharply inland and skirted the shoreline, probably to avoid the coast, which had been decreed off limits, from the Wash to Land's End, since the beginning of April.

Then what looked like a castle loomed in front of them and suddenly security was everywhere. Locked gates, sentries, soldiers, naval personnel, nothing but darkness except for low lights. Connie knew they were under orders not to speak, but she wondered about asking the Chief Wren if she, Petty Officer Wren Censor Allinson, had been posted to the incorrect place. This was nothing like HMS Holborn or the Littlewoods Building – this must be more to do with cracking codes and listening into Hitler's messages, none of which she was trained to do. She felt frantic when she thought about how foolish she would look when they had to start work the next day and Arthur, well, he would go mad.

Then they were in the castle and following the Chief Wren through a maze of tunnels that led them, at last, to a door that the Chief Wren opened. She ushered them into a low-ceilinged room furnished with bunks, a small table and five chairs. The door to a compact, spotless bathroom stood open and through another Connie saw a miniature galley: five cups and saucers stacked next to a tiny two-ringed stove.

'Petty Officer Wrens.'

'Mam,' Connie joined in with the others.

'I'm going to leave you for a quarter of an hour to claim your bunks and freshen up, but don't make yourselves too comfortable as we'll only be here for three days. When I return, I'll tell you exactly what is involved in being a mobile censor. After that, we'll go to the mess, then it's lights out. We have an early start in the morning.'

'Mam,' they recited again.

The Wrens stood to attention whilst their superior left, still unable to bring themselves to say a word. Then the door opened again and the Chief Wren put her head in, smiled broadly and said, 'Permission to speak.'

This time the Mams rose by at least an octave and when the Jennies were on their own, they fired questions and talked over each other and babbled so loudly that they would never have heard an incoming bomb.

One by one, the Wrens threw their cases on bunks and inspected the bath and kitchen. Connie followed, hoisting her belongings up onto the last unoccupied bed. 'Will you be alright there?' asked a girl with dark hair and hazel eyes.

'Yes,' Connie said. 'Fine, thank you.'

'You can have first dibs wherever we go next,' another woman chipped in. 'Presuming we'll stay together as a team. Do you think we will?'

'I'm not sure,' Connie answered. 'But it sounded as if we—'

'I suppose they'll bring the letters here and we'll have to sit around this table and read through them.'

Connie didn't think so. There was hardly enough room for a cup of tea let alone lamps and scissors and examiners' labels.

'Did you ever think you'd be bunking in a castle? I'll put the kettle on.'

'No, never. Churchill was here during Dunkirk.'

'He might be here again now for all we know.'

'Perhaps that's why there's so much security,' Connie offered.

'Could be,' the girl with hazel eyes said. 'But I'm sure it's always like this as Dover Castle is the closest point in Britain to Europe.'

That put a stop to the excited chatter. Each of them stood stock still and one girl turned towards where she thought France was situated, a mere twenty-one miles across a narrow channel of water. A shudder passed through Connie and one of the other girls rubbed her arms for warmth. So that was what they were defending. Of course an attack could come from any direction, but if the Jerries and their fellow antagonists broke the breach here, at Dover, it would seem like an insurmountable challenge to fight them off.

But they would try, Connie knew that. Churchill, who could well be in this warren of tunnels, said they would defend their island whatever the cost may be and she believed him, as did everyone else she knew. She looked around for any potential weapon that could be used should the enemy break through the fleet on the sea or the guards around the castle and knew she would make good use of a table leg, a kettle of boiling water and the scissors from her kit.

'Let's introduce ourselves,' one of the Wrens suggested.

They sat around the table holding cups of tea and said their names and where they'd been posted. Two had been at HMS Holborn and one in Liverpool but at different times from Connie, and none of them had experience of being mobile censors.

'And I,' their Chief Wren had come into the room,

'am Chief Wren Censor Patricia Burton and I have been stationed in Liverpool, Ceylon and the Bahamas.'

The Wrens rose to their feet and saluted.

'As you were,' the Chief Wren said. 'If there's one in the pot for me, we can share these.' She produced a packet of digestives and Ivy, the girl with hazel eyes, hurried to the kitchen and came back with another cup and saucer.

'Now, Petty Officer Wren Censors.'

They all listened intently.

'We are going to sweep through the principle naval ports and examine letters posted in post boxes adjoining dockyards, quays and Naval establishments with a view to detecting and preventing the evasion of naval censorship. You must remember that this is for the dual purpose of discerning leakage of information relating to operations and for promoting operational security. As always, what does not concern the war does not concern censorship. As far as logistics are concerned, we'll take the letters to the nearest post office where we'll use a back room to examine them for anything we would look out for in a censoring office. Any questions?'

'Will we have access to watchlists?' asked a Wren called Edie.

'I will have all up-to-date lists with me,' the Chief Wren said. 'Along with leaflets to add to letters that have inadvertently crossed the line and need to be reminded about the regulations.'

'Are there any specific codes we need to look out for?' Connie said.

The Chief Wren was thoughtful for a moment. 'No,' she eventually said. 'As always, you must be vigilant for all codes and for anything sinister, which would most likely relate to the movement of ships and personnel.'

'Presumably,' June said. 'Most of the mail we look at will be from civilians as the post boxes are outside the naval bases?'

'Correct,' the Chief Wren said. 'They have to be read thoroughly as they could contain vital information about ships coming in or out of port and the number of sailors around the quays. Please don't treat them lightly whilst looking for a code from someone who's trying to dodge naval censorship.'

Connie drained the dregs of her cup and tinkered with the handle whilst she listened.

'Anything else?'

Ivy put up her hand. 'Will we stay together as a group for the duration of our posting?'

'All things being equal,' the Chief Wren replied.

'And where are we off to after this?' Viv asked.

'That I cannot say, in case you momentarily forget all your training and include it in a letter.'

The Wrens around the table laughed.

'All I can tell you is that we will travel together to our next destination by train.'

'In that case,' Edie said. 'We won't be able to get our own post from family and friends, will we?'

'I'm afraid not.' The Chief Wren's mouth turned down with sympathy. 'No ingoing or outgoing post for any of us. But think how lovely it will be to get your stockpiled stash when you've finished your first tour of duty.'

No more hands were raised, so they followed their superior to the galley. Connie felt weary and ate her vegetable pasty with mashed swede and carrots for the energy it would provide rather than the taste. It was late, but the hall was quite full and noisy and Connie thought it must be open twenty-four hours a day to accommodate shift workers. Smartly dressed civilians mingled with those in uniform and two young women in neat charcoal suits sat at a table, their heads almost touching as they pored over a file.

'I didn't realise we wouldn't get post for goodness knows how long,' said Edie, who was sitting next to Connie.

Some of the others chimed in with their disappointment at not being able to receive letters, but Ivy said it was a small price to pay for doing their bit and they all agreed on that point.

'I suppose we'll be informed if anything awful happens to our loved ones.' Although cool and poised, Edie gave away the slightest hint of trepidation in her voice. 'Other than that, my letters are only filled with humdrum news, so I don't mind.'

Connie was waiting on a letter each from Norma and Marjorie and she would miss hearing from Mum, Dora and Ken, but she felt a touch of relief at not having to read through Arthur's letters, which she knew would be filled with how worried he was for her. Then remorse flooded her. He did care about her, she knew that and he wanted her to be safe and happy. He'd signed his last letter from Constance's Constant and that had made her feel close to him.

'What do you think, Connie?' Ivy asked

'Oh sorry, about what?'

'Where we'll go next.'

'Portsmouth,' she said, off the top of her head because

she really didn't care. Unless it was Liverpool or London, it would be somewhere she'd never been before and there would be a myriad of letters about other people's lives to read.

The following morning, they crammed into a small van and set off through narrow lanes and around quaysides, stopping at post boxes that were listed amongst a wad of papers the Chief Wren carried with her. Their driver was a Leading Wren who wore no makeup other than red lipstick and had a deep dimple in one cheek when she smiled. She told them she'd been a WRNS motorcycle dispatch rider and she took the corners as if she were driving on two wheels with an urgent order in her messenger bag.

'Follow me, Jennies,' the Chief Wren ordered. The gale had died down, but it was still blustery so they left their tricorne hats in the van and stood by whilst the post box was opened with a long, heavy key. Then they shovelled the contents – letters, airmail envelopes, packets wrapped in brown paper and tied with string, postcards, sealed and unsealed tomes – into postbags, threw them into the back of the van and carried on to the next stop. Every derivation of handwriting passed in front of Connie's eyes and she picked out lovely cursive shapes made with a fine pen, scrawled marks from a blunt pencil and everything in between.

A few people walking dogs stopped to stare, but no one asked what they were up to. Not many people would question the authority of a uniform, although Connie wondered if anyone who had written one of those letters would feel heartsick at the way it was being treated.

As the burlap sacks rose in mounds behind them, she began to imagine what some might contain. There might be one or two with a code, but she hoped not because she hated to think that anyone serving in the Navy could be so traitorous. That woman she spotted there, enticing a cat into her house with a saucer of something, might have written to her husband about how she'd adopted the pet after a neighbour had gone to live with her niece when her house took a packet. There might be a letter from that older man shuffling along with a pint of milk in his hands who had written to his son in the RAF, begging to know where he was stationed. The thought of learning about the comings and goings of everyone involved filled her with excited anticipation and she couldn't wait to get started.

Eventually, they came to a stop at the back of a small post office. The Chief Wren knocked and they were let in by a woman carrying a baby in her arms. 'Mrs Wilson?' the Chief Wren asked.

'That's me,' the woman answered.

'You were expecting us?'

'Yes, I received notification. Come in, I've put you in here.' She showed them into a sitting room where she'd lit a fire in the grate and pushed two tables together over a faded rug. 'I'll get you a cuppa,' she said.

Without saying much, they set out their equipment. The Chief Wren opened the first sack and handed twenty letters and packets to each of them and told them to begin.

Connie took out her first letter – written on a couple of pages of thin, waxy paper – shook the envelope then held it to the light. Nothing to worry about there. Then she started to read:

Dearest Clemmie

I went for a long walk today right out into the countryside then back again to where I could look down on the port from a distance. It was dull and quite windy, as you know it always is here, but I was wrapped up warm and I think the outing did me good. There were many more of our ships in the Channel than last week and I must say the sight was heartwarming.

Connie scritched and scratched at that sentence until it no longer existed.

I shouted, 'Good on you,' to them and saluted but my words came back to me on a generous gust of wind. I saw a lot of birds and do you know, I marvelled at how they're still nesting and flying and singing in spite of the dreadful activity in the sky and on the sea and everywhere we look. If only we could ignore what's happening, like they do and get on serenely with the necessities of life. Of course, that would be impossible to do when we have to rely on one shilling per week for meat along with two ounces of butter and tea. But soldier on we will. That reminds me to ask how your chickens are getting on? I'm down to three good laying hens and the lovely girls produce enough eggs for me to share with Mary down the road and a few I see in church.

I know you want me to visit you in Yorkshire for a rest and I truly thank you for the invitation, but I'm going to tough it out here. Thinking of the journey makes me want to lie down and have a nap and if my house takes it, I'd rather be here when it happens.

All my love to you up there on the Moors,
Your old friend,
Elsie XXX

What a lovely letter, Connie thought, and as she sealed it with her label, she wondered how long the two women had been friends and what had taken one to Yorkshire and the other to Dover. She pushed the letter into the sack of outgoing post and reached for another, which was a packet this time.

The postmistress came to the door with a tray of tea, but the Chief Wren took it from her and said she wouldn't be allowed in whilst they were working. 'Security,' she said.

'Of course.' Mrs Wilson nodded. 'Will you be all day?'

'Yes,' the Chief Wren answered. 'I'm afraid so.' She tried to gently close the door against Mrs Wilson, who was standing on her toes to peer at what was going on in her own sitting room, but the baby started to cry and the postmistress begrudgingly turned on her heel to see to him.

The tea was handed around and Connie made her way through her pile then started on another. The packet had been cough drops and a handkerchief from a mother to her son serving in the Army. Then there was a letter from a wife to her husband in the Navy that included three postcards from three children all telling their daddy how much they missed him and how well they were doing at school.

The driver came back with sandwiches wrapped in greaseproof paper and the Wrens ate without taking a proper break. They had to get through all the sacks in order for the letters to be reposted that day. Towards the middle of the afternoon, Connie came across an envelope addressed to a Mr Peter Carstairs in Tufnell Park. Turning it over, a tight knot formed at the top of her stomach when she found no return address on the back. She indicated the envelope to the Chief Wren who picked up her chair and wedged herself in beside Connie as she slit the thin paper and placed the one sheet between them. The Chief Wren adjusted the lamp and the light shone down on bold, concentrated writing.

Dear Peter

Do you remember us talking at length about the formation of flying geese? I'm sure you do. They arrange themselves in a V-shape with one goose taking the lead, then one from the back takes over when the leader gets tired. I have a strong feeling that a flock of geese will take off in the middle of next week. Here's what they would look like.

At the bottom of the page, there was a drawing that looked as if it was straight from a child's dot-to-dot comic with a letter next to each mark.

The Chief Wren's eyes widened. Connie just had time to memorise Peter Carstairs' address before her superior took the letter from Connie's damp hand and put it in a special compartment in her case. 'Well done, Petty Officer Wren Censor Allinson,' she said. 'Excellent work. Next letter, if you please.'

The lump of stone sitting between Connie's ribs turned to molten liquid and she couldn't believe she'd been the first to uncover what might very well be a written act of sabotage. The writer of the letter would probably never be traced, but she hoped the authorities would knock on Peter Carstairs' door, cart him away and leave him to rot in a cold, damp, airless prison cell – she'd gladly perform the honours if she had the chance.

Then she sat up straight, moistened her dry lips with her tongue and picked up a love letter from Harold Hargreaves to his sweet, dearest, most adored wife, Lily.

21

After lunch on Monday, Connie told Arthur she was hosting an afternoon tea for Millicent, Shirley, Susan and Mandy. 'Must you?' he said, bristling so violently the hair on his head seemed to stand on end.

'Yes, Arthur, I must,' she said. 'I can't keep having coffee at my friends' houses and not inviting them here. That would be rude.'

'But Treasure,' Arthur resorted to whining. 'All those children. They'll make a mess.'

'They won't.' Connie shooed him towards the door. 'But if they do, I'll have it cleared up before you get home.'

'I'm warning you,' he said as a parting shot. 'Something's bound to get broken.'

Luckily, Millicent brought a large plastic sheet with her and spread it out on the carpet for the little ones to play on. All the young mums produced toys and books from the huge bags they carried everywhere and the children settled down to explore them, leaving the grown-ups to their usual topics of conversation.

Mandy had just found out she was expecting a second baby and Shirley was about to burst at any minute. Connie and Millicent eased their neighbour into a comfy chair where she sat, her minidress hitched up almost to her knickers and her hands resting protectively on top of her huge bump.

'Not long to go now, Shirl,' Millicent said.

'Thank goodness,' Shirley replied. 'I'll be glad to get it over and done with.'

'Remind us of that in a year's time.' Millicent laughed. 'Many a time I've wished I could push Adie back from whence he came … Adie,' she said, as if to prove a point. 'How many times have I told you. Crayons are for colouring not for eating.'

Picking up a Duplo brick in each hand, Adrian toddled towards Connie and set them out on her lap. When he returned the smile she gave him, she noticed two clumps of blue wax on his top teeth and wiped them off with a handkerchief from her pocket.

'He would never let me do that for him, would he, Shirl?' Millicent said. 'He'd clamp his mouth shut like this …' She did a good job of demonstrating how a toddler refused to let anyone look at their teeth. 'Then he'd cry and run off. I don't know. You've got the magic touch, Connie.'

Connie pulled the little chap onto her knee, fixed the bricks together and took them apart at least a dozen times.

Then the talk turned to morning sickness, the catalogue sale and the summer break from school. Connie popped Adrian back on the plastic mat and went into the kitchen to replenish the teapot, the jug of blackcurrant squash and the plate of biscuits.

Loading the tray, she thought how different it looked from the treats served up during the war. She was thankful beyond belief for Peek Freans Assorted Biscuits, especially after enduring such delicacies as egg and bacon pie without the whole egg and very little bacon, prune sponge, mock marzipan, potato pastry and baked jam and parsnip pudding. If she offered any of those to her neighbours, they would think she'd gone mad.

A clatter from the living room made her stomach pitch – thank goodness Arthur wasn't at home to hear it.

'Adie!' Millicent shouted. 'I told you three times not to touch.' A wail from Adrian was followed by a sob from Janet and then the whole house was in chaos.

Connie carried the tea things into the living room and tried to give the impression of disregard. Which was how she felt about most of her possessions, but she knew Arthur didn't share that outlook and she would have to endure the brunt of his displeasure and I told you so's.

Adie rushed towards her, a streak of snot running down his nose, and she had to sidestep deftly to avoid another accident with the tea tray.

'I'm so sorry, Connie.' Millicent's face was puce and she looked as if she was about to cry. 'Your wedding picture.'

Smashed glass glistened on the sideboard, sharp pieces sticking up out of the carpet. The twisted frame lay on its side, one corner of the black and white photo crumpled and torn. It was so damaged, Connie was surprised that her and Arthur's faces weren't staring back at her in alarm instead of retaining their smiling countenances.

There was no chance Arthur wouldn't notice the catastrophe, but what could she say, especially to Adie and Janet who were still crying, their hands hanging helplessly at their sides. 'It's alright. No need to cry.' She kneeled and began to pick up the glass and put it on the empty tray.

When she turned on her knees a sharp scratch made her grimace but she carried on in a rather sing-song voice. 'No one's hurt,' she said. 'And that's the most important thing.'

'That's what we always say, isn't it, Millie?' Shirley said from where she was wedged into her chair.

'Yes,' Millicent said. 'But I feel so bad.' And she obviously felt sorry, too, for shouting at Adrian, because she gathered both her children to her and made a fuss of them. Then she sat Adrian down on the mat, wiped his nose and joined Connie at the sideboard. 'Here, let me help you.'

'I would leave it until later,' Connie said. 'But I don't want the little ones to cut themselves.'

'You are good,' Susan said. 'You always think of everyone else before yourself. Shall I hand round the tea?'

Connie nodded but felt guilty. Her first thought hadn't been for her neighbours or their children but for herself when Arthur came home.

'Can I pay you for it?' Millicent whispered.

'Of course not,' Connie said. How could she possibly let Millicent do that when she had a young family to think about. 'I've been toying with the idea of reframing that old photo for years.' She smiled brightly. 'And now's my chance.'

No doubt dealing with breakages was an everyday occurrence in any house with children, so when the mess was cleared away, the conversation resumed its usual pattern and the incident wasn't mentioned again. But when the mums and children trooped out, taking their plastic sheet and toys and beakers with them, Connie had to think and act fast.

First, she made doubly sure all the glass was dealt with,

then she prepared Arthur's tea because if that was late he could very well lay down the law and forbid her from holding another afternoon get-together. And once on a roll, it was likely he would shake his head and ban her from going to London again. She felt frantic, bile rising from her stomach at the thought that all she would have left was cricket matches with Elspeth and her grim gang, getting her hair done – if there was any point as she wouldn't be going anywhere – her lovely scarf, the clematis and the time she'd spent with Maude that she replayed over and over in her head.

Tears sizzled in her eyes and she brushed them away. She didn't have time for that kind of nonsense now and quickly made the decision to put the demolished photo and frame in a drawer and not mention them to Arthur. That way it would seem as if she hadn't thought the whole incident significant enough to comment on. Then when he noticed she could explain, in an offhand manner, that she'd been meaning to tell him about it at some stage and take it from there.

'Hello, you.' Connie hadn't heard Arthur's key in the lock. She just had time to stuff the damaged frame and forlorn photo between the folds of some long-forgotten table linen, close the drawer on them and pretend to busy herself in the kitchen.

Arthur released his sweaty head from his cycle helmet and watched her dry the last of the teacups and saucers and put them back in their rightful places. He didn't ask her if the tea party was successful or good fun or about any of the topics of conversation that might have come up. And she knew he wouldn't.

But what he did say was, 'Two things about cricket, Treasure.'

Connie was barely able to look at him. If she never heard the word cricket again she would have heard it one time too many. She put their tea on the table and Arthur sat down.

Looking more pleased with himself than a man about to eat a sausage roll should be, he said, 'I'll be playing in the same midfield position for the rest of the season.' He looked at her, a broad smile on his face, waiting for a reply that she couldn't bear to give him.

Eventually she sighed and Arthur carried on.

'And it's your turn to wash the whites on the weekend before you go to London.'

'Really, Arthur?' Connie's voice was harsh. 'This is too much. Cricket is your hobby and I'm pleased for you but why should I have to ...'

Before she could finish the point she was making, the doorbell rang with such urgency it sounded as if someone was leaning on it. Then there was a hammering on the door and Trev's voice reverberated through the letterbox. 'Connie, are you there?' For a moment she hesitated and Arthur sat frozen to the spot.

Sure something must be wrong, Connie gained control and sprinted down the hall. When she threw open the front door, Trev stumbled inwards. He was panting, somehow pale and red in the face at the same time and he was clutching a bewildered Simon and Tracey by their hands. 'Connie,' he said. 'So sorry. Shirl's in labour and I have to get her to hospital.' He half dragged and half pushed his two little ones into the hall. 'We had an agreement with Millie that she would have these two when the time came, but she's not home.' He carved a path through the air with his hands that ended up raking his dark beard into tufts and smoothing it down again. 'They're all out. Shirl thinks they're at a parents' evening for Janet.'

'Oh, right, I see,' Connie said, although she didn't quite understand what was being asked of her until Trev dropped the children's hands and bolted back down the path. 'I've left a note in Millie's door,' he called over his shoulder. 'She'll come and collect them when she gets home.' He blew a quick kiss in Simon and Tracey's general direction then he was gone.

The tots nudged towards each other, turned their huge, sorrowful brown eyes on Connie and felt around with their fingers until they clasped each other's hands. From the kitchen Arthur stared at Connie, too, as if waiting for her to round them all up and tell them what to do.

'Well.' She bobbed down in front of the children. 'This is a treat for me. Seeing you twice in one day.'

Simon and Tracey shuffled a bit closer together, Tracey's mouth and chin beginning to wobble. Connie felt a bit out of her depth, but knew she would have to divert their attention before they both burst into tears and carried on crying until Millicent came for them. Then they rewarded her with a flicker of a smile and she thought she would melt into the carpet. Despite the fact that she hated to see them upset or worried, this was the most exciting thing that had happened to her since her trip to London, and she was going to make the most of the time she had with the two little tots.

Gently getting in between them, she prised apart their pudgy fingers, took their hands and walked them into the kitchen. A thrill passed through her when they drew closer as they passed Arthur and although it was lovely to know they trusted her, she also felt deeply sorry for them. No, it was more than that – what she experienced wasn't merely empathy – she was sure she could feel exactly what they were feeling and as a consequence there was nothing else she could do but take care of them and protect them with every resource available to her. *That depth of feeling must be what it's like to be a mother*, she thought. And she remembered Millicent earlier, her arms around her children, protecting them from her own anger.

'Now.' Connie put her hands on her thighs and looked down. 'Do you remember the blackcurrant squash you had when you were here earlier?'

Simon nodded and Tracey followed her older brother's lead.

Arthur, who stood planted in the same position he'd been in since the children arrived, looked back and forth between Connie and the children.

'Would you like some more?' Connie asked.

Again they nodded.

'What do they drink from?' Arthur asked, suddenly springing to life.

Connie tried not to let the derision she felt show on her face. 'Glasses, Arthur,' she said.

Much to her amazement he dashed past them and into the dining room. 'I'll get two,' he said.

'Arthur won't be a minute,' she said to the tots, still standing and looking up at her.

When Arthur held out the glasses for Connie to fill, she said, 'Simon and Tracey, you know Arthur, don't you?'

Without the slightest compunction or hint of self-consciousness, they turned their heads to Arthur and gave him a hard stare. Then Simon nodded and Tracey did the same.

'Of course they know me,' Arthur said. 'I'm the chap next door, aren't I?' He smiled broadly and bobbed down to their height, as he'd seen Connie do a few minutes earlier. 'The one with the funny hat.' He jumped up, retrieved the cycle helmet from where he'd left it and put it on his head, pulling a funny face for good measure.

Simon and Tracey giggled, purple blackcurrant moustaches smeared across their top lips. Connie started to laugh, too, but almost with a sense of hysteria at Arthur's reaction to the two tiny, unexpected visitors. Had anyone asked, she would have said he'd retreat in a huff to his crossword or keep checking his watch to see how long they'd been intruding on his strict schedule. But his attitude was one of excitement and pure pleasure – his eyes were sparkling, there was a high point of colour at the top of his cheekbones and he was alive with energy. Connie was as enthralled with him as she was with Simon and Tracey.

'Are they hungry?' Arthur asked her. 'Are you hungry?' He bent towards the children again.

Simon spoke for the first time, his voice soft and high-pitched. 'Mummy was making us fish fingers but then she didn't,' he said.

'Mummy,' Tracey offered, her eyes pooling with tears.

Connie scooped her up. 'Do you know where Mummy is?' she asked. 'She's gone to get your new baby. She'll be back home soon.'

'Yes,' Simon chimed in. 'But we don't know if it's a girl or a boy baby, do we, Tracey?' He looked up at his sister. 'What are we going to call her if it's a girl?' he asked, sounding like a mini-Shirley.

Tracey furrowed her unbelievably smooth forehead. 'Carol,' she said, looking pleased with herself.

'Caroli ...' Simon prompted.

'Caroline!' Tracey shouted.

'Well done,' Simon said. 'And if it's a boy?'

Tracey thought again, her finger in her mouth. 'Ben.'

'... jamin,' Simon finished for her.

'Lovely names,' Connie said. 'Don't you think, Arthur?' She risked a glance at her husband, hoping the spell cast by these two children hadn't been broken.

But Arthur was beaming, his arms folded across his chest and watching their every move with such delight that he hadn't even fussed about their drinking glasses poised on the edge of the kitchen counter. 'They're my favourite names,' he said. 'After Simon and Tracey.'

Connie could not comprehend that this was the same man who'd spoken to her with such arrogance less than half an hour ago. The same person who wouldn't eat anything on a Saturday except steak and kidney pie and banned her from getting a job as a school dinner lady, kept her short of money and went on endlessly about what he'd fought for in the war. The man who she was compelled to lie to in order to have time to herself in London. For a moment, a heavy, claustrophobic sadness pressed down on her. To think, all it had taken for Arthur's disposition to change completely was two little ones in the house. But perhaps it wasn't so strange after all, because why should it be any different for him than it was for her?

Arthur's smile, when he looked at her, was bittersweet and she returned it with quivering lips.

'Now,' she said, setting Tracey back on her feet. 'I don't have fish fingers, but I do have this.' She rummaged to the back of the pots and pans and came out holding a jar of Nutella that she'd squirrelled away.

Arthur looked perplexed and the children's eyes widened. 'Yes, please,' they said.

'You're both so polite. I shall make sure Mummy and Daddy know what good children you are. On toast?'

'Please,' they chorused again.

Remembering how stubborn he'd been about trying a cherry tomato, she turned to Arthur, held up the chocolatey spread and half-jokingly said, 'Same for you? Or are you sticking to your usual?'

'I'm not sure what that is, but I'll give it a go with you two,' he addressed the children. 'Please, my Treasure.'

Connie was so astounded she thought she might keel over and never get up.

Tentatively, Arthur reached for Simon and Tracey's hands, which they placed without hesitating in his. 'Would you like to see the garden?' he asked. 'I could do with two helpers just like you to show me how to water the plants.'

Connie was too wise and resigned and jaded to think the bubble they were living in for a few hours wouldn't burst when the children went home. But she'd remind Arthur of how readily he'd agreed to try something different for the children when she next tried to make a change to their weekly menu.

Whilst she waited to turn the toast under the grill, she watched Arthur and the children through cloudy eyes and knew that was not the only thing about the afternoon she would hold close.

When Millie came for the children, apologising profusely that they'd treated Janet and Adrian to a Wimpy burger after the parents' evening, Connie and Arthur were both reluctant to let them go. The stunned look on Millie's face betrayed her surprise when Arthur appeared, his hands on the little ones' shoulders. They waved them down the path and when they shut the door, the quiet shouted at them.

With a bit of trepidation that the cosy, amiable atmosphere they'd been living in might burst, Connie made them a cup of tea, and they resorted to the living room where they didn't sit in silence for long. One or other of them would recall something endearing Simon had said or the way Tracey skipped or how much the children had enjoyed their Nutella on toast and they would turn to each other and smile, chuckling softly.

Connie went upstairs first, taking advantage of Arthur's good humour by daring to leave the dishes until the morning. A few minutes later, Arthur followed and when they were under the covers he turned to her, slid his arm underneath her shoulders and held her to his chest until they both fell asleep.

The following morning, Connie started on Arthur's breakfast feeling lighter and brighter than she had since the first time Richard had restyled her hair. When Arthur came down, he smelled of coal tar soap and she could see that he'd had a particularly close shave. 'Here, my Treasure,' he said, picking up the glasses Simon and Tracey had used. 'I'll pop these away.'

Connie felt as if she might be going into shock, but she didn't want to overreact and give the impression that anything out of the ordinary was happening. 'Thank you, Arthur,' she said.

She put on the kettle, measured out oats for porridge, warmed the pot, put three teaspoons of tea into it, fetched the butter and jam, set the table. Rustling and fussing seemed to be going on for ages from the living room. 'Alright, Arthur?' she called. She smiled to herself when she thought he might need help putting the glasses back from where he'd found them yesterday.

Then he appeared in the doorway and she knew the fragile orb they'd been cocooned in had splintered. In one hand he held out the mangled frame and in the other, the bent, torn photo. The features on his face had hardened once again, the heavy brows straining towards each other and his jowls were dragged down by pettiness, pomposity and an unjustified sense of betrayal.

'Oh,' Connie tried to sound flippant. 'I was going to mention that little accident to you, but then …'

He shook his head. 'You had plenty of time to tell me all about it before those two young visitors were foisted on us.'

'Arthur,' she said. 'It's nothing.'

'Nothing?'

Clearly, that was the wrong thing to say. 'Give them to me,' she tried again. 'I'll get it sorted out.' She reached for the crushed bits in Arthur's fists.

Instead of handing them over, he made a show of opening the bin and dropping them on top of the other rubbish.

'That's all they're good for now,' he said. Then he rounded on her. 'When were you going to tell me that our precious photo had been broken? Never is most probably the answer. How could you deceive me like this?'

Arthur's face was scarlet as he found his cycle helmet and fought to clip the strap under his chin. Connie wouldn't have been able to swear to it, but she felt certain she saw a film of tears cover his eyes and she thought, with pity and regret, that he must have been enjoying the bubble they'd been floating in and blamed her for bursting it.

'Wait. Your breakfast,' she said. This must be serious if Arthur wasn't sticking to his schedule. 'Let's sit down and I can tell you exactly what happened to the photo and what I plan to do about it.'

But he wouldn't be persuaded. 'I'm very hurt, Connie,' he said, his voice cracking. 'About the damage to our wedding photo and your attitude towards the whole debacle.'

Hand on her chest, Connie stood and watched him storm out, then she opened the bin and peered inside. The photo and frame were more mangled than they'd been after their first mishap and she wondered if fate was trying to tell her something about the state of her marriage. Slamming the lid closed, she decided to leave them to rot on top of old tea leaves and torn circulars and a crust of bread smeared with Nutella.

As usual, the dinner she'd processed so many times previously seemed to prepare itself. Whilst she pared carrots and podded peas and peeled potatoes, she had time to mull over how the few precious hours with Simon and Tracey had lifted both her and Arthur's moods, and how quickly Arthur had fallen back into his miserable, begrudging, trivial ways. A couple of warm, sticky tears rolled down her face and fell onto the vegetables, but all she did was shrug – the salt would liven them up.

Then the sound of the doorbell pierced her thoughts. She couldn't believe it. The hours and days and months she'd spent alone in the house with no one to talk to and now it was everything at once.

Millicent greeted her with a huge grin, Adrian clutching her hem with one hand and holding a tiny fire engine with the other. 'Morning, Connie,' Millicent said.

Adrian held up his bright red toy and shouted, 'Fire!'

Laughing, Connie put her hands up to her mouth and feigned shock and surprise. '*Nee naw, nee naw,*' she sang.

Millicent and Adrian looked at each other and laughed. 'I come with good news,' Millicent said. 'It's a boy. Benjamin William. Seven pounds four and a half ounces. Mother and baby doing fine.'

'Oh, wonderful,' Connie said. 'Thank you for telling me.'

'Well, it was good of you to step in. Trev was so appreciative. I'm sure he'll tell you so himself.'

'It was nothing,' Connie said. 'The children were delightful. We loved having them.'

Millicent's forehead crumpled under her swaying fringe. 'The children told us they'd helped Arthur water the plants.'

'Yes,' Connie said, feeling nostalgic for that lovely, uplifting afternoon. 'That's right.'

Disbelief crossed Millicent's face, but Connie held her gaze. Then she gathered herself together and said, 'Adie told his dad he'd love to help Arthur in your garden. Didn't you, Adie?'

Adrian nodded and pointed past Connie to the patio doors that led to the back of the house.

'Would you, Adie? I'll certainly mention that to Arthur. When will Shirley be home?' Connie asked.

'Not for a few days,' Millicent answered, then she lowered her voice and continued. 'There were a few complications. So it might be the best part of a week.'

'Poor Shirley.' Connie grimaced as though she knew all about childbirth complications. 'I just have to sew the buttons on a matinee jacket I knitted for the baby so it should be ready in good time.'

They said their goodbyes, Millicent and Adrian looking a bit disappointed not to be invited in, but their announcement about Benjamin had given Connie an idea.

Arthur's dinner hour was a dismal affair. He hadn't greeted her with his customary, 'Hello, you,' so there was no need to reply with a 'Yoo-hoo.' She kept her back to him as she dished up, steeling herself to hear him chase the aroma of shepherd's pie around the kitchen, then comment on how he knew the day of the week by what they were having for dinner. But no such nonsense was forthcoming today. So what if Arthur didn't pass a remark along those lines, she was well aware which day was which by the meals she cooked so there was no need to get the news from him.

The only sound in the dining room was that of cutlery on crockery. The meal was good, the meat tender and the potatoes particularly light and fluffy, but Arthur didn't offer compliments or criticism. When he finished, he stared straight past Connie into the garden and she turned, wondering what had captured his attention, but all she could see were shreds of steam dancing from the towers and the paper-thin petals on the clematis bobbing from side to side in the breeze. Turning back, she wondered if he was thinking of how happy they'd been yesterday – him in the garden with the children and her preparing Nutella on toast in the kitchen. She thought about reminding him of those few happy hours, but didn't think now was the best time.

Continuing to give her the cold shoulder, Arthur donned his leather helmet and as he bent down to pop on his cycle clips, she seized her chance.

'I mightn't be here when you get home this evening, Arthur,' she stated as matter-of-factly as possible.

Arthur seemed so shaken he had to steady himself on the worktop as he stood up. Without giving him a chance to question her, Connie continued. 'Shirley had a baby boy. Benjamin. Isn't that fantastic?'

She waited for him to respond and when he didn't, she carried on. 'She's going to be in the Royal Infirmary for the best part of a week, so I'm going to visit her there and give her the little gift I've knitted.' She forced a smile in his direction. 'I'll leave your tea under a cloth in case I'm not back in time.' Then she turned towards the sink in what she knew was an act of defiant dismissal.

Behind her, Connie sensed his eyes boring holes in her back with such intensity she thought she'd been struck by an incendiary, but she stood her ground until she heard him leave by the front door.

Of course she had no intention of visiting Shirley. She wasn't a close relative so they wouldn't let her in even if she did show up, but Arthur had no way of knowing that and he wouldn't make any attempt to find out. She set out his tea, covered the food with a cloth and left the plate somewhere prominent where even he couldn't fail to see it. Next, she sewed a row of impossibly tiny pearl buttons on the yellow cardigan, wrapped it in tissue paper and signed and attached a card with a sweet little teddy bear embossed on the front. The nurses would hand the package to Shirley and then she could have a blissful hour or two to herself in Doncaster.

She dropped off the gift, browsed through the sale at Owen Owen, joined the library and borrowed *The Gabriel Hounds* by Mary Stewart – which she determined to read every day with her feet up whilst Arthur was out at work – and sat quietly at the back of the Minster wondering why she hadn't done this before. But the only way to ensure it happened again was to either lie or manipulate days out for herself.

Letting herself into the house a few hours later, she spied Arthur through the patio doors. He was hunched over as he watered the garden, his tea still under wraps.

'I'm back, Arthur,' she called out.

Without turning to acknowledge her, all he said was, 'I've put the kettle on.'

22

The Jennies' next port of call was Plymouth where the wind whipped across the sea and they had to make sure their tricornes were firmly on their heads yet again.

'Even though we've been told we'll never go to sea, here we are getting battered by salt spray all the same,' Ivy said, trying to pull a comb through her matted waves.

Connie laughed. 'Now we know why we're not allowed hair below our collars,' she said. 'It would be completely unmanageable.'

There wouldn't be any shore leave whilst they were on active duty – they'd have to wait for that – so they'd formed quite a little band amongst themselves and that suited Connie.

'Oh dear, excuse me,' June said, yawning behind her hand. 'Who would have thought reading letters all day could be so tiring? I'd better go and wash my stockings before I fall asleep.'

'Give yourself a night off,' Viv said. She pulled out a chair and put up her feet. 'Let's have a game of cards instead.'

'We played cards yesterday,' Edie moaned.

'I'm going to wash my hair,' Ivy said, closing the door of the bathroom behind her. 'So start without me.'

June, who was softly spoken and very polite, sat with her hands folded in her lap. 'I had a heart wrenching one today,' she said.

'I hate those,' Edie said. 'They stick with you for such a long time, don't they?'

June nodded. 'I can't sleep for thinking about some of the people involved in my letters and the worst bit is getting just a tiny glimpse of a situation. The writer and addressee know the background being referred to, but we don't. We're just left in limbo after reading about a slice of someone else's life.'

'And it can be something simple,' Edie said, twisting her interlocked fingers. 'Like someone writing that they couldn't find their beloved's watch when they had to leave their flat because of a burst gas main, even though they swore they'd put it in their bag.'

'I know,' Connie said. 'That sort of thing upsets me, too. I had one in which a mother described how her little girl had tripped over what was left of their front path, skinning her knee and tearing her new dress. She described how brave the child had been and how she'd spent ages mending the hem. There was no complaining or grumbling and in fact, she made light of the whole episode, but I don't know. It gave me a lump in my throat.'

'Then it's on to the next one,' June said. '*Scritch scratch* and *snip snip*.'

'Are you in, Connie?' Viv asked, a deck of cards in her hand.

Connie nodded. 'Of course they can be sad, but the letters are endlessly fascinating, too, don't you think?' Connie looked from one to the other of her fellow Wrens, waiting for their affirmation, but none of them passed a comment.

Halfway through the post sacks the following day, Connie opened just such a letter and it made her catch her breath.

Dear Ted

Thank you for your letter, it's always wonderful to hear that you're fit and well and doing such a marvellous job for the Allies.

As I mentioned when last I wrote, Dad is quite well again now and I'm able at last to think about getting back to my job in the telephone exchange next to St Paul's.

Snip snip, Connie cut that bit and watched as the strand of paper curled into a bin.

Now, I know you've said all along that you don't like me working in London and I got the distinct impression you were quite happy when Dad took ill and I had to come home. But dearest, I enjoy my work and it's helping the war effort, so despite what you say, I shall be going back to take up my post. We're not married yet, so I didn't think I needed your permission to carry on with my work and I always thought that, married or not, you would allow me to do anything that was reasonable and well thought out, so I must admit your turn of phrase rather took me aback.

I'm going to put this hiccup between us down to how difficult it is to make oneself perfectly clear in letters – nothing is better than sitting down together and talking through a situation or sorting out a problem. How I miss doing that with you!

Oh, my darling, let's not quarrel. If we do, then Hitler and the Nazis will have won and we cannot let that happen.

Please write back to me quickly as I long for your letters. Here is my address in London in case you've misplaced it.

Your ever-loving fiancée

Beryl

Connie read the letter again and took in the names and addresses. She was astounded as Beryl Smythe could so easily have been her – and Ted, Arthur.

Laying the pages on the table in front of her, Connie stared at the peeling wallpaper in the small room above the post office that had been turned into a censoring room for a couple of days. If the curtains had been open, there would have been a much better view of the coastal landscape than that depicted in the four small pictures that hung on the wall. From a distance, the sound of heavy objects being loaded and unloaded from ships reached them along with the thin whistle of the wind finding gaps in the brickwork.

Perhaps she should have been more like Beryl Smythe and told Arthur, rather than asked him, that she was going to take up the posting in Bermuda. In the same way Beryl had proposed that there was something lost in having to constantly communicate in writing, Connie felt sure that Arthur's motivations were care and concern, although his wording sometimes came across the wrong way.

Would she have been any happier in Bermuda, she wondered. That was a question she could never answer, but she was as happy as she could be in the current circumstances. She liked each of her fellow Jennies; she travelled to a different destination every three days; she loved the work and reading about others' lives and felt confident that she knew what she was doing and made a good job of it.

'Petty Officer Wren Censor Allinson,' the Chief Wren said. 'Is there a problem? Perhaps the light is bothering your eyes again. I think you prefer to work in a bit of a shadow.'

'Mam,' Connie answered. She moved the light so it didn't shine directly in her eyes when she looked up. Then she checked around the stamp and in the envelope and smoothed an examiner's label with her number on it over the tear.

June caught her eye and lifted one of her brows in accord with Connie for reading another letter like the ones they'd referred to the night before. *Scritch scratch*, Connie thought as she reached for another envelope from her stack. *Snip snip.*

Next stop – Portsmouth. As the train approached the terminal, it slowed down until it came to a halt in a queue outside the station. The Chief Wren looked at her watch and June crossed her legs as she'd thought she'd be able to hold off using the facilities until they'd disembarked.

Peering out of the window, the Jennies saw that every line converging on the station was packed with a bottleneck of waiting trains. The tracks swarmed with railway workers and servicemen going in and out of the inner vaults of the station, but it was difficult to make out exactly what they were doing – shifting things about by the looks of it. Half an hour passed and cases that had been taken down from luggage racks were put back and books that had been stored in handbags were reopened.

'We'll be very late at this rate,' the Chief Wren said. 'I'm going to try to find out what's going on.'

'Mam,' they chorused.

'And I'll do my best to get permission for you to use the lav,' the Chief Wren whispered to June. 'Even though we are so close to the station.'

'Thank you, Mam.' June gave her superior a weak smile.

A train a few tracks over shunted backwards into a siding, followed by another then another and when the track was clear a freight train glided under the cover of the station. Masses of troops stepped down from the three sidelined trains and were led through the crisscross of tracks to where they, too, were swallowed up by the terminal building.

'I wonder if that's the only way we'll get off this train?' Edie asked.

'I don't doubt it,' Connie said. 'Something very important must be going on.'

Ivy nodded. 'Yes,' she lowered her voice. 'Closing off the coast, mass movement of troops, tons of equipment. Must all be connected.' She leaned closer to Connie and whispered, 'Perhaps they've caught wind that the Jerries are about to invade.'

Connie's stomach flipped and a chill ran up her spine. 'Or maybe,' she said. 'We're about to occupy Europe.'

Ivy's eyes widened. 'Then it would be almost over,' she said optimistically.

'Well, I suppose if either of those things happened it would soon be over.'

'I've been told we should be on the move soon,' the Chief Wren said, closing the compartment door behind her. 'June, permission granted. Anyone else? We're going to have to walk the rest of the way so we won't be near the station facilities any time soon.'

June made a bolt for the door followed by Edie.

'Mam,' Connie ventured. 'Can we know why we're being held up?'

The Chief Wren shook her head and laced her fingers together on her lap. 'No,' she said. 'I have no idea myself.'

It was getting dark when they stepped off the train into the middle of the tracks. Gusts of sea air found them even there and sea gulls squawked and swooped toward their heads. They had to stand and wait until all passengers were off the train and then follow a railway worker with a lamp that flickered across the rough ground to where they were hauled up one by one onto the platform lit by candles.

None of the Jennies turned a hair – their training wouldn't allow them to and, in Connie's opinion, it was more of an adventure than a dangerous activity. The only calamity could have been a nip from a gull, a twisted ankle or being caught very short. Even so, she wouldn't write to Arthur about it when she was allowed to send a letter. He would use the story as evidence that she really wasn't safe as a mobile censor and insist that she ask for a transfer to London. If that did happen, for whatever reason, she determined to defend herself as Beryl Smythe had done.

Again they were told by the Chief Wren not to speak about anything in public and again they followed her in twos like an order of nuns who had taken a vow of silence. Although the city was teeming with servicemen and women travelling between what must have been their various bases and quarters, the blackout was so Stygian that it was a matter of groping forward with their nerves and keeping their eyes on the very low beam of the Chief Wren's torch.

They were let into Victoria Barracks and shown directly to their quarters. Kicking off their shoes, filling the kettle, claiming their bunks and taking turns in the bathroom took a good quarter of an hour. 'Do you think we'll get anything to eat?' Connie asked.

'Never mind that,' Ivy answered. 'I'd give anything for a gin.'

The Wrens breathed out a murmur of consensus.

The Chief Wren knocked once on the door and the Jennies stood to attention. 'Sit, sit,' the Chief Wren said. 'As you were.'

They sat in various states of undress, nursing cups of tea and waiting for any news the Chief Wren might have.

'I don't know any details, but our services are not required here in Portsmouth at this particular time.'

Eyebrows imperceptibly shot up and Connie shared a knowing look with Ivy.

'Do we leave right away, Mam?' June asked.

'We leave by train at four hundred hours. So we'll have time for a quick meal and a few hours' sleep before we head back to the station. The trains will be running relatively smoothly again by then, so I've been told, but if not we'll just have to wait until we're given orders.'

'Mam,' the Wrens said.

'I'll come back in five minutes when you must be ready to follow me to the galley.'

'Mam,' echoed around the walls again.

'Where are we off to next?' Edie asked. 'Are we allowed to know?'

'Dartmouth,' the Chief Wren answered. 'Although that order could well be overridden.'

It wasn't, and on the fifth of June their train pulled into Dartmouth station, which was adjacent to the harbour. If Connie was in any doubt that there was something very grave and crucial happening, the overwhelmingly giddy sight of hundreds upon hundreds of vessels in the River Dart would have promptly changed her mind. The awe-inspiring spectacle almost caused her to gasp out loud, but she quietened herself and acted as though the dazzling display was nothing out of the ordinary.

The following morning, when the van that was driving the Jennies from one red pillar box to another passed the same vantage point from where they'd seen the anchored fleet, not a single ship or boat or battle cruiser or escort carrier was left. Connie gawped at the empty expanse and gentle waves lapping against the shore and wondered if she'd imagined yesterday's scene. But her fellow Wrens were staring, too, and they turned to each other with furrowed brows to confirm that what they'd experienced had been real. Had all of those solid, capable, durable vessels been captured by the Nazis overnight? That couldn't possibly have happened because none of them had heard a thing and, if that had been the case, Connie was sure they wouldn't be going about their censoring duties as if nothing on such an enormous scale had occurred.

At quarter to ten, the Chief Wren turned and addressed them. 'Petty Wren Officer Censors,' she said. 'An announcement is going to be aired by the BBC at ten o'clock, so we'll make our way to the post office where we can listen to the broadcast.'

'Mam,' they answered as one.

Ivy jabbed Connie gently in the ribs and when Connie turned to her, the younger girl's eyes flashed with a moment of anxiety. Reaching between the folds of their uniform jackets, Connie found Ivy's fingers and held onto them until they stepped out of the van.

They sat ensconced in the postmaster and postmistress's front room, cups of tea in their hands and a dry Madeira cake on the table waiting to be cut, whilst the postmaster twiddled the dials on the wireless until they heard the voice of the BBC Home Service presenter, John Snagge. 'D-Day has come,' he said. 'Early this morning the Allies began the assault on the north-western face of Hitler's European fortress. Under the command of General Eisenhower, Allied naval forces, supported by strong air forces, began landing Allied armies this morning on the northern coast of France.'

Decorum went out the window as Connie gasped and Ivy clung to her arm. From next door came the faint sounds of clapping and hurrahs. The Chief Wren beamed and said, 'Permission to cheer, Petty Wren Officer Censors.' They did more than that. They raised their voices and whooped and hugged each other and sang a chorus or two of 'Berlin or Bust'. The postmistress cut the cake, the postmaster danced around the table with the Chief Wren, and the dog, who'd been lying on a torn blanket in the corner of the room, ran around in circles.

After ten minutes, the Chief Wren put a stop to the shenanigans by calling them to order. 'Thank you for your hospitality, Mr and Mrs Dankworth, but now you must leave us to set about our work.'

The postmaster and his wife looked disappointed as they left the front room, but Connie heard them turn to each other when they were outside the door and talk in excited voices about it nearly being over. That's what Connie thought, too, although it hardly seemed possible.

The Chief Wren told them there was no need to censor any letters that mentioned the phenomenon of that day, or the lead-up to it, as the facts had been announced to the world by the BBC. 'However, if in any doubt please refer to me.'

That day and the next, Connie sat under a bubble of muted excitement and took great joy in reading letter after letter that let a friend or loved one know that a resident of Dartmouth had watched whilst the fleet on the river grew exponentially and then disappeared overnight. The writers' reactions ranged from amazed to frightened, curious to sceptical. Most of them had an opinion about what was going on, some of them widely speculative, others closer to the actual outcome. But now they all knew and the news was wonderful.

Almost immediately afterwards, the mobile censoring unit was disbanded. Edie and Viv were posted to Liverpool,

Ivy and June to Manchester, and after saying goodbye to her fellow Jennies, Connie boarded a train bound for London and ultimately, HMS Holborn again. She would miss them and the camaraderie they'd built amongst themselves in the strangest of circumstances. But at least Arthur would be appeased.

23

August 1967

The atmosphere between Connie and Arthur remained sour for some time until Arthur broke the ice by saying, 'I hope you haven't forgotten that it's your turn to wash the whites after tomorrow's match.'

Her turn – the remark made her seethe. Connie bit down so hard on her metaphorical tongue she was surprised she didn't taste blood.

'*You* must have forgotten that I won't be at tomorrow's match,' she said. 'I'll be having my hair done for London.'

'No matter,' Arthur retorted. 'Someone will drop off the laundry. But,' he stood in the kitchen, one cycle clip around his trousers, the other in his hand and a forlorn, lost look on his face, 'you'll miss the last away match of the season. All the rest will be at home.' He held his arms out to her as if he thought she might cry.

'Careful, Arthur,' she said, dodging his embrace. 'These plates are hot.'

'I'm sorry, Treasure,' he said. 'Perhaps I'll get in touch with Ken and postpone your trip to London for a week.'

'No!' Connie shouted so loudly that Arthur took a step back.

'Come to think of it,' Arthur said. 'I haven't heard a thing from Ken. Are you sure everything's alright for your visit?'

'Yes, Arthur,' she tried to calm her voice. 'There's no need for them to be in touch with you as it went so smoothly last time. I've had the usual letters from Dora and she says they're looking forward to seeing me. We don't want to rearrange what's working so well, do we?'

Arthur looked disbelieving for a fraction of a moment. Then he bent and released the cycle clip still clinging to his leg. 'No, Treasure, we don't,' he said slowly and deliberately.

When Connie arrived home from *New You for a Snip*, she found Arthur dragging the whites into the hallway.

'Here, let me give you a hand with those.' A smiling Trev appeared, Simon and Tracey jiggling around next to him. 'Taking in laundry now, Connie? Our house is crammed full of it so we might be able to send some your way.'

Connie laughed. 'Congratulations, Trev,' she said, giving him a hug. 'We're delighted for you, aren't we, Arthur?'

Arthur looked less than ecstatic but managed something that could have passed as civil.

The children broke away from their father's grip and flung their arms around Connie's legs. 'Hello, Simon and hello Tracey,' she said. 'How lovely that you have a baby brother. Remind me of his name. Is it Ben …?'

'Jamin,' they chorused.

'Shirl's home now, earlier than expected,' Trev said. 'We probably won't organise the christening until the spring, so a few neighbours are popping in a bit later to wet the baby's head. Please join us,' he said. 'Around six?'

'That will be lovely,' Connie said. 'Thank you very much.'

'See you then,' Trev said, turning to wave from the path.

Arthur pulled the bags of whites to the utility room and clapped the dust off his hands. 'We won't be going to the party, or whatever it is, this afternoon, or to the christening in the spring for that matter.'

Connie could not believe her ears. 'Arthur,' she protested. 'I've spent long days at *your* cricket matches, I will spend most of tomorrow laundering *your* team's whites, so I will be going to both occasions and you,' she turned her back on him and began to empty the first of the bags, 'can suit yourself.'

Arthur grunted, picked up his paper and walked into the living room to wait for his supper. Then he called out, 'If you need more time to wash, dry, iron, fold and repack the kit, I can always get in touch with Ken and tell him you're too busy to go to London.'

Angry tears spilled down Connie's cheeks, not for her London trip as she knew she'd have the laundry done on time, and not for having to make an excuse for Arthur's absence later, but for allowing herself to put up with him for well over half her life. She stopped for a moment and thought about what could have possessed her to waste so much of her precious time when Arthur made her more and more unhappy. The usual answers she gave herself about not having any of her own money or family to harbour her or Arthur not being able to help his behaviour in his clumsy attempts to keep her safe now seemed a bit lame. But more to the point was whether she was prepared to stay with him from now until death do us part, and she knew she couldn't shy away from answering that question for much longer.

She clenched her fists so tightly around a pair of grimy, grass-stained trousers that her fingernails dug into her palms. Opening her hands, she held up the grubby whites and studied them from every angle; they really were filthy. Hunting through the bags until she found another particularly dirty pair, she decided to refold them both and tuck them, unwashed, amongst the others after they'd been through the washing machine. Denise or Catherine or hopefully, Elspeth, could take care of those.

Shirley was pale and reminded Connie of the clematis petals when they trembled in the slightest breath of wind. 'Mum, Dad,' Shirley said. 'This is Connie from next door. Remember I told you she stepped in to look after Simon and Tracey?'

The children had each claimed one of their grandfather's knees and were messing lovingly with his spectacles, his receding hairline, his watch and his shirt buttons. 'Pleased to meet you, Connie,' the older man said.

Shirley's mother, wearing house slippers and Shirley's apron, was handing round plates of sandwiches and cakes.

'Pleased to meet you, too,' Connie said, the twist of a knife stabbing her ribs. Now it wasn't only young people having child after child that made her envious, it was their parents, too, as they laid claim to their adult children's territory and their grandchildren's time and attention.

She knew it would do her no good to let envy get the

better of her so when Shirley asked if she'd like to hold Benjamin, she settled herself in a chair and put out her arms. Gazing down at him, she admired the dark hair sticking up in clumps, the pimpled cheeks and flat nose that made him look as if he'd gone ten rounds in a boxing ring. 'He's beautiful,' she whispered. At that moment the little fellow stretched his tiny hands out of his blue blanket and Connie was delighted to see he was wearing the lemon jacket she'd knitted. He pursed his lips and moved his head from side to side. 'Absolutely perfect,' she said.

'Let me know if he gets too much for you, Connie,' Trev said.

'Yes,' Millicent called across the room. 'There's plenty of others here who would like a cuddle.'

'That's why we've asked all of you round,' Trev said. 'To give us a bit of a rest.'

'Where's Arthur?' Brian said.

'I would have liked to meet him,' Shirley's father said. 'The children couldn't stop talking about how much fun they had with him in your garden. Made me quite jealous.'

'Oh.' Connie played for time whilst she thought of an excuse for her husband. 'He's busy today. You know, he works hard all week so only has the weekend for … chores and … catching up.'

No remark was passed about that and Connie knew the others must have been thinking Arthur quite mad as he had no call on his time other than her and his work.

'Shame,' Trev said. 'But I don't know what I would have done without you that day, Connie.' He combed his hands through his beard. 'I'm very grateful.'

Connie looked up from admiring the baby and smiled.

Shirley's mother sat next to Connie for a few minutes and they chatted about the children, gardening, knitting and if Connie enjoyed living on the estate. 'It's certainly a different way of life,' she said.

'Very different. But moving here was the only way Trev could get on. They used to live a few minutes' walk away from us in Surrey, now it takes hours to get to them. We considered joining them here, but they'll no doubt have to move again at some point and then what would we do?' She lowered her voice. 'I do think she gets quite lonely. Thank goodness for you and Millie and the other girls.'

'We lived with my mum until she died.' A lump massed in Connie's throat. 'Then we came here for a better job for Arthur so I know what you mean. We're all in the same boat.'

'And those things,' Shirley's mother said. 'Trevor assures me they're benign, but who knows what all that steam and smoke is doing to the children.'

They focused on the inscrutable towers and a shudder passed through both of them. Connie wondered, not for the first time, what made them so threatening – their height or their girth; the way they appeared to float because of the supporting stilts they rested on; the way they seemed both solid and ethereal at the same time; the shadows they cast or the way in which they seemed to have taken on deeply disturbing human qualities despite being obviously inanimate.

Benjamin started to snuffle and he was whisked from Connie's arms to be taken upstairs and given his feed. Shirley's mother followed behind her daughter and the baby with changing paraphernalia and two cups of tea in her hands. No doubt she would sit on the bed whilst Shirley put her feet up and fed Benjamin and they would talk about the birth, Trevor's job, Simon and Tracey, what had been said that afternoon and what on earth Arthur had to do that couldn't wait.

No matter how many times Connie rolled her eyes or asked Arthur not to fuss, he carried out the same rigmarole on Monday morning that he'd gone through on her first trip to London. He chaperoned her to the station, found her seat, stowed her case, warned her about not leaving her possessions unattended. When he bent towards her, she turned her head abruptly so the peck he planted on the side of her head couldn't develop into a lingering kiss. Then, much to her surprise, he didn't shuffle around outside the carriage window but turned his back and walked away before the train departed. That didn't bother Connie one bit and if anything, it saved her the cringing embarrassment she'd felt last time when he'd waved until the train was out of sight.

Exhausted, she settled into her seat, and began to make a mental list of what she hoped to do in London. Kick her shoes off and pad around Ken and Dora's house without dinner to prepare or shopping to fetch or ornaments to dust. A wander around the shops; lunch at Peter Robinson's; high tea in a Corner House; a museum. And Somerset House. She was so looking forward to finding out about Jim Stanton, George, Peter Carstairs and Beryl Smythe and following up her research with visits like the one she'd had with Maude Grimshaw. She often thought of her and

Mikey with fondness and felt as if she'd reclaimed an old friendship.

Wandering out of the station, she passed a tiny café on Euston Road that looked as though it had survived the worst of the war but hadn't seen a lick of paint since. Through the window, she could see a row of chipped teapots hanging from nails on the wall and carousels of condiments, serviettes, cutlery, sugar bowls and milk jugs waiting on each oilskin-covered table. A group of women pushed open the door and the smell of cooking fat, burned cheese and warm milk wafted out to meet her.

Despite all of that, the place was comforting. She was reminded of a café she and Arthur had frequented when they'd both been on leave. Where had it been? Probably closer to Acton than the centre of London as that had been their stamping ground.

On one occasion, they'd sat close to each other at a table tucked in the corner, nursing a cup of tea and some sort of cobbled-together carrot slice. Their heads were almost touching in a display of intimacy and, she could hardly believe it now, they were laughing. Closing her eyes for a second, she tried to conjure up what had made them so happy. Perhaps it was the first time they'd seen each other in months so it felt as if they were on a second honeymoon. Or maybe they'd been told that the fortunes of war were turning in the Allies' favour. Delving deeper into the past, she remembered a witty remark or funny observation that Arthur had come out with, and her reaction had made him look as if he'd single-handedly won the war. That was the first time, she recalled with a jolt, that he'd used that awful phrase she'd come to despise, but then it had been said in an entirely different manner to an entirely different end. He'd watched her throw back her head and laugh out loud, and as he'd draped his arm across her shoulders, he'd nuzzled close to her ear and muttered, 'That's the reason I'm fighting this war.'

A film of tears passed over her eyes. How strange, that during those terrible years they'd somehow managed to find the capacity for light-heartedness and now – when on the surface at least they had every reason to be carefree – laughter and fun and contentment eluded them. It was as if they were ground down by each other in a way that bombs and blackouts and rations had never been able to achieve.

Silence and stale air greeted Connie when she let herself into Ken and Dora's house. She shut the door behind her, leaned against it, closed her eyes and took a deep breath. The exhilaration of unwarranted freedom and independence made her feel giddy. A bottle of gin was on the breakfast bar, a note propped against it.

Dear Connie, Cheers! There's a bit of food in the cupboards and fridge, which you're welcome to. There are clean sheets on Victor's bed and fresh towels in the bathroom. Watch the telly, put up your feet, make yourself at home. Love from Dora and Ken. X

Connie was so grateful she thought she would weep. She made a cup of tea, took her case upstairs and had a shower, read a chapter of *The Gabriel Hounds*, had a close look at the telephone and television set without touching any of the dials or buttons and decided she was hungry and would spend some of her money from Ken on tea in a restaurant.

It was a warm, humid afternoon, with dust and dried leaves swirling in small vortexes along the pavement in front of her. Connie was pleased she'd forfeited her navy mac for a light grey jacket and as there was no need to cover her hair with the lovely, silky scarf, she tied the piece of material around the handles of her bag, as she'd seen younger women do. Carried along with the crowds she could almost convince herself that she was bustling her way to an important job in a school or a hospital or a housing department. Any of those would be exciting. But at her age, without any experience or training, they would be out of reach.

Trees in a small square were heavy with blossom and their scent was pungent and heady. A group of girls in patterned skirts and dresses, their slim, brown legs crossed at the ankles, were sharing a picnic lunch on the grass. Connie smiled at them, imagining they'd raced from their office block to enjoy the sunshine during their lunch hour. She and Norma and Dotty and Josie would have done the same, if they'd been allowed, but even supposing it had been safe, it would have gone against WRNS regulations to sprawl across the ground during their breaks.

A couple of hours ago, she'd felt a rush of liberation as the restraints of her everyday life were lifted, now when she thought about the number of times she'd had to wait for permission to be granted or had been told that she wouldn't be allowed to indulge in simple things, like sitting on the grass or catching a train on her own or working a few hours a week, she began to feel resentful all over again.

The Corner House was bursting at the seams and Connie was shown to a tiny table for one right at the back where she could watch the comings and goings. The sounds of crockery, cutlery and chatter were distracting and the heady aromas of roast meat, steamed puddings and boiled cabbage drifted along in waves.

But despite all that, she felt discontented. Thoughts of rummaging through the shops tomorrow or wandering around a gallery or sitting by the river with her book, looking up from time to time at the world going past, didn't hold much of an interest for her now. All she could think about was Jim Stanton, Peter Carstairs and Beryl Smythe and as this was her weekend to do as she pleased, research in Somerset House was what she would do.

She made her way back to Ken and Dora's house, watched an instalment of Z-Cars with a gin and tonic for company and crawled between the sheets in Victor's room. Once during the night she turned over, her hand landing on the cold, empty space next to her, and she shot up, frantically looking for Arthur. When she didn't find him next to her, she sighed with a heavy sense of relief and spread herself out to the four corners of the single bed.

24

Hair by Harold and Harriet was fully booked, as was *Colette's Coiffure*, but Connie managed to make an appointment with Betty at *Nouveau Style* in Hammersmith. A fug of perm lotion assaulted her as she pushed open the door, which she then closed firmly behind her so the swirling fog she'd walked through didn't follow her in.

'Hello, Mrs Allinson,' Betty said from behind one of the basins. 'The cold's enough to cut off your legs, isn't it?'

Connie agreed that it was.

'I'll be with you in two ticks,' the hairdresser said.

Connie sat on a hard chair and unbuttoned her coat so she was ready to spring into action when it was her turn. The salon was small with three chairs, three sinks, combs, brushes, hair clips, shampoo, scissors and handheld mirrors laid out on the shelves, and blue towels draped rather chaotically on hooks.

'Right, Mrs Allinson,' Betty approached Connie. 'Let me take your coat and you can settle into this station here. 'It was a perm today, wasn't it?'

'Yes, please,' Connie said. 'I'd like a trim, too, so it lies just above my collar.'

'Righto,' Betty said, snapping a towel over Connie's shoulders. 'It's nothing but perms at the moment.'

'They're so easy,' Connie said. 'And last quite a while. But I was surprised that all the places I tried closer to where I live are completely booked up for weeks.'

Betty poured powder and two or three different creams into a bowl and started to stir them with a brush. 'Demob crazy, that's what it is. Everyone wants to look like a glamorous film star when their husband or fiancé or boyfriend comes home. As if we've had nothing else to think about.'

Connie laughed. 'I'll have to be upfront with you,' she said, pointing to her hair. 'That's what this is for, too.'

'Well, I don't begrudge you one bit. I just hope the blokes appreciate it. If my two boys were coming home I would have had a perm, so would my daughter-in-law.' She nodded towards a younger woman leaning over a customer's head.

'I'm so sorry,' Connie said, unable to comprehend how Betty managed to keep going about her daily business. The woman deserved a medal as far as she was concerned.

'They both took a packet early on.' She shrugged. 'I'm not the only one by a long shot. When's yours due home?'

'At the beginning of next week, when he's been through disembarkation and dispersal.'

'In that case you'll be able to let your perm settle for a few days without washing it. Were you in the Services?'

Connie looked down at the tweed skirt, white blouse and brown cardigan she was finding it difficult to get used to after the uniform she'd loved wearing every day for years. 'I was a Wren,' she said. 'But as you know, married women were given immediate demobilisation priority, so I was stood down almost right away.'

'To get the grate swept and the home fires burning before the men returned.'

Connie thought Betty sounded a bit cynical and hoped she never became as world-weary. But perhaps if she'd lost two sons and all the hopes that went with them, her observations would be just as acerbic.

'Oh, but the Wrens always looked so smart and well-turned out.'

Connie smiled when she remembered that was how she'd felt in her jacket, skirt and tricorne hat.

'And I suppose that's why you want to keep your hair off your shoulders,' Betty said.

'At first I didn't think I'd ever get used to it. Now I can't bear it to be longer.'

'Did you bring a book?' Betty asked. 'You'll have to sit for a good few hours before this is rinsed off and the next lotion applied.'

Connie pulled *I'll Say She Does* out of her bag.

'Oh,' Betty said. 'I've read that. It's very good.'

'I'm enjoying it,' Connie said, finding her place.

'Cup of tea?'

'Yes, please,' Connie said. 'With milk and a few grains of sugar if you can spare them.'

The perm and cut were lovely, and Connie was very pleased when she moved her head around to view the sides and back with the help of two little round mirrors.

When Connie paid, Betty said, without a shadow of envy, 'Have a lovely reunion with your husband, Mrs Allinson, and I hope we see you in *Nouveau Style* again.'

'You will, I'm sure,' Connie said. The walk to Hammersmith was well worth the result and she liked Betty, despite her barbed remarks.

Opening the door, Betty said, 'Look at that weather – it's filthy. Have you a scarf?'

'Yes, I put an old one in my bag before I left.' She shook out the square of navy-blue she'd tucked into the collar of her greatcoat in the WRNS and tied it under her chin.

The morning of Arthur's demob was cold but bright. He'd written that he would be stood down any time after twelve hundred hours and as a surprise, Connie decided to wait for him outside the Dispersal Unit in Regent's Park. Studying her face in the mirror, dark rings and a rather sallow complexion stared back at her. She'd thought the physical activity of cleaning the house from top to bottom, polishing the cutlery and crockery, changing sheets, washing windows, ironing tablecloths, baking, cooking and organising a high tea on rations would mean she'd be exhausted, but sleep had evaded her. She'd turned onto one side then the other, running her hand over the place where Arthur would soon be sleeping every night. They hadn't shared a bed for any real amount of time, other than a couple of nights here and there. Arthur snored sometimes and made grunting, growling noises in his sleep. Would that disturb her night after night? How would they carry on in their day to day lives? They couldn't try to return to how they'd lived together before the war, because they hadn't. Now they had to carve out a way of life from scratch and that life was hard to imagine, but she felt certain there would be a baby soon. They both wanted that. She and Arthur were still young and in a good position to welcome a child into their lives and into this new, better world.

She applied a thin layer of Pan-Cake, a dab of rouge, a swipe or two of mascara, outlined and filled in her lips with dark red lipstick and combed one side of her permed hair behind her ear. Nerves or trepidation, or both, made her hands shake almost imperceptibly when she bent to tie her shoelaces. When she said goodbye to Mum, she felt as if she were leaving to get married to Arthur all over again.

With a thumping heart, Connie walked the last five minutes from Baker Street to the York Gate of Regent's Park where a crowd of women and children, all with the same idea, had gathered. For some reason she'd expected to be alone except for the occasional park wanderer, watching the path for Arthur and breathing the heady, earthy smell of damp decaying autumn leaves. She joined the others, straining on tiptoes to see over their heads and hats towards the stream of released men snaking towards them, smiling in their ill-fitting suits and shirts and carrying civvy kits in bags. The ex-servicemen were being sent out in pairs or individually, or sometimes in what looked like an entire battalion at once, and Connie shielded her eyes against the low, weak November sun, worried that she'd miss Arthur and he'd disappear amongst the crowd. But that wouldn't possibly be the case, she thought. He was too tall and dark and imposing to disperse, like a wisp of smoke, towards the bus stop or the underground.

She watched as all manner of men emerged into the light, to be greeted with a warm embrace or a quick peck or a veil of barely disguised tears. Some had no one waiting for them and marched off, their faces dragged down by disappointment or lightened with relief that they could please themselves for a few hours at least.

'Have you been waiting long?' Connie asked the woman next to her who was trying desperately to keep three small children amused.

'Since yesterday,' the woman said. She swung her young daughter up into her arms.

'Yesterday?' Connie repeated. 'Were you given the wrong date?'

'I'm not sure what happened. But we've come down from Bishop's Stortford so when Les didn't show up we stayed in a B&B.'

'Oh dear,' Connie said. No wonder the poor woman looked distracted.

'But if he's not released today, we'll have to go home and wait for him there. We can't spend another night in a hotel. Well,' she smiled wryly, 'they could, but I couldn't. That would be more than I could endure. How about you, have you travelled far?'

'Acton,' Connie said, feeling guilty that she had it so easy. 'Can I help you with the little ones?'

Tempted, the woman hesitated, torn between the reprieve of sharing her burden and the risk of handing over one of her children to a stranger. She looked at her daughter and then at Connie.

'We could go and collect a few leaves,' Connie said to the tot. 'The colours look like jewels, don't they?'

The child nodded and the mother agreed. Connie held out her arms and the little girl allowed herself to be swapped between them. 'We'll stay right where you can see us,' Connie said.

'Thank you. I'm really most grateful. Boys,' she said. 'Are you watching out for daddy?'

'What's your name?' Connie asked her charge as they gathered handfuls of crimson, yellow and orange leaves and held them by their stalks to form a fan.

'Thuthie,' the little girl lisped.

'I'm Connie. It's lovely to meet you.'

'Connie,' the child repeated, managing to get her tongue around the name quite well.

Connie made a point of waving to the young mum so she'd know all was well and the vigilant mother put her hand up in reply. Then Susie squealed and ran, surprisingly quickly, towards a Jack Russell sniffing around the trunk of another tree and Connie chased after her, but just as she grabbed the child's coat a hand gripped her shoulder and spun her around.

'Treasure,' Arthur said. 'I thought that was you running across the park.'

'Arthur, I can't believe I missed you. But wait, I'm looking after a little girl.' Connie scooped Susie into her arms and as Arthur kissed her, she kidded herself for a split second that they were the family they longed to be. Confusion clouded Arthur's eyes, then they softened and he reached out to touch the little girl's sleeve. 'What a lovely welcome home,' Arthur said.

Connie's heart swelled in her chest and she imagined the same captivated look taking over his face when she could tell him, hopefully in the not-too-distant future, that he was going to be a father.

Then Susie's mother and brothers walked towards them to claim their little girl and, rather reluctantly, Connie handed her over. 'Thank you for giving me a break,' the young mum said.

'I enjoyed it,' Connie said. 'These are for you.' She handed over the bouquet of autumnal leaves. 'I hope your husband shows up soon.'

'Oh, so do I,' The woman sounded exasperated. 'I'm not sure how much longer I can manage this.'

To a chorus of, 'We have to wait for Daddy,' Arthur circled Connie's waist with his arm and they strolled towards the Tube.

'We did it,' Arthur said. 'And I'm glad beyond belief that it's all over.'

'Oh, so am I,' Connie laid her head on Arthur's shoulder for a moment. 'Although I don't suppose we'll be back to normal for ages.'

'No,' Arthur said. 'Not for a long time, and then things won't ever be the same.'

'Perhaps,' Connie said, 'some things will be better than they were before the war.'

'Everything will be better now we're together again,' Arthur said.

'Let's get home,' Connie said. 'You must be exhausted.'

When they alighted at North Acton, Connie told Arthur she had a lovely tea waiting for him. 'And Mum, Ken and Dora will be there to welcome you home, too.'

'Shall we take a walk first?' Arthur said. 'Spend a bit of time just the two of us.'

Connie shivered. It was cold and beginning to get dark and she didn't want the food to spoil. 'Isn't your bag heavy?' She looked down at the cardboard case Arthur was carrying.

He shook his head. 'All that's in it is underclothes, a spare shirt, collar and stud, a raincoat, cigarette rations and a few leads for suitable work in London. Didn't you get the same?'

Connie tipped her head back and laughed. 'Women never get the same, Arthur,' she said. 'But I did receive a small cash sum and extra rations to buy a few bits of civvy clothing.' She looked down at her tweed skirt. 'I've been living in these ever since.'

Arthur smiled his approval and steered her towards Springfield Gardens. When they tugged their collars up around their necks and Arthur drew her close, Connie had to admit she felt euphoric to be out in the crisp Autumn afternoon, warm and safe and optimistic on Arthur's arm.

'Ken and Dora are living with Dora's parents, and we'll have to stay with Mum,' she said.

'I thought as much,' Arthur said. 'All the men coming home to London or Manchester or Liverpool are in the same position. So many houses and flats completely bombed out.'

'We're lucky,' Connie smiled up at him. 'We've got each other and a roof over our heads and Mum's given us two rooms upstairs so we can have some privacy in our own little bedsit, although I wouldn't want to leave her on her own too much. I don't like to think of her being lonely.'

Arthur leaned against a tree, put his arms around her and drew her close. He smelled of regulation soap and new clothes and being in close quarters with other men who'd been waiting to be demobbed. 'When you're expecting a baby, we can look for somewhere else,' he said.

'That might happen quickly, before anything much is available.' She wrapped her arms around his waist.

'In that case, I'm sure we can make the best of things as they are.'

When Arthur kissed her, Connie felt the pulse ticking in his neck and the comforting weight of his chest and shoulders against her. Then an icy rain started and they ran for home.

Arthur allowed himself two days off, then announced he was going out to find a job. He carried himself well in his demob suit, and Connie felt proud of him as she watched him heading for the Tube. There was no shortage of work, and engineers like Arthur were needed to assist in all aspects of the rebuilding, so she knew he'd come back with a well-paid, essential position. She wanted to work, too – at least part time – and she thought her skills and experience would serve her in good stead.

While waiting for Arthur to be demobbed, she'd inclined towards a number of positions such as filing clerk, ticket dispenser at the cinema, library assistant and bookkeeper for a building firm. But what she was most drawn to was training as a researcher or investigator at the BBC, and that was now possible as the marriage bar had been lifted the year before. But instead of applying for any of those posts, Connie had thought she should wait for Arthur to come home and find a job first. Instead, she'd cleaned and polished, beat rugs and scrubbed the front steps, rehung curtains and aired bedsheets. Now that was done, and she didn't have any qualms about managing household duties and working outside the home at the same time. It would be a doddle after being a WRNS letter censor during a long, draining, horrible war.

As predicted, Arthur came home that evening full of excitement about the job he'd acquired as an engineer working on new flats being built in Holborn as part of Abercrombie's County of London Plan. 'I applied to fill one post, but by the time I'd finished with them they offered me the next step up.'

'Well done, Arthur,' Connie said, helping him off with his coat. 'I'm so proud of you.'

'It's good money, too, Treasure.' Arthur grinned, then lowered his voice and whispered in her ear. 'So, when the time comes and we need more space, I'll be able to secure us a place of our own.'

'That will be lovely, Arthur,' Connie said.

'I shouldn't have taken off my coat,' Arthur shrugged into it again. 'And you grab yours. I'm taking you for dinner in the West End.'

Connie ordered a fish pie and Arthur had a pork chop with swede and peas. A quartet in evening dress played lively music, and floor vases filled with orange and red flowers were dotted between the tables. Glasses and peals of laughter tinkled across the vast room, which was brazenly lit despite the curtains being open to a dark, winter's night – something they hadn't experienced in six long years.

They talked about Arthur's job and what it meant for their future. Between mouthfuls of red wine, Arthur covered Connie's hand with his.

'It's wonderful, Arthur,' Connie said. 'I can't believe our lives are changing so quickly.'

'Remarkable, isn't it?' Arthur said. 'All those years in the Navy have paid off.'

'That's how I feel about having been in the WRNS,' Connie said. 'And now that you're going to be out at work every day, I could use my skills in some sort of job, too. Part-time, of course. I think there are probably a lot of very interesting positions in the BBC, for example, that I'm well-qualified to fill.'

Arthur took his hand away from hers and his mouth, which had been fixed in a smile all evening, dropped to a straight, taut line. He leaned close, his forearms on the table.

'But, Treasure, we're going to have a baby.'

'Yes, Arthur, we are. But until that happens I could help towards getting our own place.'

Arthur shook his head. 'No, there's no point in you starting a job. The minute you begin you'd have to tell them you were leaving. Which is a bit unfair, don't you think?' The waiter appeared with a notepad and pencil to take their order for dessert, but Arthur dismissed him with a shake of his head.

'Perhaps,' Connie said. 'But on the other hand, whoever does the hiring at the BBC must know that's bound to happen. Anyway, if you really do think a job like that is too much, I could easily get something in an office or shop closer to home.'

'Treasure,' Arthur said. 'I didn't fight a war so you would have to work. I fought so I could come back and do that for both of us and our future family, while you stay safe at home. Besides, the house will fall into chaos if you're out at work for most of the week.'

Connie laughed out loud, eager to reset the tone of the

evening to light-hearted and amiable. 'Don't be silly, Arthur,' she said. 'I've been a Wren. I can work and take care of the home, as you'll find out.'

'No, Treasure,' Arthur was adamant. 'We must get back to the proper way of doing things. We agreed.'

Did we? Connie thought. What exactly had they agreed on?

'But Arthur, I did so enjoy my work as a...'

'Treasure, please,' Arthur said. 'Let's not spoil this fantastic moment by discussing the matter any further. What we need to do now is focus on the future, and we both have our parts to play in that – me out to work, and you taking care of the home and waiting for our children to arrive.'

Connie felt stung. Is this what she and thousands of other women had fought for? To have to obtain permission from their husbands to have a part-time job? She had taken it as a matter of course that she'd work again, as Dora and so many others were doing. She tried to raise the subject once more, but Arthur beckoned the waiter. They had a cup of tea and left the restaurant not anything like as chipper as when they'd walked in.

On Monday morning Arthur went out to work, and Connie stayed at home and waited and waited and waited.

25

August 1967

Waves of oppressive, muggy air washed over Connie. She kicked off the clammy bedsheets, nudged her head under the blind and opened the window, but if anything, what hit her was more dank and sticky than the draining atmosphere in the house.

Fanning her face with her hand, she watched a man wearing shorts plod from tree to tree with a luxuriously coated golden retriever, its long pink tongue almost dragging on the ground. In the distance, dunes of dark clouds were drifting together and when they broke, Connie thought everyone would feel better.

Barefoot in the kitchen, she drank a glass of water and filled the kettle. She found the bread and Nutella in a cupboard but when she'd spread them out on the breakfast bar, her stomach turned and she felt too hot and agitated to eat.

Or perhaps it was excitement. Maude Grimshaw had given her all the information she'd wanted, so her stomach bubbled at the anticipation of the same outcome with Jim, George, Beryl and Ted.

Peter Carstairs was a different matter. Her eyes narrowed and the same strong urge for revenge she'd felt all those years ago in Dover surfaced again. *How dare he*, she thought. She pictured him as slim and urbane, wearing a cravat and smoking jacket in a drawing room lined with books and oriental vases. He might have been part of a spy ring and perhaps still was – one of Kim Philby's sidekicks. She would confront him and insist he understand how traitors like him had prolonged everyone else's agony.

The interior of Somerset House held a chill even in the height of summer and goosebumps spotted Connie's arms whilst she waited in the queue to be served.

When it was her turn, she gave the assistant the name of James Stanton. 'He was a midshipman during the war and this is the last known address I have for him. Shall I write all that down for you?' She reached for a form.

'Please,' the attendant said. 'Then take a seat in the Reading Room and I'll find you when I've finished my search.'

'And there's another,' Connie heard herself babble. 'Peter Carstairs. I have no details for him other than this address in Tufnell Park.' She took another form and filled that in, too.

'Right you are, Madam. Anyone else?'

Connie already had another two forms ready and she wrote out the details she had for Beryl Smythe and Ted Adams.

'This may take some time,' the assistant said. 'Feel free to leave and come back later, or tomorrow. I'll keep the documents aside for you.'

'I'll wait,' Connie said. 'Thank you very much.'

The Reading Room was hushed and sombre, with the underlying intensity of deep concentration taking place. Connie claimed a table, laid out her notebook and pen and passed the time by rehearsing what she would say to each of the people she was intent on pursuing.

At last a pile of documents was placed in front of her, a note made of her table number and she was alone with the information that would, she hoped, lead to the people she'd first been introduced to over twenty years ago.

As she picked up the folder dedicated to James Stanton, her hands trembled. There was a man of about the right age, alive and married – Connie held the certificate close to her eyes and then at arm's length to make sure she was reading it correctly – to a Lucy Stanton nee Brotherton. There were birth certificates for three little Stantons, too, who wouldn't be quite so small now.

Connie rested her chin in her hands for a couple of minutes whilst she took in the information. She couldn't believe her theory had been wrong. All this time she'd been worried about Jim and George trying to negotiate their way through life as a couple, when all along they'd probably gone their separate ways towards their happy-ever-afters at the end of the war. But these certificates didn't mean conclusively that her instincts had been incorrect. Perhaps George had taken a packet or their feelings had fizzled out and Jim had thought it safer and easier to marry a woman – and who could blame him?

As she suspected, Jim Stanton was based in Nuneaton. She made a note of the address listed for him and thought that would be a good starting point for her investigations when she could plan a trip to that part of the country.

Next, Peter Carstairs. Or Sir Peter Carstairs, to give him his proper title as listed on his death certificate. She felt a sense of vindication when she remembered the image she'd had of him looking dapper in well-to-do surroundings; perhaps the spy assumption hadn't been too outlandish after all. There was always a chance that there had been another man of the same name living in Tufnell Park, but that would be too much of a coincidence. Sadness caused a lump to gather in her throat, not for his having passed away, but because she'd missed being able to take him to task by eighteen months.

There were birth certificates for a son and daughter, both born in Tufnell Park. She could follow that lead, make enquiries, perhaps find one of them, but what would she say. 'Excuse me, did you know your father was a Nazi spy during the War?' If they did, they would never admit to it. And if they didn't, was it worth inflicting that wound when she was so certain her theory was correct that it seemed as though she'd been to the elderly man's house, confronted him and heard his confession in return?

She hurriedly scribbled some details about Peter Carstairs in her notebook and moved on to Beryl Smythe. No death certificate, but there was a marriage certificate from 1949 and the bridegroom's name was Edmund Thwaites. That meant Beryl had given Ted the heave-ho or vice versa and Connie longed to find out the details. The newlyweds had lived in Islington when they married, which was easy to get to, and with a feeling of tense anticipation pressing on her chest, Connie returned the folders to the front desk and headed out to the Underground once again.

The air was heavy and felt thick and gummy to walk

through. Angry clouds tumbled and bumped and twined around each other before they parted company again. Before long, stinging needles of rain began to target her face and head and legs. She took shelter under a pub awning and tied her scarf under her chin. A soft, amber glow lit the windows and she could feel the beat of 'The Letter' by The Box Tops vibrating from under the jukebox and up through her spine. She moved to one side to let a laughing couple dart inside and as they opened the door the singer's gruff, bluesy voice came to her full throttle. She and Arthur had been like that couple once, although perhaps never as demonstrative.

Puddles began to form around her feet, but she didn't move. She felt a bit jumpy and a slick of sweat dotted her upper lip. When had that life evaporated and the rot set in? When Arthur wanted her to refuse the posting to Bermuda? When he'd been upset that she'd so readily accepted the role as a mobile censor? When the babies hadn't come? The move to Doncaster? Probably none of those things on their own, she thought, and all of them put together.

The rain eased but the air remained humid. Connie felt drained and thought she could have done with heading back for a nap; instead she pulled back her shoulders and made her way to Islington.

Number 47 Nightingale Road was hardly big enough to bring up the four children the Thwaites had, according to the certificates she'd found. Then again, people raised many more than that in two-up two-downs or one solitary room during the war.

Emboldened by her success with Maude Grimshaw, she

knocked. No answer. She knocked again and looked for a bell. Then a young man put his head around the side passage and called out a cheery greeting.

'Hello,' Connie said, stepping towards him. 'My name is Constance Allinson and I'm looking for an old friend. Beryl Thwaites, nee Smythe.' A rather high-pitched giggle escaped Connie's mouth and she tried to disguise it with a cough.

'Ooh,' the young man said, wiping his hands on a rag. His hair curled around his collar – like so many young men wore theirs these days – and it reminded Connie of the regulation length for Wrens during the war. 'Beryl hasn't lived here for some time. Years, in fact.'

Defeat crashed down on Connie and made her breathe in with a quiver.

'Last I heard she had the post office in Upper Holloway. Do you know where that is?'

She didn't, so he gave her directions and she stumbled along, a cyclist ringing his bell when she stepped into the road without looking. She hadn't had anything to eat since yesterday evening and no matter what happened next, she would have to stop for a cup of tea and a sandwich at least.

The post office was wedged between a dry cleaner's and a small grocery store, and when Connie pushed open the door, a tinkling bell made everyone in the queue turn towards the sound. Two women in their late forties were serving behind the counter and either of them could have been Beryl. Connie moved around the racks of greetings cards, flicking through them whilst she studied the likely candidates through lowered eyes. One was plump with dark hair caught in a clip at the nape of her neck and the other, the one Connie thought must be Beryl, was neat in a fawn-coloured dress and cardigan, with hair cut short like Millicent's and a tiny necklace sparkling between her collarbones.

Connie picked out a christening card and joined the queue behind three other people. She felt lucky to be called forward by the woman she thought must be Beryl and approached the counter with a smile plastered on her face. She put down the card and noticed she'd left hot fingerprints on the envelope like she'd done when she'd read a moving letter years ago.

'Just this, my love?' the woman asked. 'Do you want a stamp to go with it?'

Connie shook her head. 'No, thank you,' she said. Then she took a deep breath, lowered her voice and said, 'Are you Beryl Thwaites, used to be Smythe?'

'Beryl?'

The woman turned her head towards her colleague who said, 'Yes, Janie?'

'A lady here to see you.'

'How can I help?' Beryl asked. She wore a plum-coloured jacket over a dark pink dress and there were small, red bumps under the skin on one side of her face.

After an initial jump of surprise, Connie sidled to the other side of the counter with the card in her hand and whispered through the glass, 'I'm Constance Allinson,' she said. 'I was in the WRNS during the war.'

The only reaction from Beryl was a puzzled frown, so Connie bumbled on. 'In fact, I was a Petty Officer Wren in the letter censorship section. You were a long-distance telephone operator, weren't you?' She hoped to find some common ground.

'For a few years,' Beryl said as if she was worried about giving away too much information. 'What is this all about?'

'I was Examiner 7364.'

'I'm sorry,' Beryl said. 'That means nothing to me. Now, there's a queue waiting so shall I proceed with this card?'

'I must speak to you about a letter you sent to Edward – Ted – Adams that I opened and read during the war.'

Beryl's bemused look deepened and for one awful moment Connie thought the woman was going to laugh out loud. Instead, she asked her to move to the side where she would deal with her when she'd finished with her customers and closed the counter.

Connie paced up and down for a few moments. She picked up a pack of housewarming invitations and put them back, tried on a thimble with a picture of Big Ben stamped on it, inspected a set of coloured pens without seeing them properly.

There was the clatter of a metal screen being pulled down followed by the jangle of keys, then in a brisk, business-like voice, Beryl said, 'Follow me, please, Mrs Allinson.'

Beryl led her through a door to a small hallway with stairs going off it, which probably led to the Thwaites' living quarters. Then she stopped abruptly and rounded on Connie, her arms folded across her chest. 'You do know letter censorship no longer exists, don't you? It went out with the war. So you have no authority now.'

Connie took a step back. Beryl was very defensive, but so was Maude Grimshaw at first. All she had to do was explain herself and they'd go upstairs, have a lovely cup of tea and Beryl would tell her the whole story. 'Yes, I know,' she said, sounding less than convincing to herself. 'There's nothing to worry about.'

'You're the one who should be worried,' Beryl scoffed.

'Well, I … I can't get some of the letters I censored out of my mind.'

Beryl's eyes narrowed and she tightened her grip on her elbows. 'Go on,' she said in a cold voice.

'And yours was one of them. It was a letter you wrote to Ted Adams about him not wanting you to return to your war work in London. Do you remember? And you see, my husband, Arthur, is very much like …'

'Ted,' Beryl said. She closed her eyes and rubbed the bridge of her nose. 'That bully. You want me to explain myself to you about what happened with Ted?'

Relief made Connie's legs feel as if they were going to give way. 'Yes, please,' she said. 'If I could hear the whole story I could put it to one side where it wouldn't keep going round and round in my mind. I really would be most grateful to you.'

Beryl peered at her more closely. 'You're not well, Mrs Allinson, are you. Can I call someone for you? Or a taxi, perhaps?'

Connie shook her head. 'If I could sit down for a few minutes, thank you.'

Beryl disappeared into the post office and came back dragging a hard, wooden chair and carrying a glass of water. Connie flopped down and Beryl stood over her and watched as she downed the water in a few gulps.

'Mrs Allinson.' Beryl's eyes were softer but her voice wasn't. 'The war is over. You are no longer a Wren Censor and I am not a telephone operator working next to

St Paul's Cathedral. I'm sorry but I will not be giving you any information about my life.'

'But it would be so helpful,' Connie pleaded. 'My life would be so much easier if I could piece together your puzzle.'

Beryl's nostrils flared. 'I think you probably have some missing pieces of your own, Mrs Allinson, which I suggest you concentrate on.'

Connie felt the sharp sting of humiliation slap her hard. It had been such a simple request and Beryl's reaction had been so unexpected.

'Now,' Beryl held out her hand. 'If you've finished.' Connie handed back the empty glass. 'And if you're sure I can't call someone for you, I must ask you to leave. I have things to get on with.'

Connie trailed through the empty shop, Janie's eyes tunnelling two blistering holes deep into her back as Beryl unlocked the door and held it wide for Connie to leave. The bell chimed again as she stepped outside into the pouring rain. With clumsy fingers she tied her scarf under her chin and buttoned her jacket.

'Mrs Allinson.' The hard edge had been chipped off Beryl's tone of voice so Connie turned around, hoping she'd taken pity on her and changed her mind.

'Just a word of warning. During the war it was called censorship, now it's called being nosy. See a doctor, my dear, and think about your own family.'

'But I don't have a family,' Connie said. 'I only have Arthur and he's …'

The door was closed and locked in her face and Connie stood staring at it, tears coursing down her cheeks. This wasn't supposed to happen. She needed to go back to

Doncaster knowing at least one other letter writer's story and she couldn't imagine what she'd do with herself if she didn't secure that information.

She thought about her promise to get something to eat no matter what the outcome had been at the post office, but now the last thing she could stomach was a plate of food. Leaning against the door of the dry cleaner's, Beryl's words sunk in and shame made her break out in a cold sweat. The scarf was too tight, her jacket held the heat and her legs felt like they didn't belong to her. She stumbled along with her head down against the rain and the humidity and the raw wounds Beryl had opened. She tried to decide whether to hail a taxi or save money and sit, soaking wet, on a bus or underground train. At the corner she hesitated, trying to remember which way to go. She looked right, decided to turn left and came face to face with Arthur.

26

August 1967

Rain streamed down Arthur's umbrella, rebounded off the pavement and covered his beige trousers in wet, grimy streaks.

They stood staring at each other, Connie in a state of shock and Arthur as if he'd been waiting for her. No words would come out of Connie's mouth and when at last they did, all she could say was, 'Arthur. Whatever are you doing here?'

He was carrying a thin plastic bag by the handles as if he'd just popped out to the shops and he transferred it to his other hand, cupped her elbow and guided her away from pedestrians coursing around them. 'More to the point, Constance,' he hissed. 'What are you doing here?'

She roughly shook her arm free and scowled at him. 'Have you been following me?'

'I hardly think that's the issue. But yes, I have.'

'How dare you,' she spluttered, then wobbled and had to hold on to a post outside a shop to steady herself.

'Treasure.' He leaned in so close that Connie could smell a whole day's worth of tea and biscuits and cheese and pickle sandwiches on his breath. A dark, unshaven shadow circled his mouth and he pulled her closer until she was standing under it. 'You need to eat. Let's go in there.' He pointed to a tea shop on the opposite side of the road, a garland of plastic flowers festooned across its window.

Grabbing her arm again, he looked both ways for cars in the driving rain and marched her into the café. They found an empty table next to the window where the scene outside was cut in half by the string of pink, green and lilac daisies. A waitress appeared and Arthur ordered for both of them without giving Connie the option of deciding for herself. A spark of defiance flared in her, but she didn't care what she wasn't going to eat, so she let it go. When he'd finished thanking the young woman with a moderated, calm voice, he turned to Connie, his heavy brows meeting between his eyes and his face set in harsh lines. 'You don't look well, Connie.'

That seemed to be the message everyone was trying to get across to her today, but in case they hadn't noticed, none of them, including Arthur, looked like oil paintings themselves. 'How long have you been following me?' Connie asked.

Arthur leaned back in his chair, blowing air out in a hot huff as if he were about to explode. Then he inched forward and put his arms on the table. 'I'll be the first to ask questions,' he said.

Connie sat with her hands in her lap and felt like a chastised schoolgirl who was trying to make up an excuse for being late with her homework.

The waitress put two cups of tea in front of them and as they thanked her, they held her gaze intently as if she might pull something magical out of thin air that would save them from having to look for it themselves. When she walked away, Arthur asked Connie again to explain herself. 'Start at the beginning and tell me everything,' he demanded. 'I didn't fight a war just to have my wife …'

'Stop!' She didn't think she could take any more. 'I never want to hear any of your sayings again in my life. Ever.'

'Shh.' Arthur looked around at the other tables, the side of his mouth twitching.

Connie lowered her voice and tried to placate herself. Then it all gushed out. 'That maxim of yours that you trot out endlessly grates on my nerves, along with the meals I have to cook for you on a rota and the housework and no job and Elspeth and Clive and the cricket matches and the way I have to fawn over you for extra money to get my hair done and never going out and having to wait for your permission to do anything and …'

Arthur shook his head and was about to say something when two plates were placed in front of them. Connie stared down at the meat floating in gravy, the steaming, fluffy mashed potatoes, the peas and carrots and said, 'Shepherd's pie. It's Tuesday.'

Arthur closed his eyes as if he were trying to block out that remark. He picked up his knife and fork and, pointing to Connie's cutlery, said, 'I suggest you eat, whilst you tell me what you've been up to in London. And before you start, don't give me any of that malarkey about visiting Ken and Dora. I know you've been staying in their house but they must be away because I haven't seen hide nor hair of them. You've been wandering around, spending hours in Somerset House, hopping on and off Tubes, knocking on doors and disappearing for ages in a post office. What is all this about? I think you owe me an explanation, don't you,

Treasure?' He mixed together each of the items on his plate, took a large mouthful and waited.

With nothing in it, Connie's stomach turned on itself and she thought she'd better eat what was on her plate before she keeled over.

Arthur watched, but didn't interrupt until she placed her knife and fork side by side on the plate. He'd been right about one thing – she felt stronger with a hot dinner inside her and more able to tackle the situation logically. The waitress cleared their plates and Arthur ordered another cup of tea for both of them.

Connie took a deep breath and said, 'Do you want to hear the whole story?'

Arthur nodded begrudgingly, as if he'd already made up his mind about the outcome for her no matter what she tried to explain.

'During the war I worried dreadfully about some of the people whose letters I read and recently, their dilemmas have played over and over in my mind and I've been anxious about them all over again. It seemed as though I couldn't rest until I traced them and tried to find out how their lives had turned out.' This was the first time she'd articulated what she'd been so compelled to do and she could hear how absurd and bizarre it sounded. It made her own life appear feeble and pathetic – which it was. But that was down to Arthur, although he'd never admit it. She waited for him to say something but he sat very still, a disbelieving look on his face.

'So, this was the only way I could go about finding them,' she carried on. 'You'd never have given me permission otherwise, would you?' Connie looked down at her hands.

She felt ashamed and foolish and the explanation she'd given didn't do justice to how monumental the quest had seemed not more than a few hours ago.

'No, Connie, I wouldn't have,' Arthur said. 'Do Ken and Dora know you've been chasing around trying to find out about other people's lives?'

'No, they offered me their house for these three days because they thought I needed a break. And I couldn't tell you about that, either, or else you wouldn't have allowed it.'

Arthur studied his empty plate, a few pieces of onion and carrot clinging to the edges. When he looked up, his eyes brimmed with betrayal. 'A break from me?'

In the past she would have reminded herself that Arthur really was a caring, hardworking man who was probably a casualty of his own emotions, too, although he'd never admit it. Constance's Constant. Then gone on to mollify him whilst still trying to get her point across. But something in her broke and she no longer felt the need to do that. If she carried on in the same established pattern, nothing would change and she desperately needed to release herself from the life she'd been living. 'Yes, Arthur, that's right.'

He sat up straighter in his chair and shook his head. 'What I can't understand is why I'm not enough for you. I care about you so deeply, Connie, and all I've ever wanted is for us to have a good life together.'

'That's the nub,' she said. 'You organise our lives to meet the criteria of what *you* think is a good life and expect me to go along with it.'

'We always come to a compromise, don't we?'

Tears breached the rims of Connie's eyelids and she felt them, hot and sticky, making their way past her nose. 'No, we don't. You manipulate the so-called compromise to suit your ends. And I dare say that's very easy to do because without a job or money of my own or skills to fall back on, I'm dependent on you.'

That didn't sit well with Arthur. He fidgeted, cleared his throat and tried to bluff his way through.

'Bakewell tart or apple crumble?' the waitress asked.

They both shook their heads.

'You're not a happy person,' Arthur said when the young woman had moved onto another table. 'You haven't been for some time. I've noticed that and wondered about it.'

'If only I could have a job,' Connie wailed. 'A few days a week, that's all I've asked for.'

Arthur put up his hand. 'I've had enough of hearing that saying of yours,' he said. 'Besides, that wouldn't make you happy, would it? Nothing would. Not the house or a husband who dotes on you and provides for you, new hairstyles or coffee mornings or trips to London. It's because ...'

She guessed he was going to bring up children – or the lack of them.

'... we didn't have the family we wanted.'

She nodded. 'That's been the greatest tragedy of our lives. Things would have probably been so different if we'd—'

'And the war,' he interrupted.

'The war?' Connie thought he was clutching at straws.

'One heart-breaking experience followed by another.' Arthur looked at the wall behind her, as if what he was about to say had only dawned on him that minute.

'I'd been so scared of losing you, Treasure, and having nothing – absolutely nothing – to come back to.'

A film of tears gathered over Arthur's eyes and he rubbed them away with the back of his hand.

'When that dreadful six years was over, I was so relieved that we were both in one piece and ready to properly start our lives together. But it wasn't really over, was it? It was still in here.' He tapped the side of his head, then leaned over and tenderly touched Connie's temple. 'And in the forefront of every bugger's mind who'd lived through it. And when the children didn't materialise, there was only me and you. A family of two and I wanted you safe at home, with me.'

'I understand all of that. About the war and the terrible disappointment when a baby didn't come along, but I'm afraid,' Connie said softly, reaching across the table for his hand. 'That rather than pull me to you, you've pushed me away.'

'Everything I do is to keep us together in a nice, warm house with food on the table. It's the way I show I care.'

'But Arthur.' She took her hand from his. 'What I've wanted is for you to help me fulfil my ambitions and needs. Instead, it's all been about you fulfilling yours.'

Arthur sat back, exasperated. 'You've changed so much, Treasure,' he said.

'And you, Arthur, haven't changed at all in thirty years.'

They sat in silence for a few minutes, listening to the rain hitting the window and the steam rising from the tea urn.

'We'll have to continue with this conversation at home,' Arthur said, checking his watch. 'We have a train to catch.'

'A train?' Connie stammered. 'Tonight?'

'Yes, Treasure. The last train back to Doncaster. We'll

have to hail a taxi and pop back to Ken and Dora's to pick up your case.'

'Arthur ...' She was astounded. 'Have you not heard a word of what I've been trying to tell you? This is the perfect example of what I've been saying.'

'I've listened to every word, Treasure. Nevertheless, we have to leave now if we want to get home.'

'But, Arthur,' she said, surprising herself. 'I don't want to go back.'

'But we won't make the train if we don't—'

'*You* won't make the train if you don't leave now. I'm not going with you.'

Arthur's brow darkened. 'Oh, I see,' he said. 'You want to stay until tomorrow afternoon and find out more information about other people's lives, rather than come with me and sort out our own.'

'We won't sort out our problems at home,' Connie said. 'We'll merely go back to the way of living you've dictated for us and I want something different for myself.'

'Don't be so silly,' Arthur said. 'A few minutes ago you stated you had no independent means, so how will you go about that?'

'Ken will help me,' she said, feeling more defiant and confident now. 'And you'll have to send me a bit of money to live on.'

He snorted.

'Or sell the house and give me back the amount Mum left me that you decided to use in the way you saw fit.'

Whilst Connie stood and gathered together her jacket and bag, Arthur sat and looked stricken, as if he'd been hit by a bullet.

'Wait, Treasure, please.' Arthur grabbed her elbow before she had a chance to open the door. He pushed a ten bob note at the waitress and as she called out a cheerful goodbye, the plastic flowers lifted for a moment in the breeze from the open door then fell back against the window with a jingle.

They stood under Arthur's umbrella and Connie waited for him to tell her what she'd needed to wait behind for. In a small voice, he said, 'Are you leaving me, Treasure?'

'Yes, Arthur,' Connie said, unable to look at him for fear of his hangdog expression changing her mind.

'Forever?' His voice faltered.

'I don't know,' Connie said. 'I don't know much at the moment. Only that I have to get away and have a chance to … think and breathe and have time for myself. I'm sorry, Arthur,' she said. 'I can't continue the way we are and I don't think you can change.'

'I can.' He clawed at her arm. 'And I will. I promise you that. Just come with me now and tell me everything I need to do to please you and it will be done in a flash.'

Connie stroked the side of Arthur's face and shook her head sadly. 'I've told you so many times,' she said. 'You should have been able to sort it out for yourself before now – if you'd wanted to.'

When a taxi approached, Connie hailed it and Arthur opened the door and handed her into the back. Then he leaned into the cab and kissed her hard and long on the lips, grinding his teeth and chin against hers. He smelled of dirty rain and public convenience soap and the shadow of his beard scratched against her cheek. Before he let her go, he whispered into her hair in an unsteady voice, 'You will come back, won't you?'

Connie didn't reply. Instead, she touched her fingertips to her mouth and remembered the two other occasions when he'd said goodbye to her using the same words – the first when they were both in uniform, soldiers and sailors and WAAFs and Wrens frantically clinging to loved ones all around them in King's Cross station. The second when he'd mumbled that entreaty into her ear as she was leaving for her first trip to London. Both times she'd answered that of course she would. This time she couldn't possibly give the same answer.

Arthur slammed the door of the taxi and she felt stunned and shaken as she turned to watch him standing alone under a sodden umbrella until the waterfall of rain plummeting down the back window obscured him from her view.

27

August 1967

The rain had stopped and the promise of a bit of sun lay in wait behind a grey sky. Connie had nothing planned and nothing she needed to do – a situation that would have seemed paradisical not long ago. She could go after Peter Carstairs' grown-up children and badger them to tell her everything they knew about their father's spying activities, but that image filled her with cringing dread instead of fevered excitement. Now that her plans had changed, there was plenty of time to get to Nuneaton and seek out Jim Stanton, but the point of that had been lost. How he and George lived their lives was none of her business and if she did find out, it wouldn't make any difference to her one way or another.

There were the shops along Oxford Street or a museum or a book by the river, all of which seemed to have lost their shine. That left the restaurant in Peter Robinson, but she didn't think she could bear those murals staring down at her again.

If only she could get in touch with Ken and Dora, but they hadn't left details of their accommodation so she would have to wait until they arrived home at the weekend. She imagined their faces when they came in, luggage and souvenirs and dirty laundry in tow and found her sitting on their couch, fidgeting with her hands whilst she tried to give them an explanation of her new circumstances. She knew they'd do all they could to help her, but there was bound to be a limit and three days every couple of months was very different from her living with them for an indefinite amount of time.

Pacing around the living room, Connie knew it would be difficult to go out. Almost as difficult as it would be to stay in the confines of the house. At last she donned her jacket, scarf and shoes and decided on a walk along Regent's Canal.

Last night's talk with Arthur had left her with such a mixed bag of feelings that it was almost impossible to unpick one from the other. She felt bruised and battered and bristling with confusion, but also lighter and younger, more confident and determined than she had since she'd been a Jenny Wren. Not quite believing she'd had the courage and nerve to actually leave her husband the night before, she went over and over the conversation that had led up to her making that decision. She realised now that was what she'd wanted to do for years, unconsciously at least, and that she'd always shied away from making that move when she'd been close to it. Last night, she hadn't been able to fool herself any longer.

It crossed her mind that perhaps she should have listened to Arthur's pleas for her to go back to Doncaster with him, but once the words were out of her mouth she'd felt such relief that she couldn't rescind on them. When he'd said he could and would change, maybe she should have given him one more chance, but they were mere words, easy enough to spew out. What she needed was to see concrete evidence of that change and she certainly hadn't been witness to anything near that.

She trudged along, head down until a family of five walked past, a little girl holding a handful of conkers, two boys jostling each other until their father shouted at them to get back from the water's edge. Connie smiled and thought about Shirley and her brood and Adrian, clambering onto her lap with a book in his hand.

The mother, wearing a green cagoule and a pair of pink Dr Scholl's clogs, pointed to the periphery of London Zoo and the children started to jump up and down, trying to spy a lion or tiger or giraffe. 'You won't see a large animal from here,' their father laughed. 'Or no one would pay to go in.'

'Can we?' one of the boys begged.

'That might have to wait for another time.' Their mother cleverly diverted their attention by saying they'd soon reach Blow Up Bridge and the three children ran ahead, each wanting to be the first to see it.

Connie watched them stream away from her. She found a bench facing barges painted in bright colours, some of them with a whole garden's worth of potted plants and herbs on their decks. A lump massed in her throat when she thought about Arthur caring for her clematis from now on, if he didn't hack the whole thing down and plant salad tomatoes in its place. But a clematis wasn't worth going back for, not now she'd taken the first and hardest step towards gaining her freedom.

She wondered if Ken and Dora might advise her to return and claim the house as her own. She could see a solicitor who would insist Arthur leave the property and take a bedsit somewhere close to the power plant, but then she'd be stuck there until she sold the house and the thought of that filled her with dread. Shirley and Millicent would be a great help, she knew that, but she'd rather stay close to Ken and Dora, at least until she worked out the finer details of how she was going to move ahead. There was so much to consider and she must give herself time and take things one small step after another.

Today she would force herself to eat regularly, so stopping at a small grocery store she picked up a few things to keep herself going. When she opened the front door, the solitude of the house felt like a comforting haven. She had a bowl of chicken soup and a round of toast and as her eyes drooped luxuriously, she put up her feet, snuggled into a cushion and thought she might succumb to a nap.

Minutes later, the incessant ring of the telephone jolted her upright. She stared at the piece of black Bakelite on the small table and thought it couldn't possibly be Lyndsey, as she must know that Victor wasn't due back for a few more days. Moving towards it, she went to pick up the handset then drew back quickly as if she were in danger of getting burned. What if it was Arthur? She wasn't ready to talk to him just yet. But it wouldn't be him. He would write, or send a telegram, but not phone.

Gingerly, she lifted the receiver and whispered, 'Hello?'

'Connie!' Dora's voice sounded as clear as if she were standing next to her. 'Just calling before you leave to say we hope you had a good time.'

Connie took a deep breath and tried to speak, but couldn't find the right words to get started.

'Are you alright? I can't hear you very well.'

Connie heard pips followed by money being fed into the box.

'I haven't got much change left,' Dora said. 'And I still can't hear you.'

'I've left Arthur,' Connie managed on an exhale that ended in a small sob. This was the first time she'd said the words aloud and they sounded so final and frightening.

'You've left Arthur.' Dora was incredulous. 'Ken, our Connie's left Arthur. When? Before you came to London?'

'Last night,' Connie said. 'He followed me and when I was faced with him, that was the only conclusion I could come to. I'm sorry. I don't have anywhere to go so I'm afraid I'm going to be here when you …'

'Sister of Mine.' Ken had grabbed the phone. 'At last. I am so proud of you. Sit tight and we'll sort everything out together.'

'Thank you, Cheeky Cherub.' Tears flowed down Connie's face. 'I'm so sorry to impose on you.'

'Never,' Ken said. We've been hoping you'd do this for …'

The pips sounded and the phone went dead. Connie held the receiver in her hand then cautiously placed it back on the cradle.

There was so much to think about, so many decisions to make that Connie's head felt as if it might explode, so that was enough for one day. She poured herself a double gin and climbed the stairs with *The Gabriel Hounds* under her arm. But neither prop proved necessary as she fell into the deepest, most trouble-free sleep she'd had in years.

28

Connie buttoned up her new, camel-coloured coat with stand-up Nehru collar and stepped out of the door of Somerset House into flurries of snow mixed with stinging sleet. Digging around in her bag for her scarf, her fingers tightened around her notepad and she pushed it down amongst her purse, comb, lipstick and handkerchief to where the precious information she'd discovered that day was sure to stay dry.

It was her turn to cook tonight and she'd decided to try something called beef stroganoff followed by bread and butter pudding so she'd have to stop at the new Tesco store to buy the ingredients. A few days ago she'd served everyone coq au vin and felt very pleased with herself when Lyndsey proclaimed it the best meal she'd ever had.

She was over the moon that she'd accomplished what she'd set out to achieve in Somerset House. A couple of weeks previously, when she'd felt more settled in a routine, she'd decided to have a go at tracing some of her old pals from the WRNS and uncovered the bare facts about Norma, Dotty, Marjorie, Angelique and Ivy. She smiled when she thought of each of them, so different in their own ways but equally as lovely and fascinating.

Norma had emigrated to Australia in 1959 with her husband and daughter, but Connie had been able to find the contact address they'd listed before they left. There was a marriage certificate for Dotty dated 1948 and Connie wondered if her husband was the young man with the ears that looked like half-mast flags. If so, she pictured the four sons Dotty had registered looking the image of him. Marjorie had married and divorced and married again and lived in Winchmore Hill. A buzz of excitement fizzed through her at the thought of being close enough to meet up with her soon. As mysterious as ever, nothing other than a birth certificate could be found for Angelique so tracing her would prove to be difficult, if not impossible. Ivy was the only one who hadn't made it. Sadness overwhelmed her when she remembered the girl who'd clung to her in that tiny post office flat when they'd listened to the announcement about D-Day with the other Wren mobile censors. She'd come through the remainder of the war unscathed only to succumb to pneumonia in 1956. Poor thing, she'd left behind two tiny tots.

She would write to each of them, say how sorry she was that they'd lost touch, tell them a bit about the way her life had gone and ask about theirs. If she didn't receive a reply, she might try to find them at their last known addresses and take it from there as she'd done with Maude Grimshaw and Beryl Smythe – that last encounter making her wince all over again.

Laden with shopping, Connie let herself into Ken and Dora's house and Greg called to her from the top of the stairs. 'Alright, Auntie Connie?'

'Yes, thanks, my love. You? How's the studying going?'

'Okay,' he said. 'But A-levels are hard.'

Connie smiled up at him. 'Would you like some cheese on toast and a cup of tea?'

He grinned and stuck his thumb up in the air. 'There's a couple of letters for you on the breakfast bar.'

'Thank you,' she said. 'Now back to those books.'

Connie so wanted one of the letters to be from the local newspaper where she'd had an interview for a part-time job in the small ads department. The position entailed opening envelopes – something she was highly qualified to do – organising the forms from people selling bikes or baby's prams or plants or second-hand clothes into neat piles, making sure the cheques and postal orders were made out for the correct amount and piling them in wire baskets for the compositors. All of which she thought she could do with her eyes closed.

But when she'd sat in a chair outside the interview room and measured herself up against the other candidates, she'd lost her confidence. Four of them were straight from the sixth form and the other was probably a young mum wanting a 'little job' – as Arthur called women's work – after her children had started school.

She'd bumbled her way through the questions. '*What would you do if there were too many forms to sort through and some of the ads had to go into a later edition?*'

Connie's head had felt stiff on her neck and she was aware of her hands trembling as she clasped them together on her lap. She was sure that would never happen – she wouldn't allow it to, but she hesitated as she thought that reply would sound conceited. Then she couldn't think of anything else to say for a few minutes until she offered the idea of referring the dilemma to her superior.

They asked her what qualifications she had that would serve her in good stead and all she had to convey was what she'd done in the WRNS and how she'd successfully undertaken research at Somerset House and that, she thought, wouldn't pass muster.

Still, until she received the rejection there was hope – but she wouldn't know the outcome today as one of the letters was from Arthur and the other, also postmarked Doncaster, was in handwriting she didn't recognise.

She put the meat in the refrigerator, filled the kettle, put two slices of bread under the grill and cut slices from a block of cheese. Bypassing Arthur's letter, she picked up the other envelope and expertly slashed the short edge with a knife.

Dear Connie

I hope you don't mind me asking Arthur for your address.

Millie and I miss you very much and the children keep asking after you, especially Adie who will be starting nursery after Christmas. You wouldn't believe how much all the little ones have grown, even Benjamin.

Susan across the way has moved because Tony got a better job in Leicester and a couple with teenage children have moved in. I feel sorry for the kids because they always seem to be kicking about with nothing much to do.

Other than that, everyone is fine, but life is much

busier with three children than I thought it would be. How naïve of me. Most days it seems as though I have six.

Trev and I have booked the church for Benjamin's christening on Saturday, 20th of April at 11.00 a.m. I know it's a long way off, but I wanted to give you as much notice as possible so you could put the date in your diary and make up your mind to come along. We would love to see you.

Love and best wishes

Shirley, Trev and the Gang XXX

Connie was racked by guilt. She'd been meaning to write to Shirley and Millicent but other things had taken priority. Now she made up her mind not to let them go in the same direction as her WRNS friendships. She would write back to Shirley tomorrow and send a letter to Millicent, too. As for going to the christening, she wasn't sure if she could face Arthur again. But the date was months off – she might feel more up to it by then.

Connie buttered Greg's toast, piled it with cheese and put it back under the grill. Then she steeled herself for the letter from Arthur.

Hello, You

I hope you don't mind that I gave Shirley your address. She and Trev asked me to their house for tea on Saturday and she asked for it then. We had an unusual meal of something called spaghetti Bolognese and I pushed Simon and Tracey around the garden on their new bikes. Shirley and Millicent miss you very much, as

I do. I know I've told you that many times before, but I cannot tell you enough. I miss you with all my heart.

Do you remember me telling you that Clive and Elspeth had invited me to one of their social evenings? Well, I went along and it was tedious and tiresome. Clive did nothing but boast and as for Elspeth, she was so obviously jealous of her so-called friends that I think she would have scratched out their eyes given half the chance. I think the only reason they asked me was to get information about what's happening between us, but I wouldn't be led down that path by that nosy, prying pair. I should have listened to when you told me how obnoxious they were, but I was stubborn and hell bent on being the big head of the household. There are so many things I should have listened to you about. Anyway, last week Clive announced that they're moving to Dorset where he's got a job as a project manager. Good riddance to them, that's what I say.

Have you heard about the job you applied for at the newspaper? It sounds as if it would be right up your street, although I think you're worth much more than that and should apply for something with more responsibility. I understand that you want to contribute to the rent on a place of your own and that you need to get a job before you can do that, but my offer to send you more money each week is still open. It's the least I can do to help you.

Have you given any further thought to coming here for Christmas? I would get the food in and help with the preparation. You'd be surprised at how much I've learned about cooking since I've been forced to, including how enjoyable it is to get a meal together – I should have done that years ago, too, and given you a break.

If you don't want to come here, perhaps I could come to Ken and Dora's for a few days? Or if that would be inconvenient, I could book us into a hotel. We could have all our meals prepared for us and no washing up afterwards. Music and dancing and crackers to pull. Just let me know.

I am changing, Treasure, and I'm doing so for myself as well as for you. And I'm feeling the benefits.

Your Constance's Constant

Arthur XXX

Connie put the letter back in its envelope, turned off the grill, cut the toast into triangles, poured a mug of tea and took Greg's snack to him.

'Oh, great,' he said, taking a huge bite and letting the butter run down his chin. 'No one makes cheese on toast like you. Thank you, Auntie Connie.'

'What are you working on?' Connie looked over her nephew's shoulder.

'Advanced Maths,' Greg said through a mouthful of bread.

Connie grimaced. 'I'll let you in on a secret.' She lowered her voice. 'I still count on my fingers.'

Greg laughed. 'I don't believe you. Dad said you could have done anything you wanted to do but that Uncle Arthur held you …' He stopped, colouring from the neck up.

'It's okay,' Connie said. 'Uncle Arthur did hold me back, but I shouldn't have let him.'

Greg looked at her for a few moments, clearly

uncomfortable talking about a subject his parents must have told him to avoid. 'If you'd been able to do more, what would you have done?' he asked.

'Oh,' Connie said. 'Good question. Can I sit on your bed?'

'Sure,' Greg said. 'Sorry about the mess.'

Connie laughed and pushed aside a pair of pyjama bottoms, a t-shirt and a few odd socks. She studied the posters on the walls, the guitar on a stand in the corner, a blue and orange lava lamp on the desk. 'I've never thought about that before,' she mused.

'Why not?'

'Because when I was younger we didn't have the same opportunities you have now. Then the war started and there was no going back after that.'

Greg looked concerned, but Connie was sure he didn't really understand the implications those six years had on everyone's lives. 'But, if I'd had the chance, perhaps I would have studied History or Social Sciences or Psychology because I have a great interest in other people and what makes them tick. So be careful, I'm watching and analysing you all the time.'

She bugged her eyes and Greg laughed.

'Are you going to go for Maths at university?'

Greg shook his head. 'It's Engineering for me.'

'Same as Uncle Arthur. You should write to him and ask him about his career. He's done very well.'

'I could talk to him about it if he comes here for Christmas,' Greg said.

'I don't think he will this year, my love,' Connie said. 'More?' She held out her hand for the plate.

'If you really don't mind,' Greg said in a small voice.

Connie ruffled his hair. 'I really don't mind. Now get on with it, Brainbox.'

Alone in the house the following morning, Connie braced herself and wrote to Shirley accepting the christening invitation. If the thought of seeing Arthur proved too difficult, she could always cry off nearer the time. She also wrote to Millicent and drew a special kiss in a heart for Adrian. Then she penned short notes to Dotty, Marjorie and Norma reintroducing herself and telling them how much she'd like to be in touch.

Lastly, she wrote to Arthur and let him down gently about Christmas. *Not this year*, she said. *It's too soon for me, but I have written to Shirley that I'll travel to Doncaster for Benjamin's big day in April, so we'll see each other then.*

She found her coat amongst the others on the rack, put it on and tightened the belt. Dora had written out a list of a few things they needed from the shops and she put that in her bag along with her keys, hanky, gloves and scarf. Behind her the letterbox rattled and she picked up the post that had fanned out on the mat. A circular for Dora from a flooring business; two official envelopes for Ken; a postcard for Victor and at the bottom of the pile, a business letter for her.

She stared at it, certain it must be from the newspaper. Ripping open the envelope, she held one page of notepaper with the newspaper's logo printed at the top. Reading through the first paragraph quickly, she discovered that she hadn't been offered the job. Her heart plummeted right down to her boots; she felt so disappointed. Moving to an easy chair, she loosened her coat, unfolded the letter and started again from the top.

She took in the words: *Thank you for attending the interview. Regretfully. Many outstanding candidates.* Then the second paragraph that started with, *However …*

Connie's brow furrowed. How could there be a however? But there was. They wanted to offer her another post they thought would perfectly suit her skills. It was as a part-time archivist and if she was interested, could she please pop into the office at her earliest convenience with her National Insurance card to discuss training and a starting date? Her hand flew to her chest, then to her mouth. She shook her head and read the letter again and once again after that.

Shocked silence surrounded her. There was no question of her not wanting to take the job. She would have been mad to turn it down. Jumping up, she threw the letter in the air and twirled around the room until she was giddy and out of breath.

Her National Insurance card was in Doncaster, but she would explain the circumstances to the paper and tell them she would send for it straight away. Once that was done and she had a starting date, she could begin to view one-bedroom flats close by. She picked up her bag and hurried from the flat with a feeling of purpose she hadn't experienced since her first day with the WRNS so very many years ago.

29

Arthur had asked if he could meet her off the train in Doncaster but when she'd said no, he didn't insist. Carrying a bunch of flowers for Shirley and a little wrapped gift for Benjamin, Connie caught the bus to Barnby Dun and walked through the estate to the house she'd last seen months ago.

Nothing had altered in that short period of time, although so much had happened to her that she half-expected things to have changed in accordance. Most of the plants and curtains were the same; buggies and prams were parked in their usual places; cats paced around front doors; children raced past on bikes and roller skates. Hacking out puffs of grey smoke shot through with blackened soot, the towers followed her no matter which way she twisted and turned down paths and through cul-de-sacs, but now she saw them for no more than what they were – harmless, industrial concrete funnels. They no longer had any power over her.

Although Connie had been honest with Shirley and Millicent in her letters, her stomach turned with apprehension about meeting any of her neighbours just yet. Hoping to avoid a chance encounter, she scooted into the road from a different direction, unlocked the door and let herself in. The house was still and eerily quiet. A tremor ran through her when she stood in the hallway and took in the carpet, the coat hooks, the pictures on the walls, the kitchen cupboards and past the patio doors, the abundant clematis covering the back fence like a fountain of pink flowers. Everything looked familiar and exactly as it should be and yet, it all seemed so removed from the life she had carved out for herself in London.

'Arthur,' she called softly.

She listened, but there was no reply. 'Yoo-hoo,' she tried again.

Voices carried into the house from Shirley's garden and she thought the neighbours must have gathered there to help get things ready for the christening party. Perhaps Arthur was amongst them.

She peered into the living room, where the television Arthur had written to her about stood dark and blank in the corner. Library books were on the coffee table next to the newspaper open at the crossword page and a new photo of their wedding day stood on the sideboard in a sparkling, polished frame.

Tiptoeing into the kitchen she opened a couple of cupboards and found a large bag of pasta, a tin of tuna, a bag of rice, two cans of chopped tomatoes, crisps, a packet of Tunnock's Teacakes, a jar of Nutella and instant coffee. In the fridge there was a covered plate of leftover chicken and a paper bag filled with cherry tomatoes. A blur of tears filmed Connie's eyes and she wondered why Arthur couldn't have made those and a few more simple changes to his attitude and behaviour before their lives had come to this. It would have made such a difference to her and to them as a couple. It was too late now, but she thought that Arthur would be better off for it.

She crept upstairs and much to her surprise, the bed was made, the bathroom was gleaming and there were no dirty clothes tossed without a thought into the laundry basket.

From the window, she could see Shirley and Millicent pegging white paper tablecloths onto trestle tables and Brian blowing up balloons with a pump. Then Arthur appeared from the house, carrying a stack of chairs that he placed around the garden. When he'd finished he brushed his hands together and looked up momentarily, his gaze locking into hers. Then he disappeared from view.

'Hello, you,' he said softly from the hallway.

Connie smiled at him fondly. He took the stairs two at a time and put his arms around her, breathing in the scent of her skin and hair.

'You look lovely, Treasure,' he said, taking in her knee-length turquoise skirt and jacket, the fringed handbag over her shoulder, the black court shoes, the pale pink lipstick. 'I see you've found a hairdresser in London.' He touched her dark bob gently and smoothed a few stray strands over her double crown. 'Would you like a cup of coffee?'

'Thank you, Arthur, I would.'

She sat in the living room like a guest and Arthur didn't spill a drop of the coffee as he set down the mugs.

Sipping their hot drinks, they smiled at each other shyly a couple of times. Arthur asked her about her job and Connie asked him about his. Then he cleared his throat. 'I suppose we have a number of things to talk about, Treasure,' he said.

'Like putting the house on the market and dividing up the furniture.'

She nodded. 'Yes, I suppose we do.'

'Unless you can imagine yourself ever living here again?' Arthur asked.

'No.' Connie didn't have to think about her answer. 'I could never live here again, Arthur. As you know I was most unhappy when I did.'

'But do you think you could live with me again?' he asked. 'I have changed. Millicent and Shirley will vouch for me. And it's not just a passing phase to lure you back. As I've said in my letters, it's as much for me as it is for us. We could sell this house and move somewhere else. Somewhere that ...'

The doorbell chimed and the front door opened. 'Can we come in?' Millicent's voice carried through the house.

'Of course.' Arthur stood up and placed his mug on the table. 'Connie's here.'

'Connie, Connie.' Adrian threw himself at her.

'Hello, Adie,' Connie said. 'It's so lovely to see you.' As Shirley had warned, he'd grown but not so much that he didn't climb onto her lap and put his arms around her neck. Connie thought her heart wouldn't be able to take it. She rocked him backwards and forwards for a few moments and kissed his silky, floppy hair.

'Let me have a look-in with that cuddle, Adie,' Millicent said. She threw her arms around Connie's shoulders, her newly coloured platinum hair shimmying around her head. 'How are you?'

'I'm fine, Millie. And you?'

'Everything's okay. But much better now that you're here. Let's go next door and see Shirley, shall we?'

With a touch of trepidation, Connie took a deep breath and allowed Millicent to lead her to the gathering next door, Adrian's sticky hand tucked up in hers.

In party clothes and new, rigid shoes, the children clambered over Connie, but not for long; they soon forgot they hadn't seen her for months and went back to chasing each other with balloons and paper streamers. Shirley came forward with her arms out and Connie was pleased that the dark circles under her eyes were much less noticeable.

'Connie,' she said, giving her a hug and holding onto her hand. 'I'm so glad you decided to join us.'

'I am, too,' Connie said. 'Thank you for asking me.'

Trev and Brian and a few others said hello, but they didn't stop their chores for longer than it took to wave or nod quickly – and Connie was pleased about that.

'What can I do to help?' Connie said.

'You haven't changed much,' Millicent said. 'Always ready to roll up your sleeves and get stuck in.'

'How about holding this little one?' Shirley said, presenting her with a chubby, smiling Benjamin devoid of milk spots, unruly hair and the boxer's nose. He was angelic in a flowing white christening gown that looked as if it could be a family heirloom.

'He's adorable,' Connie said.

'He is, isn't he?' Shirley smiled at the baby and wiped a non-existent mark off the side of his face.

'Don't be fooled, Connie,' Trev said. 'He's a little imp

and tries for all he's worth to keep up with his brother and sister.'

As if to prove a point, Simon and Tracey raced past and Benjamin squirmed to get down on the floor and follow them. 'I suppose he's crawling now?' Connie asked.

'He's been on the move for ages,' Shirley replied. 'But I want to keep him off the floor at least until we get to the church.'

'Okay.' Connie laughed. 'I'll do my best.' She jiggled the baby in her arms and took him on a tour of the house. They looked at the sandwiches, cut and waiting under aluminium foil; crisps, tomatoes and cucumbers in bowls; sausage rolls laid out in sentry lines on trays ready to pop into the oven later; glasses, cups, plates, cutlery, serviettes and beakers for the children, beer, wine, tea, coffee and squash lined up on the worktops. Any worries she'd had about being around Arthur again faded into the background. She was vaguely aware of his presence, but it wasn't overbearing or critical or oppressive and the only communication that passed between them was a smile from time to time.

The doorbell rang and Trev answered it, coming back into the kitchen carrying a large box from the bakery. 'Tell me quickly where to put the cake, Shirl,' he called out.

'We've left a space in the middle of the table,' Shirley said. 'Arthur will show you.'

'Over here,' Arthur said. 'Do you want a hand?'

Stupefied, Connie watched as Arthur took one side of the box and walked backwards into the dining room, dodging children and chairs and china bowls. He did indeed seem to be, as he'd promised, a changed man. She wondered why she didn't feel resentful that it took her leaving him to make the changes she'd always hoped for, then realised that nothing would have been any different if she hadn't told him last year she wasn't coming back to live with him in Doncaster. That and the fact that she now had her own life to live in London.

There was the sound of shuffling and a burst of relieved laughter. Trev drew his finger across his throat. 'Thank goodness for that,' he said. 'Shirl would have killed me if I'd dropped it.'

'How many balloons are left?' Brian asked.

'About half a dozen,' Mandy said.

'We can leave those as spares for when we get home,' Shirley said. She stood back and surveyed the bunting across the patio doors and the figure on the cake that represented Benjamin. 'We'd better get going now.'

Connie found herself walking with Mandy and Graham, then they moved away and she ambled along with Shirley's mother. Up ahead, Adrian spun around like a helicopter propeller, spotted her, skipped to her side and put his hand in hers. Connie smiled down at him and he put two fingers in his mouth and slurped on them loudly. On their way to the Church of St Peter and St Paul, she pointed out a stunning purple wisteria forming an arch over a door and a tricycle on a path and Adrian nodded sagely whilst appraising them.

Two impish gargoyles watched their progress through the cemetery and when they passed under the church porch, a low ceiling, cool air and the powdery smell of mildewed hymn books greeted them.

They stepped reverently across Victorian tiles in the sanctuary and came into a rather large interior with light spilling through beautiful stained-glass windows. Millicent came to claim Adrian, and as Connie sidled into a pew towards the back of the church, Arthur was at her side again. 'May I sit next to you, Madam?' he asked.

Connie laughed. 'Of course, Arthur. Please do.'

They sat quietly for a few moments taking in the serenity of the flowers, the altarpiece, the images and statues. Arthur fiddled with his songbook and Connie helped him to find the right page for the first hymn. Shirley's mother and father were doing their best to keep Simon and Tracey entertained with a few little books and building blocks, but the children were more interested in swinging from the sides of the pews.

The vicar asked Shirley and Trev and their family to stand around the font along with Millicent and Brian who were godparents. He reminded them that it took a village to raise a child, and they sang 'All Creatures Great and Small' whilst Simon chased Janet with a blue and red Lego boat. In a grand finale, Benjamin cried when the water was dripped onto his forehead.

'Thank you all very much for coming,' Trev said at the end of the ceremony. 'In case I've forgotten to mention it to anyone, Shirley and I would be very happy to welcome you to our house for a bit of food and a couple of ...' He mimed putting a drink to his mouth.

As soon as Shirley's front door was unlocked, guests flooded the house and garden. Brian put *Sgt. Pepper's Lonely Hearts Club Band* on the turntable; the children chased around and screeched when a balloon popped. Photos were taken outside. The bunting came loose and Graham tacked it back up. Shirley and Millicent unwrapped the food and the guests lined up to help themselves. Brian and Trev handed out drinks and when Adrian scraped his knee on the patio, Arthur carried him into the house to have it seen to and didn't do more than grunt quietly at the streak of blood on his white shirt.

When Connie found a quiet corner to sit in, Arthur joined her with a cup of tea for each of them in his hands. Shirley was making her way amongst the crowd, handing Benjamin to some of the guests for a cuddle then confiscating him again when he started to fuss. She plonked herself down next to Connie and Arthur and with a faltering finger, Arthur leaned forward and delicately traced the contours of the baby's downy face. 'He's a handsome little fellow,' he said.

Tears gathered in Connie's eyes and she had to root around in her bag for a tissue, which she used first to hastily dry her face, then on Adrian's nose when she called him to her.

At that moment, Benjamin burped and foamy milk curdled in the corner of his glistening mouth. 'Clever boy,' Shirley congratulated him.

'I'd love to be praised for that,' Arthur said.

They all laughed and when Shirley and Benjamin moved on, Arthur turned to Connie and lowered his voice. 'Treasure,' he said. 'Something you said that evening when you ended up leaving me struck a chord and troubled me deeply.'

'Oh?' Connie said, not sure she wanted to delve into their situation in the middle of a party. What's done was done.

'You said that rather than pull you towards me, I had pushed you away. Do you remember?'

'Yes, I do and I still stand by that, but I don't think there's any point in—'

'No, you're right,' he said. 'There probably isn't any point, but will you let me get this off my chest?'

He looked at her pleadingly and despite her reservations she was intrigued. 'Of course. Go on.'

'I'm ashamed to say there were times when I knew I was behaving badly and hurting you, but I couldn't figure out any other way to keep you safe and with me. Those two things were all I've wanted for myself from the moment we met.'

'Oh, Arthur.' Sadness washed over Connie. 'Why didn't you talk to me like this years ago? We might have been able to work things out somehow.'

Arthur looked at her, then down at his hands. 'I had no idea where to start.' He sounded close to tears. 'And I thought it would make me seem weak.'

She laid a hand on his arm for a moment. 'Well, there were times when it occurred to me that you were more vulnerable than you let on. I could have asked you what was going on in your mind, but I suspect you wouldn't have told me.'

'No, Treasure,' he said. 'I wouldn't have. And I take full responsibility for that.' He threw his hands in the air then let them drop back down. 'What an almighty fool I've been.'

They sat in silence for a few moments, laughter and music and conviviality playing out around them.

'Are you going to stay the night? Or two, perhaps?' Arthur asked. 'We could take a walk into the countryside tomorrow and chat about the things we haven't had a chance to talk about today.'

She wavered. It was tempting. It might be rather nice to explore the area as they'd never done, spend some time with Arthur and find out what he was like on his own, but she wasn't prepared and had things to get back to in London.

'I'm sorry, Arthur,' she said. 'Not this time.'

He looked momentarily disappointed, then his face brightened. 'Does that mean there will be another time?'

Connie laughed out loud again. 'You're a chancer, Arthur Ernest Allinson,' she said.

'Perhaps we could meet up in a week or two for lunch. Somewhere halfway, like Grantham or Newark?'

'Where I always get hungry, like you warned me I would.'

It was Arthur's turn to laugh at that. 'Do you think that would be possible?'

Connie thought for a couple of moments. She was free now and could do whatever she chose to do. She didn't have to see Arthur ever again if she didn't want to, but she thought that it would be rather nice to meet him for lunch. They had, after all, spent thirty years of their lives together and it would be interesting to talk in more detail, especially now that Arthur had confided in her. Then there was the practical side of things they had to work out. 'I'd like that,' she said.

A beam split Arthur's face. 'When?' He seemed keen to pin her down.

'How about Wednesday 8th of May in Newark?' she said.

'Perfect for me,' Arthur agreed. 'Can we arrange the time by post?'

'Yes, Arthur.' She checked her watch. 'Now I must say my goodbyes to everyone and get to the station. My train leaves in an hour.'

'I'll walk with you, Treasure,' he said with the enthusiasm of a schoolboy.

'No, I'm perfectly capable.'

'I know, but…'

Connie put her hand lightly on his. 'I think we should leave it where it is for now.'

'Of course, Connie,' he said. 'I just have to nip to the house for a few minutes. Can you please knock on the door before you go?'

Connie said she would then made her way around her friends and promised to write and keep in touch. Adrian didn't want to let her go and clung to her hand until she picked him up and promised that when he was a bigger boy he could come to London and stay with her. 'Would you like that?' she asked.

With two fingers in his mouth, he nodded that he would.

Back at the house, she rapped once on the door and as she walked inside, Arthur rushed to meet her. 'Time for a cup of tea?' he asked.

'No, thank you. I'm going to have to belt along now as it is.'

'A bit of light reading for the train,' he said, handing her an envelope with her name on the front.

'Oh,' Connie said, a bit taken aback. 'Thank you for whatever it is.'

'And I'm really looking forward to seeing you on the date we arranged, Treasure,' he said.

'Yes, Arthur,' she said. 'We'll be in touch.'

Without warning, he scooped her up and kissed her lightly on the lips. She put her arms around his waist and smelled his coal tar soap and the christening cake he'd eaten earlier. Then she waited, expecting him to say what he'd always said in the same circumstances – 'You will come back, won't you?' Instead, he let her go and put up his hand to her as she walked down the path.

Connie made the train with three minutes to spare, found her seat and dropped into it. She breathed a sigh of relief as she watched Doncaster stream away behind her and thought about Shirley and Millicent, Adrian, Tracey, Simon and of course, the tangled mishmash of feelings she felt when it came to Arthur.

Taking the envelope out of her bag, she stared at it and hoped it didn't contain anything that would ruin the day. She turned it over a few times before opening it, then slit the envelope and unfurled one page of censored writing.

Dear Treasure

It was wonderful to see you ***** and even if you don't want to **** it, I am more enamoured with you now than I've ever been. I know I should have **** you that every single *** we were ********, but I didn't and that is a huge ******* that I will have to live with and believe me it isn't easy.

Another thing I should have said many times before and haven't is *****. I don't think I ever said that word to you the entire time we've been married, although

I should have got down on my ***** every day and begged your forgiveness for my atrocious, unreasonable behaviour and for treating you abominably. But if you give me the opportunity, I will apologise to you time and **** and **** again.

Life has dealt us the cruel **** of not being able to have ********* but instead of taking on the responsibility of lightening your burden, I made your life intolerable. But I want to make it up to you in any way *********. I don't want us to separate forever, ********. I desperately want us to stay married, living ******** in the same house and enjoying each other's company. But I'm not going to pressurise you, I *******. I'm just very grateful that you've agreed to **** me for lunch in a couple of weeks. I'm very **** looking forward to it.

With love from your Constance's Constant XXX

Connie read through the letter again then folded it and put it back in the envelope. Tears threatened, but before they could surface, she smiled and thought that it really would be good to see Arthur again – whether anything came of it or not.

Then she stood and resettled herself into the seat opposite – she didn't want to see what was fading away behind her, she wanted to look forward to where she was headed.

Acknowledgements

A huge thank you to my agent, Kiran Kataria at Keane Kataria Literary Agency, for her continued support, invaluable advice and faith in me as an author.

My thanks to my lovely editor, Bianca Gillam, at Aria Fiction/Head of Zeus for believing in this book and for being patient and meticulous through every edit.

My thanks go to everyone at Aria Fiction/ Head of Zeus for their commitment to me and my books.

A big thank you to Rory Kee and Jessie Price for the beautiful cover design.

I am very grateful to my lovely daughter, Kelly, for her invaluable feedback.

To Paula and David Horsfall for happily allowing me to steal their pet name for each other. Thank you, Treasures.

A thank you, also, to Colette Paul, my tutor on the MA in Creative Writing course at Anglia Ruskin University and Chris Gribble at The National Centre for Writing, Norwich for their on-going support.

Thank you to all my family and friends for the laughs, the love and support: Nick Abendroth, Lizzie Alexander, Basil and Maya Al Omari, Jo Bishop, Cate Casey, Barry Casey, Kathleen Casey, Erin Casey and all my Casey family around the world, Helen Chatten, Penny Clarke, Liam, Arie and Aleksia Collinwood, Jill Davis, Fiona Emblem, Jo Emeney, Ozzie, Kaan, Ayda and Alya Erdinc, Steve Farmer, Mat Garmin, Anne and Alasdair Gilchrist, Ally and Sharon Gilchrist, Danny Sonia and Cleo Gilchrist, Don Gilchrist, Duncan Lisa and Hollie Gilchrist, Tom and Toby Gilchrist, Eman Gilligan, John Gilligan, Angie Gilligan, David Gilligan, Jan and Jon Gray, Eli Heinrich, Jan and Gary Hurst, Sheila and Alan Jefferys, Maureen John, Nick John, Liz Kochprapha, Katy Marron, Tom Mathew, Stuart McKay, Fran Nygaard, Lena Nygaard, Patrice and Mark Nygaard, Liz Peadon, Liz Prescott, Dave Pountney, Martin Shrosbree, Gabby Smith, Sally Tatham, Sue and Gerald Ward, Pete Fran and Rafi Ward, Phil Helen and Sienna Ward and Bella Wordsworth.

About the Author

J AN CASEY's novels, like her first – *The Women of Waterloo Bridge* – explore the themes of how ordinary people are affected by extraordinary events during any period in history, including the present. Jan is fascinated with the courage, adaptability and resilience that people rise to in times of adversity and for which they do not expect pay, praise or commendation. Jan is also interested in writing about the similarities as opposed to the differences amongst people and the ways in which experiences and emotions bind humans together.

Jan was born in London but spent her childhood in Southern California. She was a teacher of English and Drama for many years and is now a Learning Supervisor at a college of further education. When she is not working or writing, Jan enjoys yoga, swimming, cooking, walking, reading and spending time with her grandchildren.

Before becoming a published author, Jan had short stories and flash fictions published.